I0594189

HER IMPOSSIBLE HUSBAND

RAKES & REBELS: THE RAVENEAU FAMILY, BOOK 7

CYNTHIA WRIGHT

The Impossible Husband
Rakes & Rebels: The Raveneau Family, Book 7

Copyright © 2021 by Cynthia Challee
All rights reserved in whole or in part, in any manner, without the permission from the publisher.

No part of this book may be reproduced or transmitted in any form or by any means, electronic or mechanical, including photocopying, recording, or by any information storage and retrieval system, without permission in writing from the publisher, except by a reviewer who may quote brief passages in a review.

This is a work of fiction. Names, characters, places, and incidents either are the product of the author's imagination or are used fictitiously, and any resemblance to actual persons, living or dead, business establishments, events, or locales is entirely coincidental.

Print edition published by Boxwood Manor Books

ISBN: 9781648391903

Cover Photograph by Period Images

Typeface: Le Spesse Image

Created with Vellum

BOXWOOD MANOR BOOKS

Her Impossible Husband
Rakes & Rebels: The Raveneau Family, Book 7

Copyright © 2022 by Cynthia Challed
All rights reserved under International and Pan-American Copyright
Conventions.

No part of this book may be reproduced in any form or by any
electronic or mechanical means, including information storage and
retrieval systems, without written permission from the author, except
for the use of brief quotations in a book review.

Please Note: This is a work of fiction. Names, places, and incidents
either are the product of the author's imagination or are used
fictitiously, and any resemblance to actual persons, living or dead,
business establishments, events or locales is entirely coincidental.

Print edition published by Boxwood Manor Books

ISBN: 978-1-948053-44-0

Cover Photograph by Period Images

Cover Design by Teresa Spreckelmeyer

❦ Created with Vellum

~BOOK DESCRIPTION~

He was impossible! *Yet utterly irresistible...*

Mouette's husband is a former pirate who dreams of one more adventure on the high seas, but when she needs him to join her for a summer among the London *ton*, marriage becomes the most reckless adventure of all!

Rakes & Rebels: The Raveneau Family:

1 – SILVER STORM (André & Devon)
2 – HER HUSBAND, THE RAKE (André & Devon)
a sequel novella to SILVER STORM
3 – SMUGGLER'S MOON (Sebastian & Julia)
4 – THE SECRET OF LOVE (Gabriel & Isabella)
5 – SURRENDER THE STARS (Ryan & Lindsay)
6 – HIS MAKE-BELIEVE BRIDE (Justin & Mouette)
7 – HER IMPOSSIBLE HUSBAND (Justin & Mouette)
8 – HIS RECKLESS BARGAIN (Nathan & Adrienne)
9 – TEMPEST (Adam & Cathy)

CHAPTER 1

Saint-Malo, Brittany, France
April 1829

"M'sieur," called Baptiste, Justin St. Briac's devoted manservant. "Might I remind you of the time?"

Justin paused at the top of narrow steps leading down into a labyrinthian cellar, where all his treasures from years on the high seas were stored. Even though he now lived in Cornwall with his wife and children, he would always feel a mystical attachment to this three-story mansion in the walled city of Saint-Malo. Facing the ramparts, Justin's grand residence was part of Corsairs' Row, an impressive series of homes overlooking the sea, built by the ill-gotten gains of pirates. Here Justin had long enjoyed the reckless, splendid life of a smuggler and corsair, amassing wealth, legendary adventures, and enough lovers to keep him from the altar until he was forty-eight years old.

Every year, Justin brought his family across the English Channel to Saint-Malo. For several weeks, he

1

could pretend to turn back the hands of time...a fantasy that appealed to him more the older he became.

Turning now to Baptiste, he challenged, "Stop scolding me. It is noon, is it not? My meeting with Giles Taureau is not for another hour. I am taking Anthony down to my secret storeroom to search for a particularly wonderful relic of the past."

Just then, his tall, broad-shouldered son came into the room while adjusting the cuffs of a snug forest-green coat. Something in Anthony's expression suggested that he was about to beg off the excursion to the cellar, so Justin started purposefully toward the steps.

"Follow me," he said, gesturing with one dark hand. "We have not visited the storerooms lately, and you should view the riches that will one day be yours."

Bending slightly, Justin led the way down the dark-ened stairway. Father and son continued on through a maze of vaulted stone tunnels, where lanterns hung at intervals. Occasionally, Justin glanced back to check on Anthony. Noticing that the youth risked striking his dark head as they passed under an arch, it came to Justin that Anthony might now be even taller than he was. His heart clenched as he absorbed the swift passage of time.

"It's thrilling down here, don't you agree?" he asked his son. It wasn't really a question, for surely the answer was obvious.

"Indeed," Anthony replied after a moment, polite yet hardly enthusiastic. "Thrilling." They came into a gloomy storeroom stacked high with ornate furniture and other forgotten treasures, and he blinked. "But...what do you mean to do with all this?"

"Do?" Justin echoed, wondering if he should take offense at Anthony's question. He unhooked a lantern and brought it forward to spill golden light over a life-time of memories. "Perhaps you've forgotten our past visits to these rooms when you begged me to regale you with tales of my adventures with the great corsairs of Saint-Malo! Every item you see in this cellar is infused with history and meaning." He paused to let his words sink in before adding, "One day it will all be yours."

"Ah." Anthony looked around, brows lifted, and raked a hand through his fashionably disheveled black hair. "Right. I do remember."

Justin pointed toward a carved, thronelike chair, its worn ochre velvet upholstery now spotted with mildew. "That piece once belonged to Robert Surcouf himself, the greatest Malouin corsair of all! Can you not hear it whispering to us? You used to stand on the chair seat as if it were a quarterdeck, waving your wooden sword and proclaiming that one day you too would sail to the Indian Ocean!"

Anthony looked pensive. "When I was young, I think I lived for your smiles. Making you shout encouragement felt like a great accomplishment." He paused, as if transported back to his childhood, then flashed a reassuring smile. "What a magical adventure it was, being your child."

Justin frowned. "I'm not dead, you know."

"Of course, you are not." The youth glanced away. "It's just that...it feels like a bit of a fairytale now, that's all."

"Indeed? I can assure you, it has been quite real for me, and remains so. In fact, I came down here to look for something that once belonged to the corsair I am going to meet with today." He handed the lantern to Anthony and advanced toward the jumble of furniture and other goods. Just as the object Justin sought came into focus, Anthony spoke.

"Papa, you call your friend a fellow corsair...but isn't that all in the past?" He paused. "I mean, since you married Mama and we began a new life in Cornwall, you have changed, haven't you?"

"I would have wagered that you, of all people, would not wish me to forget those glorious exploits!"

Anthony rubbed long fingers against the side of his jaw. "I suppose I thought of it all as a part of your past, a wonderful story, but then it seemed you have chosen to have a family instead."

Stung, Justin chose a cutlass from the assortment of goods and returned to display the savage weapon in front of Anthony. "This belonged to my comrade, Giles Taureau. Do you see, it is designed especially for daring hand-to-hand combat on the deck of a ship, where space is limited, and a longer sword could easily become tangled in the rigging." Justin gestured toward the short, broad blade, the faded red sash tied around the scabbard, and the initials "G.T." carved with a flourish near the hilt. His voice deepened as he added, "Once a corsair, always a corsair! It is in my *blood*."

Anthony was regarding him with concern. "Are you feeling quite well?"

"Never better. In fact, I have an idea. Giles has written to ask that I meet him on the ramparts of Saint-Malo at one o'clock. Why don't you come, too! Wouldn't you enjoy hearing bold tales of our life upon the sea from one of the bravest corsairs of them all?"

There was a pause. "Do you mean today?"

Before Justin could reply, he glimpsed a movement in the doorway, and Mouette came into view. As usual, the sight of his ravishing wife made his heart beat faster. If not for the faint glints of silver in her ebony curls, it would be hard to believe she had recently celebrated her forty-seventh birthday. Clad in a geranium-tinted morning gown with a tulle-edged stand-up collar, Mouette looked fresh and delectable.

"What are you two doing down here?" she inquired,

scanning the cluttered room. Her thick-lashed blue eyes soon settled on the cutlass.

"Anthony is always eager to see the fruits of my labor, as you well know, *ma belle*." Of course, this wasn't quite how it had happened, but Justin had always enjoyed a rather fluid relationship with the truth. He heard his son exhale, but thankfully he did not correct him. "We were just admiring Giles Taureau's very fine cutlass."

He held it toward Mouette, and her nostrils flared. "It is a gruesome thing, and that *sash* he has tied to the hilt—" She finished the sentence with a disgusted grimace. "It is filthy. I suspect some of those stains may be blood!"

"You are quite right." Justin gave a firm nod of approval. "Can you not envision the scene of battle on the deck of Surcouf's own *Revenant*? In such moments, a man feels truly alive!" He glanced toward Anthony. "More alive than you can possibly imagine."

Mouette was clearly making an effort to hold her tongue, while Anthony leaned against a stone pillar and watched his parents. For an instant, seeing him grown nearly to full manhood, Justin was transported back to a long-ago day when they were newly acquainted. They had been in a tangled Cornwall garden, and young Anthony was begging for a fencing lesson. He had danced about, holding a wooden sword, thrilled to be in the presence of a true corsair.

Justin hadn't known then that they were father and son, that Anthony had been conceived during one wildly sensual night following too many glasses of wine at the wedding of Justin's brother, Gabriel to Mouette's dear friend, Isabella. In the morning, Mouette had hidden from Justin, then taken her young son, Charles, and hurried back to her husband in London. A decade would pass before a widowed, destitute Mouette would return to Justin's life, shaking its very foundations. Anthony had adored Justin on sight, copying his every gesture, proclaiming, "I want to be a pirate when I grow up. Like you!"

By the time they had all surrendered to being a family and Emeline was conceived, Justin wondered what he had been struggling against all his life. By God, he was *happy*! Sometimes he could even forget about the deep antipathy he'd always harbored toward marriage, spawned by a lifetime of witnessing the manipulative relationship between his own parents.

The love of a good woman had healed even Justin's deepest scars, it seemed. Most of the time, he could believe it...until someone didn't behave as he expected. For instance, why wasn't Anthony responding to Justin's utterance with a grin, or at least a nod that would let him know they were of one mind. Instead, he went to his mother and kissed her cheek.

"You know how Papa is," he murmured dryly, and Mouette replied with a faintly amused smile.

What the devil did Anthony mean by that? Justin scowled. Hadn't father and son always been in league together? "I think Cambridge is making you soft. Come out with me to meet Giles Taureau so you can observe a real man who truly knows how to live."

Mouette spoke up. "All this talk of pirates makes me wonder if you are suffering some sort of crisis." Her tone was deceptively light.

"What does that mean?" he demanded.

She smiled sweetly. "Oh, you know, the kind of distress older men endure when they realize they will never be young again."

Justin could only swivel slightly to send her a warning stare. Before he could say something he would doubtless regret, ten-year-old Emeline appeared in the doorway behind her mother. Every time he saw their daughter in recent months, Justin was struck anew that she had begun to cross the bridge from childhood to adolescence.

"Hello!" She smiled at Justin before turning her attention to Anthony. "I've been waiting for you upstairs. Are you ready to go?"

"Go?" echoed Justin. He wished his enchanting Emmie would rush into his arms when she saw him, as she had done for so many years. He would stroke her soft black curls with his big hand, loving her so much it hurt...but these days Emeline seemed to have more important concerns than her papa. "Where are you going?"

Anthony cleared his throat, looking uncomfortable. "As it happens, Papa, I was just about to explain that I cannot go with you to meet your friend because I have promised to take Emmie to the beach to hunt for fossils."

Fossils. Justin clenched his teeth to stop himself from protesting, *"Mon Dieu, not those again!"*

* * *

MOUETTE WATCHED with interest as Emeline crossed to her brother's side and grasped his forearm. "Yes, we must leave, Anthony," the girl exclaimed. "The light will fade if we delay."

"There are no fossils on the beaches here," Justin declared with a note of finality. "I would have seen them long ago."

Mouette tried not to smile. Did he really think anything he could say would change Emeline's mind? She was every bit as hard-headed as he was.

"Papa, perhaps you might acknowledge that you are not an expert on this subject," Emmie dared to assert. "Villers-sur-Mer may be the superior beach for fossils

7

in Brittany, but we don't have time to travel there. Therefore, I hope to astound the geologists by discovering something wonderful, like a *trilobite,* right here in Saint-Malo!" She tugged again at her brother. "Really, there is no time to waste."

Anthony, who grew more handsome by the day, threw his father an apologetic look. "I did promise Emmie earlier this morning. Perhaps I can meet Giles Taureau another time?" After a slight pause, he added, "Even next summer."

With that, the siblings took their leave. Justin stood alone in the cellar room, holding the terrible cutlass with its stained, threadbare sash. Mouette's heart went out to him. Justin was used to exerting a magnetic power over his family, and while the children were young, that had been easy enough. However, they now had strong minds of their own and thought nothing of challenging the authority of their parents.

"Next summer?" he muttered under his breath. "Can he not fit me into his social calendar before then?"

"Our time here is ending. Tomorrow we must begin packing to return to Cornwall, remember?" Mouette reminded him. "The Easter term at Cambridge has already begun."

"I never imagined my own son would choose to spend entire *years* at a stuffy university when he could be out in the world, taking hold of life with both hands, plunging into adventures while he is young, strong, and..."

His voice trailed off, and Mouette narrowed her eyes. "What were you going to say? Virile?"

"Perhaps." Justin shrugged, but his expression was challenging. "What is wrong with that? He is coming into the prime of life."

"Oh, for heaven's sake. I have no doubt that Anthony is perfectly capable of becoming a rake, if he so chooses, whether he is studying at Cambridge or standing on the deck of a pirate ship." Sometimes it was difficult to indulge Justin's flinty moods, but Mouette loved him enough to try. Crossing to his side, she rested a hand on the sleeve of his flawlessly tailored, midnight-blue coat.

Although Justin could be impossibly arrogant and stubborn, age had not dimmed his masculine aura. Even the silk patch that slanted rakishly over his right eye added to his appeal, Mouette thought. Glancing down at her, he remarked, "I never knew it could be so difficult to be a father. No wonder I avoided it most of my life."

"You might turn your attention to other concerns," she suggested, forcing herself to look past him to the assortment of old furniture, books, paintings, and other memorabilia from the past. "Why not begin to sort through some of these items?"

Justin looked suspicious. "To what purpose?"

She couldn't help herself. "Well, do you truly need any of this? The first time you brought me to this house, these pieces were here, but ten years have passed, and I do not recall you ever reclaiming any of them."

"Reclaim them?"

"Yes. It is another word for *use*."

A storm cloud passed over his face. "Why should I do that? These are not mere *things*, but valuable artifacts!" Drawing back, Justin added, "You, more than anyone, should understand that."

"Of course, I understand, darling," she soothed. *Really, though, what value could these possessions hold?* "But I also understand that you are a very meticulous person. Every detail in our homes must be perfect or you are not satisfied, and all our servants know it. You insist on flawlessly made clothing and furnishings that reflect the latest fashions and the best of taste."

"*Oui!* I do," he growled. "What is your point?"

"Only that I find it hard to reconcile this musty clutter with the man I just described."

Justin walked away from her, staring at his hoard of memorabilia. "Many of these pieces were accumulated before I knew you, when I was a free man, engaging in outrageous adventures as a smuggler or sailing with legendary corsairs to defend France in the Indian Ocean." He picked up a large compass in an enamel case and blew away a layer of dust. "This belonged to Surcouf himself. The very sight of it takes me back to our time together in his cabin on board *Revenant*, as we planned our secret attacks on British ships in the Bay of Bengal. He was vibrantly alive." Justin paused, then added hoarsely, "We both were."

Mouette's eyes stung in sympathy. Last year, when their family arrived in Saint-Malo for their annual summer visit, Justin had gone off as usual to visit Surcouf and had been stunned to find his old friend on his deathbed. She knew this blow had meant not only the loss of a comrade, but also a stark reminder of Justin's own mortality. Surcouf had died at age fifty-four, suddenly an old man, ravaged by a wasting disease...yet Justin himself was even older. Mouette knew better than anyone that her husband resisted letting down his protective shield and becoming vulnerable to pain, but she should not encourage that resistance.

"I understand how hard it has been for you, losing your friend, Surcouf," she whispered. "Yet we cannot turn back time."

Gesturing toward the ramparts that lay beyond the windowless cellar walls, Justin demanded, "Perhaps you would have me build a great bonfire on the beach and burn everything from my past?"

Mouette knew she had pushed him far enough. "Of course not. I only ask that you think about what I've said." Embracing him, she leaned against his broad chest. The scent of Justin's warm, powerful body stirred her senses, as always. Suddenly, Mouette was hungry for him, and it came to her that they might make love in one of the ancient chairs. It was a long time since they'd done something so wickedly arousing. "I must admit, this cellar does feel like a place out of time... Perhaps we might pretend that you are a corsair and you have captured me from an enemy's ship." Even as she spoke, heat coursed through her body and she slipped her hand between them, fitting it to his crotch. Her nipples grew taut as she imagined sitting on his lap, her bodice undone, his warm mouth working its magic.

Justin made a low, primitive sound and hardened against her palm, but in the next moment, he abruptly stepped back, eyes flashing. "I do not need to *pretend*. I will always be a corsair. And now I must go to meet Giles Taureau." He picked up the old cutlass and started to turn away.

"Will you not kiss your wife before you leave?" As intended, Mouette's tone held more of a challenge than a plea.

"As you wish, *chérie*."

When he caught her against him with one strong arm, the years melted away. His mouth covered hers, burning, and Mouette responded as passionately as ever. Then, just as quickly as the flame ignited, her husband snuffed it out.

"I must go," Justin said, stepping back to brandish the cutlass with its bloodstained sash. "Giles is not a man to keep waiting!"

11

[faint mirror-image text from facing page bleed-through]

CHAPTER 2

$\mathcal{E}$merging from his home, Justin strode across the cobbled courtyard and passed through the tall green gates that opened onto Rue de Toulouse. His thoughts were far away as he started toward the Port de Dinan, where he could climb to the top of the ramparts enclosing Saint-Malo.

How long had it been, Justin wondered, since he last saw Giles Taureau? A decade? No, surely it was longer. Surcouf had told him that Taureau continued to roam the oceans, long after the rest of them turned to more civilized pursuits. It was tantalizing to wonder why his old comrade wished to meet with him again, after so many years.

What would he say if Giles proposed they join together in another reckless adventure?

His reverie was interrupted when an attractive married woman named Marie Vauvert came into view, holding the hand of her young daughter. Rue d'Orleans was nearly empty at the moment, yet she looked all around before approaching Justin. When she raised one gloved hand to smooth the fair curls partially hidden under a Breton white lace coif, he knew what was in her mind.

"*Bonjour,*" Marie greeted him softly. "I have not seen much of you these past weeks, m'sieur."

It would usually be gratifying to know he could still affect a woman in this way, but not today. "I hope you are well, madame. Look how much your daughter has grown." Justin nodded toward the child. "I am sorry to be brief, but I have an appointment with a comrade."

Marie's smile faded as she noticed the cutlass in his hand. "I hope you do not mean to use that awful weapon when you meet your friend!"

"Oh, that." He lifted it for an instant and saw the little girl back away in fear. "I don't intend to employ it...for the moment, at least."

"I thought you had retired from such dangerous pursuits."

"*Retired?*" Justin repeated acidly. "Madame, are you not aware that we Saint-Malo corsairs have danger in our very blood? We do not retire!"

"But you now live in Cornwall," Marie pressed. "Are you not domesticated, with a wife and children?"

Lifting his proud head, Justin sniffed the sea breeze. "I am here in this moment, am I not? And I must be on my way." He gave her a short bow and started off. "*Adieu!*"

What an awkward scene. He should never have stopped to speak to that woman! At times it seemed that his life, and even his own body, no longer fit him with ease. Was it... age? The very question made him want to escape, but where was he to go?

Justin's knees complained more than usual as he climbed the steps to the ramparts. When he was even with the slate rooftops of Saint-Malo, he started along the walkway. His heart pounded as he recalled the un-nerving conversations of that morning. Then came the terrible, suffocating sensation he had previously expe-rienced during episodes of strife with his devious, manipulative mother. Yet, Justin reassured himself, Cerise St. Briac was far away in Cornwall. Pausing, he put a hand on battlements, drew several deep breaths, and focused on the azure sea, gleaming in the distance.

"Papa!" cried a child's voice.

Scanning the beach, he saw Emeline waving to him from far away. She had tied up her blue skirts so that she might climb more freely among the large rocks. Anthony, meanwhile, was coatless, his shirtsleeves rolled up. Smiling, he shaded his eyes with one hand and nodded to Justin.

"Will you join us?" Anthony called.

"I cannot!" Justin held up the cutlass as a signal that he had yet to meet with Giles Taureau.

The instant his voice carried out over the city walls, a furry animal emerged from behind a rock, running on stubby legs, barking madly, clearly searching for Justin. It was Robinson, the family's corgi. Ever since the day a decade ago when the homeless dog had claimed him on one of Cornwall's hidden lanes, Robinson had dedicated himself to winning Justin's heart. It was a ridiculous situation. Everyone in the family adored the corgi...except Justin, who doled out grudging pats and greetings, yet Robinson idolized his elusive master.

"Look what I've found!" Emeline held up something gray and misshapen. It looked like nothing more than a common rock.

"Bravo," Justin called with false pleasure. *Sangdieu*, was it possible that his own children could actually be fascinated by a lot of elusive, petrified bones and shells?

He noticed then that Anthony and Emeline had already returned to picking through the rocks, clearly more interested in the possibility of finding a cursed fossil than they were in their father. Even Robinson had turned away, giving chase to a seagull that swooped down low to taunt him. *Fine then*, thought Justin. He had better things to do as well.

Giles Taureau's message had instructed Justin to meet him next to the row of cannon that lined the Holland Bastion. The grassy area nearby was quiet today. Pausing there, Justin looked around and consulted his timepiece. It was several minutes past one o'clock. Surely Taureau wouldn't give up and go on his way so soon?

"St. Briac? Is that you?"

He blinked. The only person nearby was an old man, sitting on a bench, who bore no resemblance to the wild-spirited corsair, Giles Taureau. Justin turned around and looked in the other direction, but no one else was in sight.

"Are you blind? Don't make me get up."

Mon Dieu, the speaker *was* the old man. A part of Justin wanted to pretend he hadn't heard and quickly take his leave, but instead he walked a few steps closer.

"Taureau?"

"Of course! Come and join me."

The old man wore a pair of striped, blue trousers and a short jacket. Grizzled white hair emerged from a tarred, flat-top cap with a cockade pinned to one side. With a growing sense of dread, Justin recognized the clothing from the past. Perhaps worst of all, Taureau sported a large eye-patch that seemed to accentuate his broken, sunburned nose.

Justin's chest tightened as he approached. "Sorry, I didn't recognize you."

"Well, we've both changed, haven't we? Yet I see we have one thing in common these days." Taureau touched his eye-patch and gave a raspy chuckle, revealing at least two missing teeth.

It was like a nightmare. Justin wanted to shout, *No, we are not alike, not in the least!* Instead, he sat down beside the old man on the bench and steeled himself to be friendly.

"How have you been?" he asked.

"Not so good. The injuries I suffered during our many exploits have rendered me so infirm, I am now forced to live with my daughter. Although our lives were very full, I have paid a price, as did our great comrade, Surcouf."

Justin rubbed his aching knee. "I still cannot believe he is gone."

A tear seeped from Taureau's bloodshot eye. "How well I know it. Our golden age passed all too quickly." He paused. "Yet I still revel in memories of the good times. When we were sailing the Bay of Bengal together, conquering all who dared to challenge us!"

Justin felt a sharp pang of nostalgia. "Do you remember that last adventure with Surcouf, when we captured those British ships? One of the pretentious officers dared to accuse, 'You French fight for money, while we fight for honor.'" He paused to scoff at such nonsense. "And Surcouf parried, 'Each of us fights for what he lacks most.' I will never forget the look on the face of that ridiculous, puffed-up lieutenant."

"I do indeed remember! There will never be another like Surcouf!" rasped Taureau.

"I brought something for you." Lifting the cutlass, Justin set the cruel-looking weapon on the other man's lap. As he did so, he noticed the bones of Taureau's knees outlined against his worn trousers. "For these many years, it has been in one of my cellar storerooms, waiting to be in your hands again."

"Ah, how many men fell before this cruel blade?" The frail old man sighed nostalgically. "*Merci, mon ami.*"

How had Justin ever imagined that the purpose of this meeting might have been to plan for another wild adventure? In his own mind, he had envisioned all his former corsair friends as ageless. After all, Justin himself hadn't changed much over the years...had he?

Even as he silently posed that question, a dark cloud enveloped him.

"I must tell you," he said at length, "I had the notion that you might still be living as we once did, sailing the world, gathering women and treasure with both hands."

Taureau gave a bark of hoarse laughter. "You jest. How could that be? I will soon be sixty years of age!"

This announcement was a blow, for he was close behind. "That is hardly ancient," he protested.

"For those of us who have lived every moment with the utmost passion, it is a very great age. I am grateful to have reached it. No doubt Surcouf would have given up all five million francs of his fortune to live six decades." Giles Taureau paused. "I wish I could tell you I only asked you here today so that we might reminisce about the exploits of our younger years."

"Ah." Justin leaned away from him ever so slightly. "Pray enlighten me."

"As you've doubtless perceived, I have fallen on hard times." The old man looked down, clearly ashamed. "I could greatly benefit from a bit of assistance. That is..."

Justin quickly raised a hand to silence him. "You needn't go on." The last thing he wanted Giles Taureau to do was beg. "Wait here. My manservant, Baptiste, will return to you with funds that should see you through for now. If you give him your address, I will send more at regular intervals." He forced himself to put a hand on the old man's shoulder. "You needn't worry anymore."

For one awful moment, it seemed Taureau might begin to cry, but then he managed to straighten his bent shoulders. "I'm grateful, St. Briac. More than you could ever know."

"As I recall, you saved my life many years ago. Once you are feeling better, I hope we will enjoy one last adventure." Even as he spoke, Justin knew this was a fantasy. Standing, he managed to suppress an urge to run back the way he'd come. "*Au revoir*, Giles. Until next time."

* * *

AFTER DINNER THAT NIGHT, Emeline brought out her sketchbook and began to show her family drawings of the fossils she intended to find.

"I must admit you were right, Papa. I didn't discover anything worthy of notice on the beach here at Saint-Malo. But when we return to England, I dream of visiting the Jurassic Coast."

The four of them were sitting around the candlelit table, enjoying a dessert of *crème brûlée*. The sugar coating the rich custard was crisp and utterly delicious, but Mouette noticed that Justin had pushed his dish aside and was drinking cognac instead.

"What the devil is the Jurassic Coast?" he demanded of the child. "Part of Antarctica?"

"You must be teasing." Emeline lifted her chin, just enough to send him a message. "Papa, you certainly know it is that place in England where brilliant geologists have been discovering the most amazing fossils!"

"Fascinating," Justin commented dryly.

"Emmie is quite right." Anthony leaned back in his chair, watching them, his dark eyes agleam with amusement. "It's centered at Lyme Regis, on the Dorset coast, not far from Cornwall. There's a woman there called Mary Anning, who is self-taught. She has been collecting and selling fossils and shells since she was a little girl. She's found some fossilized skeletons of completely unknown creatures. They've set the scientific world on its ear."

Justin appeared to be lost in thought, staring into his nearly empty glass of cognac, so Mouette interceded. "It does sound terribly interesting, and I know we are longing to hear more, but not just now. If we are soon to depart for Cornwall, there is a great deal to do." She looked first at Anthony. "Won't you take Robinson outside one more time tonight?" Hearing his name, the corgi appeared from under the table. "And Emmie, do you need help to pack all your books back in their special trunk?"

"Of course not!" The little girl looked offended. "No one else must touch my books. I arrange them in a special order that only I understand."

The siblings had just exited the dining room when Baptiste appeared. His steel-gray hair was windblown, and his angled cheeks were ruddy, as if he'd been outside.

"Ah, good, there you are," said Justin. He extended his glass. "Would you be so kind...?"

Mouette frowned. "More cognac? I don't think that would be wise."

"I disagree," he growled.

Of course, she was well aware of Justin's tendency to overindulge in spirits, rich food, or other sensual pleasures when he felt the world closing in on him. She had once hoped to change him, but that was folly. The question now was, what was bothering him tonight?

Baptiste cleared his throat, looking between them. "I do not wish to interrupt this – uh – private interlude, but m'sieur should know that I found Giles Taureau and gave him the envelope. He was very pleased!" The whippet-thin manservant then drew a piece of paper from an inner pocket of his coat. "And now we know where to find him, for the future."

"What on earth are you talking about?" asked Mouette.

"It is nothing," said Justin, snatching the folded paper from Baptiste. He then gave the servant a pointed stare. "I would like another cognac."

"*Bien sûr.*" Baptiste hurried from the room.

"He is a treasure, and you should not treat him that way." As Mouette spoke, it came to her that she could have said that to Justin about any of them, herself included. This thought made her heart beat fast. Turning away, she walked ahead of him up the curving staircase. When they were both inside their spacious bedchamber, she closed the door and faced him. "Please tell me what happened today so that you can release us all from your terrible mood."

Justin began to tug at his neckcloth. "I don't know what you mean."

"Clearly something occurred during your meeting with Giles Taureau. Has he persuaded you to sail away with him, leaving your family behind, and you simply don't know how to tell me?" The words were spilling out before Mouette had even fully formed the thoughts, the fears, that prompted them. Hot blood rose to her cheeks, and she turned away.

"Is that what you think of me?" His tone was outraged.

Mouette looked back over one shoulder and saw him close behind her, his waistcoat unbuttoned, a pulse beating in his strong neck. She met his compelling black gaze. "Do not try to twist the meaning of my words or imply that I do not trust you! But I must be honest." She bit her lip. "I sometimes fear that you miss your former life. That you feel constrained by the walls of our home, the duties of being a father. A husband."

There was a knock at the door. Looking relieved, Justin went to answer it, returning with a fresh glass of fine cognac. He took a deep swallow and closed his eyes. "Clearly your worries are unfounded, *ma belle*," he said. "I am here, after all, am I not?"

"Did you have a choice?" she challenged. "Justin, you have always told me the truth. What happened today with Giles Taureau?"

"Nothing! Nothing at all. First you tell me that I must dispose of a lifetime's memories from the cellar storerooms, and now you accuse me of hiding secrets. Perhaps, if I am out of sorts, it is because I bristle at your efforts to control me."

There was some truth in this. Yet, Mouette knew her husband too well to let him turn the tables. "Something happened."

"I am not allowed even a shred of privacy." Turning, Justin looked out floor-length windows to behold the star-studded view of the Saint-Malo ramparts and the distant sea. When Mouette made no reply, he muttered, "*D'accord!* Clearly you will not let this go, so I will tell you. My comrade-in-arms has been transformed into an old man...a mere shadow of his former self! If I entertained a brief fantasy of joining Giles for one more adventure, I knew better the moment I saw him again." Justin raked a hand through his thick hair, frowning.

"Are you angry at him for getting older?" she asked.

"Angry?" His voice rose. "Why should I not be! Would you have me weep instead? First Surcouf deserts me by *dying* at a mere fifty-four years of age, and now Taureau has been forced to live with his daughter like some sort of elderly invalid!"

Unwilling to let him pull further away, Mouette went closer and gentled her tone. "None of us can stay the same, Justin. Even you and I are growing older."

"Not like *that*."

"No, of course not." She swallowed, summoning the courage to ask the hardest question. "But even if Giles

21

Taureau had remained robust and presented you with plans for a wild new adventure, would you have sailed away from us?"

Justin closed his good eye and drew a harsh breath. "Would it be so wrong if I did? Many men go away for all sorts of reasons, then they return to their families. Other wives do not seem to mind in the least!"

Suddenly it seemed Mouette could not breathe. Turning, she went into the dressing room that connected Justin's impeccable suite of rooms to her own. Of course, she always slept with him, while the other bedchamber remained untouched during their visits to Saint-Malo.

Enough lamplight filtered into the dressing room to allow Mouette to see her largest trunk. Opening it, she hastily began to fill it with her clothing.

"Mouette," came Justin's low growl. "What the devil are you doing in there?"

"Packing."

"You asked me to be honest. Now I am being punished."

"Don't be ridiculous!" She tossed an exquisite lavender satin evening gown into the trunk without bothering to fold it. "I am merely sparing you my thoughts about the notion that you could sail off to engage in your former life as a corsair, then simply reappear on your family's doorstep when the adventure ends." Trying to keep the tears from her voice, Mouette continued, "I felt quite certain you understood this matter when we agreed to embark on a genuine marriage, a full decade ago. Did you not say, to me and to my boys, that you meant for us to be a *true family*?"

Justin intruded into the dressing room, his broad chest blocking the light, his face stormy. "Do not speak as if I have been anything less than a father to *our* sons, not only my own little Anthony but also Charles, who was then an adolescent. It was a challenge, for Charles remained very loyal to your first husband, Sir Harry Brandreth, who was more a villain than a true papa." He gripped her upper arms, forcing her to look up at him. "But now they are no longer boys. They are both men...and although I had dreamed that they might choose to bind their fortunes to mine, I can now plainly see that they have made other plans."

Mouette wanted to press her face against his white shirtfront and weep, for she knew exactly what he meant. Their children were leaving the nest, and she often felt that none of them really needed their parents in the same way...even ten-year-old Emeline. Their little daughter had a mind of her own, and she was already deeply immersed in her own interests that had little to do with her parents.

"Leaving us to seek adventure is not a solution, Justin," she whispered. "I am still your wife."

He looked away for an instant, pain etched on his proud face. "I hate growing old, watching my world change and being powerless to stop it."

Mouette was swept by a wave of love for this man she knew so well. "You are not going to die. Not yet," she whispered.

"Prove it, *chérie*."

In the next instant, Justin drew her into his strong arms, rendering her breathless. He scooped her up and carried her to their elegant bed. Her heart began to pound as he found the buttons on her gown and peeled it from her, his gaze raking her naked breasts as if for the first time. The fire between them had been unquenchable from the moment they had first laid eyes on each other, and when they quarreled and came back together, the blaze burned white-hot.

His hands were rough and tender all at once, stripping her bare, helping her to pull away his clothing, urging her to touch him, finding the hidden secrets of her need. Her own body had changed, but he didn't seem to notice. Mouette knew the time was coming when her monthly courses would cease. Would age render her less desirable to Justin?

"I need you," she said.

"Show me. Open your legs," he commanded, pressing her back on the bed and kissing his way down from her mouth to her taut nipples to her belly to her sensitized, swollen womanhood that ached for his mouth, his tongue, all the ways he knew to bring her to the edge of oblivion.

Soon she was climbing on top of him, pretending to master him, and he laughed up at her so wickedly that her heart skipped a beat.

"I will have my way with you," Mouette warned, smiling.

"Oh, God yes, please do," came his husky reply. "You are shameless."

She took him in her mouth, loving the illusion of power over him, making him groan and throw his big head back on the pillows. And then, as his own control ebbed, Justin gave a low roar and lifted her away from him. He turned her onto her stomach as if she weighed nothing at all, raising her hips so he could enter her from behind. As they coupled, he seemed to plunge deeper inside her than ever before, and Mouette bit the pillow, whimpering. Justin's hands reached under to find her breasts. He squeezed them, knowing just how much pressure she craved, thrusting into her, turning his roughened cheek against her shoulder.

He was still the jungle cat who would not be tamed, who could excite her almost beyond enduring. Fulfillment overtook them like a summer storm: thunder and lightning followed by an ecstatic cloudburst. Even when they both were spent and he lay holding her, his breathing husky as he slept, Mouette realized again that no matter how fiercely they loved, there would always be a part of her husband that was just out of reach.

Pushing her damp curls from her brow, she closed her eyes, inhaling his intoxicating scent. It was all so erotically satisfying that she could almost forget the many warning signs she'd sensed today.

Change was happening inside Justin, and she could not predict what might lie ahead for them in Cornwall.

CHAPTER 3

Frenchman's Haven
Cornwall, England

$\mathcal{J}$ustin usually felt a pang of sadness each time they sailed from Saint-Malo back to Cornwall, but this year he was glad, even relieved, to leave those broken dreams behind. Now, as the family's landau entered the tunnel of hedgerows and overarching trees that signaled the approach of Frenchman's Haven, Justin heard Mouette give a deep sigh.

"Ah," she murmured. "Home at last."

From the seat facing them, Anthony closed his new copy of Mantell's *Illustrations of the Geology of Sussex* and glanced out the window. "Good."

"I am very eager to see my cousin Louise," pronounced Emeline. As she spoke, she petted Robinson, who lay on the seat between the two siblings. "What if Louise has already left for the Jurassic Coast without me?"

Justin felt Mouette turn her gaze on him before she spoke. "Aren't you pleased to be home?"

Home. It came to Justin that, during all the years he'd lived in Saint-Malo, he'd worked out his restless urges by going to sea, either on a dangerous smuggling venture or as a corsair sailing to the Indian Ocean with Surcouf. And even after his marriage to Mouette, when they had settled together in Cornwall, he could tell himself that Frenchman's Haven wasn't a permanent home, for Saint-Malo continued to call him back.

Home had seemed to be always somewhere other than where he was.

"Of course, I am pleased," he told Mouette with a frown. "It's just becoming rather dull at Frenchman's Haven."

The two children were watching him, and Robinson opened one eye as well. "Perhaps you need a hobby, Papa," mused Emeline. "I could teach you about fossils."

Before Justin was forced to reply, the landau turned into the drive that led to their plain but elegant home. For an instant, he seemed to fall back in time to the first time he had come here, when he had been in search of a make-believe residence so that he might fool his mother into believing that he was going to marry. It had been her dying wish, though her imminent demise had also been a charade. *Like mother, like son*, Justin's brother had mocked, only half in jest.

The pretend home and hired bride had become quite real long ago. Yet, as much as Justin had come to want this life, a deeply rooted part of him felt compelled to continue searching for an escape route.

As the landau rolled to a stop in front of the stone manor house, the massive front door opened immediately. Justin looked forward to seeing the household staff spill out and line up to welcome them home. Margaret, their cook, would already be preparing his favorite Chicken Marengo for the evening meal, and no doubt there would be an abundance of warm brioche for breakfast. Perhaps he should be more grateful to be home.

However, it was not Margaret and her staff who appeared on the drive, but Justin's stepson, Sir Charles Brandreth. At twenty-three years of age, he wore his title of *baronet* like a halo above his head of wavy golden hair, and he was better dressed than anyone in all of Cornwall.

"Oh!" cried Mouette. "It's Charles. What a lovely surprise!"

Their coachman, Will, opened the door, and Mouette emerged first to embrace her oldest child.

Justin saw Anthony and Emeline exchange a telling glance. "All right then, you two," he said in a low voice. "Remember, Charles may be a bit stuffy, but he is your brother."

As they all disembarked, Justin went forward to clasp Charles's hand. "Ah, what a surprise! It is good to see you, son." He waited to hear how the young man would respond.

Charles stood close to his mother. "Thank you, sir," he said with a nod. "It's very fine to be with all of you again."

It hadn't been easy to forge a father-son bond with Charles Brandreth, for more reasons than one. When Justin and Mouette married, the boy had been thirteen years old and staunchly devoted to the memory of his father, Sir Harry. Justin still felt a poignant stab of emotion when he remembered the first time Charles had addressed him as "Father." They had done quite well together for a time, but when Charles reached the age of fifteen and declared that he was ready to go away to school, it became clear that the fledgling baronet was planning to one day return to London and restore his father's position in society.

"It is wonderful to have you here," Mouette was saying, "but what has brought you all the way from London to Cornwall?"

"I am eager to tell you all about it, Mother," Charles said. He wore what appeared to be a smug smile.

Justin saw the other two siblings standing off to one side, as if waiting for an opportunity to escape. "There is a great deal to do now that we are home," he said. "Perhaps we could postpone this conversation until we are all together at the dinner table?"

"That's fine," Charles said, brows lowering, "But I wish to speak to Mother *now*. You may come if it pleases you, sir."

* * *

THE MID-APRIL AFTERNOON was cool and breezy, and Mouette donned a royal blue pelisse before she went outside to join Charles. Until she knew what he wanted, she wasn't sure if she wanted Justin to join them or not.

The grounds of Frenchman's Haven were lush and green after a rainy March. The fruit trees and other ornamental shrubs planted by Justin's brother, Gabriel, were budding, and as Mouette emerged from the back of the manor house, she saw Gabriel himself standing a distance away with Tom, their aging gardener. Gabriel was a gifted botanist, and although Justin hated to admit his younger brother might know more than he did, he had long ago relinquished the planning of their grounds to him.

Before Mouette could wave to her brother-in-law and niece, a voice spoke from the stone terrace behind the house. "Ah, there you are, Mother."

29

Turning, she saw Charles, sitting in a wrought iron chair, sipping something amber-colored from a small goblet. For a moment, Mouette felt as if she were seeing Sir Harry, her erstwhile husband, rather than their son. Harry had projected an image of golden perfection, but later revealed himself to be desperately flawed. He drank and gambled to excess, secretly spending money they didn't have, and eventually he had even plotted against her own father, nearly killing André Raveneau. The hairs on the back of Mouette's neck stood up as Charles rose to greet her, impeccably dressed and wearing a familiar, proud smile.

"Will you join me?" Charles gestured toward the bottle of brandy and extra glasses waiting on a silver tray.

"Not for me, thank you. I've asked Margaret to send tea and biscuits for us." Mouette felt a pang as she heard the disapproving note in her own voice. Reaching his side, she kissed him on both cheeks. "Whatever has brought you to Cornwall so unexpectedly?"

"I have some immensely exciting news, Mother. I am to be *betrothed*."

This announcement came at her like a blast of cold air. "Betrothed?" She sat down, feeling stunned. "But...you are still young. You haven't even begun to establish yourself in a profession!"

The matter of his profession had become rather a sticking point in the family. Because Charles had been fascinated by buildings since childhood, Mouette encouraged him to become an architect. However, once her son went away to Eton, his main interests shifted to friends who introduced him to a world he longed to inhabit himself. After all, was he not *Sir* Charles Brandreth, the heir to his father's baronetcy? Whenever he had written home, going on about visits to the grand country homes of English aristocrats, Mouette had cringed, hesitating to show Justin the letters.

"I won't need a profession," Charles said, to her dismay. "I have a title...and Lady Penelope Cranford will be my wife." He paused triumphantly to let this sink in. "Yes, you heard me correctly, Mother. Penelope is indeed the daughter of the Duke of Bellingham."

Just then, Justin came through the French doors that opened onto the terrace. His hair was damp, as if he had just washed up after their journey, and he was absently knotting a fresh neckcloth.

"Ah, *bonjour*, Charles. I will join you for a drink."

"Margaret is sending tea and cakes," protested Mouette.

Justin arched a brow at his stepson and gave a short laugh. "We do not object if you have tea and cakes, *ma belle*, but Charles and I are men. We prefer something stronger."

Charles colored slightly, as if he didn't know quite how to respond. Ever since Justin had come into their family, captivating Mouette and Anthony, Charles had wavered between warming to his stepfather and holding him at arm's length. The balance had shifted toward distance after the momentous day when Mouette told both boys that she had once shared a "romantic interlude" with Justin, and he, rather than Sir Harry Brandreth, was Anthony's true father. Anthony seemed to already understand this, perhaps because of their physical similarities, but Charles had been shocked and angry.

Justin usually dealt with this by pretending the conflict didn't exist. He was always friendly toward his stepson, but never imposed himself. "Nothing I do will change him," Justin would say to Mouette when she suggested he might try harder. "I never thought I would be a father at all, and I certainly didn't learn anything from my own parents. Be glad I manage as well as I do."

"*Santé*," Justin was saying now, lifting his small glass of brandy in a toast.

"And to your health as well," came Charles's rather stiff reply. He finished his drink and poured another. "I'm glad you are both here because—"

Mouette reached out to touch Justin's arm. It would be much better for him to hear this news from her. "Charles has come to tell us that he is betrothed to Lady Penelope Cranford, daughter of the Duke of Bellingham." When he glanced at her in surprise, she put on a bright smile.

"That's right," Charles affirmed, leaning forward. "I came to not only deliver the wonderful news but also to tell Mother that she must travel to London."

"London?" echoed Justin in a tone that suggested the city was thousands of miles away, in a dangerous foreign land.

"Yes, *London*." Charles sighed. "It's quite imperative. The Season is now underway and there will be a series of balls and routs to announce and celebrate our impending nuptials. Naturally, the presence of my family is required." He paused. "Of course, my real father is dead, and I realize that the thought of spending so much time among the London *ton* would certainly fill you with dread, sir. Don't worry, as long as Mother is there, that will be sufficient."

Mouette blinked. "I would certainly hope that Justin would come with me. If I go, that is."

Justin was watching both of them, but before he could reply, Baptiste appeared with the tea and cakes. Why on earth was he serving them instead of Smythe, the kitchen maid? Even as Baptiste pretended not to notice anything they were doing, she knew better. He had been with Justin for decades, and now he ran this household with discreet efficiency. Baptiste set down the tray and poured tea for Mouette, all the while taking in every nuance of the scene at hand.

Charles addressed Justin again. "Will you not congratulate me on my good fortune, sir?"

Justin sat down in one of the woven cane chairs, and as usual it looked on the verge of collapse under his powerful body. He drank down his brandy, considering, before he said, "*Félicitations*, Charles. I hope you and your future bride will be very happy. And as for London..."

Before Justin could continue, a voice called to them from across the velvety emerald lawn. "Ah, *mon frère*! You are back."

It was Gabriel, the younger St. Briac brother, whose nearby estate, Elysium, boasted the most extensive and imaginative gardens in all of Cornwall. Looking exceedingly handsome in his gardening clothes, he held a pot containing a small tree in his gloved hands. Gabriel was accompanied by his older daughter, Louise, who had recently celebrated her nineteenth birthday. Pushing spectacles back on her delicate nose, she waved uncertainly.

"Ah, there is your friend, Louise." Justin sent Charles a keen look. "No doubt you wish to greet her and tell her your news?"

Charles coughed. "Not at the moment."

"I will go then and reunite with my brother and niece." Justin drained his glass, then lifted Mouette's hand and kissed it. "I will leave you two to make plans for the festivities in London." He said the word *festivities* as if it might conceal a poisonous snake.

As Justin strode off down the garden paths, Mouette turned back to her son. She was grateful to be alone with him. "What exactly is happening in London?"

Charles frowned. "Mother, why can you not be

happy for me? Grandmama certainly is. She vows to assist with my new life in any way she can."

This came at her like a thunderclap, for he was speaking of Harry's mother, not her own. Mouette had long ago trained herself not to think of Arabella, the Dowager Lady Brandreth. The horrible woman, who invariably looked down at Mouette in judgment, had gone to her country house in Kent after the death of her son. Meanwhile, Mouette tried to pretend her mother-in-law no longer existed.

With a sinking sensation, she thought, *Trust Charles to reopen the Pandora's box of my past.*

* * *

As JUSTIN APPROACHED THE SHELTERED, south-facing area of the garden, he saw that Tom, his head gardener, was digging a hole for the young tree.

"How kind of you to bring this fine dwarf lemon tree!" Tom said, looking up to smile first at Gabriel and then at Louise. "We do be fortunate to be able to grow citrus in Cornwall. Just like the palm trees. 'Tis a paradise here, I think."

"Sometimes," agreed Gabriel with a wry smile.

Together, they drew the tree from its pot and carefully placed it in the ground, adding one of Gabriel's secret potions before filling in the hole. Louise smiled. "It looks splendid."

Justin spared a moment to study his niece. Like her mother, Louise wore spectacles, which enhanced her reserved nature. She was tall for a female and slim as a willow, her dark chestnut hair hidden under a plain, blue bonnet. Although Louise appeared to be more interested in her studies than in young men, Justin couldn't help noticing how her pensive gaze wandered toward the terrace, where Charles and Mouette were conversing animatedly. Her small bosom rose and fell just once, as if she had allowed herself to sigh. Once upon a time, Justin remembered, the two of them had been quite friendly, sharing many obscure interests. Even during a more recent visit home from university, Charles had sat with Louise during a holiday meal. Perhaps Charles felt she understood him better than his blood relations.

"Ah, *bonjour*," Justin called, deciding to make himself known. The trio turned in unison at the sound of his voice. "It is good to be back in Cornwall." Even after a decade, he still couldn't quite bring himself to call this *home*. Pausing next to Louise, he bent to kiss her on both cheeks before accusing, "Is it true that you mean to take my little girl away to some uncivilized place to dig in the rocks?"

Her pale cheeks went pink. "But Emeline has been begging to accompany us to Lyme Regis."

"It is hardly uncivilized," protested Gabriel. Now that the lemon tree was securely in the ground, he came forward. Drawing off one doeskin glove, he clasped Justin's hand. "It will be an adventure for little Emeline, and you needn't worry. Izzie and I will be there to look after her."

Justin frowned. "It's just that I envisioned far grander passions for her than *fossils*."

This drew laughter from his brother. "Envision away, *mon frère*. Our daughters will do as they please."

"Emeline is still a child! And I am her papa."

"True. But more importantly, she is a St. Briac—and her mother is a Raveneau! If you imagine she will be ruled by you or any man, you are doomed to disappointment. Be glad she has serious interests at her young age. No doubt she will grow up to become someone extraordinary."

Justin made his chest broader. "Without a doubt!"

"There, you see, we are all in agreement." Pausing, Gabriel glanced toward Louise. "You are pale, *ma petite.* Are you feeling ill?"

She sighed again, then smiled. "I am quite well. I was just thinking how excited Emeline must be. I have a great deal to tell her about Mary Anning's newest discovery. It appears to be the skeleton of a flying reptile!" Louise's face glowed as she spoke. "Perhaps she will want to come home to Elysium to stay with us until we depart for Lyme Regis. There is so much to talk about."

"That might be wise," Justin allowed grudgingly, "since Mouette must go to London...and I am obliged to accompany her." Feeling trapped, he looked at Gabriel. "I seem to have no say in any part of my life these days. We returned home to find Charles waiting to tell us that he's now betrothed to the daughter of a bloody duke. He insists that his family must participate in whatever grand festivities accompany such announcements."

"Betrothed?" echoed Louise in a small voice.

Justin looked over to see that her golden-brown eyes were shining with what might be tears. "So it seems," he said gently. He wanted to tell her that Charles wasn't the same boy who had shared his model of Saint-Malo with her. In fact, Justin wasn't certain if Louise would even like him very much anymore.

Putting an arm around his daughter, Gabriel met Justin's eyes. "I would advise you to pay a visit to Maman. She misses you quite desperately." He paused, as if uncertain whether to continue. "I realize you may not believe this, but her health has been uncertain in recent weeks."

CHAPTER 4

*R*iding along the wildly beautiful Cornish cliffs, Justin wondered again when exactly his life had slipped from his own control. Had it begun a decade ago, when he'd arrived in Cornwall because his mother was *supposedly* on her deathbed? Or perhaps Mouette, who soon appeared on the scene, was to blame. She'd bewitched him so thoroughly that he couldn't be bothered protecting his heart.

Never mind, he told himself. It was far too late to take back his old life...yet, Justin's breathing tightened at this realization. Once he'd been free to roam the seas and challenge fate, intoxicate women and take lovers at will, and generally feel unbound by convention or anyone's expectations for him.

No more. Now others made plans for him that felt increasingly wrong.

Leaning forward slightly as Hugo, his black stallion, galloped full out over the coastal path, Justin gave himself over to the thrill of the moment. The wind was bracing, and white clouds hastened across the azure sky. In that moment, riding hard, his thighs tensed against Hugo's muscled body, Justin felt almost young again. A short distance away, the nearby cliffs dropped off, plunging down to rocky beaches that skirted the vast English Channel. If Justin squinted across the glittering water, he could almost see Roscoff, the French village where he and Gabriel had conducted so many smuggling missions. A cascade of vivid memories made him draw a deep breath and smile.

But that was long ago.

By the time they reached the outskirts of Polperro, uncomfortable emotions were at war inside Justin, none of which he cared to examine. Climbing the lane toward Elysium, his brother's eccentric estate, he looked down at Polperro. The whitewashed village was nestled in a sheltered harbor shaped like a bowl, protected by a sea-wall that bordered the English Channel. There, on a high promontory called Peak Rock, perched a long building called the net loft that Justin had owned for several years. Upstairs, his business partner, Lady Daphne Leyton, had overseen a millinery shop that employed dozens of women during a time when the fishing industry was struggling after a series of destructive storms. Justin had even brought his father-in-law, André Raveneau, in as an investor and advisor, which greatly pleased Mouette. Not only had the milliners been gainfully employed, but Justin had been able to use his profits to assist in repairing boats and houses damaged in the terrible storms of 1817 and, more recently, 1824.

Pondering all of this, Justin slowed Hugo to a walk, took the reins in his left hand, and pushed his other, gloved palm against the discomfort in his chest. Those had been good years. He had found his work to be almost as stimulating as overseeing a smuggling enterprise, and it had been surprisingly satisfying to help people rather than outwit them.

But then, last summer, Daphne announced she wanted to have children before it was "too late." Ignoring Justin's protests, she accepted a marriage proposal from the widowed Squire Callywith and went off to live in a pretty manor house near Fowey.

He looked away from the picturesque little village and the net loft, deciding he would sell the place as soon as possible. What did it matter? No one else could manage it but Daphne, and Justin couldn't be bothered to find another profitable use for the place.

"Hugo," he said in a husky voice. The horse's ears flicked attentively. "We are not going to Elysium today. Take me instead to the cottage of my parents."

Xavier and Cerise St. Briac had decamped from France to Cornwall after Gabriel married Lady Isabella Trevarre. Even though his mother's dramas and manipulations had driven him mad, when she left, a secret part of him had felt offended. Even...deserted, as he had all the times she ran away after a quarrel with their father, as if he and Gabriel didn't exist.

Or matter.

Mouette liked to point out that Cerise St. Briac knew exactly how to elicit the response of her choice from Justin. He argued that he would be happy never to be in her company again, but of course that was a lie. Loving one's parent wasn't a choice, it seemed. In the case of Justin and his mother, it often felt more like a curse.

Xavier and Cerise were spending their declining years in Woodlark Cottage, on the edge of Elysium's sprawling, beautifully designed gardens. As Justin drew near and dismounted, he was surprised to see his parents sitting together on a small brick terrace under the spreading branches of a magnolia tree.

"*Bonjour*," he called, loosely tying Hugo's reins to a post.

Xavier St. Briac, seeming frailer than Justin remembered, pushed to his feet and came toward him. "Ah, my boy. How glad I am to have you back."

They embraced, but all the while Justin was keenly aware of his mother, holding her teacup, watching him. She wore an exceedingly fashionable myrtle-green morning dress, its collar encircled by a small cape with notched edges. She even wore a stylish headdress that was accentuated by emerald-green feathers that glimmered in the sunlight. One would think she was about to entertain grand aristocrats rather than sip tea outside a tiny cottage with her elderly husband.

"*Bonjour, mon fils.* I rather expected you sooner," Cerise remarked. Setting her fragile cup in its saucer, she held her hand out for him to kiss.

Justin lifted a brow. "I wasn't aware we had an appointment." As he bent to take her hand, their eyes locked.

"But of course, I have been expecting you. I knew Gabriel would tell you I have not been well, and you would come," she said, assuming a tragic expression. "You will always be my firstborn child. Nothing can change that deep bond between us."

Justin clenched his teeth and sat down on the garden bench facing them. "Gabriel said that your health has been uncertain. What does that mean? What is wrong?"

When Cerise pinched her eyes closed, as if she could not bear to speak, Xavier leaned forward, whispering, "Your maman has been having spells."

"What kind of spells?" he demanded.

His father lowered thick white brows. "Kindly moderate your tone. She needs peace."

Peace. *Peace?* Was his father in jest? Maman had never given any of them a moment's peace in her entire life. The hairs on the back of Justin's neck prickled as he turned to look at her again. His mother peeked at him under her lashes and slowly brought a hand to her bosom.

"It is my heart..." she whispered.

Justin knew a moment of involuntary panic as it came to him what she meant. All his life, his mother had invented a variety of crises to get his attention, yet lately he had begun to realize she was old now, and really might die one day.

"Ah, there you all are!" The black mood was suddenly broken by a familiar female voice, drifting to them on the breeze. "You are enjoying this fine day. And Justin, how thoughtful of you to visit your parents so soon after your return from France."

In the distance, Justin saw his sister-in-law, Isabella, coming along the path toward Woodlark Cottage. The ribbons of her straw bonnet flew out behind her like streamers, and she carried a woven basket. At her side walked Camille, the more beautiful of Gabriel and Izzie's two daughters. The first time Justin had met her, when she was only four years old, it was clear that his little niece would grow up to be a heartbreaker.

Cerise frowned, murmuring, "Some people do not wait for an invitation before they visit."

Ignoring her, Justin rose and went forward to embrace Isabella and Camille. Holding his niece at arm's length, he observed, "You are growing up, *ma belle*. I pity my poor brother when the suitors begin to line up to beg for your attentions."

Charming dimples winked in Camille's cheeks as she smiled back at him. The girl's caramel curls shone in the sunlight and Justin found her Parisian-blue eyes more astonishingly lovely than ever.

"You should not place so much importance on beauty," Isabella scolded good-naturedly. "She has other gifts to offer the world."

41

"I don't doubt it," Justin agreed, hoping Camille wasn't a member of the fossil-hunting brigade.

"My great passion at the moment," Camille volunteered, "is *birds*. I believe I shall become an ornithologist, like John James Audubon, from America. I longed to go and see his drawings when he visited London last year. Now Mama is teaching me to paint, so that I may illustrate the birds I discover."

"Fascinating," Justin said dryly, which earned him a glance from his sister-in-law. In a kinder tone, he added, "I have no doubt you'll make a great success of anything you undertake."

Camille was staring at her grandmother in consternation. "Grandmère, are those feathers I see on your bonnet? And what is that ruby area that gleams so?"

"*Ah, oui.*" Proudly, Cerise lifted a hand and touched them. "Lady Daphne, my gifted milliner, created this embellishment from the skins of real hummingbirds!"

Camille looked aghast, but when her mother put a hand on her arm, she bit her lip and said nothing. Justin realized he had never given any thought to the more exotic items Daphne used in her workroom, but why would he?

With a sigh, Cerise continued, "How sad that Lady Daphne has given up her craft to marry. I don't know what I shall do. She was hoping to procure some rare specimens from distant lands."

Straightening her shoulders, Camille said, "Grandmère, I really must speak out. I am very opposed to killing beautiful birds merely to use for decoration. It is shocking." As if surprised at her own bold words, she added more gently, "Of course, I know *you* didn't mean any harm."

As the girl went forward to kiss her grandparents, Isabella put her basket on the bench where Justin had been sitting. "I've brought a lovely apple tart from

Madame Kerjean," she said, referring to the Breton cook whom Justin had long been trying to lure away to his own household. After emptying the basket, Izzie looked at Cerise. "How are you feeling today?"

Justin watched his mother with suspicion as she gave a plaintive sigh. "I have had no spells today, at least not *yet*...so we must be grateful." She turned her keen eyes on Xavier, instructing, "You will walk with Isabella and Camille as they return home."

"We don't have to leave yet," Izzie said. She looked as if she were about to take a seat, but paused, waiting.

"I was just about to engage in a private conversation with my elder son," Cerise said. "You understand, of course."

Justin's father rose obediently. "It would do me good to take a bit of exercise."

Gathering her things, Isabella turned to Justin. "I know you may have doubts about Emeline coming with us to Lyme Regis, but I think it will be a wonderful experience for all the girls."

Before he could reply, the little group made their farewells and left. Sitting all alone with his mother, Justin suddenly felt as if the air in the garden had become very thick. Still, he returned to his bench and reclined in an attitude of nonchalance.

"The hour advances, Maman. What is it you wish to talk about?"

She leaned forward, peering at him. "How is your eye?"

Reflexively, he brought a hand up to touch his eyepatch. "Unchanged! Why would you ask such a thing?"

"I am your mother. Each time I see you, I feel shocked anew that you have truly been disfigured in such a way. I suppose I hope that, with your great wealth, you might discover a remedy."

"There is no *remedy*," Justin said harshly. "Was there anything else?"

"We have not been together for many weeks. Now that you have returned to Cornwall, perhaps you will behave as a son ought and visit me more often." She paused. "Daily?"

Suddenly, he was overjoyed to be going to London. "I am sorry, Maman, but we have other plans. It seems that we must travel to London." For good measure, he added, "I have no choice."

"London? Whatever for? You have just returned home." Her sharp tone was designed, he knew, to make him feel guilty.

"Charles came to us today, announcing that he is betrothed to the daughter of a duke. He asks that we come back to London with him so we may participate in the festivities that are planned." Although Justin wanted to grumble about this, he couldn't admit his discomfort to Cerise.

"The daughter of a duke? Are you quite certain?" She sipped her tea, looking as if she didn't believe a word he'd said. "I thought Charles was a mere baronet. Not even a true peer!"

Justin was mildly surprised that his mother was even aware of such fine points. "All I know is what I've been told."

"But why would an aristocrat wish to marry so far below her station?"

"You are asking the wrong person, Maman." Then, knowing Mouette would wish him to defend her son, he added, "It's not as if Charles is a stableboy. He is very handsome and well-educated, thanks to my deep pockets. And he has inherited a title, after all, which is more than any of us can say."

"Hmmph," she sniffed. "And what is it *you* are expected to do in London?"

Every time his mother uttered another pointed question, the band around his chest tightened. "I am Charles's stepfather." Did he sound defensive? "Mouette wants me to be there."

Closing her eyes, Cerise gave a small shake of her head. "Listen to yourself, *mon fils*. Do you really imagine that *you* can blend into London society? You, who scoffed at my every attempt to teach you true manners? Impossible!"

Unable to help himself, Justin demanded, "Are you implying that I am some sort of uncivilized brute?"

"You may forget to whom you are speaking. No one knows you better than I do." Again, she allowed a pause fraught with meaning to settle between them. "Perhaps you imagine that you can change! That you may be accepted by *those* people. Do you long for that?" Again, the pause. "Of course not!"

"That's right, I long for no such thing. I'm only going because I have a family. It is my..." He swallowed.

"Your *duty*? It is a word that could strangle a man such as you, Justin. It will bring out the worst in you, mark my words."

He stood, remembering how Charles had also hinted that he would prefer Justin to stay behind in Cornwall. "I must be on my way now. I will send one of the servants to check on you and Papa while we are away."

Cerise smiled thinly and set down her teacup. "That would be lovely." Seizing a last chance to torment him, she slid her gaze over his physique. "If you mean to join the smart set, you should be a bit more careful in your habits, I think. Perhaps you have indulged in too much rich food during your months in France?"

"How kind of you to notice." Bending, Justin briefly kissed his mother's cheek. "*Au revoir*, Maman."

CYNTHIA WRIGHT

When he would turn away, she suddenly clutched at his hand. "Justin!"

Steeling himself, he looked back, waiting for her to claim the last word.

"Pray for me," she rasped.

Justin managed to nod, unable to speak. As he walked away, his hands clenched into aching fists, he felt his mother watching him.

Sangdieu! If only he could discover some means of escape...

46

CHAPTER 5

*D*arkness gathered around Mouette as she stood at the French doors leading out to the terrace. Feeling chilled, she drew the edges of her shawl closer and sighed. Sunset was turning to night. Violet-tinted shadows swirled like lost memories across the stone terrace.

For a few moments, Mouette was transported back to a golden afternoon when the entire family had gathered on the terrace for a festive meal *al fresco*. Emeline had been a sweet babe in her arms then. Charles had been sitting beside Louise, showing her one of the buildings in the model he was making of Saint-Malo, while she offered to make a map to identify each structure. Anthony, clutching his wooden sword, had been dashing about with Robinson. Even Mouette's parents, André and Devon Raveneau, had been among the many guests, so happy to see their daughter building a new life with a man who adored her.

And Justin had formed a fragile truce with his mother, with some encouragement from Gabriel.

Mouette wondered now if she had properly appreciated how sweet her life had been on that perfect day. Nodding to herself, she thought, *Yes, of course I did!*

She'd been grateful, brimming over with joy and love for everyone in her life, especially Justin. They'd both been suffused with hope as they began to knit together a family of their very own.

Hope, Mouette decided, had the ability to tint the future with a rosy glow not yet tarnished by reality.

A little voice inside reminded her to stop dwelling on the past and start thinking about what lay ahead. So much had happened this afternoon that Mouette had been able to push her promise to Charles to the back of her mind. But the truth was, she dreaded this forced return to London, and especially to the world of the *ton* who had shunned her after Harry's disgrace.

She turned and started toward the stairway. Emeline had already gone to Elysium with Gabriel and Louise, deprived of a chance to say goodbye to her father, who had not returned from visiting his parents. After a decade of marriage, Mouette had learned not to worry about his safety when he didn't turn up. If she had ever imagined he might adhere to time constraints, she now knew such expectations were folly.

Reaching the stair hall, Mouette paused to look at the figures from Greek mythology that marched across the long wall, seeming almost real in the plum-tinted twilight. What a labor of love it had been to restore this mural, which had looked so grimy and forlorn when she saw it for the first time. Mouette had just reached out to touch one of the figures, a woman carrying a tall pitcher, when a voice interrupted her reverie.

"Mother, is that you?"

Turning, she saw that the door to Charles's bedchamber had opened, sending a wedge of lamplight into the corridor. Since he had spent so many years away at university, often retreating with his new friends to their families' manor houses, it felt sweet yet sad to have him home again, back in his old room. Now

Charles stood in the doorway, coatless, his waistcoat half-buttoned, sipping from another glass of brandy. Robinson was lying on a rug nearby, his short back legs sticking out and one eye open as if hoping his erstwhile master might create some fun for them.

Crossing to Charles's side, Mouette indulged a maternal urge to smooth back the wavy blond locks that fell over his brow. "Goodness, how handsome you are."

Her son glanced away. "People do tell me that I resemble Father." He paused. "I mean my *real* father, not Justin."

"That's quite true. And he was very handsome as well." She suppressed a sigh, recalling the poignant moment when a fourteen-year-old Charles had first called Justin *Father*. When had the boy hardened again? Mouette tried to change the subject. "Have you seen your brother since supper? I half-expected you two to be together, talking."

"Anthony? He left to go to the Three Pilchards Inn in Polperro, to meet..." He cleared his throat and glanced heavenward. "*Someone*. You must know, Mother, that Anthony is far more like Justin than he realizes!"

Mouette tried to laugh. "A last bit of celebration before he returns to Cambridge. As for me, I was just going to see if Gwynn has finished unpacking. Is there anything I can get you?"

"Unpacking?" he echoed. "Why are you doing that? We leave for London in the morning."

Taken aback, Mouette replied, "But, most of my wardrobe is in those trunks. We were in France for months! I won't need nearly so many clothes in London."

"Why not? You'll need all those and more, Mother. Perhaps you've forgotten how many events are in store during the Season, especially when a grand betrothal is in the offing." He paused. "I had thought to suggest you visit a dressmaker as soon as you arrive in London. Thank God Justin has the means to pay for the new gowns you'll need."

She felt a rush of anxiety. "Really, I don't know..."

"Mother." He stepped closer, his expression pleading. "I am depending on you. You must realize that people who *matter* remember the past, and it's imperative that we prove to them that...all that has changed."

He didn't need to elaborate. Mouette herself tried not to think or talk about the darkest period in their lives, after Harry had committed unspeakable crimes and hanged himself in prison. Since then, it had been a delicate balancing act to allow Charles to cling to proud memories of his father, especially after she married Justin and their lives were transformed.

Oh, she thought, *why must life be so complicated?*

"Of course, I will do my very best, but..." Mouette felt sick. "You know it won't be easy to bring Justin to heel." Every time she imagined him standing in a receiving line with a lot of snobbish aristocrats—who were also the same people who had rejected her so cruelly after Harry's downfall—Mouette felt a wave of trepidation.

Charles turned away and went back inside the shadowed bedchamber. "Honestly, I wouldn't mind if he didn't come at all," he said bluntly. "But if he does, I am trusting you to bring him to heel." His voice was muffled as he continued, "Do you think it's been easy for me, existing as the outsider in your happy new family? Once you told us that Anthony was actually *his* son, I knew I would have to carve out my own place in the world, far away from here."

She drew a painful breath. It wouldn't help now to argue that he was wrong. Charles had been scarred, first by Harry's betrayals, and then by his death. He'd clung to the hereditary title of baronet, even as a boy, in spite of the way the *ton*—including Harry's pretentious mother - had snubbed them. Mouette knew that under his proud demeanor, Charles still felt that pain.

"I know it's been a challenge for you, darling," she said. "But whether you know it or not, you still have two admittedly imperfect parents who love you very much." Across the room, her gaze lit on the table where his painstakingly accurate wooden model of Saint-Malo was set up. It had been a project Charles and Justin had undertaken together, and Charles had been captivated for a time. "Ah, there is your beautiful wooden city," Mouette said, touching his sleeve. "Shall we put it in a crate and take it to London so you may have it for your own children one day?"

Charles turned away, a muscle working in his jaw. "No, I don't think so. After all, Saint-Malo is Justin's world, not mine. Perhaps, instead, my children and I will make a model of Cranford Castle. That would be much more appropriate."

For a long moment, she couldn't think what he was talking about. "Oh...is that the name of the Duke of Bellingham's ancestral home?"

"Yes, of course. And 'ere long, it will be *my* home as well."

* * *

IN THE LARGE bedchamber Mouette shared with Justin, she discovered Gwynn, her trusted maid, standing next to the trunks they had brought back from Saint-Malo. There were lamps lit around the room, bathing the stylish Empire furnishings in a welcoming glow.

"I'm sorry I have not yet unpacked, my lady, but I were waiting to ask you what I should do with your things. Sir Charles says you be going to London on the morrow." Gwynn who was stout and strong, seemed to have an infinite store of both energy and loyalty.

Mouette bit her lip. "I suppose we should leave everything as it is. My son informs me I will need all these clothes, and more. I had hoped we might only be staying for a fortnight or less, but it seems it will be much longer."

Gwynn waited, nodding. "Will you be needing me in London, my lady?" She blushed. "I mean, I have heard that your house there does not keep a staff...since you have been so little in residence."

"I hope you can come, but I must speak to M'sieur St. Briac," Mouette replied, beset by another wave of dread as she remembered the house on Bedford Square, so filled with difficult, even shameful memories. One of the best parts of marriage to Justin had been the gift of a completely new life in a new place that was unconnected to her past. But now, thanks to Charles and his lofty aspirations, the past was marching back to confront her head-on.

Meeting Gwynn's direct gaze, she allowed, "Indeed, we may well need you."

"Baptiste and I have been making lists," Gwynn announced.

This news was strangely reassuring to Mouette. "I appreciate that."

The mood was broken when the maid lifted her chin, alert, as if she could hear a distant sound. "It be the master." She scurried out the door. "He will be hungry!"

Mouette suppressed an instinctive urge to go downstairs and greet her husband. If he couldn't be bothered to join his family for supper, especially on this last evening they would all be together, why should she rush to welcome him back? Instead, she opened a drawer in her bureau and took out a soft, warm nightgown. It covered too much of her for Justin's taste, but tonight she had no interest in pleasing him.

Minutes later, as she was getting into their big Sheraton bed, Justin appeared. He had unknotted his neck-cloth, discarded his coat, and was holding a plate of squab pie. The aroma filled the room.

"Mmm," he rumbled approvingly. "I will never admit it to Margaret, but I believe she may at last be winning me over to Cornish food." He ate another bite and set down the plate.

"May I ask where you have been?" Instead of going toward him for a kiss, Mouette climbed into bed, trying to resist the carnal attraction she always felt in his presence.

Justin watched, one brow arched as he poured a cognac from a cut-glass decanter on the cellaret. He really was too sinfully handsome. "After I met with Maman, I needed a strong drink, so I went to the Three Pilchards in Polperro. You will never guess who I saw there."

"Anthony," she said. "I heard from Charles that he had gone there to see his friends."

"Is that what you call them?" Justin gave a dark laugh. "I do not think you would approve, *chérie*. Especially if you had seen the very worldly-looking, ginger-haired beauty who joined him there."

"Like father, like son, I suppose." Mouette heard the edge in her own voice. She watched as he swallowed the last of the cognac, unable to stop herself from saying, "You know you should not drink so much."

"So you have mentioned."

As he came toward the bed, Justin removed one piece of clothing at a time, until he was naked as he climbed in beside her. Although his waist was thicker, his chest remained broad and powerful, his thighs long and lean-muscled. Lifting the covers, he scrutinized her. "What possesses you to wear that garment in our bed?"

"It is chilly, and you were not here."

Justin began to undo the tiny buttons on her night-gown, his fingers dark against the snow-white fabric. "Stop scolding me. You know it won't do a bit of good."

His hand slid down to find the hem of her garment, and he slowly slid it up to her waist, his fingertips trailing fire up the length of her leg. Awash with desire, Mouette felt as if she'd taken an aphrodisiac. But of course, Justin himself was the drug. Her breathing quickened, her nipples tightened, and the warm tin-gling between her legs became a throb.

A distant part of her was again reassured by the fa-miliar response, for yesterday she'd grown flushed and hot for no reason. Was it another sign that her change of life was at hand?

"Relax," he coaxed. "You worry too much."

She let Justin turn her back into the pillows and cover her body with his, opening her legs with his knee so he might lie between them. He was hardening against her most intimate places, moving just enough to drive her mad.

"You think you can do as you please and I will al-ways relent and come to you...like this," Mouette protested, even as he lowered his mouth to her breast.

"I do," he agreed, glancing up. "Don't tell me you still have fantasies of changing me?"

"I..." She paused, facing reality once again. "I do know better."

It was impossible to hold back the tidal wave of arousal. He cupped her breast and brought his mouth to her nipple, suckling, skillfully varying the pressure until she sank her fingers into his hair and heard her-self moan. She breathed in his familiar yet intoxicating male scent. Consumed by need, Mouette was wet, arching her hips against him. Before Justin moved to her other breast, he drew her nightgown up and over her head, tossing it on the floor.

"You won't be needing that." As he spoke, he flashed a wicked smile in the shadows.

* * *

WHEN THEY LAY TOGETHER at last, spent and dozing, Justin suddenly raised his head from the pillow. They were on their sides, facing each other. He was still inside her, Mouette's pale leg hooked over his.

"Emmie!" he said in a startled tone. "She departs with Gabriel and the others for that horrible fossil place tomorrow! I must kiss her goodnight."

"She has already gone. She went home with Gabriel and Louise." Mouette couldn't help adding, "If you had come back sooner, you doubtless could have said goodbye."

Justin separated his warm, hard body from hers and lay on his back, staring at the ceiling. "I am an inconsiderate brute."

"You can be," she agreed, "but your family loves you all the same." Watching him, she kept her tone light as she dared to add, "Really, Justin, you can redeem yourself by helping me in the weeks ahead, in London..."

He didn't look at her. "*Mon Dieu*. That may be asking too much."

Mouette's stomach turned over. "But you told me you would come."

"I would probably make it all worse," he grumbled. "And I believe Charles agrees."

"Are you saying you now refuse?" When he made no response, her heart began to race. "You should not pay attention to Charles. Please, Justin, listen to me."

"It's late. Let me sleep. I will consider the matter in the morning."

After ten years of marriage to Justin St. Briac, she could guess that his diabolical mother was doubtless responsible for this black mood. But knowing that and doing anything about it were two very different things. Despair welled up inside her and she retreated to her own pillow. He had a way of erecting a barrier at times like this...a barrier she had, over the years, stopped trying to breach.

Mouette yearned to be able to tell her husband about the fear and shame reared up whenever she thought of trying to re-enter London society, of encountering her former mother-in-law again, of being back in the house where her dignity had been stripped from her with each valuable possession she had sold to feed her sons.

If Justin could stand beside her and support her through this ordeal, it would mean more than he could ever imagine! Yet the notion of saying this aloud to him was frightening, for the possibility that he would reject her plea was very real. In the back of her throat, Mouette tasted the salty tears she could not let him see.

Perhaps her husband would prove to be incapable of helping her in the way she needed. Fine. It wouldn't be the first time Mouette had gathered the inner strength to help herself.

CHAPTER 6

Ihen Justin awoke in the morning, his head throbbed as if someone had hit him with a hammer. With a groan, he recalled the indecent quantity of cognac he'd drunk last night.

"If I may be so bold, m'sieur," came Baptiste's voice from across the bedchamber. "I would observe that you had virtually given up both tobacco and strong spirits in recent years. I think it did you good."

Justin sat up in bed and looked around. The hammer became a vise that squeezed his skull. "Have you no regard for our privacy?" he demanded of Baptiste. "My wife could well have been in a state of undress."

The exemplary French servant placed a tray of *café au lait* and fragrant *brioche* on the table beside the bed. "That would be wrong indeed, m'sieur, if I did not know better. Madame St. Briac is downstairs, overseeing the many details connected to our departure for London." Baptiste paused, pursing his lips. "She seems to believe you will accompany us."

Their eyes met. "You are going as well?" asked Justin.

"*Bien sûr*! Who else can be trusted to run madame's

London home properly? It has been empty and virtually ignored for many years. In addition, do I not follow wherever you go, m'sieur?"

Justin scowled. It seemed that they all intended that he should subject himself to a lot of awful London balls where he must pretend to be just one more stiff-rumped aristocrat, cheering on Charles's plans to elevate himself to the son-in-law of a duke. All his mother's scornful predictions about his inability to carry off such a charade echoed in Justin's ears. Perhaps, he thought ruefully, she really did know him better than anyone.

"Perhaps you might have asked me what *my* plans are." He threw back the covers and rose to his feet, naked. The squeezing vice suddenly became a spear between his eyes. It was tempting to fall back onto the bed again, but Baptiste was watching as if he could read his mind, and Justin was determined to prove him wrong.

"Your plans, m'sieur?" The rail-thin Frenchman feigned confusion. "But I was standing there on the terrace, serving tea, when Sir Charles announced that madame must return with him to London. Today." He moved toward the dressing room. "And now she has sent me to rouse you and quickly pack the rest of your things."

He considered this. "Of course, you must go with Madame St. Briac. She will need you. But stop packing my clothing." As he spoke, Justin began to dress, wondering why Baptiste's gaze had the power to make him feel so guilty. "Stop looking at me like that! There is an urgent matter I must attend to here." He paused. "Concerning my mother."

Justin dressed quickly, without taking the time to shave or wash, and drank down the *café au lait*. Time to face them. The entire situation was excruciating, because how could he ever truly explain? Even the thought of being closed in that landau with his family for three long days sounded like a form of torture. No, Mouette would do much better without him. If he tried to attend one of those cursed routs, trussed up like a trained monkey, there would surely be hell to pay. Something unforgiveable would happen.

Something that would ruin everything.

Justin took a deep breath and started down the stairs, buttoning his stone-gray waistcoat and tying his neckcloth as he walked. Mouette came into the entry hall just then, looking ravishing as always in her favorite blue pelisse.

"Oh, excellent! Here you are," she exclaimed at the sight of him. "I was a bit worried you might be hiding from me." Her smile seemed tentative, even nervous. "I hope Baptiste has finished packing your things. Charles suggests that we take a separate equipage for the luggage, which seems a fine plan, don't you agree? Anthony has a shocking amount of luggage to take with him back to university. He's found some things he wants to use in his new rooms at Christ's College."

Justin reached the bottom step. He wanted to pull her into his arms and give her one of the indecent kisses she secretly adored, but something told him that would not be a good idea. Was she talking so fast because she was afraid of what he might say?

"Did you have breakfast?" she asked.

"Coffee..." His voice trailed off as the two brothers— or rather, half-brothers—came into the entry hall from the sitting room.

"Good morning, Papa," Anthony called, sending him a conspiratorial wink when Mouette was looking the other way. "I trust you slept well."

Ah, youth, thought Justin. The rogue had probably been up half the night, drinking ale and having his way with that ginger-haired lass, yet now he looked disconcertingly handsome and rested.

"Mother insisted you were coming but I had begun to wonder," exclaimed Charles. He was carrying a paper with a lot of writing; a list of some sort, Justin supposed. "We must depart within the hour."

He gave his stepson a bland nod. "I understand. Might I have a moment alone with your mother?"

Charles frowned. "A moment? Of course. But Will and the others are waiting to load the baggage." He gestured toward the trunks, crates, and other pieces of luggage stacked nearby.

When they were alone, Mouette eyed him warily. "What is this all about? Where are your things? Baptiste went up to pack for you some time ago."

Justin came closer. He reached for her hands, but she slipped free. "Ah, *ma belle*, don't be like that. I love you."

"If that is so, you will call for your baggage and come with us to London."

This was going to be harder than he'd imagined. "I will come, but not today."

Mouette narrowed her eyes at him. "I beg you, do not do this."

"You sound as if I intend to hurt you. That is not the case. If you will listen..."

"Oh, Justin!" For a moment, he feared she might sob, but then her back straightened and she merely stared at him, unblinking, waiting.

"I went to see Maman yesterday, and I am worried about her."

"I see." Mouette closed her eyes, looking very angry. "Next you will tell me she is dying!" She paused. "Again."

"Now that you mention it, she may be! She is having spells. Something to do with her heart." Even as he spoke, Justin knew that this was perhaps the least of the reasons he wanted to stay behind, but it was the only thing he could admit. "Gabriel and his family are on their way to Lyme Regis. What sort of son would I be if I deserted her now?"

Will, the coachman, came in through the front door, trailed by two liveried footmen and Robinson the corgi. Together, the servants began to transfer the trunks and other luggage to the equipage outside. Robinson stood looking between Justin and Mouette, then trotted over to loyally sit down beside his master.

Something in Mouette's face worried Justin, and he felt the familiar squeezing in his chest. Perhaps he was making a mistake. "Just give me a little time, *chérie*. I will come as soon as I possibly can." After a pause, he remembered the more practical details. "Baptiste will look after you. And you must not worry about funds. Buy whatever you like."

It seemed she could scarcely bear to look at him. Turning away without even a farewell embrace, she said in a voice that shook with fury and disappointment, "I swear, Justin St. Briac, you are *impossible*."

How many times had she said those words to him in the past? It was his custom to laugh and counter with a suggestive challenge, reminding Mouette that she didn't really want him to change, did she? And then she would soften, he would kiss the tender back of her neck, and feel her melt against him. Soon they would be in bed together, and whatever it was he'd done would once again be forgotten.

But this felt chillingly different.

Mouette was walking away, through the door, to join her sons. As he stood alone at the bottom of the stairs, Justin wondered if he had finally gone too far.

* * *

DURING THE THREE-DAY journey to London, Mouette tried to make herself numb, to harden her heart against Justin so she wouldn't suffer so much under the crushing weight of disappointment. Really, how much was she supposed to endure? If she ever let *him* down in such a way, it might be the end of the marriage, but somehow the rules seemed to be different for him. It didn't help that her two sons were with her, watching her in the close confines of the landau. Anthony wore an expression of sympathetic concern, while Charles looked rather smug, as if Justin's failure to be there with them bore out some deeper truth he had known all along.

Evening was falling when they reached London, and the landau drew up before Mouette's erstwhile home in Bedford Square. Just the sight of the narrow, three-story townhouse made her feel queasy. Or perhaps the word was *queasier*, for she had felt sick with nerves during the entire journey from Cornwall.

As Charles helped her out of the carriage, Mouette felt a surge of gratitude that her two sons were with her during this time of turmoil. There was something very bittersweet about returning here again with the two of them, for they had lived through the hardest period of their lives in this house. First, Harry had died under utterly traumatic circumstances, and then Mouette had learned of his giant debts. She had taken the boys to live in America for a time, with her parents, but eventually she had pulled herself together and they returned to London, the only real home her sons had ever known. In order to survive, Mouette had begun to sell the many valuable furnishings and works of art accumulated during her marriage. Even the servants had to be let go, one by one, until there were none. Determined to hide her shame from the world, Mouette had kept just one room, the sitting room, decorated impeccably, so if anyone came to visit, they would never guess it was all a façade.

"I've always wondered why you kept this house, Mother," Charles was saying now as they went inside. "But I suppose you realized you might need it one day...given Justin's glaring shortcomings as a husband."

In the starkly empty entry hall, Anthony put an arm around her shoulders, and Mouette felt a rush of gratitude for his support. However, when she looked up at his rakish profile, she recognized disillusionment in his dark eyes.

"I don't want to talk about your father at the moment," she said to Charles. There was a catch in her voice.

His mouth tightened, but before he could remind her that Justin was not his *real* father, Will and the grooms began carrying the luggage into the house. "Where shall we put your things, madame?" asked the coachman.

Mouette's instinctive reaction was to conceal her bedchamber from them, for all that was left was a simple bed and a table. Everything else had been sold, even the exquisite gold mirror that once hung above her priceless serpentine bureau of inlaid mahogany. The last time Mouette had seen the room, it had resembled a monk's cell...but now she reminded herself that she was no longer poverty-stricken. Marriage to Justin had changed all of that.

"Don't worry, I'll show them the way," said Anthony, patting her shoulder. "And I'll direct Baptiste and Gwynn to the service rooms."

Did he feel sorry for her? Suddenly Mouette pictured herself as an old woman who had made bad choices and now needed her sons to help her navigate life. Finding herself alone with Charles, she sighed.

"I could do with a cup of tea, but no doubt Baptiste

will have already thought of that," she murmured.

Charles was standing nearby, in the doorway to the morning room, scanning the interior. This room had once been the essence of elegance, filled with feminine pieces that reflected Mouette's fine taste. However, except for a delicate writing desk that stood in the window, hidden under a linen holland cover, everything else was now gone.

Above the mantel, there was an empty place on the wall that had once been filled by an exquisite portrait of Mouette herself. Painted by the great French artist, Élisabeth Vigée Le Brun, on the eve of Mouette and Harry's wedding, it had been her prized possession. The newly resurrected memory of the day it had been carried out of the house brought a hot tide of shame.

"Too bad about your portrait, Mother," said Charles with a shake of his golden curls. "Now that I am so much older, I can appreciate that you really must have been at the very bottom to have parted with it. How fortunate that you managed to find Justin."

Mouette felt her face grow hot. Was he implying that she married Justin only to save them all from utter ruin? "Justin and I fell in love," she said defensively. "We are still in love!"

"Oh really, is that what it's called?" Quickly, then, he changed the subject. "I must be on my way, but I'll return tomorrow. We shall discuss the extensive renovations that must be undertaken in this house."

"*Renovations?*"

"Of course! How could we possibly allow anyone to visit here, given this sad situation?"

Anthony came up beside them, holding a small silver tray with a steaming teapot, a cup and saucer, and a plate of Margaret's delicious ginger fairings that she'd sent with them from Cornwall. "Come and sit down, Mama," he said.

Gratefully, Mouette followed him into the beautifully decorated sitting room, where Gwynn was removing covers from all the furnishings. It almost felt normal to take a seat on the striped settee and watch Anthony pour tea for her.

"At least this room is still presentable," Charles said from the doorway. To his brother, he said, "Have you seen our former bedroom?"

The look they exchanged was like a knife in Mouette's heart.

"I did." A shadow passed over Anthony's face, then he lifted both brows and his mouth quirked. "It's not the best memory, but at least it's far behind us."

"I won't look at it," said Charles, sounding angry.

Were they speaking of the way their furniture had disappeared, one piece at a time? "I had been under the impression you two rather enjoyed making a tent out of blankets and pretending you were sleeping in the woods..."

"I must be on my way," Charles repeated.

"You aren't lodging here with our mother?" asked Anthony.

"No, I've been staying at Brandreth House since the beginning of the Season, and Grandmama insists I remain with her. Given my new circumstances, it is the best place for me to be." He flushed slightly. "I would invite you there, Anthony, but since it was revealed that you aren't truly a Brandreth, Grandmama's feelings are a bit bruised."

"I wouldn't come in any case," Anthony said. Watching Mouette, he added, "I will sleep here tonight, but in the morning, I must return to Cambridge. I am meeting with a new friend who may share my lodgings at Christ's College. A very interesting fellow called Darwin. He's mad for entomology." He paused before adding, "But I don't like leaving you alone, Mama."

"Oh, I won't be alone," Mouette said bravely. "Baptiste and Gwynn will be here."

Charles began drawing on his gloves. "I'll ask Will to drive me to Grandmama's residence. It isn't far. And, in the morning, I will be back, Mother." Charles said. Glancing toward his brother, he added, "Goodbye, Anthony."

When the front door closed, Anthony leaned back in his slender carved chair and stretched out lean-muscled legs. "Would it offend you if I said that I'm relieved to be rid of him?"

"Well, you've said it anyway, haven't you?" Mouette sighed. "Your brother hasn't always been like this. There were years, after Justin and I married, when he let down his shield. Don't you agree?"

Anthony shrugged, and Mouette noticed how wide his shoulders were. "I think he was jealous, though."

"Of...the three of us?"

"Yes. You were in a state of bliss, and I suddenly had a new, living father who was like a character from an adventure novel."

"But all of us were happy *together*, weren't we?"

Anthony's mouth bent in what seemed to be a rueful smile. "It was like a dream, though, don't you think? The way one feels at the beginning of a romance, before reality sets in."

"My, aren't you worldly," Mouette said before she could stop herself.

He gave a short, ironic laugh but continued, "Charles doubtless saw the writing on the wall. When he went away to Eton and began to make a lot of fancy friends, I think he was glad to learn that his title might make him superior to the rest of us."

"But don't you agree that all of his pretensions are merely a shield?" Mouette persisted.

Anthony reached for one of the ginger biscuits and

popped it into his mouth. "I suppose so, but it's what the *ton* is all about. And now all those ridiculous social rules have become Charles's religion." He swallowed the biscuit and added, "Shield or not, he's behaving like an arse."

Mouette's eyes stung as she regarded the handsome young man she and Justin had created long ago, on the first night they met. He was a product of their passion. Looking into Anthony's eyes, she realized he was speaking not only of his brother, but his father as well.

"We are all human, darling," she said gently. "You included."

"Agreed. But, I've decided, we have a choice about how close we want to get to other people. Take Papa, for example." Anthony leaned back again in his chair, gazing past her at a landscape on the wall. Mouette waited, her heart pounding. "He's rather like a fire. Mesmerizing. Radiating excitement, heat, even a kind of wild intoxication. But if one gets too close, it's very easy to be burned."

"Anthony..." Mouette cautioned.

"I'm sorry. I didn't mean to upset you." He stood, running a hand through his hair as if to shake off the sober words he'd just spoken. "Perhaps it's just as well Papa stayed behind in Cornwall. You have enough to contend with right here in this house, doing battle with the past."

When her son had gone off to wash up, Mouette sat alone in the deepening shadows. From this vantage point, it seemed that her entire adult life had been a disaster. Even her own sons seemed to think so!

And now, her fairytale marriage to Justin was cracking apart. Mouette couldn't bear to think about him, to wonder what he was doing back in Cornwall. If she let her thoughts go down that road, nothing good could come of it...

CHAPTER 7

oodpeckers!
　　Justin opened his good eye. Morning sunlight streamed across the bed, a reminder that he'd forgotten to close the drapes last night. Again.

The blasted green woodpeckers must be back, nesting in the beech trees behind Frenchman's Haven, and now the red-crowned male was sending out a mocking laugh to any competitors who might dare to infringe on his territory.

If Baptiste were here, there would be *café au lait* waiting beside the bed, but Margaret did not indulge Justin's whims so freely.

Just then, a guttural yawn emanated from the pillow where Mouette should have been. Justin reluctantly turned his head and squinted at his bed partner. Robinson the corgi seemed to smile back at him, then rolled onto his back and froze, waiting to be petted.

"How the devil did you get up here again?" In spite of his scolding tone, Justin couldn't resist the dog's comical smile. Reaching toward him, he muttered, "All right, then, here you go. But who is going to rub my belly, I'd like to know?"

Robinson emitted a series of high-pitched sounds of

joy, and Justin suddenly remembered that it had been Charles who named the stray corgi for Robinson Crusoe, the title character in his favorite novel. He'd been much younger then, claiming that he had always wanted a dog of his own, while simultaneously warming to the notion of a new family.

Throwing back the covers, Justin rose from the bed. He could think of enough ways to torture himself with right now without pondering how Charles had frozen him out. Even Robinson had been virtually ignored during the young man's recent visit home.

Justin began to don the same clothes he'd tossed over a chairback last night. This sort of thing was completely out of character for him, since he usually dressed with impeccable care. Baptiste would be aghast, but of course he was in London with Mouette and had better things to do than worry about Justin.

After glancing toward the shaving stand, he decided to forgo his usual grooming regimen. What was the point if he was going to be all alone in the house?

All alone, he realized, to do exactly as he pleased! Of course, he should visit his mother since that was supposed to be the reason he'd remained behind, but she could wait.

Humming to himself, Justin started downstairs, and Robinson followed in his wake.

The house was empty. Perhaps even hollow, if one cared to think of it that way, which Justin did not. He walked to the back of the house, where Margaret and Smythe, the kitchen maid, were making some sort of soup.

"Oh, m'sieur!" exclaimed Margaret. The plump, pink-cheeked cook immediately began to wipe her hands on her apron. "I didn't know *when* you might want breakfast." Her manner suggested that she imagined he might never emerge from his darkened bed-chamber. "What can I make for you?"

He considered this, looking around the big, sunny room. "I beg you, do not offer me a one of those awful pasties."

Smythe tittered, and Margaret sent her a sharp glance.

"Of course, I know better than that, m'sieur! Have I not been cooking for you for many years?"

This was true, but Justin was well aware that Baptiste had overseen all the food Margaret prepared, often doing the cooking himself. No one knew Justin's tastes like Baptiste, not even Mouette, who was not so quick to fulfill his appetites. Why, Justin wondered now, had he encouraged his manservant to go to London?

"I will have something delicious." He paused, watching them. "Even decadent if you take my meaning. Buttered crabs. Roasted potatoes, with those crispy edges you do so well." Glancing toward a towel-covered pan atop the stove, Justin sniffed the fragrance and added, "Some of your excellent scones with clotted cream. And fresh strawberry jam."

Margaret looked alarmed. "But...since Baptiste is not here to make brioche and the dishes you love best, the mistress has requested that I serve you other types of food."

"What the devil does that mean?" Even as Justin spoke, his stomach growled. "Am I not the master of this house?"

Smythe reddened as she watched this exchange. "But m'sieur, the mistress bade us cook eggs and plain porridge for your breakfast. She warned that you must not have too much butter." Then, as if she imagined Justin might welcome her next words, Smythe added,

"We do be making a soup with vegetables and a nice, boiled chicken for your dinner!"

"Your *mistress* is not here! She has left us to go to bloody London!" He glanced between the two of them. "May I remind you who pays your wages?" Turning toward the doorway, he added, "You may bring breakfast to my study. No *porridge*! And don't forget to add something special for Robinson."

The corgi pranced ahead, leading the way through the entrance hall and into the morning room. In his early days with Mouette, Justin had tried to claim this room as his masculine retreat, but eventually he redecorated it for her as an act of love. Remembering the look on her face when she walked in and saw her own rosewood writing table positioned where his desk had been, Justin felt the sting of tears. Quickly, he closed his eyes to hold them at bay.

All of this could have been avoided, he brooded, if Mouette had simply told Charles to go on about his life and write them with a date and time for the wedding. Why did he require his mother's presence in London for the entire Season? Was this the way it would be from now on, with Mouette rushing off to attend to the needs of her grown children, and eventually, her grandchildren? Perhaps she would spend more time in London than here in Cornwall, with him.

The room suddenly felt airless. Crossing to the tall windows, Justin pushed one open and inhaled the April breeze. Overhead, he saw that the sun was high and realized that it must be nearly midday. No wonder Margaret had looked at him as if he were mad when he began to rant about breakfast.

Backing up, Justin sat down on the emerald-silk-upholstered chair that was angled in front of the writing table. Robinson vaulted onto his lap, leaning against his chest and gazing up at him. The dog was as heavy as a sack of potatoes, and his breath smelled, but at least his devotion was unquestionable.

Everything on the surface of the writing desk was a poignant reminder of Mouette. She had special little inkpots and quills, and near one corner was her little stack of books by Jane Austen, Fanny Burney's *Cecelia*, as well as one of the geological notebooks loaned to her by Anthony. For the first time, Justin noticed a framed sketch of a spiraled ammonite, boldly inscribed: *For my dear mama from Emeline St. Briac.*

He wondered why Emmie had not made such a drawing for him.

Robinson emitted a low sound, as if he could read Justin's mind.

"They were cruel to all go away and leave us. Don't you agree?" Justin said in a low voice. He had always thought that people who spoke to their dogs were not only ridiculous but also a bit mad, yet here he was doing it himself.

The corgi's intent gaze held no sympathy. Justin wanted to protest that Robinson could not begin to understand the things Cerise St. Briac had done when Justin and his little brother, Gabriel, had been growing up. How many times, after a quarrel with their father, had she dramatically run away from home? And Xavier had always engaged in the game, chasing after her again and again. The two young boys had occasionally been left alone with servants for a fortnight or longer, while their so-called parents immersed themselves in passionate love games.

No matter how old he grew, Justin still avoided thinking about those terrible episodes. Even though he had felt quite certain that his parents would always return, eventually, there were deeper doubts that festered over the years. How could people who professed to love him behave so selfishly? His own mother still attempted to manipulate the members of her family, especially Justin himself...which made him faintly suspicious of anyone who claimed to love him.

Of course, Mouette was different.

Wasn't she?

Suddenly Justin felt compelled to open the drawer of the writing table. This was where Mouette had hidden his snuffbox a decade ago—to protect his health, she insisted. At the time, he had been furious, but gradually had come to forget about it. All his devilish vices seemed to fade a bit more from his memory with each passing year of happiness.

He thought now of all the cognac he'd been drinking of late and realized that his self-destructive habits had merely been lurking in the shadows, watching and waiting for a signal from him.

Opening the shallow drawer, Justin pushed aside a few trinkets and letters, most of them from Mouette's mother and sister, Lindsay. He reached farther back into the shadowed interior and felt a cold, familiar object. Slowly, he closed his fingers around his old friend, the agate snuffbox.

Just then, a tentative knock sounded at the door, and Smythe's thin face appeared. "Your breakfast, m'sieur," she piped nervously.

Justin's heart thundered as if he'd been caught in the midst of committing a crime. "Fine." It was hard to speak. "Just—put it over there, on my desk."

Even as Smythe entered and placed the tray across the room, she inclined her head just enough to squint in his direction...clearly wondering what he was doing. Justin closed the drawer with such force that Robinson jumped heavily down to the Aubusson rug.

"I be sorry, m'sieur, but the only crab in the larder had begun to turn," Smythe apologized, twisting her hands in her apron.

"I don't know what you mean." He kept his voice even with a great effort, for he wanted to shout at her to go away.

"The buttered crab you requested. We couldn't give you one."

Justin glared at her. "That's fine. It doesn't matter. You may go, Smythe—and take Robinson with you."

He ignored her confused glance, waiting for the door to close before he opened his fingers and beheld the snuffbox that had been his constant companion for so many years. Mouette had come along like a beam of sunlight to distract him from his darker impulses, but now she was far away, fitting herself back into London society.

God only knew what she might be doing at that very moment.

Justin opened the small agate box and saw that it contained a teaspoon's worth of old snuff. Closer inspection confirmed that the ground tobacco was, of course, quite stale. Justin closed the lid with a snap, pleased to realize that he now had an excellent reason to postpone today's visit to his mother.

Instead, he would embark on a far more urgent errand: a visit to Lewis Bates, his erstwhile snuff purveyor in Polperro. Imagining the scene inside Bates's darkened, tobacco-scented shop, Justin knew a surge of anticipation tinged with wickedness.

Ten long years had passed since he had last taken snuff. Suddenly that seemed impossible. How good it would be to reach for his agate snuffbox during moments of unease, to flick it open, take a pinch, and inhale the familiar, burning scent of his favorite blend!

There was no time to waste. Justin rose and started toward the door, passing by the tray laden with fragrant, decadent breakfast dishes.

To his annoyance, he saw that Smythe had lingered with Robinson in the entrance hall.

"M'sieur, have you already finished eating all that food?" she exclaimed.

"Eating?" Justin gave her the briefest of impatient glances. "Oh, no, there's no time for that. I've just remembered a pressing matter that requires my immediate attention..."

CHAPTER 8

" *I* feel very odd, leaving you here like this," Anthony said.

Mouette wanted to say that she felt very odd as well, looking up at her son who was now well on his way to being just as tall and sinfully handsome as his father. She felt a pang of sadness that both her boys were no longer in her charge. They were men now, and instead of listening to their mother, Anthony and Charles now wanted to offer *her* advice.

They were standing in the sitting room's bow window, watching for the arrival of the friend whose family coach would take Anthony back to Cambridge. His luggage was stacked in the entry hall. Soon Mouette would be alone in the house except for Baptiste and Gwynn.

"I'm very excited for you, returning to your new lodgings," she said. "I hope you like Mister Darwin."

"We are already friends, so it should be fine. He's brilliant." He gave her a roguish grin. "I'm hoping a bit of that will rub off on me."

Before Mouette could reply, a fine town chariot drew up in front of their Bedford Square home and a coachman jumped down from the box.

"Are you certain you'll be all right?" Anthony gently brushed the pad of his thumb over her cheekbone. "You look as if you haven't been sleeping well. Bad dreams? Being back in this house must stir up all sorts of memories."

There was a sharp knock at the door, and Mouette caught a glimpse of Baptiste as he hurried past the entrance to the sitting room.

"At least we have servants again," she said. "It wasn't easy, pretending to the world that everything was normal inside our home when, in fact, we were penniless and had let all the staff go."

"You kept up a brave face through all of it, not even letting on to Charles and me how dire our circumstances were." His jaw clenched even as voices drifted in from the entryway. "You deserve happiness, and Papa should understand that better than anyone. I hate to say this, but he can be a selfish bas—" Anthony caught himself. "Brute."

Impulsively, Mouette stepped forward to embrace her son and was reassured to feel his strong arms squeeze her in response. "Don't worry. I shall be just fine," she said. "Hasn't your papa promised that he will come to London as soon as he has seen to the situation with his mother?"

Anthony's dark brows flicked upward, letting her know he hadn't believed Justin's excuse for staying behind in Cornwall, but at that moment Baptiste appeared in the doorway.

"M'sieur Thornberry is here for you," he said to Anthony. "We have already loaded your things."

Mouette closed her eyes for a moment, resting against her son's broad chest, inhaling his scent. No wonder the women were already flocking to him, she thought. "You must go, my dear. Promise you'll write

77

after you are settled. I want to hear all about your studies."

"Remember, Cambridge is only a few hours away now. The roads have been greatly improved." He patted her back. "I'll return soon."

She walked with him to the front door and met his friend, Bernard Thornberry, who seemed to hail from a wealthy family. Smiling bravely, Mouette stood next to Baptiste and waved as the two young men climbed into the coach. Soon it was rolling away, Anthony's hand emerging from a window for one last wave before the equipage disappeared from sight.

Mouette felt Baptiste watching her. *For heaven's sake, don't cry!* She scolded herself. Avoiding his keen eyes, she turned back into the house.

"There is a great deal to do," she announced.

The Frenchman followed her into the empty morning room. Earnestly, he said, "I am at your disposal, madame. How may I be of service?"

She wanted to ask him to cast a spell on Justin, to transform him back into the irresistible, roguish husband he used to be. But of course, no one had ever been able to exert any power over Justin St. Briac. He was a force of nature...

Mouette pressed her lips together to regain her composure. "Baptiste, perhaps you do not know that most of this house is shockingly empty because I had to sell all our possessions in order to feed my sons."

He held up a silencing hand. "You need not continue, madame. Anthony has told me everything." There was deep compassion in his gaze. "Let us begin again."

"I was thinking that same thing."

"M'sieur St. Briac insists that you must purchase anything you need." He paused. "Of course, you must know that better than I."

Mouette's eyes stung again. Everything felt eerily strange, as if she were dreaming. She was back in this house, alone again, yet so much was different. A decade ago, utter poverty had been the source of her shame and fear, and Mouette had been desperate to protect her young sons. Of course, Harry was largely to blame for everything that had gone wrong, but he was dead, and she had been left to struggle with the repercussions.

Thinking about Justin, she felt so torn that she ached. How desperately she wanted him to stand up and put his own conflicts aside, to tell her that this time, *her* needs came first. Yet hadn't she always known his true nature? He had shown her over and over again how difficult he could be before she committed to making a life with him.

"I hesitate to take my husband's money to improve this house, since it was mine before we married," she murmured to Baptiste. "Perhaps, once he is here, I will feel better about it."

The aging Frenchman, who had devoted his life to Justin St. Briac, looked deeply uncomfortable. *"D'accord.* I believe I understand. But…"

She felt her chin tremble. "I see. You don't expect him to come to London, no matter what he said."

Baptiste glanced away and drew a discreet sigh. "I should not venture to guess, madame. If m'sieur promised you he would come, then we should expect him, but I suppose unforeseen circumstances could intervene." He coughed. "In the interlude, there are other, more…*dependable* resources you may draw upon. M'sieur has given me specific instructions."

Mouette felt utterly bereft, as if she had swallowed a large, cold stone. No amount of money could replace Justin's vibrant presence. "I suppose shopping for new furnishings would be a welcome distraction…but there are things I had to part with that I fear are lost forever." She looked up at the space above the mantel, thinking of the exquisite portrait Madame Le Brun had painted of her on the eve of her wedding to Harry, in 1804. Selling it to pay for her sons' schooling had been a humiliating low point, and every time she saw the empty place where it had once hung, Mouette once again felt sick with shame.

Just then, there was a knock at the front door. Before anyone could respond, Mouette heard the door open, followed by Charles's voice.

"Mother!"

"Here we are, darling." Relieved that Charles had come so soon after Anthony's departure, she went to meet him in the doorway. He was looking especially handsome in a tailored gray frock coat, light trousers, and a blue-striped waistcoat.

Meanwhile, Baptiste passed them, pausing just long enough to take the young man's top hat and walking stick.

"Good morning," Charles said. "How are you getting on?"

Usually, Mouette was a bit wary of revealing weakness to her more judgmental son, but in that moment, she was swept by a great wave of gratitude that he had made an effort to join her. "I'm so glad you came back," she said, longing to embrace him. "I confess I was feeling a bit lost."

"No doubt." Charles pursed his lips slightly, as if he wanted to say something but had decided against it. "Well, there's no need for that. After all, we have a great deal to do. Look who I have brought to help you readjust to London society!"

Mouette blinked in confusion as Charles swept an arm back, gesturing, just before another man came into view from the entryway.

"Ah, Lady Brandreth," the unexpected guest said smoothly. "May I say that, even though we have not met for many years, you are more lovely than ever?"

"Lord Redfield." Mouette said. "Can it be?"

Theodore Redfield, Viscount Redfield, bowed and gallantly kissed her hand. "As ever your servant, my lady."

Her heart began to race. It seemed impossible, somehow. One more strange episode in this ongoing dream that had plunged her, unwillingly, back into an awkward past.

Charles beamed and stretched out his arms, resting one hand on Mouette's shoulder and the other on Redfield's forearm. "Isn't this splendid? Who better to aid in our quest to restore your reputation than the Viscount Redfield, my own father's best friend?"

Drawing a deep breath, Mouette tried to get her bearings. Theo, as Harry had always called him, was smiling down at her with disconcerting kindness, his lantern jaw lending him the look of a friendly horse. He was very tall and trim, immaculately dressed, and still possessed a thick head of brown, wavy hair, tamed with bergamot-scented Macassar oil. The viscount had been Harry's best friend since their days at Eton. He had been present for their wedding and had attempted to counsel her husband during Harry's slow, spiraling fall from grace.

Later, after Mouette became a widow and had been struggling herself, Redfield had tried to offer support. But by then he had a wife and child of his own. It wasn't proper for him to be seen with Mouette, although he had visited a few times, even helping her to sell some of her valuables when there had been no other choice. She had suppressed those memories for years, but now they bubbled up again, and she felt herself flush.

Lord Redfield looked around the morning room with an expression of polite consternation. "The last time I was here, we were celebrating something or other. Don't remember what exactly, but I *do* remember this room looking very different." Redfield gave Mouette an inquiring look. "Hmm?"

Her flush deepened as she realized he was feigning ignorance about all the treasures she had relinquished to keep the creditors from their door. Was it possible he'd forgotten how many he himself had helped her sell? She didn't want to mention any of that to Charles, so she said, "I would have expected you to enlighten his lordship about my...missteps."

"Lord Redfield could only defend you," interjected her son who then turned to Redfield. "Now you can see, my lord, it's true. Mother sold everything except what was in the sitting room." There seemed to be a note of anger in his voice. "Even our beds! She told us to pretend we were living in the *forest*."

"I had accounts to settle," she whispered. Oh God, why had she agreed to come back to London and subject herself to this torment? "There were school bills, your fencing master, not to mention the butcher, the—"

"Yes, yes," Charles interrupted. "And soon, everything was gone, including the reputation of our family. But now the time has come to rebuild, and I mean to do it!"

Lord Redfield gave Mouette a faintly dismayed smile. "It seems your son has his sights set on the daughter of the Duke of Bellingham."

Just then, Gwynn appeared in the doorway, wearing an apron as if she had become a kitchen maid. "Refreshments are served in the sitting room, madame."

Relieved, Mouette led the way. After they were all seated and tea had been poured, she took a sip and felt stronger. Looking at Lord Redfield, she smiled.

"It's really lovely to see you again, my lord."

"My dear, I insist that we dispense with such formalities. You must call me Theo, just as Harry did from the time we met as boys at Eton." His smile softened further. "And as you agreed to do as well, when last we met."

She felt a surge of gratitude for his enduring friendship. "How kind you always were to Harry, in spite of his growing difficulties."

Charles stiffened beside her on the Sheraton settee. "His lordship agrees that my father was an exceptionally fine man. I rather suspect that someone was understandably envious of him and worked to undermine his good name."

"I suppose that is possible," Mouette said doubtfully, then turned her attention back to their guest. "I am longing to hear your news. How fares Lady Redfield? And your daughter?"

A shadow passed over his face. "I am sorry to tell you that my dear wife has passed on. Katherine was thrown from her horse last summer." The last words were spoken in a choked voice that caused him to pause.

Mouette wished she could cross to her friend and give him a sympathetic embrace. Poor man! "I am very sorry to hear this sad news," she said. "Please allow me to extend my heartfelt sympathy."

"You see, Mother, it will be therapeutic for Lord Redfield to assist us in the coming weeks," Charles interjected. "It will do him good, and he is just the person to shepherd you…I mean, *us*, through this process of rebuilding. He knows all the right people in the *ton*. If he brings you back into society, everyone will immediately accept your restored position."

"But," she said, "I am a married woman."

Redfield, who had been listening attentively,

blinked in surprise. "Oh yes! I do recall hearing that after you left London. Kindly remind me, who is your husband...and where is he now?" He glanced toward Charles. "I suppose I assumed you were no longer married."

Charles lifted his blond brows as if to say, *It's just a matter of time.*

"My husband's name is Justin St. Briac," said Mouette, hoping his reputation as a pirate had not preceded him to London. "He is from Saint-Malo in Brittany, but we make our home in Cornwall."

"Yes," Charles put in. "Very near Justin's brother, Gabriel, the respected botanist. Gabriel's wife is Lady Isabella Trevarre. Her father was a marquess *and* an earl!"

Although Mouette felt exasperated by her son's attempt to burnish Justin's name by bringing up the Trevarre connections and titles, she could not speak frankly in front of Redfield. Instead, she said, "My husband is delayed by family business in Cornwall."

"Ah." The viscount put his teacup back on the saucer. "I see."

"We should simply proceed with the plans to reintroduce Mother into society," Charles urged. "It is quite possible that Justin may not come at all." He glanced off to one side and added, "I have even thought that it might be advantageous for Mother to be presented as Lady Brandreth, since she previously had a respected title."

Before Mouette could protest her son's outrageous idea, Lord Redfield spoke in polite tones. "I see your point. And now, if you two will excuse me, I must retrieve my daughter from the home of her maternal grandparents, who live nearby." Another shadow passed over his face as he rose to his feet. "Frederica spent the past two nights with them. She's been a great comfort to all of us during this difficult time."

Charles stood. "But, my lord, what about our plans?"

"Is there a social engagement planned to which I might accompany both of you? As I have said, I will help in any way I can."

"As it happens, my grandmother, the Dowager Lady Brandreth, has invited us for luncheon this Thursday at one o'clock at her residence in Russell Street. Will you join us? Grandmama is most eager to discuss our strategy for the weeks ahead."

Mouette digested this information. Her former mother-in-law, Arabella, Lady Brandreth, had retreated to the country after the death of her son, Harry. Mouette guessed that she must not have recovered financially, for Arabella had always been the sort of woman who cared very much about appearances. Although Russell Street was by no means a shabby address, it was outside of May-fair, which spoke volumes to members of the *haut ton*.

"I will be very pleased to join you," Lord Redfield said with a smile. With that, he picked up his hat, gloves, and walking stick, and Mouette accompanied him into the tiny entryway. He loomed above her and reached for her hand.

"My dear, I am glad for this opportunity to tell you privately how very sorry I am for everything that happened with Harry. I wish I could have done more to assist you..."

"Please, do not apologize." She thought again of the valuables he helped her sell. "You did what you could."

"I tried, but it was a sticky situation. I had a family of my own..."

Touched, she squeezed his big hand. "Of course, I understand. How kind you are, my lord."

"Have I not asked you to call me Theo? I am at your

disposal, dear Mouette." His hazel eyes were intensely warm. "Perhaps this time, I can help to make things right for you."

She knew a sudden urge to weep, but of course she did not. If only it were Justin standing there before her instead, saying these same things.

Things Mouette longed to hear from someone she could count on.

"Thank you," she murmured.

"I will look forward to being with you again on Thursday, at one o'clock, in Russell Street."

It all felt a bit dangerous, but Mouette told herself she was being foolish. "Yes, Thursday."

CHAPTER 9

"*W*ill it be something simple, like Spanish Bran," intoned Lewis Bates, the purveyor of snuff, "or does m'sieur prefer a special mixture?"

Justin looked around the dark, tobacco-scented shop and began to wish he'd never come. He half-expected Mouette herself to throw open the door, catching him in the act. Not that there was anything wrong with a little snuff, for God's sake! On the contrary, he hoped it might restore his sanity.

"I will take the very best variety you have, but nothing cloying, like Attar of Roses." The very thought of this made him frown. He drew his snuffbox from its special pocket inside his waistcoat and extended it to Bates.

The wizened man peered at the container through his steel-rimmed spectacles. "You can't mean to buy only enough to fill that tiny thing!" He brought out a good-sized lead canister and proudly put it on the counter. "All my customers purchase at least a quarter pound of snuff at a go, enough to last them for a few weeks. A vessel like this will ensure your snuff remains fresh."

Justin felt his insides churn. He couldn't possibly

87

bring a canister brimming with snuff back to French-man's Haven! Even this clandestine act of filling his little snuffbox made him feel absurdly wicked.

In any event, he was only going to take snuff one more time.

"I do not want a canister." Justin opened the tiny box and passed it to Lewis Bates. "Just this much."

The snuff purveyor pursed his lips, clearly disapproving, but obeyed. "As you wish, sir."

Waiting only sharpened Justin's nerves. He didn't want to look out the shop window in case someone who knew Mouette might be passing by, so he examined the items on the carved wooden counter instead. Bates sold a ridiculous assortment of ornate snuff-boxes, many of them made of gold or painted with elaborate scenes. Off to one side was a special display of hares' feet.

"Odd." He plucked one of the furry things from the box and inquired, "What the devil are these for?"

"Oh, they are very much in vogue, sir," Bates enthused. "All my best customers keep a hare's foot close by to brush any lingering grains of snuff from their upper lips. Shall I add one to your order?"

"Certainly not."

"I suppose you know best, sir. Here you go then." Bates opened the agate snuffbox to display a small quantity of aromatic ground tobacco. "Less than one ounce worth of my best Spanish Bran."

Suspecting that the old man was feeling cheated because he would not be paid for a half-pound of snuff and a damned hare's foot, Justin put a sovereign on the counter. It was gratifying to watch Lewis Bates's eyes widen.

"Thank you, sir!"

When he emerged into the weak sunlight, Justin glanced right and left. The village was a maze of twisting, narrow lanes flanked by dwellings and shops of whitewashed stone and plain granite. Passersby paid him no heed. He felt a burning need to open the snuffbox and inhale a pinch right where he stood—and of course no one would care if he did so.

Still, he could not do it. It was as if Mouette were watching him, out here in the open. Or perhaps someone would write and tell her. Justin's rational mind told him such notions were mad...yet if he were going to take snuff again, no one must know.

If he continued eastward along the waterfront, he would emerge from the village and be able to climb up to find a quiet spot overlooking the glittering blue water of the English Channel. There Justin could savor his first biting pinch of snuff in a decade.

He strode along a narrow lane called the Warren, a jumble of three-century-old cottages and shops. This was the area where so many pilchards were salted and pressed, the pungent smell of fish lingered in the stones. By late summer, the Warren would stink to high heaven.

Ahead, the lane became a path as it emerged from the village. He quickened his step, keenly aware of the agate snuffbox that seemed to burn through his inside coat pocket.

But then a male voice called his name. "St. Briac, is that you?"

Forced to stop, Justin looked around and realized he was in front of Dr. Jonathan Couch's house. The young, bespectacled physician stood near his own doorway, holding a spyglass.

Justin made a short bow of apology. "I didn't see you, sir." He pointed to his eye-patch and added, "I miss a lot that happens on the right side of the street."

"I was just returning from watching the birds at Trelawne," said Couch, referring to a nearby estate.

"How nice for you." Despising polite exchanges like this, Justin got right to the point. "I am rather pressed for time."

"But, my good fellow, your father is waiting in my study. He has been kind enough to forgive my tardiness. Don't you wish to step inside and greet him?"

"My – father? I'm afraid I don't understand."

Couch adjusted his spectacles, trying to hold his gaze. "Perhaps you were not aware that I am Madame St. Briac's physician? He has come to collect some medicine for her."

Justin stopped. "Ah. *Bien sûr.*" His heart clenched, but he gestured toward the door. "Lead on."

Inside, the doctor's house was crowded, not with medical instruments or charts but an endless array of natural history curiosities. There were countless mounted specimens, mostly repulsive-looking fish and strange birds, as well as papers scattered over every surface, all of them covered with scribbled writing and sketches of fossils. From the other side of the small house, the voices of little children could be heard.

Jonathan Couch led the way into a chaotic study, where Justin beheld his father, sitting in a chair near the doctor's desk. Xavier St. Briac, now more than eighty years of age, rose a trifle unsteadily and gave his son a bemused smile.

"*Bonjour,*" he said. "This is a surprise. Were you not going to London with Mouette?"

"I am. Just not yet." Justin cleared his throat. "I had a few other matters to attend to first."

Dr. Couch cleared a lot of books and papers off a chair to make a space for Justin to sit. "It is good to have you both here, together." He poured a glass of sherry for Justin and sat down behind the desk. "How are your charming offspring? They both have excellent minds."

"Anthony?" Justin thought of his son's often middling reports from school.

"Oh, yes! If he uses his God-given curiosity rather than following the same conventional path as his friends, he will do great things." Couch rifled through some papers and brought out an intricate sketch of a moth. "He found this specimen near Tallant. Amazing!" Beaming at the paper, the doctor continued, "And your Emeline is brilliant. I couldn't be more delighted that she is spending these weeks with Mary Anning, one of the foremost experts on fossils in all of Britain."

Justin tried not to sigh. "She is barely ten years old."

"Indeed! A prodigy."

Xavier interjected, "Her grandmother and I agree."

Justin remembered now that Jonathan Couch had become more famous for his accomplishments in the field of natural history than in medicine. In fact, Anthony had shown Justin a book Couch had written: *Natural History of Fishes found in Cornwall*. Perhaps he should have shown some interest, but how could Justin know something so odd could truly be of interest to Anthony...the son who had vowed to become a bold pirate when he grew up?

"Of course," Justin managed in a tight voice, "I am very proud of both my children."

"As well you should be," Xavier put in.

Feeling trapped, Justin drank down the sherry as Dr. Couch prosed on in dreamy tones.

"Anthony, Emeline, and their cousin, Louise, are all young at a thrilling time. So many new discoveries are being made, every day, it seems! It wouldn't surprise me if Louise, or even your Emeline, becomes the first female invited to join the Geological Society of London."

"Thrilling indeed." He only spoke the words in an effort to change the subject. "I actually came to talk about my mother." He glanced at Xavier. "I assume that is what brings you here as well, Papa."

Dr. Couch sobered. "Yes. I just saw Madame St. Briac yesterday. She was able to sit in the garden most of the afternoon."

"That's encouraging." Justin paused. "And you believe her health problems are real? Are these spells she talks of a reason for concern?"

"My good sir, what do you mean?"

Justin felt almost painfully tense, and it came to him that he hadn't eaten that day. "I will be frank with you, doctor. My mother has manipulated us throughout our lives. Once she claimed to be dying in order to force me to marry. When she began talking of 'spells' I can perhaps be forgiven for wondering if they were authentic."

"They are, m'sieur." Dr. Couch frowned at him. "I fear your mother's heart is beating erratically at times. It is a serious and unpredictable situation."

"I see." As Justin attempted to digest this news, shock mingled with guilty relief. Now he had a valid reason not to travel to London. "But Maman is fine now, isn't she?"

"Precariously so." The young doctor sent Xavier a sympathetic glance. "You doubtless ought to prepare yourself for the possibility that God may call her home at any time."

Justin stared. "Is that a polite way of saying she could *die*?"

"I don't believe it!" cried Xavier. "My dear Cerise may surprise us with her fortitude, as she has done in the past."

It was impossible for Justin to believe that his mother could really leave the world, especially after all the times when he had felt real terror at that prospect only to discover that she hadn't been in danger at all.

"I'm certain you're right, Papa." He looked at Jonathan Couch. "Thank you for speaking to me, doctor. I will be on my way now."

"It's comforting to know that Madame St. Briac has a son caring enough to inquire after her condition."

To Justin's dismay, his father declared, "Indeed, my son is a very fine man!" The old man struggled up from the chair. "If you will excuse me for a few moments, doctor, I will step outside with Justin for a few private words."

Now what? Justin followed his father out of the house, wondering why it was so difficult for a grown man to simply find a place to take snuff without being bothered.

Outside, iron-gray clouds were marching across the sky and thunder rumbled in from the English Channel.

"*Eh bien*," murmured Xavier. "Soon the rain will come. I won't keep you, my son… I perceive that you are in a restless mood."

"Perhaps I should see you home." Justin discovered that he was looking down at his father. When had he begun to shrink?

"I will stay here for now. Madame Couch has kindly invited me to join them for the midday meal." He paused. "I merely wanted to tell you that you should not remain in Cornwall because of your maman. Your place is with your bride."

"I am not surprised to hear you say that," Justin replied evenly.

"I have a great deal of experience. Sometimes one must take drastic measures to keep a marriage together, waiting for the storm to pass. Perhaps it's been Mouette playing that part up to now?"

It was galling to hear this speech from a parent whose own marriage was riddled with flaws. Coolly,

Justin replied, "Of course, you are an expert on this subject."

His father paused, then a glint of anger sparked in his eyes. "Every day you delay may result in damage to your marriage!"

"Spoken by the man who spent decades allowing his wife to lead him on a series of ridiculous chases, to every corner of France, no matter what damage that did to his own *children*," Justin bit out.

Xavier blinked, shocked. "*D'accord*. Point taken! But may I remind you that your children are not at home. No one is at home but *you*." He paused as raindrops began to pelt them both. "I know you think I have no right to offer advice, but you have married a splendid woman. Have the courage to show her how much you love her."

* * *

How was it possible that this miserable day could deteriorate further? Justin wondered, even as the wind and rain swelled into a lashing storm. He and Hugo were both dripping wet by the time Frenchman's Haven came into view at the end of the tree-canopied lane.

His father's words rang over and over in his mind, taunting, *Have the courage to show her how much you love her.* How? By going to London and strutting about like a fancy aristocrat, playing by their rules, and pretending to care what they thought of him? It was mad, just as Maman herself had said.

During all of Justin's years as a pirate, smuggler, and seducer of women, he had never imagined his later life might unfold in such a manner! Even if, as Giles Taureau had insisted, his adventures at sea were over, did that mean he should roll over like a dog and allow

Mouette to lead him about in London? It might be Xavier St. Briac's style to behave thus, but Justin was a very different sort of man.

The snuffbox remained unopened in his coat pocket, but soon he would be inside his own house again, where he could do exactly as he pleased.

Justin handed Hugo's reins to a groom, instructing that he be rubbed down with warm blankets and given an extra carrot, then he dashed through the driving rain into the back entrance of the house. Margaret was standing at the worktable, looking at him with clear disapproval. This only made Justin scowl, even when Robinson woke from his nap by the hearth and sat up hopefully, his foxlike ears cocked.

Drawing off his gloves and sodden coat, Justin handed them to the waiting Smythe. "I require a hot bath and a hot meal."

"Another one, m'sieur?" Margaret dared to ask. She glanced toward the tray that was now back in the kitchen, still covered with his decadent, uneaten breakfast.

Justin narrowed his eyes at the woman. Margaret had been with them for years and had always been exceptionally kind and pleasant, at least when Mouette was present. "I think you know the answer, Margaret."

"Aye, m'sieur." Her tone was a bit too sweet. Just as he started toward the door, the cook added, "Oh, I nearly forgot. You have a guest. A lady! She waits for you in the morning room."

Justin frowned. A woman? He turned to Smythe. "Kindly inform my guest that I will be with her as soon as I put on some dry clothes." Glancing at Robinson, he warned, "Stay!"

Moments later, upstairs, he had dried off and changed into fresh clothing when he realized his cursed snuffbox was still in the pocket of the wet coat he'd handed to Margaret. *Sangdieu!* It was an impossible day.

Knotting his neckcloth as he walked, Justin descended the stairs and approached the morning room, his mind focused more on the cognac he wanted to drink than the identity of his mysterious caller.

"Ah, Justin!" A slim, petite lady was rising from the settee in a rustle of silk. "At last, you have come."

He stared in disbelief. Hurrying toward him across the Aubusson carpet was Lady Daphne Leyton, his erstwhile business partner, now the bride of Squire Callywith.

"Daphne, what a surprise." Something in her eager expression gave Justin pause. "You must be here to talk about the net loft."

She had reached his side but stopped just short of touching him. "The net loft?"

Suddenly Justin urgently needed cognac. Crossing to the cellaret, he poured a glass for each of them and returned to her side. "Only yesterday, I was thinking that I ought to sell the place, now that you have embarked on a new life." One long swallow of cognac and he felt much better.

"I have not come all this way to talk about anything as dull as business," Daphne said, gazing up at him. "Do you know, Justin, you are one of those extraordinary men who only become more compelling with age."

He cocked a brow and waited.

"Mouette is in London, is she not?"

"She is."

Looking pleased with herself, Daphne sipped from her cognac. "I need your help, my dear. You see...I desperately want to have a baby."

Her tone caused his male instincts to stir. "I know. That is the reason you married Squire Callywith."

"Indeed." She put a bare hand on his coat sleeve and

turned her striking green gaze up to him. He'd forgotten what a beauty Daphne was. "But you see, he cannot do it."

"Do *what*, exactly?"

"I think you know what I mean." She cast her eyes down, as if she were too demure to elaborate.

Justin knew from experience that Daphne was more ruthless than maidenly, and he didn't trust her to display genuine emotion any more than he trusted his own mother. "I would prefer that you speak plainly, my lady."

Drawing a deep breath, Daphne whispered, "My husband is rarely able to perform the marital *act*, despite my valiant efforts to assist. How is it possible for me to conceive a child if he cannot…"

Justin swallowed even as his heart began to pound. "Why are you telling me this?"

"Because you can help me, dear Justin. You are still a true man—in ways my husband is not. Don't you see?" A flush crept over her cheeks and she wet her lips with the tip of her tongue. "You may be alone here for weeks, and if you *help* me no one will ever know. I implore you, grant me this favor." Her expression turned sultry. "I promise you, it will not be a hardship…"

CHAPTER 10

Sitting across from her former mother-in-law at the polished Sheraton dining table, Mouette felt time shift yet again. The Dowager Lady Brandreth had aged in the fifteen years since their last meeting, before Harry's imprisonment and death, yet in many ways, she hadn't changed at all. Her curly hair, now white, was meticulously arranged. Her back was straight, and her handsome face was only lightly wrinkled. And, as always, she revealed none of her true feelings.

"Ah, Mouette, how fortunate we are that our dear Theodore is here to guide you through the balls and routs of the Season," Arabella said, her placid tone laced with steel. "My son would approve, don't you agree?"

Mouette hardly knew how to reply, for whether Harry would approve was the least of her concerns. She swallowed a bite of roast pigeon and put on a smile. "I am grateful indeed to Lord Redfield for his assistance, but—"

Before she could mention Justin, Charles broke in. "You are quite right as usual, Grandmama. As you know, it is imperative that everything come together perfectly, to ensure a successful outcome." He coughed. "For Lady Penelope and me, that is."

What did that mean? Mouette wondered. She looked at her son, who was sitting beside his grandmother, occasionally darting glances toward the old woman.

"But surely the course of your betrothal has little to do with me," Mouette said. "I am merely here to support you, Charles."

Theo, who was seated to her right, gave her a reassuring smile. "And I'm certain you shall do a splendid job of it."

Mouette felt her cheeks growing warm. "As I consider this matter, I might remind you all that I return to London society under a bit of a cloud. Charles knows better than anyone how difficult our lives became after we lost Harry." She paused, conscious of Arabella's piercing gaze, a reminder that it wasn't possible for Mouette to speak honestly about the destruction Harry had wrought before his death. "It won't be easy for me to face so many of the people who snubbed me then, but of course I will do so for Charles's sake."

"It is an opportunity for you to make a fresh start, my dear," intoned the Dowager Lady Brandreth. "You were once a diamond of the first water, one of the finest hostesses of the *ton*...in spite of the blemish of your American birth." A thin smile touched her lips. "Even today, you are still quite lovely. I hope that, together, we can all rebuild what has been lost."

Mouette was surprised to feel an instinctive flutter of hope. Taking a breath, she reflected on the life she once had lived as Lady Brandreth, filled with weekly assemblies at Almack's, invitations to balls and routs from even the Prince Regent himself, a parade of fashionable new gowns, carriages, and furnishings. Aspiring to the pinnacle of society had been thrilling, but when it all came apart, the pain had gone deeper than the cuts from her former friends and the humiliation of selling off her household. Mouette had found herself questioning everything she'd once deemed valuable.

When she married Justin and they built a new life in Cornwall, she had been relieved to sweep the last of it under the rug.

But had those old wounds ever really healed?

"I will support Charles in this new chapter of his life," Mouette said softly. "But it isn't possible for me to recreate the past." She looked at her former mother-in-law. "As you know, I have married again. My husband is not an English aristocrat by any means, and he would not try to be one, even for me."

Arabella pursed her lips and looked at Charles. "Oh, yes, I believe I have heard about this buccaneer person."

"That is an unfair characterization," Mouette protested, frowning. She wanted to speak in bolder terms, but how could she challenge this noblewoman who was not only her hostess but also her son's grandmother?

"It doesn't matter," declared Charles. "I predict that we shall never see Justin here in London. It is unlikely that he would extend himself to help me in my time of need. I am merely a stepson."

"Indeed, let us hope that is the case," said Lady Brandreth, staring at Mouette through her quizzing glass. "And, I might add, why should anyone need to know that you have wed a *French pirate*? Really, my dear, what were you thinking?"

"I'm afraid my mother has made many ill-considered decisions," said Charles.

This was too much. "Charles, how can you say these things? Have you forgotten how good Justin has been to you, for so many years?"

"He's not here now, is he?"

"You are very harsh!" She wanted to protest that, in many ways, he had been a more stable father than Sir Harry Brandreth, but they were in the presence of her former mother-in-law.

The viscount set down his fork. "I have one thing to say. I do not understand why this lovely lady, who has been through so much, must be criticized today." He turned a level gaze at Charles. "Has your mother not put aside her own life to come to help you?"

"Thank you, my lord." Mouette felt an urge to reach for Redfield's hand. It would be as warm and firm as the smile he was sending her at that very moment. Turning back to Charles and his grandmother, Mouette said, "And may I ask again, why *my* role is so important? Charles is betrothed to the daughter of a duke. I am here merely to stand in the background, as his mother."

"Be*trothed*...?" Arabella peered at her grandson.

At that moment, two footmen glided into the stuffy dining room, clearing away the dishes and serving tiny cakes and blackberry ice cream from Gunter's confectionary shop. Silence stretched among the guests, but Mouette noticed the way Arabella was looking at Charles.

When the servants had left the room, the Dowager Lady Brandreth intoned, "Charles, do you not intend to fully enlighten your mama?"

Mouette watched as a guilty flush spread up her son's neck, over his face, until it reached his hairline. Tugging slightly at his starched neckcloth, he said, "Mother, you should know that I am not actually betrothed. At least not yet! But of course, I *shall* be."

Feeling sick, Mouette said, "Go on."

When Charles finally met her eyes, she saw that a faint sheen of perspiration gleamed on his upper lip. "That's why I need your help so very much. Lady Penelope will like you; I feel it. Your presence could make all the difference!"

She shook her head. "You should have explained all of this when you came to us in Cornwall."

"The thing is, Lady Penelope has just come out this Season and suitors have flocked around her, as you might imagine. But when my lady looks at me, I can clearly see that she prefers me!" His voice rose. "So, you can see, Mother, that we must do everything in our power to show Penelope's father, the duke, that I am worthy of his daughter!"

Stunned, Mouette said, "You said that you were betrothed, not that you were merely *pursuing* the daughter of a duke, which is quite another matter. Some might consider you to have vastly misrepresented your current situation."

Into the silence that followed, Arabella Brandreth murmured, "Of course, my dear Mouette, it is understandable that you are feeling rather miffed. Yet, surely you perceive that there is much more at stake than Charles's heart. Our family has lost so much, but now *all* our lives could be transformed by this alliance."

What she really meant, Mouette knew, was that Harry's downfall had brought them all with him, in more ways than one. The Dowager Lady Brandreth had found herself without invitations from her so-called friends, and Harry's gambling debts had cost her the grand family home in Mayfair. Their title was a precarious one, for baronets were not part of the true aristocracy. If Charles should wed the daughter of a duke, it would not only shore up the family name, but their fortunes as well.

Mouette became aware that Redfield, who seemed to be the only one who remembered to eat his blackberry ice cream, was quietly watching her. When she glanced his way, he gave her the smallest nod, his eyes warm, as if to reiterate that he was there to help her in any way possible.

She was torn. Charles was behaving very badly, yet Mouette felt somewhat responsible. All the things Charles had said to her over the years, implying that she had somehow failed him as a mother, came back to her. If she could now help to make things right, perhaps she should consider it? Even as this thought passed through her mind, Mouette realized this could also be an opportunity for her to mend her own past here in London.

Of course, she didn't give a fig for the *ton*...at least not any longer. It was disturbing to realize that she was now in the position of seeking their approval once again. Yet, an inner voice argued, it might be a good thing to cleanse the stain of their rejection from her past...while helping her son at the same time.

"Yes. All right, I will do it." Mouette looked at Charles, her voice low but firm. "Of course, I regret that I was not able to make an informed decision about coming to London, but now I am here. You are my son. I will do what I can to assist you in winning the lady you love, but you must be honest going forward."

His expression softened in a way that stirred her maternal heart. "That's excellent," said Charles. "I appreciate that, Mother."

"I will not pretend to have remained unmarried all these years," she said firmly. "As if Justin were someone to keep hidden. That would be *wrong*."

Redfield was watching her, but she did not meet his gaze. It was Lady Brandreth who spoke first.

"We are not suggesting that you deceive anyone," she said smoothly. "But my dear, why say anything at all? Would you make some sort of *pronouncement*?" Her tone was threaded with disdain for any female who might make herself conspicuous in such a way. "You have a title from your marriage to Harry, and it certainly overrides the name of that French brigand. Your own son is now the baronet, Sir Charles Brandreth! When you attend gatherings, it is only fitting that you are presented as Lady Brandreth." Arabella paused to take a tiny spoonful of ice cream. "Don't you agree?"

Mouette certainly did *not* agree. It seemed that Charles and his grandmother were intent upon manipulating her for their own selfish ends, and even Justin had failed to support her in her hour of need. At that moment, Mouette longed for someone she could depend on.

"Mother?" Charles was watching, waiting for Mouette's response.

"I will agree only to think about it," she said evenly, intending to address the matter later, when she and her son were alone.

He beamed. "That's splendid, especially since the Countess of Penhurst is giving a ball next week, and the Duke and Duchess of Bellingham will be in attendance...accompanied, of course, by their daughter." His brows rose just before he added, "I refer, naturally, to my own Lady Penelope."

"Mouette shall come as our guest." The Dowager Lady Brandreth gestured approval with her fragile silver spoon, then turned to the viscount, smiling. "And Lord Redfield, I hope you will honor us with your presence as well."

* * *

WHEN THE MEAL FINALLY ENDED, and Lady Brandreth bade her guests good afternoon, Mouette felt immensely relieved. Emerging from the townhouse, flanked by the two men, she drew a deep breath of cool air.

Everything looked brighter outside in the sunshine. Hearing a cheerful trill of birdsong from the green expanse of Russell Square, Mouette gave herself a little inward shake. Why had she felt so nervous? She was perfectly capable of smiling and greeting a few stuffy aristocrats! And perhaps she should be grateful Charles and Lady Penelope were not actually betrothed. Not only would many fewer eyes be on her at the ball, but perhaps there was still hope that Charles would come to his senses and reexamine his priorities for the future.

"Allow me to accompany you home, won't you?" Redfield said, looking from Mouette to Charles. "I am assuming you two walked here, since Bedford Square is not far away."

Charles nodded. "Actually, that is an excellent plan. I have other matters to attend to." Leaning forward, he brushed a kiss to her cheek. "Thank you, Mother." He then bid them both farewell and hurried back up the steps.

During the brief stroll to her home, Mouette found that she and Lord Redfield were not at a loss for conversation.

"Now that we are alone, I must insist again that you call me Theo. It is much more appropriate, given our friendship." He smiled warmly. "Will you do that?"

"All right...Theo."

"I would imagine your head is spinning," he said. "So many plans. Did you bring a ball gown with you to London?"

She gave a rueful laugh. "I did not have time even to think of it."

"Don't worry," he assured her. "I know a modiste who specializes in last-minute gowns. My dear wife relied on Madame d'Amboise for many years."

Mouette glanced over to see that a heavy lock of

brown hair had fallen over his brow, lending him a boyish look, yet she recognized the throb of sadness in his voice. It was a reminder that poor Theo continued to grieve for his lost wife, Katherine. Impulsively, Mouette rested a hand on his coat sleeve as they walked.

"You must miss Lady Redfield very much," she said softly.

Theo closed his eyes, as if absorbing a wave of sadness, but then he looked at her. "You are very perceptive. How fortunate you were to have found another love after Harry's death. No doubt it isn't easy to be separated from your husband now." He paused. "Pardon my memory, but what did you say his name is?"

At the mention of Justin, Mouette flushed. "Justin. Justin St. Briac."

"It cannot be easy for him to be parted from you." The viscount seemed to slow his pace as they approached the west side of Bedford Square. "One hopes he will be here in time to escort you to Lady Penhurst's ball."

"Yes."

"Although," Redfield continued quickly, "if that proves impossible, you must rest assured that I will offer my support in any way possible."

"You have been so very kind…Theo."

They were now standing in front of her Bedford Square home. "Perhaps you will offer me some refreshment?" he asked in a low voice. "It's rather warm this afternoon."

"Oh, of course." It was a reasonable request, she told herself. "Please come in." It was easy enough to open the door and enter without summoning Baptiste. Mouette was in the process of hiring more servants, but for now, the Frenchman was wearing many hats. No doubt he was busy in another part of the house.

As she started toward the sitting room, Mouette realized that Lord Redfield was not following behind her. Turning, she saw him gazing around the entryway in wonder.

"Surely I must be in the wrong house. How can you have effected so dramatic a change in just a few days?"

"It's not so much," she replied with a smile. "As Charles suggested, I have begun choosing a few items to replace those I was forced to sell."

"You are a marvel." He swept one hand in a continuous arc, from the exquisite carved entry table set off by a gilded mirror, down toward the small, jewel-toned Turkey rug, then across to the corner where a new bronze pedestal supported a stunning figured Chinese bowl.

"How kind you are." Mouette felt warm under his admiring regard.

He came forward to join her just outside the sitting room, lightly holding her arm. "I have always admired your talent for decoration. Perhaps you will consider visiting my home to advise me on a few new purchases I have been considering?"

"Advise you?" Her mouth felt dry. Redfield was standing just a bit too close, gazing down at her with what might have been longing.

"Now that I am alone, I realize it's time to make some changes," he said. "There is no one whose opinion I value more than yours, Mouette."

Just as she opened her mouth to reply, a deep, sardonic voice came to them from inside the sitting room.

"Ah, *chérie*, it would seem I have arrived just in time…"

THE IMPOSSIBLE HUSBAND

CHAPTER 11

*M*ouette's stomach dropped, as if she'd just been pushed off a rooftop. Turning, she beheld Justin and blinked in disbelief. He was lounging on the Sheraton sofa, his hard-muscled legs stretched out over the fine silk upholstery as if he were master of this household.

"Justin!" she gasped. Heat flooded her face.

Lazily, he rose and made a faintly mocking bow. "Your servant, my lady wife." He looked toward Theo, then back to her, arching a brow above his eye-patch. "Perhaps you ought to introduce your *friend*."

Theo immediately stepped forward himself. "I am Viscount Redfield." He extended a hand and even managed a tight smile. "I take it that you are Justin St. Briac?"

Justin cocked his head. "I am encouraged to know that you have heard of me." He shook the Englishman's hand, his own grip dark and powerful.

Mouette couldn't help drinking him in, feeling the familiar surge of attraction, even as she tried to resist. He looked out of place in this refined setting, among the delicate furnishings she had chosen long ago, when this room had been like a stage set, a place she could bring guests while hiding the fact that the rest of the house was empty. In all the years of their marriage, Justin had never visited this house with her. Consumed by their new love, Mouette had been happy, even relieved, to cover the furniture again, lock the door, and make a new life with him in Cornwall and France.

Justin was coatless, his shirt white as snow against the dull gold of his waistcoat. His black-and-silver hair looked wilder than usual, and Mouette was keenly aware of the contrast between her husband's rough, scarred beauty and Lord Redfield's cultivated appearance.

"Of course, I have heard of you," Theo was replying calmly.

Justin's smile held a dangerous edge. "Then why were you behaving as if my wife were available to be wooed by you?" To Mouette's consternation, he reached out and took her arm, drawing her close to him. "I can assure you; she is *not*."

Redfield flushed, even as his brow furrowed. "My good man, I have done nothing improper."

"Protest if you will. I know what I saw." He paused before adding in a dangerously ironic tone, "I do not habitually socialize with the aristocracy. I presume that I am to address you as *my lord*?"

"If you choose to show me that customary respect, sir," Redfield shot back.

Mouette looked up at Justin in alarm. "His lordship has treated me with supreme kindness since I came to London."

"Oh, I can imagine," he replied.

"You should be thanking him!"

Redfield, meanwhile, was clenching his prominent jaw, nostrils flared. "My lady, I shall take my leave."

"I will see you to the door," Mouette declared and

threw Justin a defiant stare. Without waiting for his response, she led her guest from the sitting room.

In the entryway, the viscount paused to clasp both her hands. He bent his head low, searching her face as he said in a hushed voice, "I confess that I am shocked to discover you are wed to such a man. I hesitate to leave you alone with him."

As angry as she was with Justin, this almost made her smile. "Oh, you need not worry on that account. I am perfectly safe." Mouette paused. "My husband was a pirate for many years, you know. He can still adopt that threatening guise at a moment's notice, but he is no danger to me."

Redfield snorted and pressed his lips together. "That sort of behavior is quite unacceptable, especially among polite society."

"I agree." Mouette opened the door so that he might depart. "I am grateful for your concern but fear not. I know how to deal with Justin."

He wavered in the doorway. "Will you allow me to take you to meet my wife's dressmaker tomorrow? Madame d'Amboise may need several days to create a proper gown for the ball, so there is no time to waste."

She thought about Justin but refused to let his arrogant presence deter her from carrying out her own plans. "It is very kind of you to offer, my lord."

"Theo," he reminded her.

"I would be delighted, Theo."

"Excellent!" Redfield smiled broadly. "Shall we say ten o'clock tomorrow morning?"

"I will be waiting."

* * *

By the time Mouette reappeared in the sitting room, Justin had poured himself a brandy.

"What the devil is this?" he demanded after one swallow. "How can you call it brandy?"

"I don't call it anything of the kind. Those bottles have been there for a dozen years or more. It was all I could afford at the time."

Her words caused a decade-old memory to flash across his mind. He had been here only once, alone, after Mouette left him in Cornwall and ran away to London. Justin had pursued her to Bedford Square, only to find the house dark and empty. As Justin walked into a bare shell of a house, he'd been stunned to realize how low Mouette had been brought after Harry's death. Only the parlor remained furnished as if all were well, and Justin's heart had ached for her.

"Of course," he now said in gentler voice. "I suppose I had put your past circumstances out of my mind."

Looking stung, she replied, "I do not have the luxury of such forgetfulness."

"Ah, Mouette." Justin spoke her name like a caress. "Don't look at me that way. Are you not pleased to see me?"

Her eyes shone for an instant, but she made no reply. She was standing a good distance away from him, looking very fetching in a day dress of blue-gray silk with small, rose-tinted bows that resembled flower buds.

He tried again. "You look lovely in that gown, *chérie*. Come over here and let me greet you properly."

Justin recognized the storm cloud that passed over her face, though he hadn't seen it for some time. Color washed her cheekbones. It did not bode well that Mouette was not even trying to tamp down her anger. Clearly, she did not intend to come to him, so he set down his glass and took a step toward her.

"How dare you?" She raised a hand as if to ward him off.

So, it seemed she was not going to soften. Two could play this game, and he was a master. "How dare I *what*? Express dismay that a stranger is attempting to steal my wife?" His own voice was now edged with frost.

"That was not *dismay*! You were appallingly rude."

"Did you expect me to roll over on my back like a dog and welcome him in? Even Robinson would know better."

He saw her falter only a little. "Theo is hardly a stranger! He was Harry's closest friend." She paused to glare at him.

"Theo?"

"I have known him for twenty-five years, since before he inherited the title of viscount. He graciously insists that I continue to address him as Theo."

Justin lifted both brows. "Touching."

"Stop that."

He pretended to be offended. "I don't know what you mean."

"You mock him, and you know it," Mouette said. "Theo may have been Harry's closest friend, but they were not alike in the least. He tried to help Harry, to help us both!" She pointed at Justin. "You have no idea what's been happening here, or why I might need the support of a true friend, because you were too selfish to accompany me to London yourself."

All of this sounded quite ominous. Deep inside, Justin knew he had no right to accuse her of anything. He felt a sudden surge of anxiety as he thought of Lady Daphne's visit to Frenchman's Haven just a few days ago. What would have happened if Mouette had turned up unexpectedly while Daphne was inviting herself into his bed?

That was different, Justin told himself.

Aloud he said, "I'm here now, aren't I? See here, Mouette. I am your *husband!*"

"That is only a word." She was on her way out of the sitting room now, head high as she started toward the stairs. Upon reaching the bottom step, she half turned and added, "M'sieur, I have catered to your needs for ten years. Yet when I needed a real husband to support me during a difficult time, you couldn't be bothered."

It was always a bad sign when she called him *m'sieur.*

Just as Mouette disappeared from sight, up the stairs, Baptiste entered the sitting room, holding a tray. The gaunt Frenchman looked hesitant as he inclined his head.

"If I may be so bold...we were expecting to find Robinson with you, m'sieur."

This struck a nerve, for Justin had experienced an annoying sense of guilt when he left the corgi behind at Frenchman's Haven. Robinson had followed him to the stable, and when Justin mounted Hugo alone, the dog gazed reproachfully at the saddlebags as if he understood he was being excluded from a great adventure.

"I rode here on horseback!" he said to Baptiste. "I could not bring a cursed dog."

"I see." The manservant gave a stiff nod. "I recall that you did bring Robinson once before, in your saddlebag."

"I am not having this conversation with you," Justin ground out.

"No doubt you are hungry after your long journey, m'sieur. I have prepared a delicious *omelette* for you, with my own hands." He set down the tray.

"I prefer some good cognac." Justin cast a dark glance at the bottle on Mouette's sideboard. "That stuff is undrinkable. I believe that entire stock of spirits should be replaced immediately."

"*Eh bien.* I will consult with madame on the matter."

Irritated to realize that neither Mouette nor Baptiste intended to give him even a drop of power in this house, Justin reached inside his coat for the agate snuffbox. "Perhaps I should remind *madame* that the funds to manage this household come from this terrible husband!"

Baptiste stared at the snuffbox, clearly shocked. "At the risk of speaking too boldly, m'sieur, I must protest...if you return to that habit, it will not help your cause with madame."

Scowling, Justin thrust it back into the inner pocket of his waistcoat. Some inner devil drove him to take snuff and drink brandy *because* of Mouette's disapproval. But now that he'd seen Lord Redfield, he might have to rethink that approach.

"I am going to visit Deacon, my man of business. I will return by evening."

* * *

MOUETTE TOLD herself she was glad Justin had taken himself away. Her life was complicated enough without her impossible husband making waves, which was his specialty. She had so much to contend with, dealing with Charles and the Dowager Lady Brandreth, as well as her own apprehension about the upcoming social events. A great deal was at stake, Mouette reminded herself again. Not only did her son's future happiness rest on the outcome of the London Season, but it was also her own chance to repair the pain and damage of the past.

Eating alone in the nearly empty morning room, Mouette reread the letters she had received over the past two days. One was from Anthony, who continued to express concern for her wellbeing. She knew he would be happy to know that his father had finally come to London...but he would also understand that the situation would not be easy.

The second letter had arrived only this morning, from Emeline. It had been a tremendous relief and joy to hear from her daughter and know that she was all right. Opening the single page again, Mouette realized that Emmie's writing was childish but also bold, like her papa's. Mouette's heart throbbed with love for her determined, curious little girl.

DEAREST MAMA AND PAPA,

I hope that you are having a wonderful time in London. Lyme Regis is even better than I dreamed. We are staying in a cottage at the top of the town, very near Mistress Anning's own lodgings and the shop where she and her mother sell the most splendid fossils you can imagine. Louise and I have already learned so much. I follow them along the rocky beach each day, watching, listening, and helping in any way I can. Mistress Anning uncovered another large fossil fish during the winter, called a Plesiosaurus. I can't properly describe it in words, it is too amazing! Papa, I know you do not share my interest in fossils, but I think if you should see them for yourself you would understand.

Will you come to visit us here during our sojourn? I should be so very pleased to show you everything.

Aunt Izzie and Uncle Gabriel send you their special love, and Louise has asked me if I have news of Charles. Is he truly going to marry? I miss you both desperately, but I am well.

Ever your daughter, Emeline

TEARS CLOUDED MOUETTE'S vision as she read it twice. It seemed such a short time ago that the family had been together at Frenchman's Haven, their separate lives knitted securely into one whole. There had been long rides on horseback along the stunning Cornwall coast and evenings spent inventing theatricals and playing charades. A wistful smile touched her mouth as she remembered Justin's outrageous pantomimes and how he'd made the children howl with laughter.

Folding the letters, Mouette rose and started from the morning room. The late evening twilight sent shadows over the space above the chimneypiece where her own portrait had once hung. Whenever she thought of it, her heart constricted. It had been painted at a high point in her life, when she had been young and beautiful, surrounded by her family, on the verge of marriage to the golden-haired baronet, Sir Harry.

I should fill that space with a new piece of art, she thought, but could she? The lost painting by the great artist, Élisabeth Vigée Le Brun, was a symbol of how desperate Mouette's life had become when she was forced to part with it. Of all the wrenching, humiliating choices she had made during that time, selling the portrait was her greatest regret.

Somehow, a secret part of her clung to a hope that this sojourn in London might provide a chance to re-write her past.

* * *

UPSTAIRS, Mouette went into her bedroom, which connected to a small sitting room and dressing room. Gwynn appeared to help remove the intricate layers of her clothing. Styles had undergone a drastic change, and now the nearly transparent gowns of the Regency era had given way to elaborate, hourglass-shaped dresses. Her maid unfastened her full *gigot* sleeves, unhooked the back of her bodice, and untied the sash of watered silk that encircled her waist. Freed of her gown, Mouette removed her own chemisette and drawers. She had just donned a soft nightgown and was getting into bed, when a knock sounded at the door.

Gwynn frowned. "I'll see who it is, my lady."

There was a small passage between the bedchamber and dressing room, so Mouette could hear, but not see, what happened when Gwynn went to open the door.

A voice piped, "We've brought hot water. For a bath!"

Mouette realized it was one of the new kitchen maids Baptiste had hired that week. They were sisters, Joan and Barbara.

"My mistress has already bathed today," said Gwynn.

"Oh, it's not for Madame St. Briac," declared Joan. "It's for the *master*, who has been traveling by horseback on dusty roads."

Mouette gasped. She wanted to protest, but how could she? Justin was her husband. The servants would think she was mad. But if he meant to stay in this house, she would have to think about the sleeping arrangements. Did he imagine he could behave as outrageously as he pleased and yet be welcomed back to her bed?

She heard the voices of the maids and footmen who carried the water in to fill the bath. Gwynn put her head in to look at Mouette again.

"Can I get you anything else, madame?"

Mouette leaned against the pillows and picked up her copy of *Sense and Sensibility*. An oil lamp burned brightly on the bedside table. She smiled. "Thank you for asking, but you may go, Gwynn."

The maid had just turned away when another voice, deep and unmistakably French, reached Mouette's ears.

"Ah, Gwynn. It is good to see a familiar face from our *real* home."

"Does m'sieur require anything at all? A light supper perhaps?"

"*Pas du tout*, although you are very kind to ask," Justin replied. "I am looking forward to a bath and some solitude with my beautiful wife."

Mouette was shocked to hear Gwynn, who was usually so unflappable, emit a girlish titter. "Of course, m'sieur! I'll leave you to it."

The outside door closed. As footsteps approached, Mouette pressed the open book to her breasts, as if that would somehow protect her from her intoxicating rake of a husband.

CHAPTER 12

 ustin appeared in the doorway, coatless, his neckcloth unknotted. In one dark hand, he held a glass of cognac.

"I'm going to have a bath," he said. "Perhaps you will join me?"

With an effort, Mouette shook her head. "I am already tucked in and reading, as you can see. And I don't need a bath."

"No? Surely, I don't need to remind you that it's not merely a bath, my love." He started to turn away, then glanced back with a seductively masculine smile. "The invitation stands, if you change your mind."

When he was gone, Mouette leaned back against the pillows, trying to quiet the beating of her heart. Her cheeks burned. She thought of all the times they had bathed together over the years of their marriage. More than she could count, and each one a delicious adventure. It was a chance to talk intimately about the events of the day, the cares and joys and shared amusements. To wash each other's backs, and sometimes, to make love in the warm water. For her birthday, years ago, Justin had even brought an extravagant copper tub from Paris for their spacious dressing room at French-man's Haven.

"I perceive you are not going to join me."

Mouette looked up in surprise to see Justin standing in the doorway, a linen towel wrapped around his hips. She sat up straighter. "That was a very short bath."

"When I realized you were not coming, I saw no reason to linger once I had finished washing."

As Justin approached the bed, his eyes roamed the bedchamber, taking in every detail. It was, Mouette realized, nearly as empty as the rest of the house. Casually, he remarked, "Soon we will have this room looking splendid."

"You are kind to offer," she said with a slight edge, "but what happens in this house is not really up to you."

Justin perched on the edge of the bed, tantalizingly close to her. "My love, why are you treating me this way?" His voice was like the purr of a big jungle cat. "We both know you don't really mean it."

"I certainly do mean it." Out of the corner of her eyes, she saw muscles flex in his hard thigh. His skin was still damp, his silver-streaked hair disheveled. Her heart fluttered as she told herself not to notice the breadth of his chest, not to think about what was under the towel knotted at his waist. "Justin, for heaven's sake, put on some clothing."

"Clothing?" To her consternation, he gave a soft laugh and leaned closer. "That is absurd. I am about to get into bed. With you."

Mouette inhaled his addictive male scent, as distinctive as a fingerprint. She steeled herself to resist. "What makes you think you are welcome in my bed?"

The laughter went from his gaze. "Because I am your husband."

"That does not entitle you to behave as you please and expect me to simply submit to you."

"Submit? That is not how it is between us, and well you know it. Are you really determined to punish us both simply because I waited a few days to follow you to London?"

How easy it would be to relent and welcome him back into her arms. She ached to do so, but of course, that was Justin's way...and now there was more at stake than her pride.

"We must talk," she said firmly.

His knowing gaze told her that he realized she would not be able to resist him once they were touching. "That sounds deadly dull."

"It's important to me."

Justin grimaced slightly, yet he reached for her hand and brought it to his mouth. He pressed warm lips to her palm and then the exquisitely tender place at her wrist. Arousal flared inside her. Her body's traitorous response was all the more maddening because her husband knew her secret erogenous zones, doubtless better than she did herself.

"I am listening," he said. "Do you intend that I should remain here on the edge of the bed? I'm getting cold."

Mouette took a breath and reclaimed her hand. "All right. You may get into my bed." She pointed to the other pillow. "But please do not make any further advances at this time."

* * *

STANDING, Justin stared down at her and unknotted the towel at his hips. Mouette looked away, her cheeks pinkening in a way that inflamed him further. *Eh bien!* If she wished to pretend indifference to his naked body, he would not show it to her.

Not yet.

121

Instead, Justin rounded the bed but didn't drop the towel until he was sliding between the covers. Careful to remain on the other pillow, he said, "Proceed. I am eager to hear what you have to say."

Mouette turned toward him, looking utterly ravishing. Raven locks spilled past her shoulders, full breasts were outlined beneath the fabric of her prim bedgown, and her blue eyes were agleam with a mixture of wariness and vulnerability.

"Do you mean it?" she said softly.

"What a question. Of course, I would rather have you naked in my arms so that I might show you how much I have missed you, but you say we must talk...first."

"I beg you, Justin, be serious. It is too easy to use lovemaking as an easy remedy for every problem in our marriage."

"Perhaps because it has always been so effective," he parried, adding the charming smile he knew she loved best.

"I am quite serious."

It seemed that the earth shifted slightly. Remembering the way Mouette had looked at him in Cornwall, when he said he would not be traveling to London with her after all, Justin heard his own father's advice: *Each day you delay may result in damage to your marriage!* He thought of that cursed Lord Redfield, who had acted so protective toward Mouette, and felt a stab of fear.

"Perhaps..." Justin's mouth was dry, and he wished he had brought cognac with him to bed.

"Yes?" She was looking directly at him, waiting.

"I might have let you down. I mean, I can see that I *have* let you down. By not coming with you to London when you asked me." The familiar band tightened around his chest. "By being selfish...which seems to be in my blood."

To his relief, a tremulous smile touched her mouth. "I cannot believe you are saying these things."

"What did you imagine I would say?"

"Oh, perhaps that I shouldn't turn away, because you hold the purse strings. That you have brought unlimited funds to assist me—and Charles—in our current endeavor."

He prayed Mouette couldn't perceive in his face that this was exactly what he had planned to say, when given the chance. Was stunning wealth not his trump card?

Apparently not.

"Everything I have is also yours, *chérie*," he said in the low voice that had melted her resistance countless times in the past. "You know that."

"What I know is that you believe wealth is power, and you have no qualms about wielding yours."

"This would be different. I want to be your champion, to help you solve whatever problem lies ahead."

She continued to look wary. "I hope you'll pardon me for having doubts, given your recent behavior."

Sangdieu. It was worse than he had imagined. "Mouette..." He wanted badly to reach for her but what if she pushed him away? "There must be something I can say to soften your heart."

"I do not think words will do at the moment." She paused, as if mustering her courage. "I will be plain. For most of our marriage, I have put your needs ahead of my own, and I have no one to blame for that but myself. I adored you. You are intoxicating. I have catered to your moods, even the part of you that is ungovernable, I suppose, because I knew I could not change you." Her eyes glistened. "But deep inside, I always believed that if I needed you, you would put your own desires aside and step forward. After Charles came to us in Cornwall, I was depending on you. I hoped you would help me navigate the challenges here in London...but you failed me."

Her words were like tiny daggers. Why did she say she had *adored* him, as if it were in the past? He thought of many things he could say to defend himself, but it seemed that would only make things worse. She knew him better than anyone. "My reason for staying behind, concern for Maman, was not enough for you, I gather."

Mouette did not even reply to that.

"What about the fact that I am here now?"

She shook her head. "It seems you are blind to so much, even your outrageous behavior when his lordship and I came into the house today. Can you not see how wrong it was?"

His lordship. The thought of Redfield made Justin's blood boil. "I was defending my territory!"

"That's ridiculous." She looked away from him. "This is not even your house."

"You are my *wife*."

"I am not your possession! Perhaps the laws made by men may say so, but you know perfectly well that it isn't like that." She lifted her chin. "No man owns me, or ever will."

"I didn't mean it that way."

"Indeed? It is hard to imagine any other interpretation."

Justin wondered how the devil this conversation had spiraled so completely beyond his control. He took a deep, burning breath. "Mouette, I cannot undo these past days, but I see I must change my behavior."

Her eyes glistened as she swallowed. "Words," she whispered. Justin felt a surge of hope as he realized she was erecting a protective shield. It meant she felt vulnerable to him. That was all the encouragement he needed for now.

"I will show you!" he vowed. Passion throbbed in his voice. "Give me a chance."

As their gazes held, he felt her softening. "Well, I suppose I must," she murmured. "We are married."

"Exactly." Justin wanted to crow in triumph but restrained himself with a supreme effort. "Ah, Mouette, I adore you. Let me show you..." Even as he spoke the words, arousal surged through his body and his cock began to throb. This night was going to be a glorious reunion after all, thank God.

But before he could close the space between them, Mouette touched her palm to his chest. "That is how it has ever been between us. You misbehave in some outrageous manner and believe that lovemaking is the way to regain my favor."

"*Love*making." He repeated the word with relish.

"Not this time."

Justin dropped back against the pillows. "What the devil can you mean?"

"I am not ready to give myself to you in that way. Not yet. We have had this conversation in the past, you know, so you'll forgive me for being wary."

"What are you saying?"

"Demonstrate to me that your promises of change are real, and then perhaps I will feel more amorous." She smiled in a way that suggested she had all the power. It was true, he realized with a qualm.

"Are you suggesting that we share a bed without..." Justin trailed off in disbelief, unable to finish the thought.

"No. That would be cruel, I think."

"I couldn't agree more!"

She smiled. "You will have to sleep elsewhere."

This was a stunning turn of events, but Justin quickly told himself that the connecting door of the dressing room could be breeched easily enough. He knew very well how powerfully she was attracted to him. "I see. Fine. I am very tired, in any event. I'll just go through to the adjacent bedchamber."

Mouette held up a hand to stop him. "No, not there. Anthony's bedchamber has been refreshed since he returned to Cambridge. It is just down the corridor." She pointed toward the outer door. "I'm certain you'll be very comfortable there."

CHAPTER 13

*A*fter a night of tossing and turning in a bed that was too small for him, Justin awoke to the sound of drapes being flung open. Sunlight flooded the room, followed by a startled female exclamation.

"Oh, bless me! It's a *man*!"

Out of the corner of his good eye, Justin glimpsed apron strings flying as one of the new maids fled his presence. Although he was naked and completely uncovered, he'd been lying on his stomach, so the girl had been afforded a view of his buttocks rather than a more private spectacle.

Moments later, Baptiste rushed into the room.

"M'sieur?" he exclaimed.

"You sound surprised." Justin gave an ironic sigh and propped himself up on an elbow.

Baptiste replied by sending his gaze around the stuffy, sparsely furnished child's room.

"Say no more," said Justin. "I already know what you're thinking. Where is my *café au lait*?"

"Gwynn sent the tray to madame's rooms." Baptiste politely glanced away. "We didn't realize..."

"Do not feel embarrassed for me." Sitting up, Justin swung his legs over the side of the bed and rubbed his perpetually sore knee. "I can promise you this won't last long. We both know my wife cannot resist me." He flicked up one brow. "If she could, she wouldn't need to send me to a bedchamber so distant from her own."

Baptiste nodded sagely as he considered this. "D'accord."

"But now I have work to do. Mending fences if you will."

"I will fetch a jug of hot water and fresh clothing for you, m'sieur." Baptiste paused to emit a diplomatic cough. "Perhaps I should inquire of madame where she prefers that I unpack your things."

"If she tells you to put them in this airless monk's cell, you will have to move the lot by nightfall." Justin tried to sound confident, but even he heard the note of uncertainty in his voice. There was no telling what Mouette might say or do these days...

* * *

MOUETTE SAT AT A PRETTY, round table in her morning room, sunlight spilling through the window that overlooked Bedford Square. While waiting for breakfast to be served, she dipped her pen in the inkpot and added to the list of furnishings for the house.

At the top of the second column, she wrote: *A dining table and twelve chairs.*

When Justin's deep, accented voice drifted in from the stair hall, Mouette sat up a little straighter. She glanced down at the especially lovely gown of berry-tinted silk she'd chosen this morning, knowing in the back of her mind that it flattered her in all the ways Justin loved.

Of course, only Mouette would ever know how her heart raced in his presence. She had lain awake far too long last night, remembering the sight of him with a thin towel wrapped low on his hips, the flash of his smile, the way he had murmured the word *lovemaking*... After she sent him away, Mouette extinguished her lamp and moved to the pillow where Justin had reclined just minutes before. His scent worked on her like a drug. Her breasts tingled and a familiar heat grew deep in her core. She imagined the way Justin would kiss her, touch her, use his mouth on her body, and soon she was wet, aching with longing.

Thank God, I didn't allow him to stay, Mouette thought. If he had reached for her, she would have melted in his arms, powerless to resist.

"Ah, there you are."

Justin strode into the morning room, shockingly attractive for his age. He wore a charcoal-gray frock coat that emphasized the breadth of his shoulders, and a starched, expertly knotted white neckcloth contrasted with his tanned face and silk eye-patch.

Mouette put down her pen and affected an attitude of distracted surprise. "Oh! Good morning. Perhaps you will join me for breakfast."

He advanced on the round table and drew the extra chair close to hers. In a low voice, he replied, "What I have in mind is not on the menu, I fear."

"Are you planning to speak to me in that provocative manner throughout our meal?"

He sat down, dominating the fragile chair, and looked into her eyes. "I was remembering the day in the cellar storeroom at Saint-Malo, not so long ago, when you suggested we pretend I had captured you from an enemy ship." His low voice was seductive. "You wanted me to have my way with you...on top of a chest of pirate treasure."

Every intimate corner of her being awoke, warm and eager to do exactly what he was suggesting. *Stop that*, she warned her body, even as heat rose in her cheeks. "As I recall, you let me know you had better things to do."

Justin deftly brushed the backs of his fingers over her flushed face. "I am here now to make up for that."

He dropped his gaze to her breasts and for an instant Mouette imagined him opening her bodice, lowering his mouth to encircle her nipple with the tip of his tongue, and then...

"Eh...*hem.*" On the other side of the morning room, a throat was being cleared. "I have brought *petite déjeuner,*" announced Baptiste as he approached.

Justin looked annoyed. "You of all people ought to be able to ascertain when two people want to be private."

"But we are not those two people," Mouette amended with a shaky laugh. "I for one am ravenous." She felt herself blush. "For breakfast."

The Frenchman served hot, rich *café au lait* to them, and Justin visibly relaxed as he inhaled the fragrance. "I have been missing this ever since you went away from Cornwall," he told Baptiste. "Margaret will never have the gift for it."

Baptiste gave a little sniff. "Margaret is not French, as we know very well. She comes from a place called Bodmin, where even the coffee is deplorable."

"And that is why we continue to need you so much, Baptiste," Mouette said sincerely. "For your cooking... and so much more. You are truly indispensable."

"This is true, I must admit." Baptiste's thin lips flickered in a smile.

He then uncovered plates of eggs, hot-smoked salmon, and warm brioche with butter. Mouette's mouth watered in anticipation, and she began to butter her brioche before Baptiste was out of the room.

"You are spoiling him," Justin said.

"Good. He deserves it."

The new maid named Barbara appeared with a bowl of ripe strawberries. As she rounded the table and saw Justin, her eyes widened, and she blushed to the roots of her auburn hair. Quickly, Barbara set the berries between them, bobbed a curtsy, and hurried off.

Mouette narrowed her eyes at Justin. "What was that all about?"

He shrugged. "Oh, nothing much. The girl entered Anthony's room this morning, apparently unaware that I was sleeping there." He flashed a disarming grin. "She saw me naked. What could I do?"

"Cover yourself, perhaps?"

This drew only a laugh from Justin. As they both began to eat, he inquired about their children. "Have you word from Lyme Regis? Doubtless Emmie has grown bored and wishes to join us. Perhaps I should send for her."

"No, I don't think so. I have had a letter from her, and she only expresses a desire for us to visit her so that she might show us everything she has seen and learned."

"Hmm." He looked doubtful. "And Anthony?"

"He was just here overnight before leaving for Cambridge. I think he might visit again soon, though." She glanced at him over the rim of her cup. "He was very concerned for my welfare."

Justin did not take the bait. "And what of your family? I am surprised your parents aren't here to offer their support. And your sister, Lindsay. Did I just miss them?"

"No." She drew a deep breath. "Papa and Mama have not returned from Barbados, where they were spending the winter with my brother, Nathan, and his family."

"Ah, *oui*, I do remember now. I suppose your papa craves the warm weather at his age."

Mouette felt a pang at this reminder that her dashing father would celebrate his seventy-ninth birthday in the autumn. "He remains astonishingly fit and vital, as you well know."

"Yes...of course, he does."

She wanted to remind Justin that he was growing older as well, but of course he needed no reminders. His discomfort with aging had fueled their recent problems, after all. "Lindsay and Ryan have taken their children to Ireland, to visit his family there. Bridget and Sean are both old enough now to learn more about their Irish heritage." She paused to take her last bite of egg. "I do wish my family were here in London now, but how could they know I would be coming? Everything happened so quickly...with Charles."

Justin was watching her. "And his betrothal is progressing well? How do you like the young lady?"

"As it happens, I haven't met Lady Penelope yet." Mouette bit her lip. She couldn't bring herself to admit that Charles wasn't betrothed after all, at least not yet. "We will attend a ball in a few days to meet Lady Penelope and her parents, the Duke and Duchess of Bellingham."

Mouette felt a little guilty, for this wasn't a full representation of what she had learned yesterday during lunch at the home of Harry's mother. Yet it seemed the truth would only provide Justin with new ammunition against Charles. There would be time soon enough to explain more fully, she told herself.

"A ball..." Justin mused with heavy irony. "I will be counting the days."

"Perhaps you don't wish to accompany me."

"Oh no, I will be by your side. I am your husband, after all." His plate was now empty, and he set down his fork, leaning forward to focus on the paper at her elbow. "Ah, I see you are making one of your lists. I love that. It reminds me of our early days when you were helping me to decorate Frenchman's Haven."

She couldn't help smiling. "Back when you were still calling it Frenchman's *Lair*?"

Their eyes met, sharing memories, and a warm tide of euphoria swept over Mouette. This was typical of life with Justin! One moment she was burning with lust for him, the next she wanted to break something over his head, and an instant later he made her feel as if she'd just drunk a large glass of the finest champagne.

"I propose that we spend the day together, shopping. Together we'll cross off all the items on your list." He glanced up at the bare space where her portrait had once hung. "Starting with a fine piece to hang above the mantle. It should be the focal point of this room."

She felt herself flush. "Actually, the portrait Élisabeth Vigée Le Brun painted of me many years ago once hung there." Suddenly it was hard to speak. "I – I know I have told you that I was forced to sell it after Harry's death, in order to keep this house."

"Ah, yes, I remember. Who bought it?" he demanded. "I will make him an offer he cannot resist, and soon you will have it back where it belongs."

"Honestly, I cannot tell you. Lord Redfield helped me find a buyer. I don't know who owns it now."

"I will find out! And if I cannot, we will have a new portrait made of you."

She gave him a wistful smile. "That is very nice, but it could never be the same. I am very changed since Madame Le Brun painted me a quarter century ago."

"Don't think about that now. Shopping together will be an adventure." Leaning closer, Justin said, "Ah, Mouette, I have not forgotten how close we became while furnishing our home in Cornwall. I look forward to rekindling that romance..."

The way he said the word *rekindling* was thrilling, but Mouette managed to shake her head.

"I'm afraid not. I have another engagement this morning." She looked at the mantel clock. It was about to strike ten o'clock. "Lord Redfield will be here in two minutes to take me to meet his deceased wife's modiste, so that I will have a gown for the Countess of Penhurst's ball."

A storm cloud passed over Justin's harsh countenance. "Two minutes!" he echoed sarcastically. "What sort of paragon is this fellow?"

Mouette's heart was racing, but she managed to keep her tone even. "The sort who can be relied upon to keep his promises."

Just then, at the same moment the clock began to chime, the heavy knocker sounded at the front door.

Justin stared in disbelief. "I don't believe it!"

As Baptiste rushed to answer the door, Mouette rose from the table. She took only a few steps toward the doorway before turning back to address Justin. "See here. My friend has come to my aid, again, without creating a drama. I will ask you to consider my feelings and be civil to him."

Moments later, Redfield entered the morning room, holding his top hat and walking stick. He wore a warm smile that faded at the sight of Justin.

"Good morning," Mouette greeted him.

"It is a very fine morning," he replied, gazing into her eyes.

"How kind you are to make time for me today." She sent Justin a meaningful backward glance.

"Indeed," Justin agreed. He tossed down his napkin, rose leisurely from the table, and crossed to stand next to Mouette. "I am in awe of your extreme punctuality, m'sieur."

Lord Redfield's brow furrowed at that, but Mouette

gave a dismissive laugh. "Pay no attention to my husband. As soon as I gather my pelerine and bonnet, we can be on our way."

To her consternation, Justin nodded. "*Oui*. I am looking forward to this little outing." He gestured to Baptiste, who stood by in the stair hall. "Madame and I will be going out now, with Lord Redfield. If you and Gwynn will kindly bring our things...?"

Intercepting Theo's astonished gaze, Mouette gave a tiny, helpless shrug. *He is a devil.* How could she protest? As Justin kept reminding her, he was her husband. He had every right to accompany them...but Mouette could already imagine a host of mishaps that might occur during the trio's outing.

CHAPTER 14

*W*hen Lord Redfield's fine barouche drew up before a narrow, elegant shop in Conduit Street, Justin remained in his seat until the other man had helped Mouette to disembark. He imagined various ways he could forcibly take Redfield's place, but he realized that such behavior would not win any points with Mouette.

Instead, Justin leisurely lifted a brow, waiting, before emerging from the equipage to study the façade of the dressmaker's shop. The sign read simply: *Madame d'Amboise*, but there were mannequins wearing fashionable gowns visible through the gilt-edged windowpanes.

"Of course, I will take you inside and personally introduce you to Madame," Redfield was saying to Mouette. As he spoke, he opened the door. "She won't mind; men are a common enough sight inside her shop. I often accompanied my wife here when she was choosing fabric for a gown or having a fitting in one of the private rooms."

Justin decided to follow a few steps behind them and merely observe, for now at least. Inside the airy, feminine shop, there were beautifully garbed women standing behind counters, conversing with clients as they displayed fabrics and trimmings. The air held a soft fragrance that mingled fresh linen with lavender.

"Ah, Madame!" Lord Redfield called in a tone that made several people turn to look his way.

From behind the main counter, a slender, petite older woman with rich chestnut hair slowly turned from the woman she was helping and gave him a languid smile. "Ah, my lord." Her French-accented voice was refined. "How nice to see you again. If you will be so kind as to wait, I am assisting Madame Forrest at this moment."

Redfield gave her a benevolent nod. "Of course." He then began to guide Mouette around the display room, pointing out mannequins garbed in styles of gowns that he thought would suit her well. Meanwhile, Justin lounged near the doorway, watching, trying to ascertain his wife's mood. It was disconcerting to see Mouette in this world from her past, especially in the company of a man who seemed to want her to be someone other than Justin's wife.

Eventually, the impeccably garbed Frenchwoman came around the counter and approached Redfield, her beringed hands outstretched.

"Ah, my lord, how good it is to welcome you to my shop again." She gave a poignant sigh. "We have missed you, and our dear Lady Redfield…"

"It is a pleasure to be back," he replied. "I have brought a special friend to meet you." The viscount swept back a hand to bring Mouette forward. "Allow me to present Lady Mouette Brandreth. She is visiting London and must have a new gown for the Countess of Penhurst's ball this week. I told her that you were the only person I would trust to create a suitably beautiful dress in so little time."

Lady Brandreth? Justin could not believe his own

ears. How dare that self-important fool behave as if Mouette had never been wed to anyone but Sir Harry Brandreth? Justin burned to stride over and push Redfield aside, but at that very moment Mouette seemed to sense his thoughts and sent him a sharp, warning glance.

Justin clenched his fists, watching as Madame d'Amboise lifted the sapphire studded quizzing glass that she wore on a chain around her neck. As she scrutinized Mouette, the dressmaker chatted with that idiot Redfield about the gown she was making for his daughter, who was enjoying her first Season. Next, the woman brought out bolts of silk: one of rich gold embroidered with crimson flowers, another a deep emerald green.

"I hesitate to make any promises, my lord, for I have lately endeavored not to take any clients who would coerce my seamstresses to work long into the night," Madame d'Amboise explained. "I came to realize that such assignments made their lives too difficult, causing them to bend over for many hours, sewing until their hands sometimes began to bleed. It was not right."

"Precisely!" Redfield replied emphatically. "That is why I endeavored to bring Lady Brandreth to you days before the ball."

"But it is not enough time." She was studying Mouette again. "Perhaps, if you are willing to compensate *appropriately*, my two most accomplished seamstresses might be persuaded to collaborate, burning the midnight oil, just one time."

Justin bit back a smile. Madame d'Amboise was playing Redfield like a fish on her line.

"I understand completely," the viscount was mumbling. Justin had to move closer to make out what he was saying. "Have we not always been able to, uh... come to terms?"

"Come to terms?" She lifted her quizzing glass again, nostrils flaring slightly as if she had noticed a bad smell. In a low, confidential tone, she continued, "I am still waiting for full reconciliation of your account from last year, my lord. But of course, you are not the only nobleman who has expected such *terms*." Madame d'Amboise shook her head. "For the sake of my seamstresses, I now require immediate payment in full. This rule applies even to your daughter, for whom I create something quite magical at this moment."

Justin had heard quite enough. Walking forward to stand beside Mouette, he extended a hand to the dressmaker and greeted her in French. "*Bonjour*, Madame d'Amboise. My name is Justin St. Briac, and this lady is my wife." Firmly, he added, "Madame St. Briac."

The Frenchwoman blinked. "Justin?" A familiar light came into her eyes. "Can it be?"

He leaned forward slightly, temporarily speechless as recognition dawned. "Simone?"

Mouette was looking on, eyes narrowed. "You two know each other?"

"*Bien sûr!*" exclaimed the dressmaker with a girlish smile. "We once knew each other *very* well... In Paris, early in the Reign of Terror."

"It was a long time ago," Justin said, hoping to close the subject.

"Indeed. You look very different, *mon cher*. That eye-patch is quite dashing!" As she shook her head, the Apollo knot crowning her russet coiffure remained stiff, and Justin realized she must be wearing a wig. Simone Moreau had been a fetching young raven-haired Opera dancer when Justin had been enjoying Paris nightlife as a young man.

"You are now called Madame d'Amboise?" he asked.

Flushing, she replied in rapid French, "Yes. I found it necessary to take up a new life here in London, and it seemed only fitting that I should choose a lovely new name as well."

Aware that both Mouette and Lord Redfield were watching this entire exchange with surprised dismay, Justin sought to re-focus any negative attention toward Redfield. "I must not take any more of your valuable time," Justin told the woman who now called herself Madame d'Amboise. "However, I had to inform you that I alone will be responsible for my wife's accounts. When you have a total, my man will promptly send you payment in full."

He sensed Lord Redfield's discomfort even without turning to look at him. Inwardly, Justin felt victorious, but he merely sent the other man the coolest of smiles as Madame d'Amboise redoubled her efforts to create an enchanting design for Mouette's gown.

As the two men stood by, waiting, a voice called, "Ah, Lord Redfield, how nice to see you here today."

Justin saw a tall, dignified woman with a heavy bosom bearing down on them. She wore a toque decorated with the iridescent blue feathers of an exotic bird. Trailing in her wake were two strikingly lovely young ladies.

"Ah." Redfield bowed. "Good morning, Lady Penhurst."

The feather-wearing aristocrat turned and looked closely at Justin. "And *who* might this be?" A flirtatious trill crept into her voice.

Almost grudgingly, Redfield presented Justin to the Countess of Penhurst, whom he quickly realized was the lady hosting next week's ball.

"It is my pleasure to meet you, my lady," Justin said. He sketched a bow.

A flush crept over her high cheekbones, and it seemed that she swayed in his direction. "How wonderful. Tell me, m'sieur, what brings you to London? I perceive that you are used to a life of adventure. My first thought, upon glimpsing you, was that you might be a pirate."

"You were entirely correct, my lady." He flashed a roguish smile. "However, the proper term for my occupation is *corsair*. Is that not a finer word than pirate?"

"*Oui*! Indeed, it is." The lady looked dreamy.

"Ah, you speak French," he murmured, knowing he was doubtless going too far, but unable to restrain himself.

"Oh, ha, ha! Not really." Lady Penhurst's blush deepened as she held up a gloved hand and displayed her thumb and forefinger, perhaps a quarter inch apart. "Only...*un petite*."

"I have come to London with my wife..." Justin gestured toward Mouette, who was turned away from them, deep in conversation with her new dressmaker. "I believe we will have the honor of attending your ball with my stepson, Sir Charles Brandreth. I hope you will not have this wicked corsair turned away at the door?"

"Oh, m'sieur, you are wicked indeed!" The countess laughed softly before her attention wandered to Mouette, and she paused, considering. "Charles Brandreth, you say? Do you mean Sir *Harry's* son?"

At this, Mouette turned back from Madame d'Amboise, and her eyes widened.

"Lady Brandreth?" exclaimed the Countess of Penhurst. "Can it be?"

Before Justin could react, Redfield had stepped forward to take Mouette's arm and draw her closer. His demeanor was calm, even protective, which made Justin want to pick him up and slam him against the wall.

"How astute you are, your ladyship," Redfield intoned. "This is indeed Lady Brandreth, returned at last to us, her friends in London."

Justin saw red. "Lady Brandreth is now Madame St. Briac," he ground out, and firmly wrested her arm away from Redfield. "She is my wife. And we are only visiting London."

Eyebrows aloft, the countess glanced nervously among the three of them. "My, how thrilling."

Mouette, meanwhile, smiled at Lady Penhurst. "It is lovely to see you again, my lady. I am honored that you remember me after so many years."

"Of course, dear Mouette. How could I forget?" The countess looked her up and down, as if verifying her true identity. "After all that happened... none of us could have ever guessed that you ran away and married a *pirate!*"

"Life is filled with surprises," Mouette replied.

Justin interjected, "No doubt you would have expected her to choose someone far more respectable than I, a reckless corsair, my lady." His pleasant tone was laced with steel. "But who can explain the mystery of true love?"

"True, true. I suspect you swept her off her feet, m'sieur," Lady Penhurst tapped Justin's coat sleeve with her fan and began to turn away. "Such a lovely surprise to see you again, Mouette, and to meet your intrepid husband. I look forward to welcoming you to Penhurst House in the coming days." Almost as an afterthought, she glanced at Redfield. "And you as well, Theo. It will be so nice to see your Frederica again. She is out this season, as I recall. Until then, I bid you all *adieu!*"

* * *

"I HAVE SO many exciting ideas for the gown of your wife," Madame d'Amboise was saying to Justin in her charming French accent. "It will be utterly *magnifique!* I know you will be very pleased."

142

Mouette pressed her fingertips to her brow, where a headache had begun to throb. She sighed. Why was it that everywhere Justin went, he became the center of attention?

"It is very kind of you to fit me into your schedule," Mouette said to the Frenchwoman. "I am grateful to my friend, Lord Redfield, for bringing me to meet you." She felt Justin's narrowed glance but ignored it.

"I will see you soon for a fitting, madame!" As she spoke, Madame d'Amboise beamed at Justin rather than Mouette.

As the trio started toward the exit, Theo gave a little cough. "What a surprise to discover that our own Madame d'Amboise once *knew* your husband, my lady." He stressed the word *knew* in a way that suggested they'd been lovers. "She's pretty enough, I suppose, but I never thought of her in that way myself— doubtless because she is so much older than you and I."

Mouette felt the tension radiating from Justin's body and for a moment feared he might do something shocking. She tried to think of something she could say that would help Justin to understand how much she owed to Theo's kindness over the years. And now he had the ability to smooth the path forward for them that very summer. Charles had put it perfectly when he declared that Lord Redfield knew all the right people in the *ton*, and if he brought Mouette back into society, everyone would accept her restored position.

As they waited for the barouche, Mouette put a hand on Justin's arm and smiled up at him. She had no desire to inflame him further, but she yearned to make him understand her own position. "My dear, have I told you how much Lord Redfield helped me in the months after Harry's passing?"

She felt the hard muscles of his forearm tense under his coat sleeve.

Theo, meanwhile, looked tenderly at Mouette. "It was an honor and a privilege to offer my assistance," he said.

"So many people whom I had regarded as friends turned away from me in the wake of Harry's disgrace," Mouette said, hoping that Justin would listen and understand. "By the time he died, in prison, I felt engulfed in scandal. Only Lord Redfield stood by me."

Justin nodded, but he was looking at Theo. "Brave indeed, my lord," he murmured. "Were you not married, with a family of your own?"

"Just so. I was constrained by circumstances." Theo's prominent jaw tightened. "But I owed it to the wife and children of my comrade since boyhood, to try to do as much as possible. I could not bear to turn away from dear Mouette in her hour of need."

"Lord Redfield offered me very practical help," she hastened to explain, hoping to offset Theo's emotional tone. "When I had to begin selling our valuable possessions, my friend discreetly sought out interested parties among the *ton*."

"Ah, yes. How kind of him." As Justin spoke, he looked intently at Theo in a way that made Mouette feel a prickle of warning. "My lord, perhaps you remember finding a buyer for a portrait of my wife? It was made by the great Madame Vigée Le Brun."

"Really, Justin, that is a very abrupt question to put to Lord Redfield at a moment like this." In that moment, Mouette realized that the portrait had left an unhealed wound inside her, one that made the subject difficult to discuss in the light of day. Justin knew so little about that time in her life, and she instinctively wanted to keep it that way.

Theo seemed to go pale for just an instant before recovering himself. "Now that you remind me, I do believe I might have made inquiries on Mouette's behalf regarding that portrait." He tapped a gloved finger against his chin, considering. "It was an exceptionally lovely painting, was it not?"

She nodded. "Madame's talents rendered me lovelier than I ever could have been in life." Her heart tightened for an instant. "It was painted just before Harry and I were married...so long ago. It now seems like another lifetime."

"I remember those days very well," Theo said gently. "You were filled with hope." He gazed at her in a way that seemed to separate the two of them from Justin.

"Very touching," Justin interjected, an edge of steel in his voice. "If you remember it all so well, you must also know the name of the person who bought the portrait."

Blinking, Theo seemed to come back to the moment. "Now that I've had a few moments to reflect, I do recall." He sighed. "It was a very sad business, finding a buyer for a piece so infused with meaning."

"Who was it?" Justin pressed.

"Oh, a slight acquaintance of mine who later fell on hard times. I believe the fellow's name was Sir Phillip Waterstone, though I couldn't swear to that. I heard that he moved to Italy to escape his creditors and later died."

Mouette felt a surprisingly sharp stab of regret as she realized the portrait was lost, forever it seemed. "Well, it was only a possession. Perhaps it is better left in the past."

"Indeed. We can only move ahead into the currents of life!" Theo's silk top hat gleamed in the sunlight as he strode ahead toward the waiting barouche. "And now, I regret to say that we must be on our way. I have another engagement this afternoon..."

Just then, a tall, stylishly garbed young woman waved from a short distance away.

"Papa!" she called, smiling broadly, and made her way around a little knot of men who were waiting to get into the shop of Hoby, the bootmaker.

Redfield paused and looked over. "Frederica?"

"Of course, it is I! Who else addresses you as 'papa'?" She was next to him in moments, followed closely by her pale, moon-faced maid. "It seems an age that I have been staying with Grandmama. No doubt you have forgotten that today is my appointment with Madame d'Amboise. I will have my first ballgown fitting. She promises me that the moment I don the gown, I will become a princess."

Mouette saw that Frederica was a prettier version of her father. Tall and slender, she had rich brown hair, delphinium-blue eyes, and a winning smile.

Theo embraced his daughter. "What time is Madame expecting you?"

Her cheeks went pink. "No doubt you suspect that I am late. Again."

"Go, then," he scolded fondly.

Frederica nodded, but as she leaned forward to kiss his cheek, she seemed to notice Mouette for the first time. Her eyes widened, and Mouette waited for her to speak, but instead the girl turned and hurried away. It all happened so quickly that Mouette wasn't certain if it meant anything at all.

Theo stood smiling and shaking his head as he watched Frederica disappear into the dressmaker's shop, her maid trailing in her wake.

"I regret there wasn't time to make my daughter known to you," he told Mouette. "Frederica was clearly late for her appointment, and Madame d'Amboise can be temperamental, as you have seen."

"Miss Redfield is lovely," Mouette told him sincerely. "I hadn't seen her since she was a little girl."

Theo nodded. "I worry, of course. It is her first

Season and she is impatient with the strictures of society."

The coachman, intercepting a silent signal from Lord Redfield, opened the door for them. As Justin guided Mouette into the barouche, she glanced over and saw the storm gathering on his darkly handsome face. When she raised her brows in a question, Justin only frowned.

Was it possible that he thought he had grounds to be angry with her, given everything *he* had done and said inside the shop of Madame d'Amboise?

Not for the first time, Mouette thought, *Men!*

CHAPTER 15

*A*rriving back at the Bedford Square house, Justin followed Mouette inside and watched as she smiled at Gwynn and removed her frothy hat and gloves. He sensed that she was angry, but there would be no conversation between them as long as the servants were about.

He took off his own hat and gloves, waiting until Baptiste came into the stair hall before he handed them over.

The little Frenchman announced cheerfully, "You have returned just in time for a fine luncheon of lamb, spring peas, and new potatoes."

Mouette put her parasol in Gwynn's hands, looking distracted. "I regret to tell you that I am feeling unwell and cannot eat at this time. Perhaps I will improve after a brief rest."

Baptiste inclined his head, betraying surprise, since Mouette was known for her healthy appreciation of his cooking. "And you, m'sieur?"

Justin wanted to demand a large cognac, but perhaps that would not be wise. At least not until he had spoken his mind to his wife. "Not yet," he ground out.

He followed Mouette up the stairs. The fact that she

had banished him from her rooms did not discourage him in the least. Arriving in the corridor, he heard a door click shut, but suddenly he could not remember which bedchamber was hers. Several doors were closed, and they all looked the same. He knocked on a likely one but received no response.

"*Sangdieu*," Justin muttered under his breath. How maddening it was to feel like a deuced stranger in the home of his own wife!

Moving to the next door, he knocked again. When silence greeted him once more, he barked, "Madame St. Briac, kindly open to your husband!"

As the seconds ticked by, Justin detected a faint rustling sound inside. Curse her, did she intend to ignore him? He considered breaking down the paneled door, but it looked awfully thick.

"Mou-*ette*," he growled. "Let me in."

Long moments of deafening silence followed, then suddenly the door opened in a rush. His wife stood before him, blue eyes flashing, cheeks pink. Her raven curls, arranged so carefully just a short time ago, were now unbound, flowing around her shoulders.

Hot desire surged through Justin. He knew just how Mouette would smell, taste, and respond to him...once he had compelled her to surrender. When there was tension like this between them, their eventual love-making was potent and fiery, and in that moment, Justin couldn't think of anything else.

"You are very rude," Mouette said, yet she did not close the door in his face. Instead, she turned on one stockinged foot and went back into the sparsely furnished sitting room.

This reminded him of the reasons for his earlier outrage. "You are very bold to pretend that I am the one at fault!" He stalked after her. "How do you think I

149

felt when that fool Redfield presented you as *Lady Brandreth* and you said not one word to correct him?"

This brought her up short. She stopped next to a chaise and glanced back over one shoulder. "I tried to speak, but I was interrupted by that elderly Frenchwoman."

"Elderly?" He felt his face darkening. "She is nothing of the sort."

"Naturally you would say that since she was once your lover!"

Justin came up behind her, close enough to inhale her warm, heady scent. He ached to kiss her, to taste her, to change her mind in the language he knew most fluently. The very thought sent hot blood surging to his loins, but Justin clenched his jaw and forced himself to think of something else. "You are very clever, using Simone to divert me from the real issue, but I know you." His voice was husky as he repeated, "I *know* you, Mouette."

"Indeed? Sometimes I think you know me not at all."

"And I suppose you believe that buffoon Redfield does?"

"He treats me with respect and kindness. Why do you persist in insulting a man who has never been more than a dear, devoted friend to me?" They were facing each other now, and Mouette reached out to push lightly at his chest. "In truth, Theo was a friend when my own husband was nowhere to be found!"

Justin caught her wrist. Did she call Redfield by his Christian name, *Theo*, just to torment him? How badly he wanted to pull her into his arms and kiss her until she was dizzy with arousal, pulling up her skirts, begging him to... *No! Stop it*, his inner voice commanded. *For God's sake, not yet.*

"That idiot—" he began.

"Theo is not an idiot!" Mouette took a step back.

Fury burned through him, but he managed a tight smile. "Fine then. But hear this: *His lordship* is not your friend! He wants you for himself. I see it." For good measure, Justin added, "Men know these things."

"Oh, yes, you men profess to be so wise. But for you, everything is reduced to base desire."

"Perhaps," he agreed with an ironic shrug, adding, "Yet there was a time when you liked that about me, *chérie.*"

"I will not dignify that with an answer. Instead, let me say that it is refreshing to know a good, kind man who sees and admires me as a person, someone with talents and a fine mind."

"Can you really believe that? You are a fool if you do." As soon as the words were out, he regretted them.

Mouette stormed off toward the window, then whirled around and started back. "M'sieur, *you* are the fool if you imagine you can recapture my affection by speaking to me thus!"

He could see her breasts swelling under her thin, embroidered bodice, and the yearning he felt for her took on a bittersweet edge. It came to him that the gulf between them was widening. A memory returned from early in their relationship, before they were married, when Mouette had frequently spoken of her intention to return to London and pick up the life she'd left behind. Such talk had rankled Justin, but once she had clearly fallen in love with him, all that was forgotten.

Or had it just been swept away, under the rug? Maybe she really did have a life here that she secretly missed. Now that their children were growing up, was she having second thoughts about what—or who— would make her happy? Justin felt a stab of terror.

"Perhaps I have it all wrong then," he said in a low voice.

"Yes! You do."

"Are you telling me you prefer this life in London to our marriage?"

Her eyes flashed. "No! I am saying that I am here in London to help Charles, not to indulge your moods. Just last night, you swore that you intended to become a different man, that you would change your behavior and be someone I could rely upon during this precarious time." She took a breath, meeting his gaze. "If you truly want to prove your love and worthiness to me, you will put your own ego to one side."

"I see." His heart pounded. "It sounds as if I am the one who is in the way, not Redfield."

Mouette's eyes blazed. "How dare you speak as if our marriage is disposable, as if we might simply throw it away during an argument or because you feel threatened?"

He reached out and caught both her forearms. "Mouette, you make my head spin. What the devil are you saying?"

"Simply...that I have a great deal to contend with." For an instant, her voice seemed to break. "Really, you cannot imagine."

Tell me then. He very nearly spoke the words aloud but sensed that Mouette was in no mood to reveal her deeper feelings. Later, perhaps. He released her, realizing that his urge to solve their problems in a blaze of passion was a fantasy.

It remained impossible to convince Mouette that Redfield was not to be trusted, even though Justin knew this in his gut. She would say he was jealous, which was true enough. Yet could he not be jealous—and right as well?

* * *

WHEN JUSTIN HAD LEFT her to seek out a drink, Mouette felt like weeping. She summoned Gwynn to help her take off the berry silk morning dress and draw the drapes. Mouette then lay down on her bed, longing for a restorative nap.

She closed her eyes, but a flurry of thoughts began to go round in her mind. Thoughts of Justin, of course. Sighing, she wished desperately that her mother or sister were there to talk to.

During her years with Justin, he had always been the unpredictable one who gave vent to his impulses, and Mouette had let herself be swept along under his spell. She loved him madly, almost addictively. And although she knew he was mad for her, too, it would certainly be disaster if both of them tried to hold the reins. Hadn't she known all about him when they married? Yes. Marriage was like a sublimely thrilling dance between them, day in and day out...until Justin started behaving erratically in Saint-Malo, yearning to be young again.

And then Charles had turned up unexpectedly, demanding his mother's attention.

Mouette couldn't blame Justin for being confused and frustrated by the harsh words she had just spoken. But how could she explain to him that she felt cornered on many sides? Charles had even convinced her not to divulge the truth about his betrothal, or lack of one. And seeing the Countess of Penhurst today had stirred up so many old feelings. It felt like yesterday, rather than a dozen years ago, that she had last encountered Lady Penhurst at her annual ball. The woman and her little group of friends had glanced away as if they didn't recognize Mouette.

She knew none of that should matter now, but the hurt and humiliation clearly ran deeper than she had realized.

Mouette took a deep breath and brought herself back to the present, reminding herself how much stronger she had grown over the years. *I am no longer that woman!* She closed her eyes and made herself imagine scenes of triumph for all of them at the Countess of Penhurst's next legendary ball. Charles would claim the affections of Lady Penelope, Justin would behave himself for her sake, and Mouette would move gracefully among the *haut ton* with her head held high.

At the end of the splendid evening, she and Justin would return home together, kissing in the darkened carriage. Back inside the house, they might sit together in the shadowed parlor, sipping wine, surrendering at last to their potent mutual attraction.

Lying alone now under the sheet, Mouette let one hand drift up to her breast as she imagined him touching her, kissing her, and finally carrying her up the stairs to bed. The intimate part of her that she had struggled to deny for days surged back to life, tingling in heated anticipation at the prospect of being in Justin's arms again.

Of letting herself love him.

Soon, soon, Mouette promised herself, just moments before she drifted off to sleep.

CHAPTER 16

The next morning, Mouette allowed herself to soften toward Justin. She looked at him across the breakfast table and her heart began to beat faster, just as it always did when he was near.

He fed her a bite of his salmon and murmured, "You look ravishing."

Mouette glanced down at the peacock blue silk gown he had seen at least a dozen times this past year. Today, she had chosen it not only because it flattered her, but also because she remembered Justin loved it on her.

"I may have been a bit too harsh yesterday," she said, almost afraid to let herself meet his gaze. "When we talked."

"Ah. *Oui*, I must agree." His voice was seductively low. Waving Gwynn away, he picked up the pot and poured more coffee for Mouette, adding just the right amount of sugar and rich, warm milk. "You were angry with me—for being who I have always been."

It was true, she realized. "Perhaps. But I beg you to remember the promises you made when you arrived here from Cornwall."

Justin leaned back in the delicate chair. "As you

might imagine, it was not easy for me to say those things. And at the time, I did not anticipate that I would have to battle a stiff-chinned nobleman for your attentions."

Tilting her head slightly, Mouette replied, "It seems that you do not hear anything I say. Once again, I must assure you that Theo is but a loyal friend to me. I need such friends right now."

"*Eh bien.*" His dark eyes flashed, but then she saw him visibly bring himself under control. "I will try to tolerate him."

Impulsively, Mouette reached across and covered his strong hand with her own. He was so vital, so alive, and just the feeling of his warm skin sent a little shiver of arousal to the core of her. "I will be very grateful if you can refrain from insulting or taunting Lord Redfield."

"I will try...for you, *ma belle.*"

She had to admit, it was thrilling to feel the love in his gaze.

Before Mouette could find her voice, there was a commotion in the entry hall and Charles appeared, unannounced. Her heart sank as he strode into the morning room, still carrying an umbrella that dripped rain over the Aubusson carpet. Of course, Mouette loved her son, but he had become a divisive force in her relationship with Justin. Just as things were beginning to mend between them, Charles might very well be bringing trouble.

"What the devil—" muttered Justin, rising, but Mouette lifted a hand in warning, and he fell silent.

"My dear, do come in," she said. "Will you join us for breakfast?"

Baptiste appeared behind Charles, eyes wide, and accepted the wet umbrella and beaver hat that were thrust into his hands. Mouette felt Justin's outrage, but he somehow managed to refrain from speaking his mind to her son.

When the young man drew near to the table, he reached inside his coat and drew out a rolled-up sheet of paper.

"I have something to show the two of you!" Eyes blazing, Charles unfurled the paper and held it up for them to see. "Look what everyone in London is talking about," he exclaimed before narrowing his eyes at Justin. "Or should I say, *whom?*"

Mouette's skirts rustled as she rose and went toward him for a closer look. She felt suddenly queasy at the sight of a vivid satirical print in the unmistakable style of Thomas Rowlandson. She was conscious of Charles's ragged, angry breathing as she stared at the depiction of an outlandish pirate surrounded by several refined ladies. A colorful parrot teetered on the one shoulder of the man, who sported not only a black eye-patch, but also an exaggerated peg leg. The broad-shouldered pirate was grinning, his old-fashioned tri-corne hat tilted slightly over black hair drawn back in a queue. He brandished an evil-looking cutlass at a styl-ishly garbed female with feathers in her hair, who Mouette guessed was meant to represent Madame d'Amboise.

An assortment of richly garbed, aristocratic ladies circled around the outrageous buccaneer, watching aghast. A few of the women held quizzing glasses aloft, while others exchanged comments behind their gloved hands.

"These outrageous drawings are displayed in the windows of every print shop in Mayfair this morning!" shouted Charles. "What must the Duke and Duchess of Bellingham think?"

Justin leaned forward for a better look at the print

before remarking, "I don't see what it could possibly have to do with them."

"This sullies the name of my family, sir."

"Why?"

"Do you not see? That ridiculous pirate is you!"

Justin's handsome visage darkened slightly, but his tone remained mild. "That fellow looks nothing like me."

Fearing that Charles might have an attack of apoplexy, she touched Justin's arm. "It is a caricature, my dear, as I think you know."

Her son cried, "Have you not seen the caption?" He pointed to the words, ornately written across the bottom of the print: *Lady Brandreth's new Pirate Husband takes London by Storm!* "How can I ever show my face in society again?"

Mouette felt a familiar wave of pain and humiliation as she remembered the cruel satirical print that had made the rounds after Harry went to prison. It had depicted him wearing a black cloak and mask, paying criminals to murder his own father-in-law, André Raveneau. It had been a horrible time for many reasons, not least because the aristocrats Mouette had once deemed so important whispered about her whenever she entered a room.

"This is a cruel drawing," she murmured. "But we should not be distressed. The people who mock Justin are not worth our attention."

"How can you say that?" Charles exclaimed. When he swiveled to stare accusingly at Justin, Mouette sent him a warning look. In that moment, she wished she had been more forthcoming with her husband. Why had she postponed telling him that Charles was not really betrothed after all?

"Dear son, may I remind you that you are not perfect either? In fact—"

He interrupted her, grasping her arm tightly. "Mother, I must speak with you alone. Urgently."

Once again, Mouette felt pulled in two directions. She wanted to call Charles out, to put him in his place, to tell Justin every bit of the truth, but the look of desperate pleading in her son's blue eyes gave her pause.

"We are eating breakfast," she managed.

"I require but a few moments of your time."

Glancing back at Justin, she saw the scar on his cheekbone whiten but he gestured toward the newspaper that lay folded beside his plate. "Pay me no heed. I will read the *The Times* until you return," he told her and promptly shook it out.

Mouette lost no time in leading Charles through to the sitting room. When they were inside, she turned to face him. "What is so important?"

"You must not say anything to Justin about the…situation with Lady Penelope," he said in a low, strident voice. "Promise, Mama."

Her son so rarely called her Mama that she faltered, but only for a moment. "By *situation*, do you mean the way you misrepresented your betrothal to both of us when you came to Cornwall?"

Glancing toward the door, Charles took both her hands and drew her away, closer to the windows. "You will never know what I went through when I was a boy and I discovered that Justin was Anthony's true father. Every time I watched the three of you together, sharing a story or a jest, I felt as if a wall had been erected that I could never cross. Even my fair hair set me apart," he said urgently.

"Charles, I am sorry about that, but really—"

"Do you think it's easy for me to talk about this now? But I want you to understand why I must maintain some dignity with Justin. I already feel inferior.

Isn't your place, as my mother, to support and protect me?"

Mouette felt torn about Charles's situation, right up to the part where he demanded her protection. Suddenly, she wanted to tell him that he was a grown man, and that she was also Justin's wife, and it wasn't fair to ask her to keep secrets from him.

"I just don't see what Justin has to do with any of this. Why can't he know the truth?"

"If he were a true gentleman, it might not matter. But he is not, and you know it, Mother. His words can be weapons. Just the thought of how he would look at me, the things he might say, the way he would remind me every day that I am not truly betrothed to the daughter of a duke..." Charles broke off with a shake of his head.

"I think you misunderstand Justin. He can be very caring, even kind."

"Not to me," came her son's stubborn reply. "And you must see that his very presence in London complicates everything. Damnation, that deuced buccaneer print will make me a laughingstock when people realize he is my stepfather!" Abruptly, Charles's tone softened. "I am simply asking for a bit of time. I promise you that by the evening we attend the Countess of Penhurst's ball, my betrothal to Lady Penelope will be quite real. And then it won't matter what I did or didn't reveal before."

Mouette closed her eyes, utterly torn. In that instant, she had a vision of Charles as a boy of ten, struggling to understand what had happened to the father he adored. Perhaps she had been partly to blame for not being more honest with him about Harry's faults and crimes, but it seemed cruel to add to his torment during that terrible time. It had been impossible then to foresee how Charles's need to enshrine his father's memory would distort his values as he moved into adulthood. Was there still hope for him? Mouette felt that he needed support, if only because he believed he hadn't received enough after her marriage to Justin. Hadn't her own parents always supported her, even when she made bad decisions as an adult?

"All right. I will hold my tongue, but only until the ball," she said quietly, and was gratified by the expression of relief and joy that lit her son's handsome face. "But if you have not won Lady Penelope's hand by then, I must share the truth with Justin."

To her surprise, Charles made an awkward attempt to embrace her. "Oh, Mama, you have no idea how much this means to me." His voice caught. "I sometimes feel so alone, rather like an orphan… but it seems I do have a mother after all."

"Of course, you do!" Tears pricked Mouette's eyes as she felt her son's heart beating through his fine clothing. Drawing back to look into his eyes, she said, "You must never forget that I love you very much."

Even as Mouette spoke, she resolved to have a very serious conversation with Charles if matters had not improved by the time the ball was over. It was one thing to stand behind her child, but quite another to enable bad behavior in a son who had grown to adulthood.

* * *

JUSTIN COULD HAVE SWORN that Mouette was avoiding him, but he couldn't corner her long enough to demand an explanation. It wasn't until the afternoon following Charles's visit that he managed to find his wife alone. She sat at the desk in her morning room, bathed in sunbeams that slanted through the windowpanes.

"Ah," he said from the doorway, "there you are."

Mouette looked up, a sheet of white paper in one hand, and smiled. "I was just reading a letter from our daughter."

This was all the invitation Justin needed. Crossing the room, he pulled up a chair next to Mouette. "What does Emmie say?" Just speaking of her caused his heart to squeeze. "No doubt she begs that we hasten to Lyme Regis with all possible speed to rescue her from the drudgery of searching for *fossils*."

Even as Mouette shook her head, he saw a dimple wink in her cheek, a sign that she was succumbing to his charm. "She says nothing of the kind. This letter is even more enthusiastic than the last. Emeline has found some vertebrae that Mary Anning herself does not recognize, so that is very exciting." Mouette passed the letter to him.

Justin read the words penned in his daughter's childish yet intense hand. "I've been trying not to think of her very much," he said softly. "I confess...it hurts."

"She will return to us, perhaps sooner than we hoped," Mouette assured him, and her use of the word *us* lifted his spirits. "Isabella has written as well. It seems that Mary Anning may come to London soon. She has been invited to visit the geologist Roderick Murchison and his wife, and if it all works out, Izzie will bring the girls along as well." Mouette reached out to touch his coat sleeve. "Wouldn't that be wonderful?"

Their eyes met and held, and Justin's heart gave a mad thump. "Of course." He wanted to cover her hand with his and then bring her over onto his lap. But just then, Mouette glanced away.

"You ought to write to Emmie," she said.

"I know. I shall." He sighed. "It isn't easy, being a parent."

To Justin's surprise, instead of encouraging him to try harder, Mouette's eyes moistened, and she nodded slowly. "That's very true. It sometimes feels like I am feeling my way in the dark."

"You are a splendid mother." He hoped to make her smile, but instead she began to turn away. Justin touched her hand. "Let us speak of other things. Come with me to visit a cabinetmaker in Upper Marylebone Street. His name is Fawley. I've heard very good reports about his work, and he keeps a selection of fine, ready-made furnishings."

Mouette looked tempted. "I have an appointment with Madame d'Amboise for a fitting at three o'clock."

"Excellent. I will take you there as well." Justin leaned close enough to feel her response, like an ember glowing in the space between them. "Perhaps we might take a turn in Hyde Park while we are out. Wouldn't you like that?"

She gave him a tentative smile. "Will you behave yourself in the company of others?"

"Madame, have I not given my word?"

"You have." Mouette rose, smoothing her skirts. "But I know you all too well, m'sieur."

"Yet you will come."

"Yes." Turning, she tossed him an enchanting smile over one slim shoulder. "It will be a test…"

CHAPTER 17

"*I* have never heard of this cabinetmaker," Mouette said to Justin in a soft voice.

They stood inside the shop of Josiah Fawley on Upper Marylebone Street. "It is possible there may be a few things you do not know, madame," he teased lightly.

She looked around at the examples of French-influenced furnishings displayed in the large room. "I once fancied myself an expert on the very best merchants in London," she said wryly. "And I had the bills to prove it."

Justin gave a low laugh and slid a hand around her waist, drawing her closer. She could feel sparks catch fire, charging the air between them. "*Chérie*, will it not be a pleasure to spend freely without fear of the bills?"

"But it doesn't feel right that you should finance renovations in this house. I mean, it really has no connection to you."

"No connection?" His tone was faintly suggestive. "You are my wife."

In that moment, he turned slightly toward her, and Mouette imagined that if their bodies met, she would feel the carnal proof of the bond between them.

164

Warmth tingled enticingly at her intimate core. "Yes, but..."

Justin touched a silencing finger to her mouth, and she breathed in his scent. "I have a selfish interest in this matter. You have banished me to a mean little bed in Anthony's room that isn't fit for a potboy. If I must live in *your* house in London, I mean to be comfortable."

As he spoke, it came to Mouette that even though she had avoided the Bedford Square house during their marriage, perhaps she had kept it just in case things didn't work out with Justin...in case he committed an unforgivable act, and she needed a place of her very own to which she might escape.

Yes, she admitted to herself, *and it might still be true*. Life with Justin felt as dangerously unpredictable as it had been in the early weeks of their relationship.

Just then a tall, heavy-set man appeared from a doorway at the back of the shop. He wore a leather apron over his breeches, shirt, and waistcoat, and his sparse sandy hair was damp with perspiration. "My apologies! I did not hear the bell." He wiped his hands on a cloth and added, "I am Josiah Fawley."

Justin walked forward to meet him, one strong hand extended in greeting. "My name is Justin St. Briac." He turned back to bring Mouette to his side, but before he could speak, Fawley made a sound of delighted surprise.

"Why, it is Lady Brandreth! What a pleasure to see you after so many years." And then the cabinet maker bowed to Mouette.

"Mister Fawley, I beg you to refresh my memory," she said with a smile. "How do we know one another?"

"Oh, my lady, you would not remember *me*! I was but a lowly apprentice in the shop of the great Thomas Sheraton. You visited us many times and were always

165

very kind to everyone whose path crossed yours." The big man reddened. "Once I had the privilege of carving a footstool you ordered for your husband, Sir Harry, and I brought it out to you myself. I've never forgotten the compliments you paid me that day."

"Oh, yes, I do remember." Mouette beamed at him. "You made charming lion's paw feet. They were very lifelike."

"Indeed, my lady! I am honored that you recall."

She wanted to tell him that she still had the footstool but in truth it had been sold along with the other Sheraton pieces she had purchased during those extravagant, early days of her marriage to Harry.

"I am forced to remind *her ladyship* that a great deal has changed since then," Justin interjected in a sardonic tone.

"Oh, yes, that's right." Mouette's face felt warm. "I should explain that I am no longer Lady Brandreth. You doubtless knew that Sir Harry is no longer...that is to say, he is..."

"Quite dead," Justin supplied coolly.

"It is true," she agreed. "And I am now Madame St. Briac."

"What my wife means to say," Justin said, "is that she has been my wife for a full decade."

"Ah, I see." Fawley shifted into a more deferential posture. "In that case, how may I be of assistance to *you*, sir?"

"We are in need of new furnishings for our London home," Justin said.

Mouette flushed. Perhaps Josiah Fawley wondered what had happened to all the costly and valuable furniture she had purchased originally? Drawing a deep breath, she said, "Indeed we are. Styles have changed."

Fawley seemed to be studying her. "Some things never go out of fashion," he observed.

"That's true," declared Justin. "We have come to you, sir, because you make fine furnishings in the French style." He pointed to a magnificent fourposter bed that gleamed in the morning light. "I am particularly drawn to that piece."

"Oh, aye, sir," Fawley beamed. "Your taste is excellent. The bed is solid mahogany, and the spiral turnings are made in the very latest fashion." He pointed to the beautifully carved posts as he spoke.

"We must have it. I see that you also do upholstery. How soon can you have bed linens and draperies made for us?"

"There is a linen draper across the road who keeps exceptionally fine fabrics in stock," the cabinetmaker replied. "If you and Lady Brand—" He broke off and cleared his throat. "That is, if you and Madame *St. Briac* make choices today, we will do our best to have it all ready for you by week's end."

Justin nodded slowly, considering. "I suppose that might be soon enough." He paused as if realizing that Fawley was wondering about payment. "When we finish here today, you may send me a bill. My man of business will see that you are compensated in full when we take delivery."

"Excellent!" The cabinetmaker's eyes lit up. "Might I show you other pieces, sir? In fact, we have several new items that are not yet on display. Allow me to step away for a moment to procure a current list."

No sooner had Fawley left the room than Justin turned his compelling gaze on Mouette. She knew him well enough to realize that he was imagining them together in this new bed, and suddenly it was difficult to breathe.

"I think sapphire-blue for the hangings, don't you agree?" he murmured.

"Hmm. Perhaps. Although, I would favor emerald-green," she managed to parry.

"Would you?" A seductive smile touched his hard mouth. "Then green it shall be."

Her pulse raced. Surely this was the first time Justin had ever surrendered immediately to her opinion. Although a small concession, it might be a sign that he really did mean to change. Was it possible? Mouette realized she should know better...yet hope caught fire in her heart.

* * *

AT MIDNIGHT on the eve of the Countess of Penhurst's ball, Justin lay once again in his son's uncomfortable bed. The air was warm, too warm, and a moonbeam broke through the parted curtains to disturb his fitful sleep.

He thought he could hear Mouette moving around in her rooms. Perhaps she was feeling just as unsettled as he was! What if she was missing him, longing for him to appear in the doorway, to take her in his arms and make passionate love to her? As the scene played in his mind, Justin rolled onto his stomach. His stiff cock pulsed beneath him, taunting him to put on his dressing gown and hunt down his wife.

These thoughts were interrupted by an admonishment from his higher self. *Don't be a fool! Patience. Wait one more night and all your longings will be fulfilled...*

Justin closed his eyes, aching but determined, and soon sleep crept up on him. It seemed only a moment later, as he began to snore softly, that a hand shook him awake.

"What the devil!" a loud voice exclaimed. "Who are you, and what are you doing in my bed?"

Instincts rooted in Justin's years as a corsair caused

him to open his eyes in the darkness, bolt upright in the bed, and reach for a dagger, but of course there was no such weapon here in civilized London. Heart thundering, he whirled and tried to focus on the shadowy form that loomed above him.

"*Sangdieu!*" Justin scrambled to his knees and roared, "I will kill you!"

Powerful arms restrained him with surprising ease. "Papa, stop! It's me, Anthony! For God's sake, you mustn't kill me!"

Was it possible? As he came more fully awake, Justin began to make sense of what was happening. Perhaps his son really had come home from university, never expecting to find his own father in his bed.

"What are you doing here?" Justin demanded.

"I might ask you the same thing," Anthony replied with heavy irony. "You're the one sleeping in *my* bed." Even as he spoke, he went out to the corridor and returned with a softly glowing oil lamp.

Justin reached for his trousers, his bad knee aching as he dressed. Clearly, he wasn't going to sleep any time soon. "Why aren't you at university? Is your mother expecting you?"

"I am deuced thirsty. Join me for a drink?"

Anthony casually reached into the cupboard where he had once kept toy soldiers and produced a bottle of brandy and two glasses. Justin watched as the boy, who now suddenly appeared to be a man, dropped into one of the chairs near the moon-silvered window and propped his booted legs on a low stool.

After pouring himself a brandy, Anthony enjoyed a long sip. "Mama wrote to me that you came to London after all. I had just finished an examination and had some free time, so I thought I would pay a visit and see how the two of you were getting on."

Justin sat down in the other chair, frowning. "We're getting on splendidly."

This statement elicited a crack of laughter from his son. "Oh, right. I can see that."

He was about to concoct a tale about sleeping here for a perfectly legitimate reason, but Anthony was watching him with such keen dark eyes that he stopped himself. Suddenly the prospect of talking to someone else about what had been happening was extremely appealing.

They sat together in the shadows, drinking brandy, as Justin unspooled the tale of his adventures since arriving in London, including his efforts to win Mouette's trust and the frustration he'd been enduring because of Viscount Redfield.

"My suspicions about him were confirmed when I learned that he has not paid his account at the dressmaker," Justin muttered. "He had the effrontery to act insulted when she called him on it."

"I remember Lord Redfield," Anthony said, nodding. "He was a friend of... my other father." He looked a bit uncomfortable, as he always did when attempting to speak about Sir Harry Brandreth, the man he'd thought was his true parent for more than half his life. "At least that was the reason he always gave for visiting us when I was a little boy. He said he had come to fulfill a duty as Papa's friend, that he had to check on all of us."

"But?" Justin heard himself prompt. As always, the mere mention of Redfield made him want to challenge the viscount to a duel to the death. Failing that, Justin wished his snuffbox was at hand. "Were you about to say that Redfield lusts after your mother?"

Anthony shot him a glance that mingled surprise with wry amusement. "I wouldn't have put it exactly that way, but...perhaps you've got it right."

"It's a relief to hear someone else confirm my instincts. Your mama is convinced that he is some sort of gallant knight, always ready to come to her aid. She thinks I am jealous and petty to suspect his motives." Leaning back in the too-small chair, Justin glanced over at his son and realized again that Anthony had crossed the bridge into manhood. He had a roguish air that was new. His black, curly hair was fashionably disheveled, his shoulders were wide, and the boyish lines of his features now looked chiseled. "Do you remember the portrait of your mother that she prized but was forced to sell years ago? I learned it was Redfield who helped her find a buyer. I mean to discover its whereabouts, pay the owner off, and restore it to her."

"Of course, I remember it." A wry smile curved Anthony's mouth. "No doubt you dream of the moment when you hang it back above the mantel in her morning room and she throws her arms around you in gratitude."

"Exactly," Justin agreed, flashing a grin. "Which brings me back to Redfield. It develops that he found a buyer for the portrait: a fellow called Sir Phillip Waterstone. When we quizzed Redfield further, he insisted the man had gone to Italy and is now dead." He shook his head. "I am convinced there is more to it."

"Fascinating." Anthony rubbed the side of his jaw. "Perhaps we should investigate."

"I was hoping you would say that." Justin smiled.

"Suddenly I am very fatigued. Just one more drop of brandy..." His son poured an inch of liquor into each of their glasses. "And what of Charles? Have you met his betrothed yet? I confess that I am curious."

"Charles has been difficult, to put it generously." Justin relayed the tale about the satirical print and shrugged. "Tomorrow night, we will at last meet Lady Penelope, and it is expected that the Duke of

Bellingham will announce their engagement. One hopes Charles will then unclench his jaw and cheer up."

Anthony nodded, considering. "Yes, Mama wrote me that tomorrow is the Countess of Penhurst's annual ball. No doubt you are dreading it."

"*Au contraire.*" Justin drained his glass. "I am counting the minutes! Tomorrow night, I intend to make your mother fall in love with me all over again. I have been slowly making progress toward regaining her favor, and I mean to finish sweeping her off her feet at the ball." He sent his son a sidelong glance. "Then you won't find me in your bed any longer."

"Clearly I have come home at just the right time," Anthony murmured with wry amusement. "I thought I might attend the ball as well. You never know; you might need me if something goes wrong."

"Wrong?" Justin gave a derisive laugh. "Impossible! I mean to guard my every word and deed. Your mama will be powerless to resist me."

"Hmm." Even as Anthony nodded, one side of his mouth cocked upward. "That should be entertaining..."

CHAPTER 18

It was going to be a wonderful day, Mouette decided. Her beloved son had come home to surprise them, the Countess of Penhurst's annual ball was tonight, and her finished gown of rich plum silk had arrived. Mouette held her breath as Gwynn helped her try it on.

"Madame, how beautiful you are," breathed the maid as she did the last tiny button and they both looked at Mouette's reflection in the cheval mirror. "Wait until tonight, when your hair is dressed, and you have the proper jewels."

Before Mouette could reply, a knock sounded at the door and Gwyn bustled over to admit Justin. He entered without an invitation, bringing the intoxicating energy that was his alone.

"Ah, Gwynn, how faithful you are to stay by your mistress's side today," he said.

"I take great pleasure in serving her," the young woman beamed.

"You deserve a reward. Baptiste has prepared a special breakfast tart with the first peaches of the season." He added a low sound of pleasure. "You must hurry before it is all gone. Anthony has already had two pieces."

Moments later, they were alone. Mouette's heart leaped as Justin came toward her, as roughly, deeply appealing as ever. Reaching her side, he bent to inhale the fragrance of her hair, his breath warm against her ear.

"That gown provides an excellent showcase for your beauty, *chérie*," he said. "It is elegant, but not over-powering."

He was right. At Justin's insistence, Madame d'Amboise had kept the design simple. Fashion dictated excessive decoration with lots of little bows, froths of lace, and hems padded with wads of cottonwool. After consulting with Mouette and Justin, Madame embellished the plum gown with only golden silk embroidered with tiny leaves, twisted into buds that trailed diagonally from one side of the gown's waist to the opposite hem. The effect was restrained yet striking.

"You speak as if I were still in my first flush of youth," Mouette said wistfully. "In truth, just the opposite is true."

Justin shook his head. "Your beauty and experience have a richness that no immature girl could match."

She swayed closer when he encircled her waist with one hand. The bodice of her gown grazed his chest, and her nipples tingled under the thin layers of fabric. Did he really mean it? When Mouette looked up into his face, she believed him.

"I have brought you a small gift, for tonight." Justin lifted his free hand and she saw that he was holding a blue velvet pouch. "But you must turn around and close your eyes."

Mouette obeyed, alive with anticipation. His fingertips were deft and cool on her neck. She felt the weight of a necklace before he fastened the clasp. Opening her eyes, she looked at their reflection and saw him standing close behind her, his hands lightly touching her bare shoulders. At her neck gleamed a beautiful choker of square-cut amethysts set in rich gold, colors that perfectly matched her gown.

"It's exquisite," Mouette's mouth was dry, her heart pounding. "Thank you."

"There are earrings as well." His gaze met hers in the mirror, and as always it seemed both of his eyes were on her, even though one was covered by a silk eye-patch.

As Mouette watched their reflections, she felt his long fingers slide down from her shoulders, over the fashionable beret shape of her short sleeves, tracing the contours of her arms. Then his hands encircled her waist and slowly drew her back so that they were touching, full-length.

"I have missed you so much," he said, raw need in his voice.

Tears pricked her eyes. She let herself melt into him, aching.

"I have just received word that our new bed arrives today," Justin said, his voice infused with temptation. "It is perfect timing, *oui*?"

"I…" Mouette found it hard to breathe. "Well, perhaps." Between her legs, all the longings she had suppressed since leaving Cornwall swelled. She was warm and wet there, and if she turned just a bit and lifted her face, he would kiss her. How she had missed his masterful kisses! Every inch of her yearned for his mouth, his deft fingers…

Just as one of Justin's dark, strong hands slid up and was about to cup her breast over her bodice, the sound of insistent barking reached them from outside.

"Did you hear that?" Mouette froze. "If I didn't know better, I would say that was Robinson."

"Fortunately, that is impossible." Justin shook his dark head, but she could feel that his body had tensed. "Robinson is in Cornwall, at Frenchman's Haven."

The mood was broken. As the barking continued, Mouette started toward the window. "We should see, though, just to be certain."

"*Oui.* You are right, of course." With long strides, he reached the window first and stopped Mouette before she could look for herself. "*Mon Dieu!* A liveried servant has just brought a dog that does resemble Robinson to the door."

"Whose livery does the fellow wear?"

She saw Justin go pale under his tan. "I have no idea. And what does it matter? I will go down immediately and find out what's happening. I'll send Gwynn to help you get out of that gown."

When the door shut behind Justin, Mouette hurried back to the window, but no one was there.

* * *

By the time Justin reached the stair hall, Robinson had begun to bark again, straining at the tether held by a footman who looked all-too familiar. Of course, he had known the moment he looked out Mouette's window to glimpse the servant's distinctive bottle-green livery.

Daphne. A powerful wave of dread rose inside him. Ever since the day she had appeared at Frenchman's Haven, imploring him to help her conceive a child, he had tried to blot her from his memory. *Mon Dieu, please don't let her come here.*

Anthony, who was standing off to one side, came forward to take charge of Robinson. The corgi leaped into his arms, smiling broadly.

"Good day, milord!" said the footman, bowing his head to Justin. "My mistress has bidden me return your little dog to you."

"I wasn't aware I'd lost him." It felt as if the bottom had dropped out of his carefully planned morning. "Why is Robinson *here* instead of in Cornwall?"

"Lady Daphne has sent you a message," the young man proclaimed, and Justin wanted to clap a hand over his mouth to stop him from saying her name. The servant produced a small, folded envelope with a bottle-green seal. On it was written, in bold, flowing script: *Justin.* Thank God Mouette hadn't come downstairs yet!

"Fine, *merci.* I suggest that you go out this way." Justin steered him toward the kitchen, hoping to prevent him from passing under Mouette's window again. "Tell Baptiste, my steward, that I've said you should have a reward."

When the footman was gone, Justin tore open the letter.

My dear Justin,

As I was preparing to travel to London, it came to my attention that your servants were very concerned about dear Robinson. It seems he was languishing there at home, without you. One cannot blame him! I succumbed to their pleas and agreed to bring him with me. It was the least I could do, given the many favors you have bestowed upon me.

Yours as ever, Daphne...

"What's all this about?" Anthony inquired in a deceptively mild voice.

The familiar band was tightening around Justin's heart. "How should I know? The woman is quite mad." He glanced down, scanning the message again. "Still, I must insist that you say nothing to your mother. She might misunderstand."

One of Anthony's dark brows flew up, but he made no reply.

Just then, Mouette herself appeared above them on the landing. Clad in a lace-edged dressing gown, she hurried down the stairs, gazing in wonderment at Robinson.

"Oh, you handsome fellow!" she exclaimed, and the corgi squirmed out of Anthony's arms and ran to greet her. Mouette crouched down to embrace him, accepting his wet kisses, laughing. "How I have missed you."

Justin realized he ought to join in this reunion. "Only this incorrigible beast could find a way to travel from Cornwall straight to this very house," he muttered, stroking Robinson's thick fur.

"And how exactly did he manage that?" asked Mouette. Although her tone was light, she watched him intently.

Across the stair hall, Anthony coughed.

Justin tried to gather his wits. "According to the footman who made this unusual delivery, our servants at Frenchman's Haven said Robinson was suffering without us, and so they begged a neighbor to bring him along on his journey to London." He rose and started toward the kitchen, hoping to escape before Mouette could quiz him further. "I will go and talk to Baptiste about this new addition to the household."

"Wait!" she said. "Which kind neighbor brought Robinson all this way? We must send a note of thanks."

"What?" Justin gave her a distracted glance, feigning utter indifference. "Oh, do you know, in all the excitement, I forgot to ask. Robinson demanded all the attention for himself, of course."

On cue, the dog left Mouette, his nails clicking on the marble floor. Reaching Justin's side, Robinson gazed up as if waiting to hear what escapade they would enjoy next.

"How odd." Mouette's brow furrowed with a trace of suspicion. She looked at their son. "Anthony?"

Justin held his breath.

"Don't look at me," Anthony said with an offhand shrug. "But now that Robinson is here, does it really matter who brought him?"

"Hmm." Mouette looked doubtful but turned back on the steps. "I suppose it is a mystery that can wait until tomorrow. The Countess of Penhurst's ball is just a few hours away and there is still a great deal to do."

CHAPTER 19

*M*ouette stood on the edge of the glittering ballroom at Penhurst House, looking out over elegantly garbed masses of waltzing aristocrats.

She blinked, and a door swung open in her memory, carrying her back a dozen years to the last time she had stood in this ballroom…newly returned from America after seeking refuge there with her parents in the wake of Harry's crimes, imprisonment, and death.

On that long ago night, Mouette had known she was making a mistake by coming to the ball. People were staring at her. Whispering. The Countess of Penhurst herself had glanced over and lifted her lorgnette, frowning.

Mouette and Harry had once been embraced by the *ton*, and Mouette hoped enough time had passed that she could now be welcomed again by these sought-after aristocrats. But instead, she had suffered a series of disapproving glances, and then the sting of her erstwhile friends literally turning their backs on her. Each blatant snub felt like a blow.

Only Theo had crossed to her side, insisting that she come out to dance with him.

Aching, Mouette returned to the present.

"Ma belle." Justin's whisper was husky. He grazed her cheek with one fingertip. "What's amiss?"

Mouette opened her eyes, suffused with relief at the sight of her husband. "It's nothing. Just a memory." It came to her that she had never truly confided in him about all she had endured, first because of Harry's crimes, and then at the fickle hands of the Beau Monde. She had glossed over those memories, preferring instead to leave the past behind, to live in the moment with Justin, grateful that he had no connection to London society.

Mouette drew a breath. What irony to be here among the *ton* again, this time with Justin by her side.

"Will you dance with your husband?" he was asking with a roguish tilt of his dark head. "When the other men see you in my arms, they will all be filled with envy."

She decided then to surrender to the present moment and do her best to enjoy the evening. As the musicians struck up a waltz, the ballroom at Penhurst House glowed with light reflected by the dangling prisms of magnificent, cut-glass chandeliers.

Justin clasped her hand. He wore white kid gloves that fit like a second skin, and it seemed that he was touching her for the first time. She caught her lower lip between her teeth and Justin arched a knowing brow.

Tipping her head back, Mouette basked in his intoxicating nearness, fully aware that her husband was more ungovernable than a lightning strike.

Justin bent, his mouth brushing her ear as they turned and whirled together to the lyrical strains of the waltz. "Relax, *chérie*. I have you."

She drank in his scent. Starched linen and soap, a whiff of brandy, and a masculine essence that was his alone. Mouette relaxed in his arms, let him lead her, as their bodies melted into the music.

"You look...very handsome tonight," she heard herself say.

"If so, it is for you, my love."

Mouette's gaze shifted to admire his impeccably tailored dress coat of midnight blue. Other men might be similarly clad, but none with her husband's effortless *savoir faire*. His snow-white neckcloth, flawlessly executed in the formal Ball Room style, was fastened with a gold pin set with one narrow, octagonal emerald. His London tailor had suggested padding, which was currently in fashion, but Justin had flashed a smile and refused. His impressive shoulders and chest needed no artifice.

"We have not had an occasion to wear formal clothing for some time," she ventured. "I'd forgotten how easy you are in it."

"I am a corsair." He drew her closer, staring at her mouth. "We are easy in all that we do."

In that moment, Mouette was hungry for his kiss. She knew she should verbally push back a little against his bold self-assurance, but tonight she longed to give herself over to the spell he cast. As her gaze skimmed the other men who were dancing near them, she realized that Justin was more recklessly attractive than any of them, even the arrogant young bucks.

"Later tonight," Justin said softly, "we will christen our new bed properly, yes?"

Mouette felt a rush of warm desire between her legs, and for a moment she was breathless. "That remains to be seen," she managed.

A knowing smile touched Justin's mouth before he lifted his gaze, turning slightly. "Ah, look over there. Charles has arrived. It seems we are going to meet his betrothed and her exalted family, at last."

A sigh pricked Mouette's romantic mood. *Charles.*

The waltz ended. As Justin guided her from the

floor, she saw Charles standing with Anthony, engaged in tense, unsmiling conversation. Her sons were as different in every way as the two men who had sired them.

Just then, Mouette sensed that someone was watching her. Turning her head, she saw the Dowager Lady Brandreth, pinched yet elegant, standing near their hostess, the Countess of Penhurst. Harry's mother raised her quizzing glass, reminding her of all they had discussed during luncheon. *Together*, the dowager had insisted, *we can all rebuild what has been lost...*

Justin settled a warm hand at the small of Mouette's back, sending a possessive message to anyone who watched. With a nod, he greeted Charles. "*Bonsoir*. I can't tell you how much I've been looking forward to this evening. Am I about to meet Lady Penelope, our future daughter-in-law?"

Spots of color flared on Charles's cheeks. "All in good time, sir."

"You'll pardon my impatience, I hope," Justin said smoothly. The tension between the two was thick enough to cut with a knife. "We have waited so long for the announcement of your betrothal. I know you won't disappoint us—especially your mother."

Mouette intercepted the glance Charles sent her. "The night is young," she said, attempting to lighten the mood. "We can wait a little longer." Her heart was beating fast. She prayed Charles would not fail to keep his promise, tonight of all nights! All Mouette wanted was for Charles's betrothal to be announced to Lady Penelope, releasing her at last from their secret. Then, later tonight, she could open her arms and heart to Justin without any reservations.

"I assume that Lady Penelope is present tonight?" asked Anthony, looking around. His expression was a reminder that he wouldn't be here if his brother's betrothal announcement was not imminent.

Charles pressed his lips together. "Of course! She is over there, chatting with her very devoted friend, Miss Amelia Thatcher." He lifted his gloved hand to indicate the two young women who stood together on the other side of the ballroom. "My Lady Pen is the beauty in green, with jeweled feathers in her hair."

They all turned to look. Mouette saw two young ladies who appeared to be deep in conversation. Lady Penelope was rather plain, but animated. The mint green shade of her gown complemented neither her hair nor complexion, but she was still young and would doubtless gain polish with age.

"Your lady looks very amiable," said Mouette diplomatically. She thought it was odd that Charles was not by Lady Penelope's side, nor had he found an opportunity to introduce her to his family. "Perhaps she would like to dance with you?"

"Right. Of course!" Charles nodded. "I was just about to claim the next dance."

Mouette watched the two young women until she caught sight of Theo coming toward them with his daughter, Frederica, in tow. Justin made a sound under his breath that caused her to send him a sharp glance.

"Ah, look!" cried Charles, clearly happy for the distraction. "It is our good friend, Viscount Redfield, and his lovely daughter." He poked an elbow toward Anthony and queried in an undertone, "Do you see how Freddie has blossomed in recent years? The spotty, gangly duckling has become a swan..."

* * *

COULD anyone tell that Justin was suffocating at this damnable ball? Of course, he didn't really care if others guessed, as long as Mouette thought he was enjoying every moment with her.

The last bit was true enough. He was putting himself through this ordeal because he loved her more fiercely than ever before. Had he taken her devotion for granted? He drew a harsh breath. *Perhaps.* But now he would do whatever was necessary to regain Mouette's love…and trust. God knew he'd made his share of mistakes, right up to the moment of his recent departure from Cornwall, but a man was never too old to change. This time Justin had *truly* seen the error of his ways.

The last thing he wanted to do was deal with Lord Redfield, but it seemed he had no choice. Justin told himself that soon enough this torture would end, and he could take Mouette home.

To bed.

"Psst." Mouette gave him a gentle nudge, and he looked up to see Anthony speaking to Redfield's daughter, Frederica. It was rather startling to realize that his son was already fully aware of his power to charm. Miss Redfield was gazing at him with thick-lashed dark blue eyes and her cheeks pinkened as she nodded and rested a hand on his arm.

"I wasn't expecting that," Justin said under his breath.

Mouette nodded. "Neither was I."

The young couple went to join the others, including Charles and Lady Penelope, on the dance floor. As the orchestra struck up a country dance, Justin noticed Redfield's worried frown. Outrage burned inside him. He wanted to announce that the chit should feel damned lucky to attract the attention of a young man like Anthony St. Briac.

Mouette, meanwhile, had moved closer to the viscount. Beaming, she said, "My goodness, Theo, don't they make an attractive couple?"

"Couple?" He blinked at her. "I must protest. My daughter is a young lady of the highest quality."

Justin couldn't stop himself. "What the devil is that supposed to mean? Are you impugning the character of our son?"

"I was referring to his true ancestry, not his character. For many years, it was assumed that Anthony was the son of a baronet, but now we know that wasn't the case." Redfield lifted his eyebrows. "Frederica has noble blood, on both sides of the family. Her maternal grandparents are the Earl and Countess of Justmore. My daughter has long been expected to make a very fine marriage."

Justin's hands fisted, but he managed a tight smile. "I see." *Sangdieu!* He bit his tongue to keep from remarking that Redfield meant to sell his daughter to the highest bidder. What fatherly devotion!

Mouette tugged at his arm. "Darling, let us not forget that his lordship is our friend."

His lordship! Every time she called Redfield that, Justin's entire body clenched. To make matters worse, the other man gazed back mildly and dared to smile.

"Indeed, I have been a devoted friend for many years." The viscount looked at Mouette as he spoke, and Justin wished he had a pistol.

Or, better yet, a wicked rapier. It would be a great pleasure to dispatch Redfield in a duel to the death.

"Justin," came Mouette's cautionary whisper.

He forced himself to turn and focus on her rather than this cursed Englishman. She squeezed his hand and leaned closer, her eyes speaking to him without words. *Breathe*, he told himself. *Don't allow him to distract you from what you really want.*

Just as Justin felt his heartbeat slowing, a female voice rose above the music from a short distance away.

"Oh, look, Edgie! I believe that may be our own Justin St. Briac standing there, as dashing as ever."

A cold chill of dread skittered down Justin's spine as he turned to see Lady Daphne Leighton gliding toward them, escorted by her brother, Viscount William Edgecumbe. As Daphne stared directly at him, Justin bit back a curse.

Tonight, of all nights, she was the last person he wanted to meet.

CHAPTER 20

" $\mathcal{H}$ ow lovely to see you two here at the ball,"
Lady Daphne greeted them. Then, to
Justin's consternation, she extended a hand for him to
kiss.

"Quite unexpected," said Justin, refusing to meet her
shrewd gaze. Because everyone seemed to be looking at
him, he lifted her hand and pretended to kiss it.

Always polite, Mouette nodded first to Lord Edgecumbe, and then to Daphne. "Indeed, this is quite a surprise. What brings you the considerable distance from
Cornwall to London?"

"You must know that we have a family home, just
across the way in Half Moon Street," Lord Edgecumbe
said in lofty tones. Justin knew that the man disliked
their encounters, for the mere sight of Justin was a reminder of all the priceless heirlooms he'd been forced
to sell to keep his country estate in Cornwall from
passing out of the family. Justin could admit he'd
driven some hard bargains while acquiring them, but
Lord Edgecumbe's treasures looked so much better in
Frenchman's Haven than they had at Leighton Court,
Edgecumbe's drafty tomb of a manor house.

"Perhaps you didn't know, since you are so rarely in

London, but I still have a very active social life here," Daphne told Mouette with a trace of condescension. "I would never miss Lady Penhurst's ball."

Justin's head began to bang like a drum. Every time Daphne sent a covert glance his way, he feared that she was on the verge of saying something that might deal a death blow to his marriage.

Even as he madly sought some means of escape, Justin realized the country dance had ended and the musicians were beginning another waltz.

"*Ma belle*," he murmured to Mouette, praying she couldn't hear his thundering heartbeat, "Listen to the music. It was created for us." He gathered her near and glanced briefly toward the others. "You must excuse us. I have promised my wife that we will dance every waltz tonight."

As they circled away, blending into the crowd of other dancers, Justin took a deep breath.

"What causes your nerves to be wound so tight?" Mouette asked.

He bent his head just enough to inhale the stirringly familiar scent of her hair. "I've been in this state ever since you banished me from your bed."

She looked unconvinced. "Really, Justin, you forget how well I know you." Pausing, Mouette reached up to touch the furrow between his brows. "*This* has nothing to do with my bed."

He was on the verge of saying something very rude about her dear friend Redfield. It was easy enough to summon outrage when he recalled the way the man had acted as if Anthony wasn't good enough for his precious daughter! But before the words could spill out, Justin bit them back, reminding himself of his higher goals for tonight. *Seduction. Conquest. Love.* Of course! Were these not his specialties?

189

Unfortunately, seducing his own wife was not as easy as it should have been.

"I want to be alone with you," he said, pinning her with his smoldering gaze. "Those people keep interfering with our romance."

"Do you mean Lady Daphne?" she inquired sweetly.

His nostrils flared. Why did Mouette have to make this so difficult? "Naturally I was not expecting those two to make an appearance here tonight, but I am more bothered by Lord Redfield. Doesn't his attitude toward our son annoy you in the slightest?"

She gave a little laugh, and he felt her breasts swell temptingly against his chest. "Theo is just being a protective papa. No doubt he would feel that way about almost any young man who invited his daughter to dance."

Justin bristled at her words but forced back an argument. "I suggest that we leave now," he said suddenly, surprising even himself. "I promise you, there are many better ways for us to spend this night."

An alluring blush tinted her cheeks. "Justin, really, we cannot simply leave in the middle of the ball."

He drew her closer as they turned to the music. "But you want to. You are looking forward to being alone with me." His voice turned smoky on the word *alone*. "I can feel it, Mouette. You want me as much as I want you."

"You must not say those things here, in company. Someone might hear you."

"*Eh bien.* We will speak openly when we are together, as man and wife. As soon as the Duke of Bellingham has announced the betrothal of his daughter to Charles, we shall take our leave. Agreed?"

To his surprise, Mouette looked away, clearly avoiding his gaze.

"Lady Penelope and Charles *will* be officially betrothed tonight, *n'est-ce pas?*"

"Well." She glanced over to the corner where Lady Penelope had rejoined her friend. "I assume so."

Before Justin could press her further, he caught sight of a familiar figure dancing nearby. He blinked. It was Lord Redfield, waltzing with Lady Daphne Leighton! They were conversing intently, and his heart constricted as he considered what they might be talking about.

There was something about the surprised yet gratified expression on the viscount's face that set off a loud warning bell inside Justin. Seized by trepidation, he had to remind himself that he had faced far more dangerous situations than this. Was he not a legendary corsair who had fought duels to the death with countless evil villains? Still, his mouth was dry as the Sahara.

He was so preoccupied that he barely noticed Anthony waltzing past with Miss Redfield in his arms.

"Goodness, did you see that?" Mouette asked.

"See what?" he managed.

She nodded discreetly toward the young couple. "Anthony and Frederica are dancing again, and this time it is a waltz! I'm rather shocked that Theo allowed it."

"Perhaps they didn't ask him."

Mouette didn't seem to notice his sarcastic tone. "Look at the way she blushes under his regard. I suspect Theo won't approve."

Theo, Theo, Theo! Justin burned inside, itching to throw Redfield from the balcony. But no! If he truly wanted to be rid of him, the rooftop would be a better starting point.

At that moment, as the waltz was ending, Lord Redfield glanced over, and their eyes met. The exchange lasted a mere instant, but the light of triumph in the nobleman's eyes was clearly visible even from a distance.

Mouette was watching, taking it all in. Justin considered offering a diversion or excuse but realized that his Mouette would not be so easily placated. Again, her voice rang in his ears: *Really, Justin, you forget how well I know you.*

* * *

AS THE WALTZ concluded and they were leaving the floor, Justin said a bit too casually, "It's deuced hot in here. What about a turn in the gardens?"

"No." Mouette shook her head. "Not now." All the while, she watched Theo and Daphne, feeling that something awful might well be about to happen yet determined to face it.

Her palms were damp as they drew near. Theo's expression was censorious, and he turned to look directly at Justin, brows aloft.

Daphne spoke first. "How lovely it has been to renew my acquaintance with Lord Redfield. We've had an excellent chat."

"Indeed, we have." Theo looked down at Mouette, his hazel eyes momentarily pitying, and her skin prickled with foreboding. "Lady Daphne has been telling me about her recent visit to your *home* in Cornwall." He let the words hang in the air until their meaning could be fully absorbed.

Mouette, filled with cold dread, brought a hand to her mouth.

"Lady Daphne and I have long had business dealings," Justin said defiantly.

"Well, yes," Daphne allowed, "that was once true. But now we are *friends*." She turned to Mouette. "I must tell you that I adore what you have been doing at Frenchman's Lair."

"We call it Frenchman's Haven now," Justin interjected, clearly desperate to redirect the conversation.

Mouette couldn't look at him. "Yes, Lady Daphne, perhaps you forgot that my husband and I chose a new name when we married, many years ago."

"Oh, but I always adored the word *lair*! Only Justin could contrive such a dashing name for his house. It is so perfectly descriptive!" She laughed in a way that made Mouette feel sick. "I must say, the house is looking terribly civilized these days. I particularly enjoyed the elegant daybed in Justin's study."

Before Mouette could reply, Justin spoke, his voice edged with panic. "Lady Daphne, you are confused. That is no longer my study, but my wife's morning room."

"But the daybed is divine," she kept on, twisting the knife. "It is comfortable enough to *sleep* on. I must have the name of your upholsterer."

As the woman spoke, Mouette seemed to be paralyzed. She felt trapped in a scene of increasing horror.

"I say," drawled Theo, staring at Justin with loathing. "It seems that M'sieur St. Briac was quite the host in his wife's absence."

"Guard your tongue," Justin ground out, stepping toward him.

"Do you dare to threaten me?" Theo taunted. "But I have done nothing wrong! On the contrary, I have protected dear Mouette while you remained behind in Cornwall, *amusing* yourself with Lady Daphne."

"Are you suggesting that I have betrayed my wife?" Justin's tone was deadly. Surely the next words out of his mouth would be a challenge.

As heads began to turn all around them, Charles appeared at Mouette's side, distracting her from her own personal crisis. His color high, he whispered urgently, "Mother, what has Justin done this time? Does he mean to cause a scene amid the grandest ball of the Season?"

"Of course not." Even as Mouette spoke, she feared her son might be right.

Charles gripped her arm. "First there was that satirical print featuring Justin in pirate garb, and now this! Is it his intention to utterly ruin my chances of marriage to Lady Penelope?"

Mouette wanted to point out Charles's own questionable behavior and Lady Penelope's apparent lack of interest in him, but she quickly realized that this was not the time. Instead, she stepped forward to put a hand on Justin's arm.

"You must not do this here."

He looked around, as if seeing for the first time how many guests were watching him. Nodding, he spoke to Theo through clenched teeth. "Let us take this discussion to a place of privacy."

"Indeed." Viscount Redfield lifted his chin and started off toward one of the alcoves tucked into the far side of the ballroom. "Follow me…"

* * *

EVEN AS HE seethed with white-hot fury, Justin felt proud of the restraint he had shown by not murdering Redfield in the middle of the ballroom. Soon enough he would have this matter out of the way, and he and Mouette could go home and sort it out.

However, the moment Justin followed the viscount into the lamplit alcove, the other man whirled around, eyes blazing.

"See here," Redfield thundered. "Mouette doesn't deserve the treatment she has gotten from you, *m'sieur*! I won't have it!"

Something exploded inside Justin. How dare this self-important Englishman presume to give him orders, especially concerning *his* Mouette? "You have no right to an opinion about our marriage!" Justin reached out with one strong hand and grasped Redfield's starched shirtfront, pulling him near so their faces were inches apart. "Listen to me. I want you to stay away from my wife. I've had enough of you lurking about, behaving as if you are just waiting for me to turn my back so that you may attempt to court her yourself. Mouette is Madame St. Briac, my wife."

"You are an *adulterer*," Redfield flung at him.

Mon Dieu, what had Daphne said to this man? Terror speared Justin as he realized he'd left Mouette and Daphne together in the ballroom.

"I am no such thing," he replied through clenched teeth.

Redfield gave a mocking laugh. "*Adulterer!* And when Mouette learns the truth, she will find the courage to leave you once and for all. She deserves a man of honor in her bed."

Now there was no going back.

"Bastard!" Through a crimson haze, Justin drew back his arm and hit the man. He could have decimated his pompous face if he'd wanted to, but he found the restraint to merely make a point. Painfully, he hoped. "You don't know a thing about her!"

Redfield stepped back as blood began to drip from his prominent nose. "Good God, look what you've done!"

Justin produced his own immaculate handkerchief and handed it over, watching as the viscount pressed it to his face. *This is not good*, Justin realized. Crimson drops spattered the front of Redfield's cravat and soaked through the lawn fabric.

It seemed that his carefully planned evening had plunged off a cliff like a runaway coach.

* * *

MOUETTE'S HEART pounded erratically as she waited with Anthony and Charles for the two men to emerge from the alcove. Fortunately, once they had taken their differences to a private location, Daphne had wandered off with Lord Edgecumbe to greet old friends and find new waltzing partners.

Theo was the first to reappear. Mouette drew a shocked breath at the sight of him holding a blood-spattered handkerchief to his nose. Whispers buzzed again among the guests, louder than before, punctuated by horrified gasps.

"Good God, what's Justin done to poor Theo?" Charles exclaimed. Yet he didn't rush to the aid of their old family friend and seemed relieved when Theo strode off through glass doors leading to the gardens. A pale Frederica followed her father outside.

Mouette wondered why Justin had not yet emerged from the alcove. Perhaps he was injured or even un-conscious. But in the next moment, he appeared, his face unmarked but grim as he wound through the clus-ters of staring guests on the perimeter of the dance floor. Watching him approach, Mouette was swept by a hot tide of anger. How could Justin have allowed this to happen on this night when she had hoped to make a new beginning among the people who had once shunned her? Was he incapable of behaving like a gen-tleman, even for her?

And what about the veiled suggestions Theo had made regarding Daphne's visit to Frenchman's Haven, after Mouette's departure for London? Tears pricked her eyes as she imagined, even for an instant, the two of them alone in her morning room.

Justin drew near, his slightly askew eye-patch the only sign that he had just had any sort of altercation. Reaching toward her with one hand, he spoke in a husky voice. "Mouette…"

She couldn't look at him. It seemed that the past and present were blurred together, and she was reliving the horrible night of this ball a dozen years ago…once again humiliated by a husband who paid no heed to her feelings.

"See here, Mother," Charles exclaimed, "surely you agree that this time he has gone too far."

Mouette straightened her spine and stepped forward, looking at each of the three men. Her eyes stung but she would not betray the strong emotions she felt. "I will not discuss this matter further while so many people are watching and whispering. I want to leave, now."

Nodding, Anthony rested a supportive hand on her shoulder. "Completely understandable. But wasn't there going to be an announcement of Charles's betrothal?" Turning slowly, he looked at his brother. "Isn't that why we've been forced to endure these hours of torture?"

Charles blanched but did not meet Anthony's sardonic gaze. "Mother is right," he declared. "Justin has ruined everything! Why, I would not be surprised if the duke forbids our union. Who could blame His Grace for refusing to let his daughter marry into this uncivilized family?"

Mouette glanced toward the Duke and Duchess of Bellingham, who stood with the elusive Lady Penelope and her friend, watching and whispering along with their aristocratic friends. In that moment, the last of her dreams for this night crumbled into dust.

CHAPTER 21

hen Justin, Mouette, and Anthony arrived
back at Bedford Square, the sounds of
Robinson's agitated barks came to them from inside
the house. No sooner had Baptiste opened the front
door than the corgi rushed forward.

"Do not dare to jump up on us," Justin warned
sternly, pointing for emphasis. "And stop making noise.
You can plainly see who has arrived. There is no need
to threaten your own family."

Reluctantly, Robinson closed his mouth but cast a
hopeful glance toward Mouette. Her expression was
distant, as if a hundred other thoughts were vying for
her attention.

"Welcome home," Baptiste intoned. "We did not expect you to return so soon."

"Not soon enough," muttered Anthony under his
breath. "It was one of those evenings that seemed to be
two days long."

"I am going upstairs," said Mouette. She started toward the stairway, nodding toward Gwynn to
follow her.

"I will give you a few minutes to refresh," Justin said

198

and was rewarded with only a cold stare from his departing wife.

"Hmm," Anthony observed. "That didn't look promising."

Baptiste stepped forward, hoping no doubt to cool his master's temper. "Perhaps you would care for something to eat? I have made an exceptionally fine *cotriade*." He referred to the fish stew, cooked with chunks of potato and onion, that Justin loved.

"Later perhaps." It came to him that he should stay close to Mouette so that he might gauge the right moment to speak to her. "I will take a bottle of wine, however. Bring me one of madame's favorite vintages."

Baptiste hurried away, followed by Anthony, who could be heard calling, "Robinson and I would be happy to sample your *cotriade*," as the corgi barked in agreement.

* * *

MOUETTE SAT at her dressing table, wearing a nightdress of thin ivory muslin under a *robe de chambre* with full sleeves. She looked at her reflection in the mirror as Gwynn removed the pins from her carefully arranged curls, watching as her hair tumbled down along with every hope she had nurtured for the evening.

"I hope nothing be amiss, my lady," Gwynn ventured.

"Amiss?" Her laugh was hollow. "Have you ever put your trust in a man?"

The maid pursed her lips. "Aye, madame. I will admit that I have been foolish enough to do so when I were younger." She paused, brushing Mouette's hair. "But I have learned better of it."

"I have not been as wise as you." In the lamplight,

she saw with a pang that more silver strands glinted among her raven locks.

Just then, a forceful knock sounded at the door, and Gwynn rushed to answer it. Mouette's heart accelerated at the sound of Justin's deep, French-accented voice.

"You may go, Gwynn. I will see to my wife's needs." After a moment, he added through the partially open door, "Let me in."

Eyes wide, Gwynn glanced back to Mouette, who frowned and shook her head.

"Oh, m'sieur, I cannot do that," the maid objected.

"Nonsense. It's quite simple." He walked right past her, bringing a potent dose of his special magnetism into the room. "And now you may leave us."

Gwynn blushed and hurried out without another word.

Torn between outrage and grief, Mouette drew her robe more firmly around her body. "You should not have done that. She was trying to protect me."

Justin ignored this challenge. "You are not the sort of coward to hide up here from me," he said, and perched on the edge of her dressing table, so close that she could feel the heat of his powerful body. "We are married, Mouette. If you mean to keep me from *our* bed again tonight, I cannot force you." He arched a brow ever so slightly. "But we must at least talk about the things that are upsetting you."

Her heart hurt. Tears burned her throat, but she refused to let him see them. She wanted to tell him that nothing about him upset her in the least, but it would only be a waste of breath. "It should be evident to you that I would be in turmoil." Her mouth went dry. "About—you know...that woman."

"I take it you are referring to Lady Daphne." Justin rose and wandered over to the cellaret near the window, where he opened a decanter of claret and poured himself a glass. "Will you join me?"

His nonchalance pricked her. "No," she replied, though she wanted to say yes. And, maddeningly, it seemed he could read her mind, for he brought a small helping of the ruby-red spirits to her.

Justin then continued across the room and sat down on the edge of the new bed. *How dare he?*

"It looks very fine here, don't you think? And it is exceedingly comfortable," he approved, touching the emerald silk counterpane she had chosen before adding, "You were saying?"

"I was saying that I don't want you in this room. With me."

He made himself comfortable, loosening his starched neckcloth, removing his coat and shoes, and leaning back against the pillows. "Go on."

Mouette realized that he was inviting her to give voice to her anger. She felt a barrier give way inside. Drawing a deep breath, she summoned her courage to say what she really felt.

"I was shocked to hear Daphne announce that she had been inside Frenchman's Haven—*our house*—when you were there alone, and I was in London." Speaking the words aloud gave her a terrible pain in the center of her being. "It felt like...a terrible betrayal."

"That's a very strong word." His face hardened slightly. "Daphne was in the morning room, not our bed."

Mouette would not be deflected. "To be clear, it especially felt like a betrayal because I had to hear it from that woman. In public! If you had nothing to hide, why didn't you tell me the truth yourself?"

She felt a little sick when he glanced away. One dark hand came up to the front of his waistcoat, touching the pocket where he had once kept the snuffbox she despised. "I didn't tell you because I knew you would be in a temper and misunderstand the situation."

Rage welled up inside her. How many times had she suppressed her fury over the years when Justin had misbehaved in some way? She always told herself she couldn't change him, that getting angry would only drive him away, but tonight was different. Lifting the feather-light skirts of her robe and night-dress, she rose and crossed to the bed, pointing at him.

"Do not imagine that you can escape this night, m'sieur," she said coldly. "I will not allow you to turn this around, to imply that I am somehow to blame for you keeping the truth from me. I am a woman. I saw her face tonight and I saw *yours*! Something happened at Frenchman's Haven, and I demand that you tell me. All of it."

* * *

JUSTIN'S HEART stopped as he met Mouette's icy-blue eyes. *Sangdieu*. He felt like a condemned man, but he could not let her see that his hands were sweaty, his mouth was dry. He took a long swallow of claret, wishing his snuffbox were at hand.

"*D'accord*. The truth." This was no time to lounge on the bed and pretend carelessness. He swung his legs over the side and sat up, facing her, hoping that she would sit down beside him so he might look at her as he spoke. "First, I concede that it was selfish of me not to travel to London with you. I couldn't bear to give myself over to this nonsense with the *ton*."

To his relief, Mouette perched nearby, but not close enough to touch. She nodded. "I already know that. You forget how well I know you. I was quite aware that you were too self-involved to meet the moment when I was leaving Cornwall, but I had other, more pressing concerns."

He swallowed. "I knew I was being called on to step forward as your husband, but it seemed that some inner demon was holding the tails of my coat. My mother didn't help, telling me that it isn't possible for me to change, to blend into London society, to be guided by duty."

Mouette angled her head. "Please tell me you are not going to blame Cerise for your own transgressions."

"No!" He scowled. "But I was in turmoil when Daphne turned up. She told me that Squire Callywith cannot perform in the bedroom any longer, and she is very eager to have a child."

"What a tragic tale!" Bright color stained Mouette's cheeks. "I can only guess whom she has chosen to solve this problem!"

"I told her it was impossible because I am married." He fixed her with a look that had always been guaranteed to melt her resistance. "To you."

For a long moment, she only stared back at him. "Justin St. Briac, we both know that is not the whole story. If you love me even a whit, you will tell me all of it."

He dared to move closer and take her hands. She was trembling a bit, and her fingers were cold, but she did not break the contact between them.

His chest burned when he tried to breathe. All his instincts urged him to lash out, to turn the argument around and accuse her of seeking to control him. Then he could stalk from the room and hope that might end the matter.

But what if his marriage was at stake?

"Fine. Here it is. No excuses." He swallowed and drew her a little closer. "I kissed her."

The raw pain in Mouette's tear-filled eyes stabbed him like a dagger. She put a hand up to her own lips. "I *knew* it. And then what? Oh, I cannot bear it." Closing her eyes, she demanded, "Go on."

He shook his head. "Nothing. That's all. I swear!"

"Oh, Justin, do you really expect me to believe that? I am no fool! Was it just *one* kiss? What sort of kiss? Were you two lying on the daybed in my morning room?" Her voice broke on a sob.

"*Chérie*, you do not really want to hear such details. You need only know it meant nothing." He closed his eyes dismissively. "Nothing!"

"Tell me."

"I can't remember," he insisted. "The moment we touched I knew it was a terrible mistake. You must believe me. In fact, it is what brought me to London. I realized that everything I was doing, beginning with my ill-conceived choice to stay in Cornwall, was wrong. All wrong! I had to be a better man. I resolved to come to you."

She was weeping. He gathered her into his arms and felt her heart beating against his, through the gossamer muslin. Love and desire mingled inside him, flooding his body. "Say you believe me."

Mouette made no response, but when he looked into her stricken eyes, he saw that she wanted to say, "Yes." *She loves me still!* Words paled compared to the language their bodies could speak to one another. He brought a hand up to cradle the back of her head, sinking his fingers into her silky curls, and kissed her.

After a moment, her soft mouth opened to him. *Mon Dieu*, she tasted like honey. How long had it been? Forever, it seemed. "I love you," he murmured hoarsely. "I love you." Mouette made a tiny sound he recognized, and Justin deepened their kiss. He stroked her tongue with his. She arched closer. He brought her down onto the bed with him, so hungry for her his cock ached and throbbed.

"This is all that matters," he told her, deftly untying the ribbon of her dressing gown. "The two of us."

"The two of us matter, yes…but I want us to be two lovers who *trust* each other and—"

He slid his hands over her pale, satiny arms. "How can you not trust this?" He sought to touch her just the way she loved best. He pressed light, burning kisses down her neck and cupped her breasts over the fragile stuff of her nightdress. She did not protest. On the contrary, Mouette strained closer while fitting her hips to the hard shape of his sex. He dared to expose her breasts and groaned at the sight of her taut, dusky nipples.

Mine, he thought. As he circled one nipple with the tip of his tongue, she whimpered and caught the back of his head, urging him closer. He suckled, alternately bathing the sensitive peak with his tongue then pulling at it with his lips until he heard her pant softly.

"Ah, Mouette, how beautiful you are. More a woman with each passing day." Justin lifted his head for a moment, meeting her fevered eyes. "I have missed your breasts. The scent of you. The wildness in you that only I understand." He kissed her again and felt her urgent response. "I will make it all up to you in the many wonderful, wicked ways I know you love best."

Arching a brow, he glanced down below her waist and slid a hand to the hem of her nightdress. He had just begun to draw it upward when Mouette stopped him.

"Wait." She put a hand on each of his shoulders and pushed him back against the down-filled tick. Then, in one smooth movement, she was on top of him.

* * *

MOUETTE LOOKED DOWN AT HIM, her hands on his wide shoulders. "You must swear."

He blinked, and she knew that he understood what she was asking. "I swear. I kissed her just once."

Her bare breasts were so close to his face that she could feel his warm breath. It was achingly tempting to lower herself just enough to allow Justin to carry on with the delicious things he'd been doing. But then it came to Mouette that this was always what happened after he misbehaved in ways big and small. He cast a sort of carnal spell on her and, as she lost her reason, all was forgiven.

"You believe me, don't you?" The sight of him, so magnificent, made her heart squeeze with longing. His silver-streaked ebony hair curled in disarray, and the scar on his cheek was shadowed in the faint glow of the lamplight. "One kiss," he was assuring her. "It meant nothing."

Summoning her resolve, she drew the bodice of the nightdress back over her tingling breasts. "Do not say that. It meant *something*, not nothing. You knew perfectly well that you were betraying me, having her there in our house, in my morning room!" Tears threatened anew. "And to think that you held her, kissed her... Truly, it breaks my heart."

"Ah, but I know how to mend your heart," he coaxed. His tanned fingers traced the line of her hip, then curved daringly over one side of her bottom, brushing near her intimate parts. "We have all night. I will do my very best to make you forget, *ma belle*."

"I have no intention of forgetting, not now at least. We have much more to address than your interlude with Lady Daphne. There is still the matter of tonight, at Penhurst House, and the horrible scene you created with Theo."

He made a show of looking contrite. "I took him away, though, out of sight."

"And then you struck him, causing him to bleed all over his evening clothes! Everyone saw it. Really, Justin, how could you? You may have ruined everything for Charles. It's quite possible the Duke of Bellingham has decided to withdraw his permission for their engagement."

The mention of Charles caused his eyes to narrow. In the next instant, Justin easily reversed their positions, and Mouette found herself on her back, lying under his big, hard body. As he regarded her, her outrage gave way to a sense of foreboding.

"Hmm. How convenient for Charles." he mused with heavy irony. "After seeing the way Lady Penelope behaved toward him, I suspect that there never was any engagement to be announced tonight."

Feeling the hot blood climb up her cheeks, Mouette wished she could cover her face.

Justin leaned closer. For a moment, she hoped he might kiss her again, but instead he only hovered there, watching her like a jungle cat with his prey. "Perhaps I am not the only one who has been keeping a secret. One might suspect that you already *knew* there was no engagement—and you were keeping the truth from me."

She squirmed, her heart racing. "Let me up!"

"Aha! So that's how it is." Now it was Justin's turn to be outraged. "You are a fine one to lecture me about honesty. How do you say it? The pot calls the kettle black."

Mouette watched as he climbed off the bed and gathered his coat. "Justin!" She wanted to protest her innocence, but the words died on her lips.

At the door, he glanced back at her over one broad shoulder, his black eye flashing. "Sleep well, madame."

CHAPTER 22

*E*ven before Justin knocked at Anthony's door, he heard Robinson make a low sound inside. The dog seemed to sense when the people he loved were within range. Justin had to admit, he'd missed the beast...a little.

After a long minute, his son appeared, clad in a dressing gown. His raven hair was disheveled, and he held a large, open book.

"What are you doing here?" Anthony asked. "You're supposed to be with Mama. The new bed, and all that." His brows flicked upward suggestively to make his point.

"I can't stay there. We've had a row." Justin took a step forward, but his son didn't budge. "Aren't you going to invite me in?"

"You kept me awake last night, talking in your sleep to the pirate Surcouf. I think the two of you were planning an attack in the Indian Ocean. That's a lot of drama to bring into a place that ought to be restful." Anthony paused. "Besides, Robinson has taken over the other bed. Why don't we go into the sitting room and have a drink? Perhaps Mama will call you to return to her."

208

"What are you reading?" Justin squinted at the open pages filled with tiny print and an engraving of what appeared to be a mountain.

"It's Charles Lyell's new book, *Principles of Geology*. My friend Darwin procured one of the first copies. Utterly fascinating." Anthony held up the open book and pointed to the engraving. "That is a volcano. Can you imagine? One day I intend to see them for myself."

"If I didn't know better, I would think that both you and Emeline were sired by another man. The studious Dr. Couch of Polperro, perhaps. His house is littered with fossils and preserved animal specimens."

"You jest." Anthony arched a brow in a way that reminded Justin of himself. "The truth is quite simple. You sailed off to be a corsair when you were young, and I dream of making similar journeys to discover the wonders of the world. Our spirits are the same." He led the way to the sitting room. "Science is making tremendous advances. You should read more about it all, Papa, and then you could converse intelligently with your precocious daughter."

Justin glanced over, trying to decide whether Anthony was more serious than his light tone suggested. "Did you know Emmie is coming to London? Soon. With Isabella, Louise, and that odd woman, Mary Anning."

"I hope I will still be here to see all of them." Anthony's eyes gleamed. "I would particularly like to meet Miss Anning."

Justin poured each of them a liberal helping of cognac and sat down on the striped settee. When Robinson lay down on one of his feet, solid as a bear cub, he bent to rub behind the corgi's ears. "At least there is someone in this house who still regards me with unstinting devotion."

Anthony laughed and stretched out his long legs. "I thought you and Mama were working things out."

"We were. At least, I was trying, but her dear *Theo* keeps turning up, being incredibly annoying. Your mama refuses to see what I have known all along, in my bones. Lord Redfield is not the paragon he pretends to be."

To Justin's surprise, Anthony sat up straighter, nodding. "I think you may be right. I had an interesting conversation with his daughter, Miss Redfield, when we danced tonight. After the ensuing drama, I nearly forgot to tell you."

"Good God." In his excitement, Justin rose halfway from the settee, splashing drops of cognac from his glass onto Robinson's head. "Tell me."

"I think she likes me," mused Anthony. "She insists that I address her as Frederica, ostensibly because we first met as children."

"Of course, she *likes* you! Every young woman in London would have danced with you tonight, given the chance."

This only drew more laughter from his son, and it came to Justin that, at twenty years of age, Anthony was just beginning to realize what power he had over the fair sex.

"Frederica told me a great deal about herself in the space of that one dance," Anthony continued. "And as we danced, I noticed that her gaze went to Mama each time we passed her. Eventually she revealed, almost by chance, that her father has long carried a torch for Mama."

"Aha!" Justin exclaimed triumphantly, earning a wary glance from Robinson. "I knew it."

"I asked if this were merely a suspicion, and Miss Redfield's face grew shadowed. She was quite emphatic, assuring me that she knew this to be a fact."

"That cur." Adrenaline coursed through Justin's veins. "I *knew* I was right about him. What proof does she have?"

"I haven't discovered that yet." Anthony set down his glass. "I thought I might invite Frederica to ride with me in Hyde Park. Perhaps she will elaborate about her father's feelings for Mama."

"Brilliant," laughed Justin.

Yawning, Anthony asked, "Why not go upstairs and try again with Mama? She might let you back in."

"No. It wasn't like that. I am actually the one who stormed out." His good spirits evaporated. "We argued first about my altercation with Redfield, but then it turned to Charles."

"Ah. Charles is on the wrong path, I think. In every way." A muscle moved in Anthony's chiseled jaw. "I've known him all my life, and I can perceive when he's behaving oddly. Something doesn't smell right about this entire betrothal."

"*Oui.* And I think your mama has been colluding with Charles."

"Colluding? That's a rather sinister word."

"She knew there was no engagement, I believe, and she perpetuated his lie to protect him. Perhaps Charles hoped he could manufacture a betrothal if everyone rallied round him here in London, but it was all a sham. And he had the effrontery to lecture me about my own shortcomings!"

"No doubt Mama could explain, if you let her."

"I grew tired of being called a villain tonight." Justin shrugged, leaning back against the settee. The cognac was doing its work. "But for once, I am not the only one at fault."

Anthony gazed off into the distance, pensive in the flickering lamplight. "If no one takes my brother to task, he'll find himself in trouble...like our father."

"I believe you mean *his* father." Stretching out on the narrow sofa, Justin made a pillow of his midnight-blue frock coat. "For better or worse, your own papa is here before you."

Just as Justin was drifting off to sleep, Robinson jumped up and squeezed in beside him, sighing.

From a distance he heard his son's ironic voice. "It is fortunate Mama can't see you two at this moment, defiling her precious Sheraton settee."

* * *

MOUETTE AWOKE BEFORE DAWN, almost surprised to find herself alone in the big bed. All the emotions and longings she and Justin had stirred up together had lingered on in her dreams. Turning her head, she looked at the empty pillow next to her and drew a painful sigh. Justin should have been lying there, gazing into her eyes, holding her... making love to her as only he could. When Mouette thought of the moments of intimacy they had shared the night before, she ached not just for his touch but for the full restoration of that powerful connection between them.

Then an image of Justin kissing Daphne reared up, scorching her mind. She closed her eyes, trying not to imagine them together, trying not to wonder what else might have happened between them that she would never know. How could she ever stop wondering if his vow of "only one kiss" had been made to spare her the painful truth?

This was a special kind of hell.

He thinks we are on equal footing because I also kept a secret, she reminded herself. *But they are not the same!*

Her first order of business was to deal with her own transgressions. Rising, Mouette donned her robe, crossed to the small writing table in one corner of her bedchamber, and took out her pen and paper.

My dear Charles, she wrote.

* * *

"M'SIEUR!" Baptiste whispered urgently. "What is this?"

Justin opened his good eye just enough to focus on his faithful servant's face just inches away. "What do you mean?" he answered groggily. "It's me. I've been sleeping, as you can plainly see."

"Bien sûr. But you are in the sitting room." Baptiste looked alarmed. "On madame's prized settee!"

Just then Robinson lifted his head from the burrow he'd created between Justin and the back of the settee. *"Ahhroo,"* came his drowsy yawn.

"Anthony brought me here," Justin explained. "No one seems to want me in their bedchamber. It is a sad situation, *n'est-ce pas?"*

Just as Justin caught a whiff of his nearly empty glass of cognac, resting on the rug near his face, Baptiste scooped it up along with the bottle. The little Frenchman was standing there, clutching them both, when a female voice spoke from the doorway.

"My, Baptiste, isn't it a bit early for spirits?"

"Oh, madame, these were not for *me...*"

Justin smiled to himself and sat up, heedless of his disheveled appearance, and met Mouette's startled gaze over the top of the settee.

"Bonjour," he greeted her huskily. His wife looked delectable, clad in a morning gown of sky blue that set off her coloring to perfection.

"Goodness!" Her beautiful mouth made an O. "I certainly didn't expect to see you—"

Before she could finish the sentence, Robinson leaped up, paws over the back of the settee, and barked.

Baptiste interjected, "I was just trying to tell them, madame, that they should not be sleeping on this very fine piece of furniture."

Justin sent him a warning glance. Who did Baptiste think had been paying his wages for years and years? "Don't you have something important to do, like organize my breakfast?"

When Baptiste had bustled away, Justin plucked Robinson from the settee and looked over at Mouette. "I didn't plan to fall asleep here," he explained. "Anthony and I were talking, and suddenly it was morning, and you were standing there." His voice grew husky as he added, "So beautiful."

Mouette came around the back of the settee and stopped before him. Robinson craned his elongated body, hoping to lick her face, until Justin set him on the rug.

"Go away," he told the corgi, not unkindly. Robinson obliged by sitting down close enough to watch them with interest.

"About last night..." Mouette said.

"I should not have left you so abruptly," interjected Justin. He deeply longed to draw her into his arms, to hold her against him, to smell her hair and feel her warm body soften. "I suppose I was hoping to end our interview on a note of victory."

"I know that." She reached up to smooth his sleep-tossed hair. "I realize that we both were at fault."

His eyes burned. "Of course, my share of the blame is much greater. It always is."

"If you say so." Something flickered in her eyes. Was it pain? "But, about Charles..."

Before Mouette could finish, there was a sound like thunder at the front door. The knocker cracked against the portal—once, twice, three times. Robinson opened his mouth to bark but Justin pointed at him, frowning, and the dog obeyed.

Their newest footman, a stocky older man called Softlaw, appeared in the doorway and intoned, "Sir Charles Brandreth!"

Charles stalked into the sitting room and handed his walking stick and top hat to Softlaw. "What could possibly be so important that you required my presence at this hour?" he asked, then turned to Justin. "I am surprised you have the nerve to show your face after the spectacle you created last night."

Justin itched to show him the door, but Mouette sent him a quelling look. And Robinson, who had once adored Charles, made no move to greet him now.

"Do not speak to either of us in that way, Charles," Mouette said. "I did not ask you here today to talk about Justin."

"By Lucifer, we certainly ought to be talking about him!" he exclaimed. "Can you not understand how deeply humiliating it was for me last night, surrounded by all the people whose good opinion I value, waiting to hear the Duke of Bellingham announce my betrothal to his daughter...only to have my own stepfather ruin everything? At the grandest ball of the Season, Justin behaved as if he were on the deck of a dashed pirate ship!" He threw out his arms in despair. "I fear all my dreams are crushed."

Justin stared. Did Charles really mean to blame *him* for the problems that the pretentious pup had created all by himself? It took every ounce of self-control to let Mouette handle the situation.

"Let us be seated," said Mouette, a quiet note of steel in her voice. She looked at Justin and added, "All three of us."

Charles frowned but obeyed, taking a chair across from his parents, who sat at opposite ends of the settee.

"If you did not call me here to apologize for *him*," Charles said, sending Justin a dark look, "do please explain."

"The time has come to speak the truth," Mouette said. "Justin could not ruin your dreams because you and I both know that your supposed betrothal was not real. You intentionally misled us, beginning in Cornwall when you told us the duke had approved your suit and we must come to London to support you during the ensuing celebrations."

Her son went pale. "But…I did need your help."

"There will be no more prevaricating, Charles. We both know that the matter was not settled at all. Do you think I would have traveled to London if I'd known that everything you told us was a lie? Not only was there no betrothal, but you were merely angling for an advantageous marriage to secure a place among the *ton*! Furthermore, your quest was unrelated to any tender feelings for Lady Penelope herself." Her voice shook a little.

Charles had gone white as a ghost. "But, but—"

"Allow me to finish. Once I arrived in London and realized what was happening, you—and your grandmother—altered your story, persuading me that Lady Penelope was on the verge of accepting your proposal. You begged me to keep your secret until the ball." Mouette leaned forward, forcing Charles to meet her gaze. "I am your mother. I love you, and I am sorry for your unhappy childhood. I wanted to believe you, but last night it was clear that Lady Penelope is not enamored of you in the least. You have used me, and now I realize how wrong I was to be drawn into your charade. My involvement has only compounded your mischief."

"Mother!" He glanced toward Justin as if to remind her that they were not alone. "Must you say all these things aloud? In company?"

"It doesn't matter," Justin said. "I already surmised that there was no engagement."

Mouette raised a slim hand to silence them both. "This secret has been damaging to my own spirit, to my bond with my husband...but most of all to you, my son."

A warm glow spread inside Justin as he considered her words and what they meant to him, to their marriage. It seemed that one reason Mouette had convened this meeting was to begin building a bridge between them.

Her side of it, at least...

Charles jumped to his feet. "How can you say that? What could be harmful about aiding in the achievement of my greatest dream?"

"Your dream is misguided, and I should have told you sooner," she said firmly. "It isn't Lady Penelope you love, but the social prestige that you would gain by marrying her. I can tell you from my own bitter experience that such aspirations will bring you only hollow pleasure that does not last or satisfy. On the contrary, it will eat away at your very soul."

He turned his handsome profile away and said stiffly, "Grandmama would disagree with you. Perhaps you have forgotten that I endeavor to restore the good name of the Brandreth family."

There were tears in Mouette's eyes. "Oh, Charles, can't you see that you are on the wrong path? Nothing good can come of this."

He looked away. "We shall see. I am not one to surrender easily."

Just then Anthony passed by the wide doorway to the stair hall. He was immaculately turned out in riding clothes and polished Hessians, his neckcloth boasting a deft Corsican knot. Justin felt a surge of pride as he regarded his son, who wore his good looks with careless ease.

"Ah, there you are," Anthony said. Seeing Charles, he came into the sitting room. "Hello! Have I missed an exciting piece of news?"

Robinson went to Anthony and flipped over on his back, stubby paws pointed heavenward. "*Raworh*?" the corgi inquired hopefully.

"We've been having a conversation," Mouette said in a tone that brooked no further questions. "Where are you going?"

"I'm off to meet Miss Redfield to ride in Hyde Park." He flashed a smile. "How do I look?"

"Splendid," said Justin with an approving nod.

"It's too early in the day for that," Charles told him. "It isn't done until at least five o'clock."

"According to the *ton*?" Anthony sounded amused as he bent to scratch Robinson's furry stomach. "I thought it best not to give them more reason to talk about our families, given the scene between our two fathers last night at the ball. If none of the Beau Monde see us riding this morning, so much the better."

When he had left them, Mouette looked at Justin. "I wonder what that is all about…"

He flipped both palms up, feigning ignorance. "Perhaps he feels drawn to her."

"To Freddie?" scoffed Charles. "I doubt that."

Mouette sent him a quelling glance. "I think Frederica is a lovely girl, but I wonder if Theo knows they are meeting? After all, it is her first Season. I am not certain Theo would approve, even if he hadn't just been physically attacked by Anthony's father."

Justin lifted both brows. "Perhaps Miss Redfield will not care. Given a choice between her father's approval and her attraction to our son, I suspect Anthony will win the day…"

CHAPTER 23

$\mathcal{B}$urnished sunlight filtered through the leaves of oak and chestnut trees shading Hyde Park. It was quiet, as Anthony knew it would be, especially since most members of the *ton* were still abed, sleeping off the Countess of Penhurst's ball.

He leaned forward to stroke the regal head of his father's prized stallion, Hugo, as they came into the bridle path known as Rotten Row. Frederica had agreed to meet him here at nine o'clock but there was no sign of her. What if her father had discovered her plans and kept her at home?

"Hello!" called a female voice.

Anthony looked over to see her coming around him. She rode a spirited chestnut filly, and her smile was as bright as the sun.

"Good morning, Miss Redfield." He returned her smile and doffed his hat.

"Have I not given you leave to call me by my Christian name? It's very tiresome to be formal."

"You took me by surprise, Frederica."

"I was very quiet." There was mischief in her tone, and Anthony glimpsed a dimple in her left cheek. "I sent my groom back to fetch my riding crop and I don't want him to discover where I've gone. So many people want to supervise me! I pride myself on being elusive."

"I see." Bemused, he cocked his head. "You are possessed of an independent spirit."

"Exactly! I was drawn to you because I sense that we are alike."

This almost made him laugh out loud. "Are we? Then you must tell me more about yourself. Perhaps you are different from other young ladies enjoying their first Season in London."

"Oh, yes, vastly different!" Frederica held the reins lightly in her gloved hands as they rode slowly, side by side, along Rotten Row. "Unlike the others, I am not engaged in a husband hunt."

"No?" Amused, he cocked a brow. "Does Lord Redfield know this?"

"It would do me no good to tell Papa how I feel." She rolled her eyes ever so slightly under the brim of her feather-trimmed riding hat. "Since my mother's passing, he dwells far too much on making an excellent match for me, especially since I am an only child."

"He hopes you will marry someone wealthy?" Anthony remembered what his father had learned about Lord Redfield's unpaid debts to the dressmaker.

"Oh, perhaps, but I believe it has more to do with a lofty title." She paused. "May I share a secret with you?"

Anthony put a hand over his heart. "Of course." He felt a pang of guilt, knowing that he had lured her there for that very purpose. All he had to do now was uncover the useful bits, and Frederica was making that easy.

"You will be shocked." Frederica fixed her striking blue eyes on him. "I do not wish to marry."

He blinked. "Ever?"

"No! Although I suppose it is possible that I could change my mind." She looked doubtful. "For the moment, I must pretend to indulge Papa. It's not very difficult because I do enjoy most of the entertainments I am obliged to attend." Her cheeks pinkened as she added, "Dancing, especially, is pleasurable."

"Is there a reason why you feel this way?"

Her blush deepened, but her gaze was direct. "I enjoyed dancing with you at the ball."

He was surprised to find her so beguiling. "I too enjoyed it, but I was referring to your aversion to marriage. Are you against it because you have other ambitions, like my cousin Louise, who studies fossils?"

Frederica glanced away for a moment. "I grew disillusioned, watching my parents. Knowing that Papa was secretly in love with another woman yet pretending to the world—including me—that he was devoted to Mama. It has made me suspicious of other marriages, especially knowing that most within our class are arranged for reasons other than love."

"I don't blame you. May I ask you a question?" He gazed at Frederica, wishing he didn't have to do this, but knowing that his father was depending on him. "What led you to believe this about Lord Redfield's feelings for my mother?"

They stopped under the spreading branches of a plane tree. Anthony could smell the green leaves, the grass, and a hint of meadowsweet that drifted to him from Frederica.

"It is painful to speak of it." When she stopped smiling, some of her beauty faded.

"I only ask because...well, we are speaking of my mama." He arched a brow.

"Yes. And I believe I can trust you, Anthony." Tears sprang to her eyes. "Papa has a portrait of your mother." She frowned. "After Mother died, he brought the painting out and hung it in his study!"

Anthony's heart began to gallop, and he feared

Frederica could see the shock of emotion on his face. With an effort, he said, "How odd."

"Odd indeed!" she cried. "When I asked questions, he told me he had owned it for several years. He even explained that he'd kept it stored away because Mother didn't like it! Can you imagine? Of course, she didn't like it! It must have been agony for her. The portrait is simply gorgeous, signed by one of my favorite artists, Élisabeth Vigée Le Brun. When I saw how Papa gazed at it when he thought he was alone, I knew he must be in love with the woman in the portrait. To this day, I pass in the corridor and find him sitting in the study, looking at her above the mantelpiece as if she is real and they are alone together!" Her voice broke. "I hadn't seen your mother since I was very small, so it wasn't until we met outside the dressmaker's shop that I realized *she* is the woman in the portrait!"

"God, I am so sorry," Anthony said, and he meant it.

Frederica accepted the fresh handkerchief he proffered, wiped her eyes, and returned it. Straightening her back, she said, "Thank you for listening. I must say I feel better having shared this secret with you. Perhaps you can now understand why I am not interested in finding a husband among the *ton*. I believe they are all quite lacking in the deeper emotions required to be truly devoted to another person. They think wealth and position are far more important than love and fidelity!"

"True enough." He allowed himself to reach over and brush her cheek with the backs of his kid-gloved fingers. "And you are right. We are alike, for I have no wish to marry either."

"Even when you are older and have finished university?" She seemed to be holding her breath as she regarded him.

Anthony shook his head. "No. I intend to travel the world, experiencing true adventure while discovering new species of birds and animals." He gave her a wry smile. "You are not the only one who has been disillusioned by the marriage of your parents. There is a great deal of drama in my own family, beginning with Sir Harry Brandreth, the man I thought was my father until a few years ago."

"Yes, I know. Sir Harry was Papa's dear friend. It was after his death that I first came to know you and your brother. Imagine my surprise to discover later that Monsieur St. Briac was in fact your father." Color washed her cheeks again. "Of course, I didn't understand how such a thing might be possible until I grew older."

"I'm glad to know *you* understand," he said ironically. "It's all too complicated for me. I love them, but their marriage is fraught with drama. Now that I am grown, I choose freedom from such entanglements."

Frederica opened her mouth to reply, but they were interrupted by the sound of hoofbeats, and a moment later a young man riding a gray gelding rode up alongside them.

"Miss Redfield, bless me!" He paused, breathing hard. "I feared I'd lost you!"

"As you can plainly see, Billings, I am safe and sound, in the company of Mr. St. Briac."

"I brought your riding crop, as you bade, but when I went into the house to get it, his lordship asked me quite strongly where you might be." Billings sent Anthony a pointed glance and furrowed his brow.

"I see. Kindly wait for me at a distance," Frederica told the groom. After he obeyed, she turned to Anthony and sighed. "It seems I must leave...just as I was beginning to sense a true sympathy between us. Did you feel it as well?"

Surprised anew by her refreshing candor, he smiled. "Yes. I did." Then, unable to resist, Anthony reached

over, lifted her hand, and kissed it. "You are a remark-
able young woman, Frederica. I hope you will remember your vow to resist an arranged marriage."

Their eyes met. She started to speak but seemed to
think better of it.

Moments later, Anthony watched Miss Frederica
Redfield ride away with her groom, the feathers in her
hat aflutter in the morning breeze.

* * *

MOUETTE, who had slipped away into the garden to
assemble flowers for a bouquet, felt Justin's approach
before he spoke. That sixth sense was part of their
powerful connection.

"I can't stay in our son's bedroom any longer," he
said. "Anthony won't have me. I would ask you to welcome me back…"

She looked back at him over one shoulder and lifted
a questioning brow.

"To your bed," he clarified.

"I see." Mouette clipped a magenta peony and added
it to an array of blooms in her basket. "Or?"

He blinked. "Or make me comfortable in another
room. That is, unless you want me to leave London?"
Justin angled his strong head in a challenge. "No doubt
I could find—" Breaking off, he closed his mouth.

She could see the effort it took for him to swallow
what he badly wanted to say. "Do you really mean to
deprive me of your quick wit?"

"I don't want to deprive you of any part of me,"
came his low reply, and he leaned close enough so that
she could inhale his scent. "As for my wit, I don't think
you would have liked what it was urging me to say. Can
we leave it there?"

"I suspect you were about to say that you could

easily discover another woman who would not banish you from her bed." His expression told her she was right.

"What is important, I think, is that I did not say it. It would have felt good to toss out such a remark, like wielding my rapier to flick off an opponent's buttons during a duel. But it would not help my case with you." He gazed deep into her eyes.

Mouette's heart ached. *He is trying.* "I just don't think I am ready yet."

"What else can I do? I confessed my sins in a way that left me exposed. Surely you know how hard that was for me." He paused for a moment and pressed long, tanned fingers to the silk patch covering his right eye, a reminder that it still pained him. "I discovered that you had a secret as well, but I realized I could not continue to be angry. Why can you not do the same?"

Her eyes stung, and her throat felt thick. "I am not able to talk about it. Not now."

"That isn't fair." Justin reached for the basket and put it down on a low stone wall that bordered the garden before capturing her hand with his. "We cannot go on this way!"

"At first, I thought as you do. That we had each made needed confessions, and yet today I find that the dull ache will not leave me." Lifting her free hand, she pressed it to the place beneath her breasts, where the pain hid. The words spilled out. "Don't you see? My secret was about Charles. My son! I kept it from you, which was very wrong, but it was not a betrayal of our love. You, on the other hand, brought another woman into our home—"

"I did not bring her in!" he shouted. "She just *appeared!*"

"You knew. You knew what it would mean to me, but because I could not see it, you allowed her to stay.

To be in my morning room. To proposition you!" She was weeping now, as all the emotions that had been swirling inside broke free. "And still you let her stay. You *kissed* her!" Silently, Mouette added, *and God only knows what else...*

Still holding her free hand, Justin tried to bring her into his arms. "*Sangdieu!* I have said I know I was wrong!" He was drawing her closer, caressing her back, his mouth burning the softness of her temple.

She drew her head back. "If you think you can kiss *me* now and somehow banish these painful feelings I have, you are sadly mistaken, m'sieur!"

A cool voice interrupted them from the slate terrace near the house.

"It never ends, does it?"

Mouette turned her head to see Anthony standing there, effortlessly handsome in his riding clothes. Sitting beside him was Robinson. The corgi looked wary, as if he couldn't decide whether it was safe to rush over, as usual, and gather his family together.

Justin drew a harsh breath and released Mouette.

"We were just—" he started to explain.

"Oh, no, never mind," Anthony interrupted, raising one hand to silence his father. "This new drama is no surprise to me. In truth I thank God for it. It's one more lesson in the perils of marriage."

CHAPTER 24

*A*s Anthony reached the doorway, he looked back and said, "When you two have concluded this altercation, I have some information about Lord Redfield that you should hear."

Watching his son disappear into the house, Justin felt the weight of his own tangled problems. Perhaps it had been a mistake to come to London, to think that he could take life by both hands here the way he did in France or Cornwall. It was ridiculous to imagine he could gain acceptance in the *ton*, even if he wanted it.

Justin realized that he was a fish out of water here, and his efforts to fit in for Mouette's sake were only making matters worse.

"I suppose we should go in," Mouette said softly.

"*D'accord.*" He nodded and met her eyes. "I have been thinking…perhaps your life would be easier if I return to Cornwall. Once everything is sorted out with Charles, you'll come home, and we can decide where things stand between us."

She searched his face. "Are you in earnest?"

"No." His heart twisted. "I don't know."

Mouette turned away and started toward the house. "Woof."

It was Robinson, stubbornly remaining at Justin's side, urging him to join his wife and son, and so he let the corgi herd him inside to the morning room, where Mouette and Anthony were already seated on a newly delivered rose-striped settee. Baptiste had just set a tray with tea and little apricot tarts on the low table before them, and the Frenchman gave Justin an encouraging look as he left the room.

"Ah, Papa, there you are." Anthony flashed a smile that seemed to contain a secret message. "Sit down, won't you?"

He took a chair facing them and waited, suddenly longing for his snuffbox. He'd put it away so Mouette wouldn't know he had it, and now he couldn't remember where the devil it was. It came to him that quite possible that Baptiste had found the thing and thrown it away.

"As you know," Anthony was saying, "I went riding in Hyde Park this morning with Miss Redfield."

Mouette's brow furrowed. "Yes. I will confess that I feared Lord Redfield would not approve if he knew about your plans."

"Frederica has a mind of her own," came Anthony's amused response.

"But she was accompanied by her maid?"

"A groom was there," he said enigmatically. "In any event, we are not here to discuss Frederica's reputation."

"Has she given you leave to address her by her Christian name?" Mouette persisted.

"She has." Anthony laughed softly and patted his mother's arm. "Stop this now. I want to talk about our old friend, Lord Redfield. Mama, I have learned something about him that is related to your lost portrait; the one he helped you sell many years ago."

She blinked, clearly trying to piece things together. "How do you know about all of that?"

"I told him," Justin said. "We have talked, during these past nights when he had to share his bedchamber with me. I confided my distrust of Redfield—"

"Oh, for heaven's sake." Mouette turned to Anthony. "You surely remember Lord Redfield's many kindnesses to us in the past, and you must realize that your father is being unfair to him."

Anthony nodded. "I do remember, but I believe Papa is correct. There is more to it than mere kindness."

Justin badly wanted to give a shout of joy, but he managed to remain silent, waiting as his son took one of the apricot tarts and ate it in two bites.

"Mama, you must hear the truth," said Anthony, and then he went on to tell Mouette about his conversation with Frederica at the ball. "She is convinced that Lord Redfield has carried a torch for you for years," he finished. "But it wasn't until today that I learned more."

A flush crept up her face. "How very mysterious."

"I know this is awkward for you," Anthony said, and took her hand. "But it seems that Papa's instincts are sound. Lord Redfield has a deeper motive for drawing close to you here in London...and for trying to drive a wedge between you and Papa."

Justin held his breath, almost afraid to hope.

"Frederica explained to me this morning that her father has a portrait of you that he gazes at in secret," said Anthony, pausing to drink a cup of tea.

The air was suddenly heavy with tension. When Justin stole a glance at Mouette, he saw shock but also dawning comprehension on her face.

Their son leaned back against the silk upholstery. "The portrait upset Lady Redfield, so he put it away... but after his wife's death, he brought it out again. Frederica sometimes saw him sitting all alone in his study, staring at it above the fireplace, but she didn't realize the woman in the painting was Mama until she saw her outside the dressmaker's shop." He looked at Justin, explaining, "We were living in Cornwall, and Frederica had not seen us since she was a child. Also, Mama was very young in the portrait."

"I can scarcely take it in," Mouette said, her expression a mixture of disbelief and hurt. "How can this be? Theo helped me find someone to purchase the portrait when we were virtually destitute. I was heartbroken to part with it, and he knew very well that was my lowest point. This means that..." Her voice trailed off in disbelief.

"Right," Anthony said briskly. "He's been lying to you, I'm afraid. Lying to you and pretending that he is only your friend, when in truth--"

She held up a hand. "You don't need to say it."

"I've already said it for you," Justin interjected, unable to stop himself. "Many times."

She seemed not to hear him. "I could have sworn that Theo was my caring friend, my port in a storm. That his motives for helping me were wholesome." Tears gathered in her eyes. "Men! Why are you all so... so *carnal?*"

Justin met his son's eyes, silently warning him not to attempt to answer such a question. He knew, too, that he would be on very thin ice if he made any further attempts to castigate Redfield, given his own recent transgressions.

Anthony cleared his throat and turned to his mother. "Perhaps, more to the point, one might ask how we will regain possession of the portrait that means so much to you. Not only is it a veritable family heirloom, but it also is the work of the great Élisabeth Vigée Le

Brun. It belongs in your morning room, hanging above *that* mantelpiece." With a dramatic gesture, he pointed to the mirror that was such a feeble replacement.

Mouette stared into space for a long moment before giving a little shudder, and Justin knew she was imagining her trusted Theo making a secret shrine out of the painting he had supposedly sold to someone else. "I don't feel well. I would like to go upstairs and lie down."

With that, she rose and hurried from the room, leaving Justin and Anthony alone together once again.

"Do you think it was a mistake for me to include her in this conversation?" asked Anthony. "I thought it was important that both of you know, so that we may begin planning how to get the thing back. I didn't expect her to react so strongly!"

Justin had no intention of telling their son about his lapse with Lady Daphne, but he did allow, "I think your mother may be angry with men in general. Why don't you tell me what sort of plan you have in mind for Redfield?"

"I thought it might be both amusing and satisfying to steal it from him, the way he stole it from Mama," Anthony replied with a roguish grin.

It was impossible not to laugh. "I admire your thinking. But he did pay her, even if he lied about buying it for himself." Even as he spoke, Justin saw a plan in his own mind's eye. "Perhaps we might leave something in place of the portrait."

"Exactly!" Anthony ate another tart. "I am famished."

"The more I think about this, the better I like the idea of drawing an unsuspecting Redfield into our web." An intoxicating sense of anticipation rose in Justin, reminding him of the surges of adrenaline he'd gloried in before an attack at sea. "*Mon Dieu*, that coward deserves it!"

"True," Anthony agreed with a lazy smile. "I thought we might persuade Mama to be our bait…"

"Bait? I'm not certain I understand what you mean."

"Why not have a bit of fun with him before we spring our trap? I would think that Mama, of all people, might enjoy toying with him, given what he did to her."

Justin arched a brow. "I like it."

"Good. Let us work out the details of our plan, and then you can go upstairs and persuade her to join in with us."

"I see." Justin swallowed. "You make it sound so easy but unfortunately your mother and I have a few problems between us… like boulders in our path."

"Papa, are you not a great corsair, renowned for using your wits and swordsmanship to dispatch anyone who dares to defy you?" Anthony jumped to his feet and struck a fencing pose, just as Justin had taught him long ago, in Cornwall. "How difficult could it be to persuade your own *wife* to soften her heart toward you?"

* * *

"Go on," Anthony whispered, pressing the tray against Justin's chest until he was forced to take hold of it. They were standing in the corridor just outside Mouette's bedchamber door.

"This might not be a good idea." Justin looked down at the aromatic, covered dishes and the bottle of their favorite wine, made from the finest Chinon grapes.

Anthony shook his head. "Have courage! Explain that you've brought her dinner so that she doesn't have to come downstairs tonight. Pour a bit of wine for her. Tell her…" He broke off with a soft laugh. "I must be mad. You of all people don't need any advice in the art of seduction."

Justin felt his face heat. "You should not speak thus to your papa."

"Fine." Anthony's dark eyes gleamed with amusement. "But kindly remember who you are, Papa! Men envy you, and women desire you." He gave him a little push. "Go in there and do what you do best."

* * *

MOUETTE PACED across her bedchamber to the small entryway then back again to the new bed Justin had purchased from the shop of Josiah Fawley. She felt like a caged bird with no place to fly. Why had she come up here? She should have gone for a walk, but in the next moment, she realized that there was no place where she could escape from the ongoing cascade of revelations. Daphne, Charles, and now Theo. And tangled up among them was Justin, who stirred so many potent emotions and longings deep within her.

A knock sounded at the door. Perhaps it was Gwynn, bringing food to distract her.

But when Mouette opened the door, she saw Justin standing there, holding a tray laden with aromatic covered dishes and a bottle of wine. His expression, halfway between a frown and a smile, was endearing.

"*Bonsoir*, madame. I have brought you sustenance, to soothe your soul."

What could she say? The food smelled wonderful, and Mouette realized how hungry she was. "All right. Thank you." She stepped aside so he might enter. Unable to help herself, she added, "I must say, you cut a dashing figure as a footman."

Justin set the tray on the tea table near the window. "Is there an open position on your staff?" Glancing back over one shoulder, he flashed a smile, and her world was suddenly a hundred times brighter. No one else made her feel like Justin, who made each moment vibrant in ways she couldn't begin to explain.

She smiled at his jest, but still the swirl of emotions continued in her heart. "It's been a difficult day. Perhaps we can talk tomorrow?"

"Mouette—" Justin took a step toward her but stopped, hands fisted at his sides. She could feel how badly he wanted to use the force of his will to try to change her mind. "*Eh bien.* I will leave you."

But he had taken only a few steps toward the door when there was the sound of a key turning in the lock. Justin's face darkened. "*Anthony,*" he growled.

Mouette stared. What could it mean? She went to stand beside him at the heavy door, watching as he turned the knob, back and forth, in frustration.

"Anthony St. Briac!" Justin thundered. "Unlock this door!"

"I will be glad to do so," came their son's amused reply. "In the morning, after you two lovebirds have sorted your differences."

"That is outrageous!" exclaimed Mouette. "As your mother, I demand that you open the door."

The only response was the sound of Anthony's footsteps, retreating down the corridor.

CHAPTER 25

*M*ouette stared as Justin walked back inside the bedchamber. "He cannot do this!"

"Yet it seems he has," came his ironic reply. He held up the bottle of Chinon wine, and time fell away as he inquired softly, "Do you remember, *chérie?*"

"Yes." She nodded, awash in memories.

Soon after their first meeting, they had been sitting alone together in the sun dappled garden behind the home he called Frenchman's Lair. Justin had poured Chinon wine, telling Mouette that she would taste the essence of raspberries in it. Everything about him had warned her of danger, heartbreak...and unimagined sensual pleasure.

Now, the memory brought a frisson of arousal that made her ache for him all over again.

Justin poured the deep ruby wine into two small glasses and held one out to her. He was coatless, Mouette realized. His starched neckcloth was slightly loosened, and the snowy linen of his shirt outlined powerful shoulders. He wore a striking waistcoat of bronze and sapphire-blue striped silk, his eye-patch a slightly deeper shade of blue. She nearly sighed aloud, mesmerized as always by his sinful good looks.

"Don't worry," he said in a low voice, "I will not attempt to make love to you."

She blinked. "What?"

"That what you're worried about, is it not? We are alone together, locked in, with a new bed that is crying out to be properly christened. Yet you have made it clear you do not want that."

Heat pulsed at Mouette's core. "I am not *worried*."

"Ah, good." He paused to sample the Chinon wine and allowed himself a slow smile. "I can taste the memories."

She sipped from her own glass and lifted the cover from one of the dishes. Baptiste had arranged a beautiful assortment of French cheeses, surrounding the wedges with bright, plump strawberries, blackberries, and raspberries. Mouette nibbled at one of the berries. It was juicy and sweet, but she discovered nerves had banished her hunger.

Hooking his goblet between two elegant fingers, Justin crossed the room. He seemed to be avoiding the bed entirely as he settled into one of the chairs near the windows overlooking the garden. "Since we won't be making love, perhaps you would like to have a conversation?"

Was he toying with her? "You needn't make that announcement every time you speak," Mouette said, feeling annoyed.

"Do you mean the reminder that we will not be making love?" His wicked brow arched. "Would you prefer that I call it something else?"

She took the chair next to his and set her glass on the small side table. "As a matter of fact, I approve of your notion that we should have a conversation. Shall we talk about Emeline? It will be wonderful to see her tomorrow."

"Of course, I agree about Emmie, but don't you think we should talk about *us*?"

His direct gaze made her mouth go dry. "Perhaps…"

"The very fact that you don't want to talk about what you're feeling tells me that we must do it." Leaning across the space that separated them, Justin traced the top of her hand with one forefinger. "I don't like it either, but how else are we to bridge the chasm between us?"

She swallowed. "I suppose it's necessary if we are to persuade Anthony to unlock the door."

"*Oui…*" His voice was smoky. "And more to the point, if we want to be husband and wife again." He gazed into her eyes. "Do you want that, *chérie*?"

Mouette's palms were damp. "Yes."

"Tell me then. What is really bothering you?"

It came to her as she looked at him that it was so much simpler to hold Justin at arm's length than to be vulnerable, opening herself to the possibility that he might break her heart – again.

Tears thickened her voice, burned her eyes. "I am afraid, and I don't like that. Not now, at this stage of my life." Feelings and thoughts swirled inside her, and she tried to make sense of them. "I am afraid that you may be incapable of being truly devoted to me, only me."

"Go on," he said evenly. "Tell me everything."

Something seemed to crack open inside her. "I am afraid that I will discover something more about you and that woman…and the thought of that is so painful, I can't describe it."

She reached for his hand and felt a surge of relief when he braided his fingers with hers. "Our love has always felt thrilling, even volatile, but it holds risks. A part of me has always feared you could not be utterly true to me…the way I have been to you."

"And this disclosure about Daphne confirmed your fears."

"Yes." Her heart was racing, and she felt hot and cold all at once.

"You are afraid to trust me again."

Mouette nodded. "Since we spoke last night, I have *tried* to let go of my darker thoughts, but they keep circling back, over and over. I imagine her with you, kissing you, lying with you on the daybed in my morning room..." Once again, tears blurred her vision. "It is like a bruise inside me, and my heart keeps touching it, hoping against hope that it might be healed."

"I understand." Justin rose and drew his chair around to face her. "My darling, I wish I could turn back time to the morning of your departure to London. I would climb into the coach with you, Anthony, and Charles, as I should have done." After a moment, he added ruefully, "I would change myself and be a different sort of man."

"I don't want you to be a different sort of man." The words spilled out before she could think.

Leaning forward, Justin took both of her hands in his, lifting them to his mouth. Head bent, he looked up at her under his lashes, silver-streaked hair agleam in the soft evening light glowing through the windows. "Perhaps the same, yet better? I need you to trust me."

His mouth, touching her hands, was like a drug. How she craved it! And his words were deeply comforting. "I want that."

"Shall we try then, day by day?"

Mouette felt the tears on her cheeks. "Yes, please."

He turned one of her hands so that he might kiss the sensitive heart of her palm. Arousal blossomed under his touch, tightening her nipples and warming every secret corner of her body. His French accent was mesmerizing as he continued, "It hasn't helped that I have been feeling edgy ever since coming to London. I have tried, but it's as if I've been wearing an ill-fitting suit of clothes. Every day, I feel like I'm trying to button someone else's coat. The sleeves are too short." As he spoke, he reached up to loosen his neckcloth and gave a dry laugh. "Am I making sense at all?"

"Yes." Mouette ached with longing for him. "I know exactly what you mean. I feel it too!"

"Let me take you away, then. Soon."

"Soon," she agreed.

He arched a brow. "In the meantime, I would like to dispose of these ill-fitting London clothes, for tonight at least."

Mouette watched, burning, as Justin removed first his neckcloth and waistcoat before he unbuttoned his fine linen shirt. The emerging view of his very male chest made her breath catch. She yearned to bury her face in the wide, warm expanse of him, breathing in his scent...

Their eyes met in smoldering recognition. Justin pulled off his fine Hessian boots and cast them aside. When he knelt before her, he winced slightly as his left knee touched the carpet, and Mouette's heart swelled. She found his battered body irresistible.

He reached down to remove her silk shoes, dyed sky-blue to match her gown. His hands on her stockinged feet were warm, his fingers deft as they caressed her toes and the soles of her feet, before sliding up to find her garters. The hidden, tender place between her legs began to pulse, readying her for his lovemaking. *It's mad*, she thought. *He has barely touched me.*

Very slowly, Justin removed her stockings. When he looked up and their eyes met, Mouette felt the full force of his love for her. He pushed her silk skirts up her legs,

239

watching her cheeks pinken, and then he was kissing the sensitive insides of her knees, her thighs, and Mouette wanted to slide down the chair and into his arms. Justin leaned forward, reaching around to cup her bottom and bring her to the edge of the chair.

"Really—I don't think—" she stuttered, face blazing. "Someone could come in!"

He snorted softly. "The door is locked." His mouth was nearing the opening in her drawers.

"But—" she gasped, thinking of Anthony, who had a key.

Justin drew the silky fabric apart, exposing her, and made a low, appreciative sound. "Stop thinking, love."

Her legs quivered as his breath touched the curls between her legs. In that moment, it seemed they had never shared anything so outrageously erotic before. Heat pulsed at her core. He kissed here and there, taunting, until his tongue found her swollen bud, slowly probing, stroking, claiming, and Mouette could have wept.

"Mmmm." Justin breathed again against her, muttering, "I love you. Madly."

She reached out to sink her fingers into his thick hair, holding him near as he deepened his kisses, suckling, licking, skillfully bringing Mouette to the very edge of cascading bliss. She teetered there, his prisoner, panting. When at last her hips began to shudder against him, he pushed his fingers inside her, feeling her contractions, knowing ways to wring out the last drops of her pleasure.

"Oh, oh," she murmured, shaking her head, nearly insensible, "you are very bad."

He grinned up at her, ever the rake. "That was just the beginning, madame. Now I intend to undress you and make love to you properly…in *our* bed."

* * *

JUSTIN HELD out a piece of fresh, crusty bread spread with delicate cheese and offered it to Mouette, loving the sight of her mouth as she bit into it.

"Food has never tasted better," she proclaimed. With a dreamy smile, she sank back against the deep feather pillows. A candle burned on the table beside the bed, illuminating two of the dishes he'd brought on the tray hours before. "Is there dessert?"

"I thought I'd already given you that," he teased. "More than once."

"Yes indeed." She ran her fingertips down the front of his silver-flecked chest, continuing lower, past his naval, to the dark nest where his sex lay, sated. When she brushed his manhood, it stirred. "It was delicious."

Justin's smile gleamed in the shadows. "A different sort of sustenance, yes?" They ate a few more of the berries before he set the plate aside and gathered her into his arms. "Ah, Mouette, you will never know how I've missed you. I love you with my heart and soul."

She heard the throb in his voice and knew they had crossed over to a thrilling new land, even after a decade of marriage. Lifting her face, she searched for his mouth, kissing him lingeringly. In their bed, while the rest of London slept, time seemed to have stopped. How many hours had they made love, tangling together, kissing, panting, thrusting, licking, surging, daring, then lying joined and sharing whispered words of love until one of them couldn't resist beginning again. Mouette's intimate places felt sore in the best way possible.

"May I tell you a secret?" she asked softly.

"Of course, chérie. Anything."

"Sometimes I worry that I am not as attractive to you as I once was," she confessed, breathing in his arousing scent. "My belly is softer; my breasts not as high as they once were."

Justin responded by turning her into the pillows and cupping one breast with his strong hand, caressing, before he bent to take her nipple into his mouth. "*Magnifique*," he breathed. "I wouldn't change an inch of you."

"Will I be less of a woman when I am no longer fertile?" Giving voice to her doubts seemed to rob them of their power, and she suddenly knew the answer to her own question.

"I cannot believe my ears." He was kissing his way over one full breast, lingering in the valley, before pleasuring her by suckling her other nipple. His mouth was so deft that she felt another orgasm building. He nudged her legs apart and slid a hand between them, one fingertip circling and grazing the spot that craved him most. "You are a goddess, Mouette. But I am a dozen years older than you. Should I worry that you mean to put me out to pasture?"

As Justin moved over her, she ran her hands down his tapering back, from his wide shoulders to his strong buttocks. She felt his scars and a bit of thickening at his waist. Every inch of him was more alluring to her than ever. "Perhaps one day we'll wander off to pasture together, but not yet," she said, smiling against his mouth as her hand drifted lower.

"Touch me. *Oui*, exactly like that." He groaned. "You are a sorceress."

After more languid minutes of love play, he nudged at her core, and Mouette opened to him, arching up to meet his slow, deliberate thrusts.

Later, half-dozing, they shared a glass of wine.

"I wonder what I am going to do about Theo?" Mouette mused. "It is a very tricky situation. I can hardly confront him about the portrait."

"Ah. I am glad you mentioned that. As it happens, our son has a brilliant plan."

She lifted her head. "For dealing with Theo?"

"We discussed it, earlier, after you went upstairs." He put a cherry into her mouth. "You and I will pretend to be estranged, as we were just a few hours ago, and then, as Anthony phrases it, you will be our bait."

"I see! What exactly does that mean?"

Justin gave a low laugh. "There are details to be worked out, but the plan is for you to distract Redfield while we retrieve your portrait."

Propping herself on an elbow so that she might look at him, Mouette arched a brow. "Do you mean *steal*?"

He shrugged, looking every inch a pirate against the moonlit pillows. "It isn't his, is it, so there's no stealing involved. And just to be fair, I plan to leave him something of equal value in its place."

"You and Anthony are two of a kind! No doubt, you two rogues would revel in such an adventure."

"So would all *three* of us. And it won't be the first time you and I put on an act for the world. We are very good at pretending, are we not?" Justin leaned closer and tasted her mouth, smiling. "After all, we fell in love because of a make-believe marriage."

CHAPTER 26

Sunlight was pouring through the bed hangings when a sudden jostling caused Mouette to stir and open one eye. Her limbs were entwined with Justin's, her cheek against his broad, warm chest. A sense of deep contentment filled her. It had been, quite possibly, the best night of their marriage. The unbroken rhythm of Justin's breathing told her he was still asleep, but the movement came again, on her other side.

Turning her head, she saw Robinson, sitting inches away on the edge of the feather tick, staring.

"Where did you come from?" she whispered. The door was locked. Had he entered through a window?

The corgi made a small sound of greeting and rolled over on his back beside her, waiting for his usual morning rub, and Mouette saw a folded note attached to his collar. She managed to tear it free with one hand and open the small paper. Inside was a boldly scribbled message:

Good morning! Assuming you two are still alive, Baptiste has sent you breakfast, and I was good enough to unlock the door. When you are free to come downstairs, you'll find my sister and other relatives have arrived.

I am, ever your meddling son,
Anthony.

From the open door leading to the passage area, the aromas of strong coffee and fresh, warm brioche mingled, stirring her senses. Mouette blushed at the realization that it must be mid-morning—and they had been oblivious to the late-night arrival of their daughter and other family members.

"Justin," she murmured, "wake up."

He turned slightly and nuzzled her neck, eyes still closed. "For a price," he murmured huskily.

Robinson stepped on the silk counterpane to force his way over to Justin, licking his face with gusto.

Justin bolted up from the pillow, fully awake *"What are you are doing?"* He sent Mouette an accusing stare. "You should have warned me. For one shocking moment, I thought that was your tongue."

She couldn't help laughing, covering her mouth with one hand. Robinson began to bark, pushing back into his master's arms, and soon Justin was laughing as well.

"You should have seen your face," she said, wiping away a tear.

"Mon Dieu, it was terrible." He shook his head, attempting to look serious *"Not only was I assaulted in my sleep, but when I smelled his breath, I feared you had developed a dreadful problem."

As their eyes met, more laughter bubbled up. Robinson wriggled his way between them, woofing, until Mouette held up a hand. "Wait. We must stop this. We haven't time."

"That's right," Justin agreed. "Send this beast away so we can return to what we are meant to be doing." He quirked a brow to make his point.

"No, darling. We must get up, dress, and go down to meet our guests." Mouette held out Anthony's brief note. "Emmie has arrived, in the company of Isabella and Louise."

Even as she spoke, a familiar voice called to them from the corridor.

"Mama, Papa! Will you *never* come out to embrace your daughter?"

* * *

LOOKING AROUND THE DINING ROOM, where a splendid table and twelve chairs were newly installed, Mouette took a bite of perfectly poached egg and smiled. It seemed she had never been happier. The sideboard was lined with a mouthwatering assortment of breakfast dishes, and everyone had a full plate. Of course, it was regrettable that Gabriel and Camille had stayed behind in Lyme Regis so the females could travel more comfortably, but the sight of Emeline, Isabella, and Louise filled Mouette's heart with joy.

Was it possible that her little girl had grown taller in just a few weeks? Mouette drank in the sight of Emmie, who sat between Justin and Anthony, chattering away to them about all the adventures she had enjoyed in Lyme Regis. Raven curls fell around her shoulders, and her chin was as stubborn as her papa's.

"Miss Anning has a *dog*," she was announcing. "His name is Tray, and he is brilliant! He scrambles around the rocks as we hunt for fossils, and often it is Tray who finds the most wonderful bits. Miss Anning has even trained him to guard her discoveries if she has to leave for a bit."

"What sort of dog is he?" asked Anthony.

Emmie wrinkled her nose. "Sort?" She looked at Isabella, who sat beside Mouette.

"Tray is a spaniel, I believe," Izzie said, "though he might have something else mixed in."

"He has lovely black and white markings," confirmed Emeline. "And he is utterly devoted to Miss Anning. I wish we could find a dog like Tray."

From his nearby position on the Aubusson carpet, Robinson gave a plaintive woof, gazing at his young mistress with liquid brown eyes.

"You've hurt Robinson's feelings," Anthony laughed. "How will you make it up to him?"

"I never meant that I would want to replace him," the girl protested. "But perhaps he would like a companion." Plucking a kipper from her plate, Emmie offered it to the corgi, who sat obediently and cocked his head.

Tomorrow they would all go to the Geological Society to meet Mary Anning and view the bones of her winged reptile, said to be unlike anything ever seen before.

"I am so pleased that we could accompany Miss Anning to London," said Izzie. "It's a proud day, but it is shocking that she will not be able to step foot inside the Geological Society, even though *she* was the one who discovered and identified the fossil."

To Mouette's left, Louise nodded. "You are so right, Mama. At least her friend, William Buckland, will make the presentation on her behalf."

"And all those men will credit Mr. Buckland with the discovery!" exclaimed Emeline. She shook her head. "I am grateful that my own family doesn't hold such medieval beliefs about the value of females."

Justin laughed, his hardened face alight with love. "If we did, *ma petite*, you would doubtless set us straight."

"Indeed, Papa!" Emmie leaned over to kiss his cheek.

Emotion welled up in Mouette. Thank heaven he

had not said anything to disparage their daughter's interest in fossils!

Isabella squeezed her hand. "Emmie has been missing all of you, so much."

"Oh, I have missed her desperately as well, and I know Justin feels the same." Mouette felt teary again. "Perhaps, when the rest of you return to Lyme Regis, Emmie will want to remain here with us."

Louise shook her head. "I don't think so. Little Emeline is a born geologist, or as she likes to call herself, a *fossilist*. She has a natural talent for discovering things the rest of us sometimes overlook, and some are quite amazing." Reaching for a fragrant brioche, Louise continued casually, "I rather expected to see Charles here this morning. Where might he be?"

Mouette looked over, surprised by the sudden mention of Charles. "He is staying with his grandmother, the Dowager Lady Brandreth. I was told that she would be able to help him in his quest to win the hand of Lady Penelope, but so far Charles has been unable to reach his goal."

"What do you mean? I thought he was already betrothed when he came to you in Cornwall." Louise furrowed her brow.

"No, I later learned that he was hoping my support might prove valuable…"

"Do you mean that he *lied* to you?" Louise was frowning. "I must confess, I am quite out of temper with Charles. He is behaving like a complete ninny, aspiring to a position among the *ton* that will never bring him happiness."

"I completely agree. Honestly, I haven't even seen a sign that Lady Penelope is interested in him, let alone inclined to accept his suit, but he refuses to give up."

"You have spoken plainly to him? It's the only way, you know. He's very stubborn."

"Indeed, I have been extremely frank with him, but I am his mother. I suppose it isn't surprising that he would rebel against my advice." Mouette studied Louise as she spoke, noting the sparkle in her brown eyes and the warm flush in her cheeks. "You and Charles have been friends for many years, and clearly you know him very well. Perhaps he would listen to you."

Fiercely, Louse replied, "I fear he must do so if our paths cross here in London. I couldn't possibly mince words with someone I care for so much." She blinked behind her spectacles as if suddenly realizing what she was saying. "As a friend, of course!"

"Of course," With an effort, Mouette suppressed a smile. "I understand completely."

* * *

AFTER BREAKFAST, Emeline held court for her family in the parlor. She sat between her parents on the elegant sofa, leaning against Mouette as she detailed their daily excursions to the rocky beach at Lyme Regis.

"It is a place where all manner of fossils can be discovered with patience and a sharp eye," Emmie declared. "Miss Anning tells me that I am naturally endowed with both, but I must strive to improve."

Justin smiled at Mouette over their daughter's head as if to say, *Look at this living miracle, wrought of our love.* She returned his smile, her heart swelling.

After Emmie had regaled them with a few more tales of her adventures amidst the Lyme Regis shale, she rose to present her parents with an ammonite she had discovered herself. The fossil, coiled and frilled, resembled a ram's horn, and Emmie explained that they were called 'serpent stones.'

"I found this one myself, but Miss Anning has

others in her shop, the Fossil Depot, where she sells curiosities to help fund her serious pursuits. It is filled with wonders like Devil's toenails, angel's wings, thunderstones!"

Indulgently, Louise interjected, "Those are merely the names bestowed by people, not science."

"I will make a drawing for you of Miss Anning's great discovery," Emeline said, fetching her sketchbook and a pencil. Mouette, Justin, and Anthony looked on in wonder as the girl drew the misshapen vertebrae, ribs, an elongated beak with teeth like a crocodile, and bat's wings. Its front talons, three on each stubby leg, were hooked.

"It's as long as I am," Emeline explained. "And it has scales, like an iguana!"

"They have named it a Pterosaur," added Louise. "But we call it—"

"The flying dragon!" Emmie interjected, clearly relishing the chance to make this announcement "Can you imagine? Nothing like it has ever been seen before."

Mouette stared at her daughter's sketch in wonder. "Where did you learn to draw like this?"

"From Aunt Izzie, of course…she sets up her easel and paints by the sea nearly every day. And Miss Anning spends each evening making sketches of her fossils, until the light goes. She calls them 'scratches.'" Emmie beamed.

As Emeline and Louise related more tales about their adventures in Lyme Regis, Isabella bent over to whisper in Mouette's ear.

"I have been longing to ask you something ever since we arrived. Might I steal you away for a few minutes?"

* * *

Mouette led her sister-in-law across the entry hall, into the morning room. Once inside, she stood back to have a good look at Isabella and realized that she had grown plump, and her bosom was fuller.

"You are looking very well," Mouette said tactfully.

"I know I must appear quite Rubenesque." Izzie gave a rueful little laugh. "Perhaps it will sound mad, but I am expecting another child."

For a long moment, Mouette couldn't breathe. Jealousy unexpectedly squeezed her heart. "Goodness, what a surprise." She embraced Izzie, hoping the turmoil she felt didn't show on her face.

"Perhaps you think we are too old for this." Isabella drew back, blushing. "But it just…happened."

"You look beautiful." Mouette's gaze touched Izzie's golden curls and registered her glow of inner happiness.

"I already feel as big as a barouche, but Gabriel always tells me I am more alluring when I'm *enceinte*." She laughed, but a moment later her expression sobered. "Are those tears I see in your eyes?"

"I – I confess that I am feeling a trifle envious," Mouette said softly. "I have been rather grieving the end of my childbearing years, knowing I'll never hold a new baby of my own again."

"I understand." Isabella embraced her and smoothed dark curls back from her temple. "But you and Justin will be off enjoying adventures while Gabriel and I are pacing the floor with a crying baby. We are wondering how we will cope at our ages."

"You'll be splendid parents, as always," Mouette assured her, sighing.

"Is everything else all right? What about you and Justin? I was rather concerned about him the last time we met, at Cerise and Xavier's cottage. He was as skittish as a wild stallion."

Mouette longed to confide in her sister-in-law, who knew Justin so well. But if they were going to pretend to be estranged, it seemed better not to share the whole story with anyone.

At least not yet.

"It hasn't been easy," she said, grateful that much was true. "And he is completely out of place here in London." Mouette told her about the satirical print, featuring an outrageous pirate at the dressmaker's shop. "Once matters with Charles are sorted, we can return to Cornwall. Being back among the *ton* has only reminded me of all the terrible lessons I learned after Harry's death."

"They were awful to me, too!" exclaimed Izzie. "Do you remember? Every time I went to an assembly, those wretched dowagers would whisper behind their fans about my figure." She patted the curve of her hip and gave a rueful smile. "Speaking of those days reminds me why I wanted to speak to you. I am longing to see the portrait our friend Madame Le Brun made of you on the eve of your wedding to Harry."

Mouette's cheeks burned. Isabella had been with her in the Frenchwoman's London studio on the memorable, golden afternoon she'd sat for her portrait, along with Mouette's mother, Devon. It seemed another lifetime, before either Izzie or Mouette had married or borne children. They had been completely unaware of the joys, challenges, and heartaches that life held in store.

"The last time I was here, before you came home with me to Cornwall, I asked about the portrait, but you said an art student had borrowed it," Isabella continued. "I have especially looked forward to this visit so I might see it again, at last. Of course, Madame's creations are all treasures, but your portrait has so many extra layers of meaning." She smiled. "And beauty."

Mouette swallowed, feeling sick. "I have a confession to make. I lied about the art student having the painting." Her heart was pounding. "In truth...it was gone."

"Gone! Whatever can you mean?" Izzie exclaimed.

"Just before you took me away to Cornwall, I was forced to sell the portrait to pay my creditors." Her mouth was dry. "Or rather, my friend Viscount Redfield offered to sell it for me. I believed I could trust him." Mouette explained a little then of what Anthony had learned about Theo and the portrait. "He has told me he sold it to a nobleman who later died in Italy, but now it seems it may still exist, inside Theo's own house!"

"That is outrageous! He must return it to you at once! You should have him arrested!"

Mouette managed a wan smile. "Justin would doubtless agree with you, but of course it is complicated. Please don't say anything about it to anyone for now. I hope that the next time we meet, the portrait will be hanging above the mantel once again."

Isabella's eyes flashed behind her delicate, gold-rimmed spectacles. "It is shocking. I hope he at least paid you a very grand sum for the painting."

Mouette nodded. "Yes, I think so." She named an amount.

"What? Are you certain?"

"I believe so but let me check." She went to her writing desk and opened the ledger she had always kept in the drawer. Thumbing back to the year 1818, she found the transaction, carefully noted in ink, and showed it to Isabella. "I was afraid I might lose this house if I didn't sell, and it seemed a very good price."

"And Lord Redfield knew how desperate you were?"

"Yes. I confided my circumstances to gain Theo's assistance in finding buyers. He had acted as a go-between for many of my valuable possessions, but the portrait was the last one." Her voice thickened with emotion. "For a very long time, I hoped I wouldn't have to part with it. I believed Theo was acting as a loyal friend. It has been a blow to discover that he wasn't truthful about the portrait...and that he may have had feelings for me, all along, while married to Lady Redfield."

Isabella's cheeks were flushed. "Lord Redfield is *not* your friend! The sum he paid for your portrait was barely half of what it was worth at that time...and today, its value is doubtless three times that amount!"

"My God." Mouette went cold. "That is shocking. But perhaps Theo didn't really know its true value?"

Izzie narrowed her eyes in response. "Do you believe that?"

"No. Yet it is possible." She took her friend's hands. "No doubt Justin would be quick to believe the worst—and kill Theo in a duel before the next sunrise."

"I wouldn't blame him," fumed Isabella.

"Please don't say anything to Justin, at least not yet. His temper could be lethal, endangering his own life as well as Theo's." Mouette glanced toward the ledger. "It is only money after all."

Looking skeptical, Isabella nodded. "It isn't my place to interfere, but I hope you know what you're doing."

254

Standing before the imposing façade of Somerset House, Justin accepted an umbrella proffered by a footman and held it above Mouette and Isabella. The sky was weeping gray, drizzly moisture which didn't bother him, but the four females were another matter.

"Louise and I are quite used to dismal weather," Emmie proclaimed. "We have learned from Miss Anning never to be deterred by rain or wind."

As if on cue, a rather odd-looking woman emerged from a hired chaise. She wore an unadorned, wide-brimmed bonnet and a drab cloak. Her shoulders were broad, and as she started toward them the wind blew her cloak enough to afford them a glimpse of her plain cornflower-blue dress.

"Miss Anning was raised a Dissenter," Isabella said softly. "She makes her own clothes and shuns excessive decoration."

Louise and Emeline both went forward to greet Mary Anning, leading her back to Justin and Mouette for introductions. The woman regarded them with a thin smile and nodded.

"Your young girl has a good mind, and she is learning discipline. You should be proud."

Justin studied Miss Anning. He had heard that she was thirty years of age, but exposure to the sun and the elements caused her to look older. Her face was tanned, and there were lines beside her mouth and bright blue eyes. Although Justin was prepared not to like her, he found himself enjoying the woman's direct manner.

"*Bien sûr.* We are very proud of our daughter." Justin felt Mouette glance up at him, and he knew she was remembering all the disparaging remarks he had made about fossils. When he sent his wife a self-deprecating smile, she touched her gloved fingers to his.

Another carriage drew up and a couple emerged. Moments later, Mary Anning introduced her friends, Roderick and Charlotte Murchison, explaining that she was a guest in their home near Regent's Park.

"It is a pleasure to meet you," Murchison said to the assembled members of the St. Briac family. He was tall and lean, and as he spoke, he tipped his top hat to them, revealing a high, broad forehead.

"Mr. Murchison is a very fine geologist," said Miss Anning. "Since my arrival, I have been happily occupied studying his collection of bones."

"Utterly fascinating," Justin murmured.

Amused, he arched a brow toward Mouette. Although she would not be tempted even to meet his gaze, she did bite her lower lip in a way that sent a surge of lust through Justin. Perhaps, he mused wryly, his wife meant that as a private sign. They had agreed before leaving Bedford Square not to display any romantic feelings in public. It was more important that the *ton* believe they were estranged, and then, as soon as Isabella, Louise, and Emeline returned to Lyme Regis, they would set their trap for Redfield.

Justin allowed himself a frisson of anticipation as he imagined the viscount's downfall.

Meanwhile, Mouette watched as a few other scientists greeted Mary Anning, including William Buckland, who would present the flying dragon to the Geological Society. The gentlemen were all very learned and had been trained at the best universities, but none could claim to have made discoveries to rival those of Miss Anning. She was simple and plain, her education limited, but she had a brilliant gift that could not be taught.

"I will wait with you, Mary, while the men endure the speeches inside," said Charlotte Murchison.

Miss Anning turned to watch as two large footmen carried the trunk containing her newest fossils into Somerset House, where the relics would be shown at today's meeting of the Geological Society. A shadow passed over her weathered face.

"A walk might do me good." She pressed her lips together and tried to smile at Mrs. Murchison. "After the meeting begins."

Out of the corner of her eye, Mouette glimpsed a parade of dignified-looking men on their way to the entrance of Somerset House. Trailing near the back were Charles and Theo, chatting as they strolled along together.

Mouette caught her son's eye and inclined her head. Charles paused before coming toward her.

"Hello, Mother," Charles said, pointedly ignoring Justin. He was looking dignified in a black frock coat and gray trousers strapped under his elegant shoes. A fine mist clung to the golden curls that were not covered by his top hat. "Why do you look surprised? I am certain I told you I am a member of the Geological Society."

Emeline hurried forward to her brother. Charles

looked uncertain for a moment, but then he bent to embrace her. For a few poignant moments, his pretensions shed, he was once again a member of their family. Maternal warmth washed over Mouette, and she briefly indulged hope for her son's future.

Emmie was chattering about her adventures and introducing Charles to Miss Anning as Theo approached. A white bandage covered his bruised, swollen nose, and Mouette felt an involuntary pang before reminding herself that he was not the person he had seemed for so many years.

"Hello, Mouette," he murmured.

She made a point of glancing over her shoulder to be certain Justin was conversing with the others before she turned back to Theo and whispered, "Could you spare me a moment after the Geological Society meeting?"

He seemed to grow taller as he regarded her, blinking hopefully. "Of course! But..." His gaze flicked toward Justin.

"Don't worry. I will make myself free to speak to you."

As Mouette turned back to the others, the sun peeked out from behind a bank of smoke-gray clouds, and her heart lifted. Their plan was now truly in motion.

* * *

EMELINE, Isabella, Louise, and Mary Anning were strolling together along the River Thames while Mouette and Justin walked behind them. The morning's misty rain had given way to a humid, warm afternoon. Boats of every description plied the waters, and white sails fluttered in the rays of sunlight that pierced the clouds.

Justin looked down at Mouette, aching for her in every way possible. He had never felt more fully connected to her, not even in the early days of their marriage, when so much of their love was heated with euphoria. Recent events had forced him to strip naked and expose all his emotions, and worse, his vulnerabilities, to Mouette.

And yet, here they were. She seemed to love him more than ever!

Lovers, comrades, parents. He paused, smiling as he thought again: *lovers*. Was it possible for deep contentment and fiery lust to mingle? All of it felt like a splendid miracle.

Mouette glanced up at him under the brim of her summer parasol. Seeming to read his mind, she mouthed the words, "I love you."

Justin needed no further encouragement. He caught the back of her leaf-green silk gown and pulled her behind the drooping branches of a giant willow tree.

"I want to do wicked things to you," he threatened, drawing her close against him.

"You are outrageous," she protested, and made a halfhearted attempt to push him away.

"You are my wife. We are meant to be wicked together."

"Stop saying that *word*!" Mouette was laughing as he covered her luscious mouth with his and kissed her, deeply.

After one sharply arousing minute, Justin forced himself to stop. They would, after all, be alone tonight in their own bed, where they could pleasure one another for hours. His cock throbbed insistently at the thought. "Tonight…"

"Yes." With her delicate hand, Mouette covered the hot, hard ridge that pressed against the front of his trousers. She licked her lips.

He saw stars. "You are a harlot."

This made her laugh again. "Indeed. But my darling, we must join the others before someone sees us. Remember, we are supposed to be estranged."

"Tell them your barbaric husband forced himself on you," Justin said.

Mouette stepped back. "I look forward to that later tonight, but today we must not let anyone see how we really feel. I have made an appointment to speak to Theo after the meeting is over." She paused. "He took the bait quite easily."

"I feared you might lose your nerve when you saw his pitiful bandages."

Mouette sent him a wry smile. "I admit I faltered for an instant, but I quickly recovered. I am very strong, you know."

He took her arm and brought her back out onto the walking path. "Ah, madame, I know very well how strong you are. It's one of the reasons I love you so much."

* * *

LOUISE ST. BRIAC had been able to think of little else but her friend, Charles. She had pretended to socialize outside Somerset House, but as usual she was occupied with an entirely different line of thoughts.

Now, watching her childhood comrade emerge from the Geological Society rooms, she straightened her spectacles and started forward. How serious and self-important Charles looked! Memories flickered of their early encounters in Cornwall after Uncle Justin and Mouette were married. Charles had been resistant to his new family, but Louise always sensed he was hurting inside. Her interest in the model he was making of Saint-Malo, Justin's walled city in France, had sparked their friendship, and the easy connection between them had continued until he went away to Eton. During those years, he had visited only occasionally, and Louise had been put off by his new airs, his attitude that he was somehow better than the rest of his family. They had drifted apart...but as Louise studied him now, she realized he was still that insecure boy who tried to build himself up with a lot of frippery.

Charles stood outside Somerset House, lips pursed as he conversed with a spindly, distinguished older man. A liveried groom approached, spoke in a low voice, and then the older man nodded, turned, and went off without another word to Charles.

Louise lifted one gloved hand and saw him look her way. "Hello, Charles."

"Why, it is Louise!" He blinked, walking a few steps toward her. "But of course, you must be here from Lyme Regis with the others."

She felt unaccountably disappointed by his greeting. "I suppose I should be grateful you remember me."

"Have I offended you?" He swept off his hat and bowed. "Please accept my apologies."

Looking past Charles, Louise saw the spindly older gentleman getting into an elegant open landau, a ducal crest emblazoned on its door. "May I ask, who was that man you were speaking to a moment ago?"

"You must mean His Grace, the Duke of Bellingham!" Charles seemed to swell with pride. "I am exceedingly fortunate to now move in his circle."

"Oh, that's right." Louise paused before adding, "You are betrothed to his daughter!"

Charles flushed. "Not quite. But I soon will be."

"In that case, I am surprised your future father-in-law's manner was not more friendly toward you."

"The duke was distracted by the arrival of his carriage," he said, frowning. "Is that why you wanted to speak to me? I thought you might wish to congratulate me on my elevated circumstances. I have come a long way since those long-ago afternoons in Cornwall when we made maps together."

Louise felt her face growing warm. "Might you make room in your schedule for a brief walk with me? I would like a private word." As she spoke, she glanced toward a tall man with a lantern jaw and a bandaged nose who stood nearby. He was watching them, but pretending otherwise.

Charles gazed at her for a moment, and their eyes met. Louise drew a breath as she took in his physical beauty. Curly golden hair, sculpted features, crisp blue eyes, and a mouth that might be sensual if he allowed himself to relax.

But then he broke the spell.

"All right, I suppose I owe you that much. Long ago, you were the only person to whom I could talk...before I returned to my true place in the world." He guided her over to the man with the prominent jaw. "Lord Red-field, I would like you to know Miss Louise St. Briac." After greetings were exchanged, Charles continued, "Miss St. Briac and I are distantly connected through my mother's *other* family. If you will excuse us, we are going to take a brief stroll. I shall return shortly."

"Of course," said the viscount. "I will wait for you, and we'll ride together back to the Dowager Lady Brandreth's house in Russell Street."

As they walked toward the River Thames, Charles glanced over at Louise several times, and she was suddenly conscious of her outdated gown of yellow cambric and the haphazard way she had tied her bonnet.

"I suppose I am not properly dressed for London," she explained. "As you know, I've been in Lyme Regis these past weeks searching for fossils."

He smiled unexpectedly. "Actually, I was just

thinking that you look rather fetching. The sea air must suit you, Louise."

Shocked to feel her heart begin to race, she gave herself an inward shake. "It is kind of you to say so, but I asked to speak to you about something more important." Louise drew a breath. "I hope you know that I care for you, as a friend…"

"I am glad." His blue eyes seemed to soften. "For quite some time, you were the only person I felt at ease with."

"That is why I must be frank with you now." Oh, how much harder this was than she had imagined! "Charles, you are making a cake of yourself."

"I beg your pardon?" he exclaimed. "What has come over you, Louise?"

"I am your true friend. I have wanted to say these things to you for years, ever since you first returned home from Eton and behaved as if we were all beneath you." Even as she spoke, Louise saw that his attention had wandered to the open landau passing nearby. Inside, the Duke of Bellingham faced two young women on the opposite seat. The closer female, wearing a pink silk headdress decorated with fresh flowers, glanced toward them for a moment.

Charles raised his hand a trifle uncertainly. "It's Lady Penelope, with her friend, Miss Thatcher," he said dreamily. After a moment's hesitation, he waved to her.

Upon spying Charles, the young woman nodded politely, then turned back to her companion as the carriage passed out of sight. Charles was left to stare at empty space.

"Don't you see? That is just what I meant," Louise exclaimed. She caught his coat sleeve. "Look at me, Charles. You are deluding yourself if you think that girl cares for you. Even if she did agree to marry you, you would not be happy."

He seemed to freeze, and then his eyes grew wet. "None of you think I can make this happen, but you underestimate me. I intend to wed Lady Penelope, no matter how long it takes, and in the process, I will reclaim my family's lost position among the *ton*."

"But what about *you*? I know who you really are. You can be so much better than this." Suddenly Louise wanted to throw her arms around his neck and kiss him, as if that might reawaken his true self. "Charles, I implore you. Do not continue down this path. You have forgotten the people who really love and value you." She shook her head, blinking back tears. "You lied to your own mother about your betrothal."

He stepped backward, nearly stumbling over a piece of wood. "Mother made you do this."

"Your mother only cares for your happiness!" Louise heard the tremor in her own voice. "In any case, I have wanted to say these things to you for years. You have real gifts. You could be an architect and design buildings that would enrich the world, but instead you are putting on airs, turning yourself inside out to be someone you're not, and chasing after a lot of people who don't give a fig for you!"

All the blood had drained from his face. "Are you quite finished?"

Louise felt sick. She had gone too far. But before she could try to soften some of the blows, Charles turned and strode away without a backward glance.

* * *

ALTHOUGH THE MEETING of the Geological Society had ended, many of the members continued to gather just outside Somerset House. Mouette stood with her family members, watching as several refined men paused to doff their top hats and speak to Mary Anning. It was heartening to see that some of them realized the importance of her work, but just as many never glanced in her direction.

Nearby, Theo paced back and forth, apparently waiting for Charles to return from his chat with Louise. When Mouette looked the viscount's way, he lifted his prominent chin in an invitation.

"Psst," whispered Anthony, nudging her, and tapped the side of his nose.

She remembered then that the nose-tap was the secret sign her roguish son had devised for them to use during their "covert operation," as he called it. Mouette wanted to smile. He might be too charming for his own good.

Justin bent to murmur in her ear, "Pretend to be annoyed with me before you go to join his lordship."

Raising her voice, she declared, "You are not my master." And with that, Mouette walked off to join Theo, head held high.

Theo regarded her a trifle anxiously. "Are you all right?" He paused to clear his throat, periodically glancing toward the glowering Justin. "That pirate isn't going to assault me again, I hope."

"He knows that if he does, it may cost him his wife," she replied, striving for an expression that mingled outrage with anguish.

"My dear, I hope you don't feel you are in danger. Is there something I can do to assist you?"

"May I be frank with you?" Mouette held Theo's gaze as she angled her parasol, blocking the two of them from her family's view.

"I insist!"

"I am so angry with my husband over his treatment of you at the ball, I cannot stop thinking about it. He is impossible! There have been rifts in our union for some time, but that scene made me question my vows."

She swallowed as if overcome. "I am not certain I will return with Justin to Cornwall."

Theo looked as if he had just received a gift from God. In a low, passionate voice, he replied, "I must own that I have wondered how you could pledge yourself to such a man." He started to lean closer, then stopped himself. "Tell me, dear Mouette, what can I do to help you?"

"I need time to think, of course, before I make a decision, but I know I must establish my independence. Not long ago, you asked me to aid in the decoration of your London home. Would you still welcome my assistance?"

Theo's nostrils flared at the base of his bandaged nose. "If you agree to do this, I would be a very happy man. When can you visit Redfield House?"

"On Tuesday next, Justin will be shopping for horses at Tattersall's. Might I come that afternoon?"

"Of course." Theo's eyes were wide as he considered her meaning. "I will send a carriage round to fetch you. One o'clock?"

Mouette nodded, smiling, even as her heart pounded. "As always, you are the kindest of friends."

For an instant, he caught her hand. "I look forward to our time together."

CHAPTER 28

*J*ustin leaned against the back of the elegant Sheraton sofa in the parlor and glanced over at Mouette. "You are quite the actress," he remarked, aware of the edge in his voice. "I especially liked the bit where you used your parasol to block my view. No doubt your dear friend Theo noticed as well and took it as a sign that you mean to embark on a secret liason with him."

Anthony looked over at them, brows aloft. "I hope you two aren't about to engage in another verbal sparring match." He stood at the cellaret in the parlor, having just poured three small glasses of sparkling wine. "I was about to toast our successful outing."

Mouette would not be distracted. "Your jealous papa seems to be a bit confused. Was I not instructed to entice Theo, so he would let me into his house?"

"I am not jealous. Or confused." Justin scowled. "And what exactly do you mean by entice? I would never instruct you to entice anyone." He leaned closer and murmured, "Except me, of course."

Anthony gave them a stern look as he served their wine and took a chair. "See here, let us agree on our mission. We intend to retrieve Mama's portrait and bring Redfield to his knees in the process."

"Bring him to his knees?" Justin repeated doubtfully. "Hmm. That sounds rather vague. I thought we agreed that, by the time we are finished, his lordship would be utterly ruined, disgraced, and—preferably—in prison."

Mouette gasped softly. "On what charge?"

"Theft!"

She shook her head. "I did not agree to anything so harsh. I know, the evidence is strongly against him, but really—theft? Besides, we still have no real proof that he meant any harm."

"*Mouette,*" Justin warned in a low growl.

"I only mean that it's quite possible his motive was simply unrequited love." Hoping to cool down the temperature, she pointed to herself and added, "Really, can you blame him?"

Reflecting on Izzie's revelation that Theo had vastly underpaid for the portrait, Mouette knew she should tell Justin and Anthony, but she also knew it would only further inflame her volatile husband. They did not know Theo as she did or remember the times when he had appeared to help her when the rest of the world had turned away. Perhaps Izzie was wrong about the value of the portrait, or Theo simply hadn't known. Of course, it was disturbing to think he had lied to her and kept the painting for himself...but she needed more real proof of his wrongdoing before she could condemn him completely.

Justin's brows lowered. "As long as you still intend to help us get into his house so that we may retrieve your portrait, I trust that the truth about his character will be revealed."

"I want that as well."

"You needn't fear that we're going to murder Lord Redfield," said Anthony, setting down his empty glass.

"But don't forget that he has deceived you many times over."

"I suppose he has." The truth of what her son was saying sank in. "You are right."

"Why don't you ever utter those words to me?" Justin wondered.

Mouette straightened her back, ignoring his light gibe. "As long as you both promise not to commit violence toward Lord Redfield, I will wholeheartedly do my part when I visit him on Tuesday."

Justin leaned closer. "Don't be too wholehearted, *ma belle*."

Before she could reply, they were interrupted by the sound of Emeline's voice as she hurried down the stairs. "How soon shall we dine? I am famished. Isn't it exciting that Miss Anning and the Murchisons will be joining us?"

Mouette moved over so that their daughter could snuggle in between them on the sofa. "Yes, it's wonderful that all of us can be together this evening."

Emeline rested her head on Justin's chest for a moment. "Papa, you have not replied to the letters I wrote inviting you and Mama to come to Lyme Regis. I am longing to take you on a real fossil hunt!"

Mouette stared at Justin, praying that he would not make another disparaging remark about their daughter's interest in fossils.

He held Emmie close and stroked her curls, as he had since she was a baby. "I was waiting until we were together to tell you that I would be honored to visit you in Lyme Regis, *mon petit chou*. I will bring your maman there as soon as possible."

"Oh, Papa, I am so glad you are interested after all. I know you will come to adore fossils as much as I do."

Justin glanced at Mouette above Emmie's head, sending her a wry, secret smile that made her fall in love with him all over again. A moment like this was worth more than a hundred promises that he would change.

More footsteps sounded above them, and soon Isabella and Louise were entering the parlor. By the time Baptiste appeared with a question about the dinner menu, the room was buzzing with conversation and laughter.

* * *

ONCE THE ST. Briac females had returned to Lyme Regis with Mary Anning, Justin turned his attention to their plan to retrieve Mouette's portrait and bring Redfield to justice.

On Tuesday, Mouette and Justin watched as Viscount Redfield's tasteful green landau drew up in front of the house in Bedford Square, pulled by a matched set of grays. As a groom leaped down from the back and approached the front door, Mouette tied the ribbons of her bonnet.

"How do I look?" she asked, gesturing to her dove-gray gown that featured large *gigot* sleeves. Lace-trimmed lappets dangled over the curves of her breasts. "Competent, I hope."

Justin gave a snort. "You must mean ravishing, in spite of that costume."

"You are extremely biased, m'sieur."

A sharp knock came at the door.

"Be careful." He could not resist the urge to draw Mouette in against his chest, so she could feel the force of his heartbeat. "I wish I could be there with you the entire time. Perhaps I should disguise myself as your manservant."

Mouette fondly shook her head. "Really, there is no reason for you to worry. Although Theo's fine character is clearly a façade, I'm certain he is harmless. While I am there taking measurements and making notes, he will doubtless be occupied with tasks of his own."

"Right. Like seeking ways to elude his creditors."

She pretended not to hear him. "I can't imagine that I would have any trouble finding the study where Frederica says he keeps my portrait, but if it will make you feel better to involve yourself today, I understand."

He let out a harsh breath. "I feared you might change your mind."

She reached up to touch her soft fingertips to his hard jaw. "I have agreed to the plan you and Anthony concocted because I don't want you to worry."

"You are the most splendid of women. I have no doubt you can manage on your own, but I don't trust Redfield. If I leave you alone there too long, I'll go mad." Justin bent to press a brief, scorching kiss to her mouth. "Thank you for indulging me, *chérie*."

Mouette picked up her slim satchel filled with an assortment of decorating accoutrements and started toward the door. "I know you and our son both crave adventure. You are two peas in a pod!" One of her delicately arched brows flicked upward. "Just don't get carried away."

Justin watched from the bay window as Mouette went out to the open landau and let the groom hand her inside. Even as his heart swelled with pride for her ingenuity and courage, a cold chill crept over him. Would his Mouette really be safe with Lord Redfield, who was more devious and lovesick than she could imagine?

* * *

STANDING with Theo in the exceedingly drab formal dining room of Redfield House, Mouette looked over the notes she had just written.

"I believe I have everything I need to get started," she said, gesturing toward her list. "You wish to make the initial changes in the formal rooms, so they may be suitable for parties during Frederica's come out this Season."

"That's correct." He gazed at her intently. "Nothing has been done since I brought Lady Redfield here after we were married, more than two decades ago. Of course, I gave her carte blanche to make any changes she wished, but as you can see, Katherine lacked your exquisite taste." With one pale hand, he gestured around the room with its draperies of muddy green velvet, dark furnishings from the shop of Thomas Chippendale, and worn carpets.

Mouette felt sympathy for Theo's deceased wife. "Katherine had many fine qualities, and no doubt this was the height of fashion when she planned these refurbishments."

"You are gracious as always."

"I am quite sincere. Now then, I must begin my work. Do you mind if I move around among the rooms on my own?" She kept her tone light. "I like to make my notes and take measurements without any outside distractions."

He looked crestfallen. "Perhaps we might take some refreshments in the drawing room before you begin? My cook has made little iced cakes with candied violets."

"That's very kind but I am here to help with your home decoration," Mouette said with a smile. "I must try to keep to that task."

Theo stepped closer. "My dear, I know that you are going through a difficult time with your...spouse." He said the last word reluctantly, as if he still didn't want to admit she was married to Justin. "I want to tell you that I know how that feels. For many of the years I was married to Katherine, I felt rather numb. My heart wasn't in it, but what could I do?"

Mouette had to remind herself that it was important for Theo to believe she and Justin were estranged. However, she didn't want to encourage his attentions, and finding a balance was more challenging than she had expected. "You are quite right. Marriage can be a great challenge, especially if one's spouse is...difficult." Then, she said, "I am grateful for the distraction you are providing me here. And now, I should begin my work..."

Theo started to reach for her but stopped and fisted his hands at his sides. "I see. If you must, I will leave you to it." He turned toward the door.

"Should I need to speak to you, will I find you in your study?" Mouette tossed out the question as casually as she could, almost as an afterthought, but her heart was pounding as she waited for him to respond.

Theo stopped and looked back, his head cocked to one side. "My study?"

"Yes. I assume you would be occupied there, at your desk." Could he sense her nerves?

"No, my desk is in the library. My study is a more... private retreat." His eyes darkened.

Mouette said, "I would love to see your library! I have always been fascinated by the books people choose."

"I would be happy to show you. If you think it has possibilities, perhaps you can turn your talents to the library once the other rooms have been refurbished."

He led the way down the shadowy corridor, pointing out the drawing room as they passed but ignoring another door that was securely closed. Inside the library, Theo showed her the shelves of dusty books, explaining that most had been part of the family collection for nearly a century. In one corner stood a large desk that appeared well-used, for the surface was stacked with documents secured under paperweights, and there were quills and an inkwell.

Theo regarded the books and sighed. "My father constantly urged me to read, but when I tried, something in the pages made me sneeze," he confessed. "I keep them because one must, of course."

Mouette peered at the worn, embossed letters on the book spines, feigning interest. "Do you mind if I look at them before I get on with my work?"

"Go right ahead. I must go downstairs to the kitchen and tell them we have no need for refreshments." In the doorway, Theo paused. "I will leave you to it then."

"Thank you."

At last, he left her, and when his footsteps died away down the long corridor, Mouette moved quickly toward the desk. Perhaps she might find something there that related to her portrait! Her heart was racing, for she was in full view of the doorway, but she felt compelled to look. What if they couldn't get into the study, where Frederica had said he kept the painting? Also, she would love to report a discovery of her own to Justin and Anthony. They seemed to believe they were the only ones capable of carrying off a cloak and dagger scheme.

Mouette's fingers trembled as she opened the center drawer of the desk. Inside was a jumble of papers, old pen nibs, leftover stubs of sealing wax, and other items which should have been discarded long ago. Another drawer held stacks of what appeared to be unpaid bills. It was a bit of a surprise to discover that Theo was not only disorderly but purse-pinched, as Charles would say.

Hearing voices in another room, Mouette quickly opened one more drawer. Her mouth went dry. Inside were assorted messages written in her own hand. Invitations to routs and dinners, given during her marriage to Harry. Other small notes, presumably thanking Theo for his various kind deeds after Harry's downfall and death. There was a small, dried posey wrapped in one of her signature emerald-green ribbons. Where had he gotten it? It seemed her heart would burst from her chest as she fumbled through the artifacts Theo had saved. Then, at the back of the drawer, Mouette saw a letter...written in Theo's sprawling hand but addressed to *Lady Brandreth* at her Bedford Square address. Hands shaking, Mouette drew it out and opened it just enough to see the date: *9 April 1818.*

Her thoughts spun. That was virtually the same day, eleven years ago, that Isabella had come to Bedford Square with Mouette's sister, Lindsay! Perceiving how destitute and desperate Mouette had become, Izzie had persuaded her to travel to Cornwall...where Mouette had met Justin, and her entire life had turned upside-down.

Clearly, she had left London before Theo could post his letter!

Footsteps sounded at the other end of the corridor.

Mouette pushed the drawer closed and hurried back to the bookshelves, still clutching the paper. She heard Theo speaking again, this time to a male servant. Opening the letter he had clearly never posted, she scanned the page, phrases leaping out as if they were aflame: *"I cannot bear to wait another day to reveal my true feelings...My marriage is empty, I have adored you for years...I know of your reduced circumstances and I want to take care of you, to provide for you...let me come to you, my beautiful Mouette, and prove my love..."*

Bile rose in her throat. How could Theo write such a letter, when he had been the one to contribute to her "reduced circumstances!" Izzie's words about the true value of the painting rang in her mind. He had pretended to help while cheating Mouette out of the monies she should have received, making sure that she was utterly desperate and afraid before he had written offering to "take care" of her. Her eyes stung with fury and the pain of one more betrayal. Furious, she folded the letter into a small square and pushed it up into her padded *gigot* sleeve.

"I couldn't stay away."

Mouette nearly gasped aloud. Looking up, she saw Theo's tall frame filling the doorway. How long had he been there? Had he seen her with the letter? She gave a shaky laugh. "I was just admiring your library...and thinking what a pity it is that no one seems to be reading these books. Unless Frederica is secretly a bluestocking?"

Theo seemed not to hear her. Instead, he crossed to stop in front of his desk, leaning over to move some of the papers. His eyes narrowed slightly as he opened the center drawer, then stepped back to scan the entire desk. Apparently satisfied, he turned to her.

Mouette swallowed, feeling faint. Could he see that she had touched his things? Would he look for the letter and discover that it was missing? Quickly, she picked up her satchel and started toward the door.

"I know that you are very busy, my lord."

He was before her in an instant. "Have I not insisted that you address me as Theo?"

Just then, a loud series of knocks sounded at the front door and an all-too-familiar voice shouted, "Redfield, I demand that you admit me!"

"Dear God, that is my husband!" Mouette said in an urgent whisper. "He cannot find us alone together. I must go to the drawing room and be clearly engaged in the task I came here for, or there is no telling what he might do."

Theo blinked and brought a hand up to his still-bandaged nose. "I say! That buccaneer cannot simply burst in here and lay waste to my home! Is he truly some sort of heathen?"

Mouette was already crossing to the drawing room. Once inside, she opened her satchel and took out the notebook in which she made notes and sketches of her design ideas. When Theo followed her, she turned and said, "My husband is a very jealous man. He is determined to force me to return to Cornwall with him."

As she spoke, Mouette saw Redfield's ancient butler totter past, on his way to greet the viscount's unruly caller. There was fear in Theo's hazel eyes, but he seemed to realize that this was his chance to become a hero. "That uncivilized brute cannot simply do as he pleases, shouting and bursting in here as if this were the deck of one of his blasted pirate ships!"

When he started toward the door, Mouette called, "No, please, you must not incite him further!" A moment later, she managed to trip over a low stool and tumbled forward.

"Dash it all, what's happened, my dear?" cried Theo, horrified. Turning back, he knelt beside her. "Are you hurt?"

The butler appeared in the doorway and had just opened his mouth to speak when Justin slipped past him, looking wicked and dangerous with his eye-patch and tousled silver-streaked hair.

"What are you doing to my wife?" Justin shouted, pointing at Theo.

"I?" cried Theo, clearly shocked by Justin's accusatory tone. "*You* are the one who has upset her so that she stumbled and fell! I merely came to her aid."

"I have twisted my ankle," said Mouette. "But I will be fine. Justin, you should not have come here! I thought you were at Tattersall's today, buying a new horse."

His nostrils flared. "Ah, *oui*, that's where you would like me to be, far away from your little tryst with this aristocrat who seeks to cuckold me!"

"You have no right to push your way into my home and behave in such a brutish manner," shouted Theo. "Your wife is here in a professional capacity! I will ask you to leave, sir." As he spoke, he helped Mouette up into a velvet-upholstered chair where she promptly pretended to swoon.

"Yes, Justin," she said weakly. "You must go."

She let her head drop back against the back of the chair and closed her eyes. A moment later, Theo called to his butler, "Adkins, don't just stand there! Get some smelling salts and a cool cloth. And perhaps a spot of brandy!" Then, to Justin, he ordered, "Can't you see that once again you are only making matters worse? Do as your wife bids and leave my home. I will see that she arrives safely back in Bedford Square after she comes around."

Justin took a step closer, as if to refuse, but when Mouette gave a moan, he stopped.

"*D'accord*. I will leave. But I don't like it!" With that, he made a noisy exit, stamping away and closing the front door so forcefully that Mouette thought she could feel the floor shake slightly.

She wished she could look to see what was happening. Had he truly left? A few moments later, Adkins returned with the smelling salts, a damp cloth, and a small glass of brandy.

"Has that despicable Frenchman gone?" Theo asked Adkins.

"He must have done," replied the butler. "I saw no sign of him in the corridor."

"Good. He isn't fit to set foot in my house." He waved the smelling salts under her nose, and Mouette blinked and smiled.

"Oh, my," she murmured. "I am sorry for that. Perhaps I should go home before Justin does something else outrageous."

"I will take you myself!" Theo caught one of her hands and brought it to his mouth, kissing her a bit longer than was proper. As Adkins backed out of the room, he told her, "I cannot abide the notion of you living with that man. The situation with Harry was bad enough, but this is beyond belief! I hate to say it, but I fear for your safety."

She gave him a tremulous smile. "I have a few matters to sort out first, and then you and I will talk."

"Oh, my dear." Theo looked nearly overcome with emotion. "Do I dare to hope you may be going to free yourself of that man?"

Mouette sighed and patted his cheek. "Soon enough, you will know my plans."

CHAPTER 29

"I fear something terrible has happened to your papa." Mouette paced back and forth across the warm, sun-dappled garden courtyard, while Robinson sat nearby, watching intently. Her fashionable rose silk shoes pinched as she walked, but she didn't care.

"Nonsense," said Anthony from his place on the garden bench, sketch book on his lap. He pointed with his pencil to a large insect poised on a nearby branch. "Look at this. I've found a rare crucifix beetle that will make my friend Darwin green with envy. He's obsessed with beetles, you know. He even has attendants who carry the equipment during his hunts."

Mouette glanced at the rust-colored insect marked by a distinctive black cross who was posing unknowingly for her son. "Goodness. What sort of equipment?"

He shrugged. "Lug nets, boxes, traps…that sort of thing." As he spoke, Anthony returned to his sketch, wielding the charcoal pencil with long, deft fingers.

Bemused, she remarked, "You are meeting the oddest people at Cambridge."

"I suppose I am." He laughed, then added more seriously, "Don't worry about Papa. We both know he will walk through the door at any moment, completely unharmed."

"I know nothing of the kind." She shook her head. "Your papa pretended to leave Lord Redfield's home, but no doubt he slipped into one of the rooms and was hiding while his lordship escorted me home. You know how reckless he is, and how he has been craving danger. Anything could have happened to him if he was later discovered!"

"But was that not the point of him going there, to get into the study while you created a distraction?" Anthony stopped drawing for a moment and watched Mouette.

"Yes, of course, that was our plan...but it felt much riskier in the moment. Theo wouldn't let me near the one closed door, which I feel certain led to his study. And...I found something that made me realize you and your papa have been quite right about Theo's true character."

"What was that?"

Before Mouette could reply, a sardonic voice spoke from the direction of the house. "Yes, do enlighten us."

She whirled around and beheld her husband's tall, broad-shouldered form haloed in the sunlit doorway. Robinson barked and hurried forward to greet his master, while her heart clenched with joy. "Justin! I have been so afraid."

"Afraid?" He wore an expression of mock-consternation. "But you know me better than that, my love." And as Mouette rushed toward him, he caught her in his arms and murmured, "*Much* better."

She soaked up the warmth of his solid torso, the familiar and arousing scent of him, the reassuring beat of his heart against her ear. Tears threatened. "You should not jest at such a moment."

Across the courtyard, Anthony picked up the crucifix beetle and set it under a tree. "Mama was certain Lord Redfield had done away with you."

Father and son exchanged amused glances, and Mouette protested, "I didn't say that. But when you didn't return home, I couldn't help worrying a bit. That house, and even Theo himself, felt threatening to me today."

Justin tightened his fingers around her waist. "I agree. Threatening...like an irksome fly. Anthony, you should have seen the dramatic scene your mama enacted today. She has hidden talents." Then, seeing her serious expression, he moderated his tone. "I am glad you worry for me, love. But there was no need. I was out of there before Redfield returned from seeing you home."

"Did you manage to find the study?"

"Of course." He smiled. "You mentioned that one door was closed, so I tried it first. I couldn't linger there, tinkering with the lock, since the butler might return at any moment, so I went outside and located the window."

"The window? But the study is up a flight of stairs."

"I know. I climbed a tree."

She didn't know whether to laugh or scold him. "You are mad."

"Did you go inside?" Anthony pressed, rising to join them.

"I'm not *that* mad," Justin replied with a laugh. "But I did see enough through the window to know that it was definitely a man's study." He paused. "And I glimpsed a painting above the mantelpiece, where Frederica told Anthony her father had hung it."

Mouette thought her heart would stop. "Oh, Justin, was it my portrait?"

"I couldn't be absolutely certain. The view was restricted by a lot of draperies...but I made out the corner of a gilded frame, and something green. A gown, I think."

"Yes!" breathed Mouette. "I was wearing a gown of sea-green muslin in the portrait." She paused, feeling a pang as she added softly, "Trimmed with silver cord."

Anthony was focused on his father. "Was the window unlocked?"

"It was," Justin confirmed. "I could see that it was slightly ajar. Now all we need to do is discover an opportunity."

Baptiste appeared then, carrying a tray of refreshments. "M'sieur! Sir Charles has arrived." The Frenchman waggled his brows meaningfully. "I thought you would like to know."

"My son, Charles?" Mouette looked perplexed. "I was not expecting him."

Quickly, Justin took his hands from her and moved to sit on a bench several feet away. Robinson followed and planted himself on his master's booted foot. "Have a care, mongrel," Justin muttered fondly. "Do you have any idea how much those boots cost?"

Mouette watched as her older son emerged from the house, impeccable in his midnight-blue coat with gilt buttons, golden curls agleam in the afternoon sunlight.

"Ah, Mother, there you are," he said, seeming not to notice the others.

Anthony went to join Justin on his bench, and they both accepted glasses of wine from Baptiste. They greeted Charles but appeared to be absorbed in a more serious conversation. From time to time, Anthony gestured toward his beetle sketches, and Justin would nod as if utterly fascinated.

"Hello, Charles," Mouette greeted her son. She moved to embrace him, but he gave her only a brief kiss on the cheek. "What a lovely surprise."

"Actually, I can't stay," he said. "Lady Penelope likes to ride in Hyde Park at four o'clock, so of course I want to be there. However, I thought I might pop in on my way to bid Louise goodbye." His tone was offhand, but Mouette knew him well enough to read the intensity in his gaze. She longed to ask why he only wished to say goodbye to Louise and not his sister or Isabella.

"That's very kind of you, my dear, but I'm afraid they left for Lyme Regis yesterday morning."

"Oh!" Charles blinked, and for a moment disappointment showed on his handsome face. "She's gone back then? Well, never mind. It was just a thought." He shrugged, accepting a small glass of wine from Baptiste. "While I am here, I might mention that Grandmama is having a small number of guests over for supper on Friday, to celebrate her birthday." Charles lowered his voice before adding, "She wondered if you might like to join us, Mother, but I don't think she cares for...him." He finished the sentence by glancing toward Justin. "Also, Lord Redfield and his daughter will be there, so that is another reason why *he* cannot be present."

"I agree." Mouette leaned closer to Charles, as if to share a secret. "I know better than anyone that Justin can be quite impossible, and he has created a great deal of friction with Theo. They despise one another."

"You agree that he is a problem?" Charles whispered, as if he couldn't believe his ears.

She gave a small, resigned nod. "This interlude in London has opened my eyes to a great deal...Yet I must go on with my life! Will you escort me on Friday?"

He widened his blue eyes. "Why, yes. I'd be delighted to do so. I am hoping that Lady Penelope will attend as well. It would be a perfect opportunity for us to grow closer."

"Lovely." Mouette patted his coat sleeve. "I look forward to it."

After settling on a time for Charles to collect her, she then walked him to the door and bade him good-bye. On impulse, Mouette decided not to return to the garden. She knew they were waiting for her to come back and reveal what she had found at Redfield House that had convinced her of Theo's darker motives, but it came to her that this was a conversation she and Justin must share alone.

Later.

* * *

JUSTIN HAD SO MUCH on his mind that he nearly forgot what he'd heard Mouette say as he came into the garden that afternoon. *I found something that made me realize you have been quite right about Theo's true character.*

Later that night, as they made love in the moonlit bed, her words came back to him. She was especially passionate, welcoming his intimate caresses, returning his kisses with fervor, and crying out when he thrust deep inside her, joining their bodies. Her legs were wrapped around his hips, and she was damp with per-spiration at the moment of her own release. In the blissful afterglow, Justin watched her face, awash with love.

He spoke in a husky whisper. "Now that you've gotten that out of your system...are you ready to tell me what you discovered?"

Their eyes met, inches apart. "Yes," she said and nodded. "I have a letter to show you."

After a bit, they rose and donned robes. Justin lit a lamp and poured them each a small glass of Chinon wine, while Mouette retrieved a folded paper from a drawer in her bureau. Then, they sat together on the side of the bed amidst the rumpled covers, sipping their wine.

Mouette sighed. "You were right."

"I *was*?" He resisted the impulse to smile. Instead, he gently rubbed her back and waited.

"About Theo." She began to unfold the paper. "I was a fool to hold out hope that his only crime might have been caring for me too much."

"Do not be so hard on yourself. You thought he was your friend at a time when you needed someone to trust. I love the optimist in you." Justin squinted at the letter she held out, remembering the many times Mouette had urged him to order a pair of spectacles for reading. "The light is too dim. Just tell me what it says."

"It is from Theo, written in April of 1818, the month I traveled to Cornwall…and eventually agreed to become your make-believe bride. It seems that he wrote it just before he learned that I had left London, and then he must have put it away in his desk, saving it no doubt for my imminent return." Mouette looked up at him and bit her lip. "Oh, Justin, that is the other thing. I discovered a drawer in his desk where he seems to have saved every note, invitation, or keepsake related to me. It was chilling!" She shivered. "And then, in the back was this letter…"

Justin unconsciously stopped breathing as he waited for the rest, still holding her against him so she wouldn't doubt his support.

"His wife was alive then, of course, yet he was confessing that he had loved me for years. He wrote that he wanted to take care of me." Mouette's voice broke. "You needn't remind me what Theo meant by that! You were so right. He cheated me when he took my portrait and other valuables to supposedly sell to someone else, and then after he saw to it that I was finally destitute, he wrote this offer to 'take care of me.' But what he really wanted was to make me his mistress!"

"I want to kill him," Justin said in a low, deadly voice.

"You must not do that." She shook her head, almost smiling. "Instead, we will steal back my portrait."

"And make him *pay*, like the thief he is. Newgate is too good for him."

Mouette tossed her long black curls, and he saw the determination in her eyes. "You must leave that part to me. I was the one he duped, and I will see that he pays for it properly."

Justin cast the odious letter onto the carpet and took her in his arms. "You would have made a glorious lady pirate, *chérie*." Kissing her, he added, "Hmm...Perhaps it's not too late."

CHAPTER 30

"*S*hhh." Justin balanced precariously in the elm tree outside Redfield House and turned to look down through the moon silvered branches. There, below him, was Anthony. As Justin pointed to the large window, looming just a few feet away in the darkness, he suddenly felt a sharp twinge in his lower back. *Sangdieu.* It crossed his mind that he might be growing too old for such adventures, but he gave himself a mental shake. Never!

"Let me go first," whispered Anthony. He gestured toward the gap between their position in the tree and the edge of the window casement.

Was his son implying that he couldn't leap nimbly to the window? "That's not necessary."

But Anthony climbed up beside him, his smile flashing in the shadows. "If one of us is to fall, it should be me. My bones are still flexible."

This almost made Justin laugh, even as he felt a surge of love for his boy...who was now a man. "*Eh bien*, if you insist. But I will hold onto you, just in case."

"You are welcome to do so if it makes you feel better, Papa."

Anthony leaned recklessly toward the window, but

his long arms could not quite reach the glass. He then braced one booted foot on the edge of a branch, and Justin grasped him round the waist, providing an anchor. Still, the situation was fraught with risk. Just as Anthony pushed the window open with his fingertips and prepared to make the leap across, Justin heard a groaning sound, followed by a snap as the branch beneath his son's feet gave way. In that instant, Anthony threw himself over to the brick ledge outside the window, shoved the casement more fully open, pulled himself up, and disappeared inside the study.

Justin's heart was beating as if he were about to be eaten by a tiger. After what felt like an hour, Anthony's head emerged again, and he gestured for Justin to join him.

"Can you make it, Papa?" he called softly.

Justin sent him a warning look. Had his son forgotten who taught him everything he knew about hazardous exploits like this? In that moment, Justin imagined that he was high in the masts of Surcouf's ship *Revenant*, swinging out to catch a line that was just out of reach. A thrilling surge of power filled his body. With a deep breath, he flexed his knees, tightened his powerful thighs, and leaped from the tree to the window ledge. Fortunately, Anthony was there to grasp his hand at the crucial moment, pulling him up until Justin could gain purchase on the sill and climb the rest of the way himself.

Inside the darkened study, they blinked at one another, laughing softly.

"Papa," whispered Anthony, "you were splendid!"

"*C'est vrai.*" He smiled and patted his son's broad shoulder. "Like father, like son, as your mama likes to say." Turning toward the fireplace, he said, "And now, let us take the portrait down and endeavor to leave with it through the front door. Thank God everyone is out tonight, and we don't have to try to go back the way we came in."

"What about the servants?"

"The only one I saw when I burst in the other day was a withered butler who appeared to have one foot in the grave. Even if the fellow should totter out of bed to investigate, he could never catch us."

Together they went forward through the dense shadows, but as they reached the mantelpiece, Anthony gave a muffled groan. "I don't see any portrait. Where the devil is it?"

Justin went closer, peering up, but all he saw hanging there was an ugly oval mirror. "That was not here when I climbed the tree on Tuesday." Feeling Anthony's skeptical glance, he added, "*You* were the one who said we would find the portrait in the study, above the fireplace!"

"That's what Frederica said! She specifically told me—"

"Shh!" Justin cut him off, heart pounding, as he listened. Were those footsteps in the corridor? Clearly, Anthony had heard it as well, for his eyes widened as he looked around the room. Turning, Justin saw a long, low sofa squatting just in front of the wall of bookshelves. Father and son virtually flew across the study and flung themselves behind the hideous piece of furniture.

A moment later, the door opened a few inches.

"Papa?" queried a female voice. "Is that...you?"

Anthony groaned softly and prayed Frederica would turn around and leave. Why wasn't she at the birthday dinner with Lord Redfield? The door opened further, creaking on its hinges.

"Someone is in this room," Frederica said more firmly. She raised her lamp and it cast eerie shadows behind them on the paneled walls. "Make yourself known to me!"

Anthony looked at his father and saw his silent command. *Go on!*

He rose from behind the sofa and went forward, straightening his coat sleeves.

Frederica gasped. "Anthony St. Briac!"

"You are doubtless wondering what I am doing here, hiding behind the furniture in your house." He gave her a smile that he hoped was charmingly sheepish.

She was wearing a soft muslin nightgown under a matching robe. The fragile, pristine fabric was embroidered at the edges with delicate flowers and leaves. Her vivid blue eyes met his unflinchingly as he approached. Of course, it was completely inappropriate for him to be here, in this darkened room, especially given her attire.

"I thought you and his lordship were out, at the Dowager Lady Brandreth's birthday dinner..." he began.

"I was ill with a headache this evening, so I remained behind." Frederica said. "But I do not owe you an explanation, do I? It is the other way around."

"I will be honest with you," he said, standing a bit too close to her. "Since the morning in Hyde Park when you told me that my mother's portrait was hanging in this study, I have wanted to see it for myself. It seemed an adventure, getting inside, but I meant no harm."

"Are you alone?" She lifted her chin slightly. "I heard voices."

Damn. Anthony moved a bit closer until he could inhale the fragrance of lily-of-the-valley soap that clung to her visibly damp skin. It came to him that she had just bathed, and suddenly he was hard, aroused. "I will tell you a secret," he murmured.

Her guarded expression seemed to soften slightly. "I am listening."

"You heard voices because...I have been known to talk to myself."

Frederica looked surprised, then she gave a little laugh. "I don't believe you."

He sensed that she didn't seem to care about the voices any longer, so he moved on. "I came not only to see my mother's likeness, but also because I am a great admirer of the artist, Élisabeth Vigée Le Brun."

"Oh, so am I!" she exclaimed.

"My aunt, Isabella St. Briac, is her friend. That is how Madame Le Brun came to paint my mother on the eve of her first wedding." He projected self-assurance, as if it were perfectly natural that he had climbed in through the window of her father's study to converse about art.

"I did not know of your connection to Isabella St. Briac," Frederica replied in wonder. "I am an admirer of her paintings as well!"

"I would be pleased to introduce you if the opportunity presents itself. She was here in London just a few days ago, but I was unaware then that you were a lover of art."

"I truly am." She lowered her voice. "That is one reason why it has vexed me so that Papa keeps your mother's magnificent portrait hidden from the world."

"Miss Redfield..."

"Frederica," she interrupted him.

"All right." He smiled into her eyes, feeling the sparks flare brighter between them. "I know it is improper for me to be here with you, Frederica, but I hope that before you send me away you will allow me to see the portrait of my mother. Just once." Anthony dared then to reach for her bare hand and bring it to his mouth, grazing her delicate fingers with his mouth.

She stared at him, lips parted, and he could see her nipples tauten tantalizingly beneath the thin muslin. "I have long wanted to see what she looked like when she was young, before life tested her so severely."

"That is lovely." Frederica took a step closer so that their bodies were nearly touching. Anthony knew she would allow him to kiss her, and he ached to do so, but of course his father was behind the sofa, so it was out of the question.

"You will show me the portrait?"

"Well, you can see for yourself..." Turning, she pointed toward the space above the fireplace and made a little shocked sound. "Oh! Where can it be?" Before Anthony could respond, she narrowed her eyes and said, "Papa must have put it away after your mother was in the house yesterday. She has come to help him with the décor, he says, but of course all he really wants is to be alone with her."

Anthony saw pain in her eyes. "It hurts you that he – uh – carries a torch for her."

"Yes! This obsession he has besmirches the fine memory of my own mama. And he cannot have Lady Brandreth, can he?"

This seemed to be a rhetorical question, but Anthony thought he heard a low grunt of protest from the other side of the room. Quickly, he said, "No, no, she will not return his regard, I am quite certain. And of course, she is no longer Lady Brandreth. My parents' marriage may be bumpy at times, but I think Mama enjoys the passion. He is a French pirate, you know."

"Everyone knows," Frederica replied with a soft laugh. "Your father is the talk of London."

In an effort to turn the conversation back to the painting, Anthony asked, "Where do you suppose Lord Redfield has put the portrait? I hope no harm has come to it."

She looked toward a small door at the back of the study, only a few steps from the place where Anthony's father crouched behind the sofa.

"I suppose he locked it in his little anteroom," Frederica said. "Unbeknownst to him, I know where he keeps the key. He never realized how many of his secrets Mama and I discovered over the years."

As Anthony followed her toward the little door, he felt a wave of panic at the prospect of her spotting his father crouched behind the sofa. Before he could speak, however, Papa suddenly cleared his throat and rose to his feet.

"Miss Redfield, I apologize for my intrusion," he said in his deep, French-accented voice. "As you can see, Anthony was not alone when he climbed through the window tonight."

Frederica cried out in surprise, then whirled on Anthony. He saw anger and hurt in her eyes. "You deceived me," she accused.

"I am sorry." He tried to take her hand, but she stepped back, out of reach. "When Papa hid there, we didn't know who might be outside in the corridor. And then—"

"I trusted you. I thought you were my...friend." Her eyes said, *And more.*

"I am!" He felt as if he were on a sinking ship. "But I owed this to my mother, to find the portrait and see that it is returned to her."

"Yes. Your desire was not only to see it, as you insisted earlier, but to *take* it. And so, you used me." Her eyes gleamed, but her expression was resolute. "In Hyde Park, and now tonight..."

Anthony's face grew warm as he remembered the feelings he'd encouraged in her just minutes ago. He opened his mouth to protest, to explain, but caught a glance from his father that stopped him. He knew then that Frederica was not the sort of person who could be placated by charm or excuses. The fact that she was clearly attracted to him only underscored that point.

"I am deeply sorry, Frederica. I did not mean to offend you."

"You may address me as Miss Redfield," she said coolly and crossed her arms over her breasts, closing herself off from him.

Across the room, Justin watched the young couple. Although his heart went out to them, he reminded himself that they were both very young. At Anthony's age, Justin was just embarking on a long series of *affaires de coeur*, culminating in his almost-accidental marriage to Mouette at the age of forty-eight. Their son, no doubt, still had a lot to learn about women and love.

Justin cleared his throat. "I hesitate to interrupt but time is of the essence. Miss Redfield, I am hoping that you will still consent to help us retrieve my wife's portrait. As you doubtless know, Mouette was forced to part with it in order to pay her creditors. Your father led her to believe that he had sold it to someone else, that it was lost to her forever. Will you help us return Mouette's portrait to her?" Coming around the sofa to face her, Justin took something from his pocket and held it out in his open palm. "I will repay Lord Redfield for his monetary investment with this rare Colombian emerald, from one of my own treasure chests. Your father can sell it for many times the amount he paid Mouette for the portrait."

Frederica stared at the priceless gem, glowing in the lamplight. The emerald was the size of a robin's egg. "I would agree, even if Papa would be left with nothing. That portrait has caused a great deal of pain in my family, not only because it came to him through dishonest means."

Justin saw the telling glance she sent Anthony as she uttered the word *dishonest*, but in the next moment she had turned toward the little door in the far wall. Frederica opened a drawer in a nearby writing desk and took out a large key. Fitting it in the lock, she opened the door to what appeared to be a storage closet.

"Ah, there it is." Frederica pointed into the murky darkness.

Anthony came forward with the oil lamp and held it up to illuminate the contents of the tiny room. There were old, dusty wooden chests and stacks of books, but in the middle was what appeared to be a framed painting, covered by a linen cloth. Justin brought it out into the study and took off the covering.

"Yes," said Anthony, a catch in his voice. "I remember! I haven't seen it since Lord Redfield came to get it when I was a little boy."

In spite of the dark, shadowy surroundings, Mouette's likeness seemed to glow on the canvas. Justin's heart hurt as he looked at her, so innocent and beautiful.

"We may not have much time," he said, and turned his attention back to Frederica. "Miss Redfield, I am sorry to make you a party to this night's exploits, but will you allow us to remove the painting from your house?"

She seemed to grow paler but nodded. "I will. Let us go out now, before Papa returns."

Justin went back into the antechamber and placed the emerald in the spot where the portrait had been. Then Frederica locked the door and replaced the key.

"He won't suspect that you helped us?" asked Justin.

She shrugged. "He has no idea that I am aware of the key, but even if he does guess, what can he say? I think he will not want to speak openly of his little secret to me or anyone else."

With that, she turned, took the lamp, and went to the study door. Anthony was carrying the painting as they followed, but no sooner had Frederica opened the door to the corridor than muffled voices reached them.

"It's Papa!" Frederica whispered. "He is outside, speaking to the coachman."

A part of Justin longed for a violent confrontation with Redfield. He had brought a dagger, sheathed beneath his coat in the event of a crisis, but now it came to him that such a fantasy was impossible. Too many other people were involved.

"I will meet him and take him upstairs," Frederica said quickly.

"What about that ancient butler of yours?" asked Justin.

"Adkins goes to bed early. He has done so since his eighty-fifth birthday. Papa will expect to let himself in." Her eyes were poignant. "Goodbye then."

Anthony spoke up suddenly. "I will visit you tomorrow."

"Please do not," Frederica replied. Her dignity was impressive for one so young. In the next instant, she had disappeared into the corridor, closing the door behind her.

Justin and Anthony, who still held the draped portrait, retreated into the shadowed depths of the study, waiting. Soon they heard the sounds of Redfield coming into the house.

"Oh, Papa, you have returned early!" Frederica was saying. "I revived a bit and so I had just come down to the library to choose a book. Look, it's one of your favorites."

"I was feeling blue-deviled and decided to come home. There was nothing for me there tonight," Redfield said, his voice slurred, as they reached the study.

"P'rhaps I'll have a brandy. You'll excuse me if I pause here for a few minutes?"

The study doorknob rattled, sending a cold chill down Justin's spine. Looking over, he saw Anthony's dark eyes go wide, and it seemed the sound of their heartbeats reverberated through the room.

"Perhaps you have already imbibed enough tonight, Papa," Frederica was saying on the other side of the paneled door. She sounded completely natural and re-laxed. "Come upstairs with me, won't you? I want to hear all about the Dowager Lady Brandreth's birthday dinner."

When the first floor went silent, Justin met Antho-ny's uncertain stare and flashed a smile. "Let's be away. Quickly!"

Opening the door, Justin peered out into the dimly lit corridor. There was no sign of anyone about, so he went first and gestured for Anthony to follow. They hurried down the steps to the ground floor, opened the front door, and father and son emerged into the balmy summer night. Justin was acutely conscious of the rush of adrenaline and the thrill of adventure that he'd missed in recent years.

Park Lane still bustled with enough vehicles, horses, and pedestrians that Justin and Anthony were able to blend in, unnoticed, as they carried their bundle to-ward the waiting carriage. Will, the coachman, took the wrapped painting from Anthony, put it inside, and held the door for the two men.

When they were seated inside and the horses drew the carriage out onto the thoroughfare, Justin allowed himself to savor the moment.

"We've done it, thanks to you, *mon fils*! You were splendid."

Anthony's handsome profile was pensive. "Yes, it

was quite an adventure...but I suppose the real credit should go to Miss Redfield."

Justin knew better than to press his son further. Instead, he leaned back against the plush squabs and rubbed his bad knee, watching the fine, lamplit townhouses as they passed by.

His thoughts immediately turned to Mouette. Suddenly, all that mattered was his need to tell her everything that had happened, to hold her and feel their hearts beating in unison. Overtaken by a sense of urgency, Justin wanted to order Will to hurry.

Where, he wondered, was Mouette at that very moment?

CHAPTER 31

*M*ouette studied Charles's shuttered face as they sat together in his grandmother's aged, musty-smelling barouche. It was hard to know what to say to him, but soon they would arrive at her home in Bedford Square and the opportunity for conversation would be over.

She knew how much her son had been looking forward to this evening, especially once he learned that Lady Penelope planned to attend with her friend, Miss Amelia Thatcher. Charles would never say so, but Mouette sensed that tonight had felt like a last chance to make his consuming dream a reality. However, it had not turned out that way.

"There are other women, you know," she said gently.

"Mother, will you answer a question? Honestly?" His blue eyes blazed with confusion.

"Of course."

"It's unnatural, isn't it? I mean, what is between Lady Pen and her *friend*."

Mouette's heart sank. She had seen the two young ladies together, chatting intimately in the drawing room as if they were alone in the world, and the nature of their relationship had become clear to Mouette. She felt their romantic joy, yet her heart also went out to them, for such an attachment would prove challenging, even impossible, in London society. Perhaps, she had mused as she watched Miss Thatcher gaze into Lady Penelope's eyes, they could live abroad.

"I don't think we can know exactly what is between them," she said carefully, "but I do think it is quite clear that Lady Penelope is not interested in marrying you, and that is what really matters. You and your grandmama must stop pretending otherwise."

Charles flushed as he said, "Mama, I saw them *kissing*." In a choked voice, he added, "I went out to the garden, hoping to steal a private moment with Lady Pen, and…"

She leaned over to put a hand on his arm. "This is not a personal affront toward you, Charles. Nor does it mean they are wicked, as some might claim. It is simply the way they are made, and we must hope that they can find happiness in this world."

"The duke will keel over dead if he discovers this!"

"I hope not. But we cannot predict the outcome. I hope he will love his daughter and wish her well. And if given the opportunity, we must stand up for those two young women."

Charles rolled his eyes. "You are suggesting that I pitch the gammon when the truth will be plain to see on my face!"

"Nonsense. Be grateful that Lady Penelope did not encourage your suit. Wish her happy and go on with your own life." They were drawing up in front of her home. "Thank you for inviting me this evening, my dear. And please try not to harbor ill will toward those two lovely young women. When your real future becomes clear, you'll be grateful for this night."

301

* * *

JUSTIN STOOD AT THE WINDOW, watching for Mouette, his whole body tensed with a mixture of joy and pain. In the past, when he had experienced genuine happiness, he'd thought he might be dying. Or he would have reflexively reached for his snuffbox to calm his nerves. Thank God he at last knew better.

All he needed was the woman who stepped from the barouche, glancing toward the house even as she embraced her son and bade him goodnight. Mouette. Justin loved her so much it hurt. But surely that was a good thing! It meant he had opened his heart in a way that had been impossible for most of his adult life.

He threw open the front door as she approached, a vision in an evening dress of white crêpe over an azure satin slip. She wore a wreath of satin bows in her dark hair that was especially fetching, setting off her expressive blue eyes. This was his *wife*. A wave of mingled love and desire swept over him.

"Goodness," Mouette said, beaming, as he reached out for her. "What's come over you? Do you have designs on Baptiste's position as steward?"

Justin brought her inside even as he watched Charles's carriage roll off toward Russell Street. "Devil take Baptiste. I have designs on *you*." His voice was husky and seductive.

"How lovely!" She laughed up at him, but her eyes shone with love.

"Where have you been? I was beginning to worry."

"Oh, you needn't fear that Theo had me in his clutches." As she spoke, Justin pressed her against the wall and caressed her through the delicate fabric of her evening dress, reveling in the sensation of Mouette melting under his touch. "I was perfectly polite to him, so I don't think he guessed anything was amiss, but I

302

did not encourage him in any way. I think he was quite disappointed, in fact."

"I know. I didn't see him when he arrived back at Redfield House, but from what I heard, he was fuddled. Or, as Charles would say, drunk as a wheelbarrow." Smiling, Justin pressed a slow, burning kiss to the side of her neck and heard her emit a small moan. "I have some very special plans for you tonight." He breathed in her scent. "I wish there weren't so damned many things to talk about first."

"Do you have exciting news?" She gazed at him. "I've been hesitant to ask, but of course I long to know."

"Yes, we do. Anthony is waiting for us in your morning room." He kissed her, exploring the sweetness of her mouth.

"If he is waiting, you should stop doing these things," she teased.

He took her hand and pushed it against his crotch, groaning. "I want..."

"Don't say it now," Mouette cautioned as a dimple winked in her cheek. "Tell me later, when we are alone." Standing on tiptoe, she whispered against his rough cheek, "In our bed."

A voice came to them from the morning room. "What's happening out there? Did you two make a wrong turn?"

After hastily rearranging their clothing, Justin took Mouette's arm and guided her inside the morning room. When he saw Anthony pacing in front of the fireplace, the linen-draped painting propped up nearby, Justin felt the weight of the moment.

None of them could ever really know what Mouette had quietly suffered during the years after Harry's disgrace and death. She had been forced to part with her treasured possessions, one by one, in order to feed her sons and maintain a semblance of normalcy in the eyes of the *ton*. The rooms of her house had gradually emptied, except for the sitting room which had remained furnished like a stage set for the benefit of aristocratic guests. Yet instead of showing Mouette kindness, they had whispered behind her back, crossed her off their guest lists, and gradually forgotten her completely.

How had Mouette felt that long-ago day when she had been desperate enough to part with the portrait by Madame Le Brun? As Justin watched his wife enter the morning room, he imagined that scene and became achingly aware of her feelings, and he even understood why she had needed to trust Redfield. She had badly needed a friend; one person who would turn toward her instead of away.

"Mama, we have brought your portrait back to you," Anthony said, gesturing for her to come forward.

Mouette stood there with one hand pressed to her mouth. Her beautiful eyes swam with tears as she looked between Justin and Anthony. "I'm not certain I believe it."

Justin put an arm around her and brought her toward the fireplace. Anthony held up the portrait with both hands, allowing Justin to pull away the linen covering.

Mouette blinked, staring at her much younger self. It was an eerie moment, Justin thought, as if past and present were joined.

"You are even wearing the sea-green gown with the silver cord," said Anthony, as if she might be doubting that this was the right portrait. "How beautiful you were."

"And still are," interjected Justin.

"It is just as I remembered," Mouette said softly, still staring. "Yet it is bittersweet to see myself again. I think now that I attached too much importance to that hopeful young girl...as if I lost something precious the day Theo carried the portrait out of the house." Turning, she gazed at Justin. "But I was confused. I thought if I could be accepted among the *ton*, I would be happy, but just the reverse happened. Later, I clung to this portrait as a sort of talisman, hoping that as long as I had it, I might still achieve that foolish dream." Mouette shook her head and reached for his hand.

It was Anthony who broke the spell. "Well, now you can leave all that behind. It's a magnificent portrait, Mama, and it is back where it belongs."

Leaning against Justin, she regarded their son. "And what of you? Did you enjoy your adventure tonight? I want to hear all about it."

He shrugged, and a lock of his thick, curling black hair fell over one eye. "It was well enough."

Justin murmured, "We will tell you everything over the delicious meal Baptiste has prepared."

She was watching Anthony, her brow slightly furrowed. "But...?"

Sighing, Justin allowed, "We were discovered in Redfield's study by his daughter. It was she who eventually helped us discover the portrait's hiding place and get it out of the house." He paused before adding, "Yet in hindsight our son might have a few regrets."

"Frederica did the right thing, no thanks to me," said Anthony, staring out the window. "I don't think she will ever speak to me again." He seemed to give himself a mental shake then, for he straightened and smiled at them. "But that isn't what really matters, is it? I knew all along that I was cultivating our friendship with the goal of finding Mama's portrait. I succeeded. And soon I'll be leaving London." He flicked a bit of tree bark from his coat sleeve. "Really, it can't be soon enough."

As their son turned away, Justin and Mouette exchanged glances. It was hard to see Anthony spouting the same sort of self-protective nonsense that Justin had uttered himself...for decades. But this was not something a parent could teach a child, especially one who had grown to manhood.

"Let's move on, shall we?" Anthony suggested as he took down the mirror from above the mantelpiece and replaced it with Mouette's portrait. "There, you see? All's well that ends well."

* * *

LATER THAT WEEK, Justin and Anthony were walking in the central garden of Bedford Square with Robinson, who was on a tether. Overhead, the skies darkened with the threat of rain.

"I will be very glad to leave London tomorrow," Anthony said.

"Not as glad I will be," Justin replied. "Tonight, we will pack up your mama's portrait and Baptiste will see that it is taken to Frenchman's Haven until our arrival."

Next to them, Robinson raised his head, ears standing straight up, and barked. On the walkway nearby, Justin saw Charles waving to them. After a moment's hesitation, he gestured for his stepson to join them.

"What are you two doing out here?" Even as Charles spoke, raindrops spattered on his beaver hat. "Can't the footman exercise Robinson?"

"*Bonjour*," said Justin, extending his hand. "Your mama has a guest and we are making ourselves scarce until he leaves."

"It's our erstwhile friend, Lord Redfield," Anthony put in.

"Oh, right." Charles nodded. "I heard about that terrible business with Mother's portrait, and all the rest. I would have never imagined that Theo could turn out to be a villain." He looked glum. "One never knows about people, it seems."

Sensing an opening, Justin said, "Is everything all right?"

"Trouble in paradise?" Anthony chimed in, brows flicking upward.

Charles frowned. "I must confess that it's not going well with Lady Pen." He took out his snuffbox and helped himself to a large pinch. The raindrops fell faster. "In fact, I have given up. She – uh, well, she seems to be happier in the company of her friend, Miss Thatcher, than with me."

"Ah." Justin gave a sage nod. "When I saw them together at Lady Penhurst's ball, I thought as much." Charles gave him an intensely curious look, and so he decided to be honest. "Lady Penelope may be one of those women who like other women, if you take my meaning. When you spend more time in the world, you'll understand."

"Better that than losing her to another fellow!" Anthony said, and momentarily put an arm around his brother.

"You don't understand," Charles said morosely. "My entire future depended on this match!"

"Nonsense," said Justin as the three of them let Robinson lead the way through the green central square. "You must give up those false notions of what will make you happy. Is there anyone among the exalted *ton* who gives a damn about Sir Charles Brandreth?" He gave him a sidelong glance. "You witnessed what they did to your mother, and now it's happening to you."

Charles went pale and looked at Anthony, who only nodded his agreement. Warming to his speech, Justin continued, "I am saying these things because I care about you." A mad urge caused him to add, "Like a father. I urge you to leave these schemes behind and choose a better path."

"I suppose you would suggest that I become a pirate," muttered Charles.

Justin nearly laughed at that, yet he saw the glimmer of hope in the young man's eyes. "No, but I believe you have gifts of your own. Why not return to university and study architecture?"

Charles looked suspicious. "I thought you believed universities were dull, boring places, and any fellow who spent his time studying was missing out on the real meat of life?"

"I may have held those views, but I was wrong."

The two brothers blinked at him in disbelief.

"*C'est vrai.* It's true; I am fallible." He gripped Charles's forearm, smiling. "If you return to university, you can make your own way in the world rather than settling for scraps from some cursed duke."

Charles stopped walking and seemed to think for a long moment. "And…you would be willing to help me?"

"Of course, I will…if you endeavor to succeed and behave properly toward your mother. Perhaps you might consider thinking of me as a father again, as you once did." Justin's tone was casual, but he held Charles's gaze.

As if hoping to lighten the mood, Anthony said, "This is an excellent plan. And in the meantime, I suggest that you stop hanging about here. Show the London *ton* that you don't give a damn. Come with us! We are going to visit Emeline in Lyme Regis. She wants to show us her fossils."

They began a second circuit of the garden square. With forced nonchalance, Charles inquired, "Louise is still in Lyme Regis, isn't she?" His face flushed. "The last time we met, she told me off."

"That's only because she cares." Anthony lowered

his voice to a confidential tone. "In any event, she may soon be too busy to dispense advice to you. I happen to know that Lord Rupert Featherstone fancies Louise. He met her when she was here, and when I saw him at Whites, he asked a lot of questions about her." Behind Charles's back, Anthony sent Justin an almost imperceptible wink. "I think Featherstone might be packing to go to Lyme Regis himself."

"What?" Charles's jaw dropped. "But Featherstone is a twit! Do you think there is any chance Louise would be taken in by his attentions?"

Anthony shrugged. "With women, one never knows."

"Dash it all! As her friend, perhaps I should intervene." Charles looked at Justin, his flush deepening. "But I wouldn't want to intrude."

"Intrude? *Pas du tout.*" Warmth spread through Justin, and he thought again of Mouette and how wonderful it would be to share this news with her. "Are we not a family?"

* * *

MOUETTE STOOD ALONE in the morning room, waiting. All around her, the furniture had been draped in holland covers in preparation for their departure. Soon, their sojourn in London would be ended, but first Mouette had to attend to one more piece of unfinished business.

The bell at the front door rang, followed by muffled voices.

Mouette's heart began to pound and her palms were damp. She knew that she had every right to confront Theo, but it was hard to be certain what he was capable of. Clearly, he was not the man she had always believed him to be.

When she had written to Theo, asking him to come today, Justin declared that he wanted to be present. Mouette had refused.

"You have had your share of duels of honor," she had told him. "Today I must fight one of my own...and in my own way."

Now, as she listened to the approaching footsteps, she willed her spine to stiffen.

Baptiste appeared in the doorway first. "The Viscount Redfield," he announced.

Theo came into view. He looked as genial as ever with his long chin and big hazel eyes. "Good afternoon, Madame St. Briac. How kind of you to invite me for a visit." Glancing around the room at the linen-draped furniture, he blinked in confusion. "By Jove! It appears that you are preparing to leave London."

Mouette went forward to meet her guest, but Baptiste didn't budge from the doorway. In the distance, she saw Softlaw, the footman, standing guard as well and realized this must be Justin's doing.

"Hello, Lord Redfield. Please come in," Mouette said, then looked at Baptiste. "You may leave us."

The Frenchman backed away, out of sight, but she knew he hadn't gone far. This was a comfort, for she saw that Theo was focusing on her portrait. He visibly swallowed and went very pale.

"So, that's where it went," he said hoarsely.

Mouette had made up her mind not to discuss the means by which the portrait had returned to her possession. He had been well remunerated for it...and he must know that she could see him ruined if she so desired.

"Lord Redfield, I do not wish to prolong this interview," Mouette said. "However, there are a few things I need to say to you."

He made a sudden lurching movement toward her.

"Mouette! You must understand...for years I have *adored* you from afar. Even during my marriage to Katherine, I was secretly in love with you, the exquisite wife of my best friend." Stopping in front of her, he begged, "I know I should not have kept the portrait for myself. Yes, I plead guilty! Guilty to the crime of loving you too much."

Theo was breathing hard and Mouette feared he might drop to his knees and begin to sob.

She felt nothing. "I happen to know differently." From her silk reticule she withdrew the letter he had written to her more than a decade earlier, proclaiming his love, acknowledging her desperate circumstances, and offering to 'take care' of her. Smoothing it open, she held it out at a distance for him to see. "I now understand that you not only deceived me when you said you had found other buyers for my valuables, including this treasured portrait, but you also underpaid for them in order to create in me a growing sense of desperation." As Mouette spoke, her resolve hardened.

Theo had begun to sweat. He took out a handkerchief and mopped his brow, staring at the letter. "How did you get this? It belongs to me. It is my private property!"

"But it was clearly addressed to *me*." She showed him the small envelope. "I know you would like to turn this situation around somehow, to paint yourself as the victim, but I will not allow that. You watched me suffer for years after Harry's death, yet you toyed with me like a spider. And you dare to speak of love? Clearly your plan was to make me so frantic to keep a roof over the heads of my beloved sons that I would be forced to come to your bed."

"You make it sound sordid! It would not have been like that. You had been married, after all. You know, a woman of experience." Theo looked around, wild-eyed, as if he expected Justin to burst in again, this time wielding a deadly weapon. "I...I beg you to forgive me. Because of Katherine, I could see no other way for us to be together. I would have helped you, I—"

Bile rose in her throat, and she raised a hand to stop him. "Do not say another word." She paused, shaking. "If it were up to my husband, you would be in Newgate at this moment, or better yet, dead. But we agreed that Frederica would then suffer for your crimes, as you allowed my boys to do after their father's death." Mouette paused as tears stung her eyes. "For her sake, I will not endeavor to see you ruined. I cannot change the past, only look to the future. I would ask that you turn your attention to your lovely daughter, who is coming into womanhood. Try to smooth the way for her and make certain that she has everything she needs to succeed."

Theo stared as if waiting for a death blow, but Mouette only turned away, unable to look at him for another moment.

A deep, French-accented voice spoke from the doorway. "Redfield, it is time for you to go."

Mouette waited, watching through the window. When she saw Theo climb into his curricle, snap the reins, and drive away, a profound sense of relief washed over her. For Freddie's sake, she prayed he would do the right thing going forward.

She turned back to find Justin standing a few feet away, brows raised as if waiting to discover if she was all right. Tears came as she went into his arms. She wept against his starched shirtfront, letting the joy of her present life wash away Theo's stain on her past.

"What a woman you are, *ma belle*," Justin murmured. "You clearly were victorious in your duel of honor."

Mouette looked up at him. "It's a relief to have it over. Now we can finally leave Bedford Square. Although this house has lately felt almost like a real home, today I only want to go far away and never come back."

"Ah, no doubt you will change your mind." His powerful arms held her fast. "Who can say what the future holds?"

EPILOGUE

Frenchman's Haven, Cornwall
September 1829

Mouette stood next to her parents, André and Devon Raveneau, in the morning room at Frenchman's Haven. Golden sunbeams streamed through the windows, illuminating the portrait that now hung on the wall behind her rosewood writing desk.

"It is even more exquisite than I remembered," said Devon as she gazed at Mouette's younger likeness. "Thank goodness Justin and Anthony were able to retrieve it from that awful Viscount Redfield."

A rueful smile touched André's hard mouth. "Your husband showed more restraint than I would have done, I think, by not killing Redfield. If I had known what he was doing, I would have put a stop to it myself, years ago."

Mouette smiled. Today her father would celebrate his seventy-ninth birthday, surrounded by family. Although she was uncertain if he could still effortlessly

314

dispatch enemies who were foolish enough to incite his wrath, it was certainly possible. Still lean and strong, his thick hair now white, Raveneau continued to cut a dashing figure. His only concession to age was the polished ebony stick he leaned on when his hip needed a rest.

"I vividly remember the day we were together at Madame Le Brun's for your sitting. Nearly twenty-five years ago!" Devon said wistfully. "It is a reminder that we never can know what lies ahead."

Mouette nodded. "That is very true. How little I understood then about life or love. I did not know that the things I yearned for would never make me happy. I wouldn't go back, even to be young and beautiful again."

"You are more beautiful than ever, *chérie*," Justin said as he came up behind her and slipped his hands around her waist.

André glanced over with a grudging smile. "I am beginning to approve of you, St. Briac. I confess I have had my doubts over the years, fearing you were too much like me."

This caused Mouette and Devon to shake their heads in amusement. Before Justin could reply, Emeline burst into the room. She wore a pretty blue dress, part of the new wardrobe Mouette had ordered when Emmie came home from Lyme Regis. Not only had she outgrown most of her clothing over the summer, but she'd spent weeks climbing around on the rocky beaches with her skirts tied up around her waist, so her dresses were in sad condition.

"Grandpère and Grandmama, won't you come out and join us? Louise, Camille, and I have brought out our natural history treasures, and I wanted to show you the nearly *perfect* ammonite I discovered with Miss Anning."

CYNTHIA WRIGHT

Devon beamed, and Mouette thought that time had not dimmed her mother's inner glow. Her dawn-colored hair was threaded liberally with silver, but otherwise she seemed ageless.

"Grandpère and I would love to see your ammonite," Devon replied.

Emeline excitedly led her grandparents from the room, leaving Mouette and Justin alone. She turned in his arms and reveled in the warm mixture of contentment and pleasure that washed over her. Gazing up at him, she ran a fingertip over the scar on his cheekbone.

"I suppose you are a bit like Papa…"

"No woman has ever compared me to her father." He pretended to frown. "But in the case of André Raveneau, I will allow it."

Mouette laughed and gave herself over to his passionate kiss. As always, desire flared up between them. Her breasts ached for his touch, and she felt warmth blossom at her core. "We should go outside to join the others before…"

"I could draw the drapes, lock the door, and take you on the chaise," he whispered.

For an instant, Mouette remembered her dark fears about Lady Daphne being in *her* morning room, on this very chaise with Justin…when he had kissed her. She felt a stab of pain. And then it was gone.

That was no way to live, she told herself, and they both deserved better.

"That is a very tempting proposition, m'sieur." She kissed him. "But there are too many people about. When we are alone…yes."

Justin made a low, predatory sound. "I will hold you to that promise."

"Until then, let us go out and join the others."

Emerging from the morning room, they nearly

bumped into Anthony, who was reading a piece of paper as he passed by.

"Oh! Sorry." He stopped, looking distracted. Focusing on his parents, he flashed a reckless smile. "I've received a letter from my friend Darwin, presenting me with a scheme for just the sort of adventure I crave."

Mouette looked at him, thinking that the older Anthony got, the more he became a potent mixture of St. Briac and Raveneau. He wore his riding clothes with casual elegance, and his black hair was appealingly windblown. All that was missing was their edge of danger, but no doubt that would come with time...

"Adventure?" Justin echoed, lifting his brows hopefully.

"Exactly! He hopes to join a voyage to the Canary Islands as a naturalist and urges me to apply as well. Our botany don, Reverend Henslow, would be along, so you needn't fear that we would sail off never to return." He laughed and held up the letter. "I've never known Darwin to be so excited, writing on and on about Teneriffe, a perfect example of tropical scenery and vegetation." His eyes gleamed in a way Mouette recognized all too well. "We will begin learning Spanish in preparation when we return next week to Cambridge. In addition, Reverend Henslow is planning weekly botanical excursions as far afield as Wales, to solidify our geological credentials."

Mouette looked at Justin, who wore a bemused expression. "So, the purpose of this voyage to the Canary Islands would be to capture...what? More beetles?" He paused. "Not *fossils*, I hope."

"I am told the Canary Islands are famous for their beautiful women," Anthony parried with a jaunty grin as the three of them began to walk toward the back garden. "More seriously, I think our aim will be the collection of botanical and geological specimens, but I will write when I have more information." He met Mouette's eyes for only an instant. "After the past summer in London, I will be glad to be back at university, in my element."

He tucked the Canary Islands letter into his coat pocket as he went out to the terrace. Mouette's heart ached a little. She thought of Frederica and reflected that Anthony was much more like his father than he could ever know.

Her reverie was broken when Baptiste came out of the kitchen, carrying a tray of glasses filled with sparkling wine. Justin took two and handed one to Mouette.

"Wait until you see the lemon tarte Margaret has made for the birthday celebration," the little Frenchman announced. A rather dreamy smile spread over his face. "Margaret's skills have undergone a metamorphosis! When I smelled it baking, and later beheld the finished work of art, I thought for a moment that I was in France."

He made a sound of sensual pleasure and went on his way outside, but Justin and Mouette lingered together at the glass doors, watching the scene outside.

"One might almost imagine that Baptiste is feeling drawn to Margaret," mused Mouette.

Justin snorted. "*Drawn*? What the devil does that mean? If you suspect that he wants to have some sort of romance with her, I can only laugh."

"Because he is like a monk, devoted only to you?"

His brows flew up. "Margaret is not his type."

"What is his type? In all the years I have known Baptiste, he has never indulged in romance, so it is a mystery," she replied, sipping her champagne. "I only know what I saw in his eyes."

On the terrace, the long table was covered with a crisp white linen tablecloth. Isabella was arranging bouquets of purple heather interspersed with daisies, bright dahlias, and rose campion while Cerise and Xavier sat nearby, having already claimed their favorite chairs. As Isabella finished each bouquet and moved on to the next, Cerise rose to rearrange her daughter-in-law's handiwork.

"Maman has obviously recovered from her *spells*," Justin observed dryly.

Gwynn and Smythe were placing generous platters of food on the nearby serving table, a sign that everyone would be called to eat very soon. Where were the others? Mouette looked out over the lawn, now sprinkled with coppery leaves from the beech trees. Anthony and Gabriel were walking together, talking, Robinson bounding along on his stubby legs through the crisp leaves. A short distance away, her parents sat on a low stone wall with Emeline, Camille, Louise, and...Charles. Louise was pointing to the ammonite Emmie displayed, and as the girls animatedly described the fossil, Charles carefully shifted so that he was sitting only a few inches away from Louise.

"Hmm," Mouette murmured.

Justin looked dubious. "Well said."

"People can change, you know. Even Charles, if he wants it."

"Perhaps you have forgotten that I am financing his return to university to study architecture?" He cocked a brow. "I would not do so, even for you, if I didn't hope for that very thing."

Mouette looked outside one more time. Although the scene was reminiscent of countless other past gatherings, she felt a warm, new appreciation for each family member and the bonds they shared. After all, only a few weeks ago she had stood in this very spot, achingly alone as she watched twilight gather over the empty terrace...and today everything was different.

As if sensing her thoughts, Justin curved a hand around her waist and drew her firmly against him. "None of this would be happening without you, love."

Mouette couldn't resist asking, "You don't wish for a return to the past, when danger and passion were waiting for you around every corner?" She was teasing him, but only a little, and when he stared outside for a long moment before answering, her heart beat faster.

"Of course, you know the answer," Justin replied. For once his voice was quietly sober. "I think I have finally learned that life is wasted longing for the past. And as we regard our family, I understand that this moment is precious." He paused. "You see, even I am capable of change."

He embraced her, and Mouette leaned against his broad chest, soaking up their shared sense of love and gratitude. "You won't change too much, though, will you?"

Justin's deep, passionate kiss was an answer in itself. "Not in the ways you love best," he promised, his tone irrepressibly wicked. "In fact, I was thinking that while your parents are here to watch Emeline, we might go to Saint-Malo for a few days. Just the two of us."

"My, that sounds wonderful."

There was a gleam in his eye as he continued, "*Eh bien*, I would like to clean out my cellar and dispose of a lot of the clutter I've been hoarding. Decrepit old relics from my past, you know."

"Oh yes," laughed Mouette, "I do know."

"Perhaps you would like to help me?" He bent, his breath warm against her ear. "This time, we might engage in the little drama you once suggested, wherein I would capture you at sea...and have my way with you on top of a chest of pirate treasure."

A thrill of arousal coursed through Mouette. "Yes, please, m'sieur," she managed to whisper.

Justin straightened with a triumphant smile. *"Excellent."* He pronounced the word in the French way. "And now, let us go out and enjoy this splendid afternoon. Suddenly I am famished!"

As he opened the glass door and they emerged into the golden air, Mouette drew a deep breath and savored the moment with her impossible, irresistible husband.

~ THANK YOU ~

Thank you so much for reading HER IMPOSSIBLE HUSBAND. I am honored that you've chosen my book and I sincerely hope you enjoyed it.

If you'd like to stay in touch, please join my newsletter! It's where I occasionally share news about my new releases, special sales, giveaways, and personal news. You can sign up here: www.cynthiawrightauthor.com

If you'd like to see the real-life people and places in HER IMPOSSIBLE HUSBAND and my other books, please visit the Galleries on my website and also my Pinterest boards.

You are invited to join a special "Cynthia Wright's Rakes & Readers Group" on Facebook. You'll be the first to see my coziest posts, be included in special previews and giveaways, and have a chance to interact with others who enjoy reading my books. I hope you'll come by now and join us—just click HERE.

You can also follow me on Twitter @CynthiaWright1 and on Instagram

Many readers have asked for a Family Tree for my characters. It's HERE now!

If you enjoyed , please consider posting a REVIEW, which will help other readers make a choice.

HER IMPOSSIBLE HUSBAND is Book 7 in the series Rakes & Rebels: The Raveneau Family:

1 – SILVER STORM (André & Devon)
2 – HER HUSBAND, THE RAKE (André & Devon)
a sequel novella to SILVER STORM
3 – SMUGGLER'S MOON (Sebastian & Julia)
4 – THE SECRET OF LOVE (Gabriel & Isabella)
5 – SURRENDER THE STARS (Ryan & Lindsay)
6 – HIS MAKE-BELIEVE BRIDE (Justin & Mouette)
7 – HER IMPOSSIBLE HUSBAND (Justin & Mouette)
8 – HIS RECKLESS BARGAIN (Nathan & Adrienne)
9 – TEMPEST (Adam & Cathy)

The Raveneau Family series intertwines with Rakes & Rebels: The Beauvisage Family:

1 – STOLEN BY A PIRATE (Jean-Philippe & Antonia)
a novella prequel to RESCUED BY A ROGUE
2 – RESCUED BY A ROGUE (Alec & Caro)
3 – TOUCH THE SUN (Lion & Meagan)
4 – SPRING FIRES (Nicholai & Lisette)
5 – HER DANGEROUS VISCOUNT (Grey & Natalya)

If you've not read HIS MAKE-BELIEVE BRIDE, in which Justin & Mouette fall in love, you won't want to miss it!

I'm excited to tell you that an audiobook of HER IMPOSSIBLE HUSBAND is in the works and I know that you will love Tim Campbell's inspired performance as much as I do. Tim has already brought the St. Briac family vividly to life in his performances of THE

SECRET OF LOVE and HIS MAKE-BELIEVE BRIDE. You can listen to samples of my audiobooks here.

The next book in the Raveneau Family series is HIS RECKLESS BARGAIN, set in 1818. Join rebellious Adrienne Beauvisage, whom you met as a girl in THE SECRET OF LOVE, as she takes a position in an English castle where danger lurks. Her father hires Mouette's brother, Nathan Raveneau to masquerade as her bodyguard – and keep her chaste until her twenty-first birthday!

If you haven't yet read SILVER STORM, the mega-bestselling romance of Mouette's parents, André and Devon Raveneau, you can download your copy now!

Once again, my heartfelt thanks for your support & friendship. I welcome your comments and suggestions, and I hope that you'll write to me at Cynthia@ CynthiaWrightAuthor.com. I promise to reply!

Warmest wishes,
    ~ Cynthia

~ MEET CYNTHIA WRIGHT ~

Cynthia Wright is the *New York Times* and *USA Today* bestselling author of the two *Rakes & Rebels* series, 14 intertwining historical romances starring the irresistible Raveneau and Beauvisage families. She has also written beloved series set during the Renaissance in France, England, and Scotland, and in the 19th century American West. Cynthia has won numerous awards over the years, and Romantic Times Magazine hails her novels as "Romance the way it was meant to be."

Cynthia lives in northern California. She enjoys riding a tandem bike and taking road trips in an airstream trailer with her Colombian-born husband, Alvaro and their corgi, Watson. She is also devoted to her two adorable grandsons who live nearby.

You are invited to visit Cynthia's website (where you can sign up for her newsletter and peruse the Books Page):
    http://cynthiawrightauthor.com/

You can join Cynthia's Facebook Reader's Group here:
https://www.facebook.com/cynthiawrightauthor/

View her "Behind the Books" boards on Pinterest:
    http://pinterest.com/cynthiawright77/

~ BOOKS BY CYNTHIA WRIGHT ~

RAKES & REBELS
The Raveneau Family
SILVER STORM
HER HUSBAND, THE RAKE
SMUGGLER'S MOON
THE SECRET OF LOVE
SURRENDER THE STARS
HIS MAKE-BELIEVE BRIDE
HER IMPOSSIBLE HUSBAND
HIS RECKLESS BARGAIN
TEMPEST

The Beauvisage Family
STOLEN BY A PIRATE
RESCUED BY A ROGUE
TOUCH THE SUN
SPRING FIRES
HER DANGEROUS VISCOUNT

* * *

CROWNS & KILTS
The St. Briac Family

~ BOOKS BY CYNTHIA WRIGHT ~

YOU AND NO OTHER
OF ONE HEART
ABDUCTED AT THE ALTAR
RETURN OF THE LOST BRIDE
QUEST OF THE HIGHLANDER

* * *

ROGUES GO WEST
BRIGHTER THAN GOLD
IN A RENEGADE'S EMBRACE
THE DUKE AND THE COWGIRL

* * *

BOXED SETS

RAKES & REBELS: THE RAVENEAU FAMILY 1
(Silver Storm, Her Husband, the Rake)

RAKES & REBELS: THE RAVENEAU FAMILY 2
(Smuggler's Moon, The Secret of Love, Surrender the
Stars)

RAKES & REBELS: THE RAVENEAU FAMILY 3
(His Make-Believe Bride, His Reckless Bargain,
Tempest)

THE RAVENEAU FAMILY IN CORNWALL
(Smuggler's Moon, The Secret of Love, His Make-
Believe Bride)

RAKES & REBELS: THE BEAUVISAGE FAMILY 1
(Stolen by a Pirate, Rescued by a Rogue)

RAKES & REBELS: THE BEAUVISAGE FAMILY 2

~ BOOKS BY CYNTHIA WRIGHT ~

(Touch the Sun, Spring Fires, Her Dangerous Viscount)

CROWNS & KILTS: COLLECTION 1 – CROWNS
(You and No Other, Of One Heart)

CROWNS & KILTS: COLLECTION 2 – KILTS
(Abducted at the Altar, Return of the Lost Bride, Quest
of the Highlander)

ROGUES GO WEST
(Brighter than Gold, In a Renegade's Embrace, The
Duke and the Cowgirl)

www.ingramcontent.com/pod-product-compliance
Lightning Source LLC
Chambersburg PA
CBHW011449100726
47899CB00010BB/3215